AN OUTPOURING OF PRAISE FOR
JULIA ALVAREZ'S ¡YO!

"A HILARIOUS, HEART-WRENCHING, SATISFYING BOOK . . . We fall right back in love with Yo, with writers, and with the way they steal from us in order to tell us the truth about ourselves."
—*Elle*

"AN ENTRANCING NOVEL . . . Alvarez's canny, often tart-tongued appraisals of two contrasting cultures, her inspired excursions into the hearts of her vividly realized characters, are a triumph of imaginative virtuosity."
—*Publishers Weekly* [starred review]

"THERE ARE THREE WAYS OF LOOKING AT JULIA ALVAREZ'S LIVELY AND ENGAGING NOVEL. It's like the kind of fireworks whose first explosion is only a prelude, sending invisible rockets out to go *pop! pop! pop!* around a wide perimeter. . . . It's a portrait of the artist."
—*Los Angeles Times*

Julia Alvarez is the author of two previous novels *How the Garcia Girls Lost Their Accents*, which won the PEN Oakland/Josephine Miles Award, and *In the Time of the Butterflies*, a National Book Critics Circle Award Finalist. Julia Alvarez has also published two highly acclaimed books of poetry, *The Other Side/El Otro lado* and *Homecoming* (all available in Plume editions). She lives in Middlebury, Vermont.

"Yo becomes the artist as wandering trickster, fomenting trouble or falling into it wherever she turns up. Her adventures make excellent reading."   —*Atlantic Monthly*

"Alvarez's storytelling is virtuosic and beguiling, deftly shifting gears from high humor to pure terror. . . . *¡YO!* is certain to send readers scurrying back to meet the whole clan in *García Girls*."   —*Houston Chronicle*

"The title character of Julia Alvarez's exhilarating, sometime heart-piercing third novel is so hot, hot, hot . . . she almost seems on the verge of . . . spontaneous combustion."   —*Miami Herald*

"Fans of *How the García Girls Lost Their Accents*, the acclaimed 1991 novel by Julia Alvarez, will cheer the return of the García sisters."   —*People*

"A stylish and accomplished novel about the often literal risks of storytelling and imagination."   —*Ms*

"The many voices of these characters impress and delight. . . . As much as anything, the novel is about the nature of storytelling, its joyous rewards and sometimes unexpected pitfalls."   —*Dallas Morning News*

Also by Julia Alvarez

Poetry:
The Housekeeping Book
The Other Side / El Otro Lado
Homecoming

Fiction:
How the García Girls Lost Their Accents
In the Time of the Butterflies

¡Yo!

Julia Alvarez

A PLUME BOOK

for Papi

PLUME
Published by the Penguin Group
Penguin Putnam Inc., 375 Hudson Street, New York, New York 10014, U.S.A.
Penguin Books Ltd, 27 Wrights Lane, London W8 5TZ, England
Penguin Books Australia Ltd, Ringwood, Victoria, Australia
Penguin Books Canada Ltd, 10 Alcorn Avenue, Toronto, Ontario, Canada M4V 3B2
Penguin Books (N.Z.) Ltd, 182–190 Wairau Road, Auckland 10, New Zealand

Penguin Books Ltd, Registered Offices: Harmondsworth, Middlesex, England

Published by Plume, an imprint of Dutton Signet,
a member of Penguin Putnam Inc.
This is an authorized reprint of a hardcover edition published by
Algonquin Books of Chapel Hill. For information address
Algonquin Books of Chapel Hill, P.O. Box 2225, Chapel Hill, NC 27515-2225.

First Plume Printing, December, 1997
10 9 8 7 6 5 4 3 2 1

 REGISTERED TRADEMARK—MARCA REGISTRADA

LIBRARY OF CONGRESS CATALOGING-IN-PUBLICATION DATA
Alvarez, Julia.
    Yo! / Julia Alvarez.
        p.   cm.
    Sequel to: How the García girls lost their accents.
    ISBN 0-452-27918-6
    1. Dominican Americans—New York (State)—New York—Fiction.
    2. Women authors, American—Fiction.   3. New York (N.Y.)—Fiction.
    4. Dominican Republic—Fiction.   I. Title.
    [PS3551.L845Y6   1997b]
    813'.54—dc21   97–39937
                                                                    CIP

Original hardcover design by Bonnie Campbell
Printed in the United States of America

BOOKS ARE AVAILABLE AT QUANTITY DISCOUNTS WHEN USED TO PROMOTE PRODUCTS
OR SERVICES. FOR INFORMATION PLEASE WRITE TO PREMIUM MARKETING DIVISION,
PENGUIN PUTNAM INC., 375 HUDSON STREET, NEW YORK, NY 10014.

*M*any are those who deserve my heartfelt thanks—but most especially, to Shannon Ravenel and Bill Eichner for their faith and help with this book; to Susan Bergholz, my friend and literary guardian angel who watches over my work; to my colleagues at Middlebury College, especially those at the reference desk at the library, for their help with finding answers to my questions; to those students—you know who you are—whose editorial help on some of these stories was beyond the call of workshop commentary, may the muse be with you; to my friends and family, old and new, whose loving support inspires my life and work; and always y siempre to la Virgencita de Altagracia, mil gracias.

Contents

Prologue

The sisters

fiction

Suddenly her face is all over the place in a promo picture that makes her look prettier than she is. I'm driving downtown for groceries with the kids in the back seat and there she is on *Fresh Air* talking about our family like everyone is some made-up character she can do with as she wants. I'm mad as anything, so I U-turn the car and drive back home and call her up and I get her long-winded machine that says she can't come to the phone right now, to please call her agent. Like hell I'm going to call her agent to give her a piece of my mind. Instead, I call up one of the other sisters.

"She's now on to Papi in the Laurentians, imagine."

"Jesus! Doesn't she have any sense?"

"She has this whole spiel about art and life mirroring each other and how you've got to write about what you know. I couldn't listen to it, it was making me sick."

The kids are running around, screaming, knowing it's a heyday because their mother's mad at somebody else. And then little Carlos comes up and says, "Mamma, am I really in Auntie Yoyo's book? Am I going to have my picture in the paper?" And then he's begging to bring his auntie's book to Easter show-and-tell so that the whole third grade of little Christians can get their ears burned to a crisp with the doctored-up family story.

"No! You cannot take that book to school!" I snap at him. And then more gently because those sweet chocolate-kisses eyes are blinking back tears, "It's a grown-up book."

"So can *I* take it in?" the eighth grader chimes in. She has started wearing her hair all fluffed out like her aunt's.

"You kids are going to drive me crazy. When I end up at Belle-vue—" And then I have to stop myself because that sounds more than vaguely familiar—it's what the mami in the book always says. "Are you still there?" I say to my sister, who has gone strangely silent. Now I'm the one blinking back tears.

"I tell you, if she gets into my personal stuff, I'm going to . . ."

"But what can we do? Mami's saying she's going to sue her."

"Ay, come on, Mami's just pulling her usual. Remember when she used to pile us in the car as kids and drive over to the Carmelite nuns and say she was going to leave us in the convent unless we'd promise to behave? Remember? We'd be kneeling by the car and all these Carmelite nuns, who weren't supposed to show their faces, were at the windows wondering what the hell was going on!"

We're both laughing over that old story. I don't know if we actually feel better about being fictional characters or if it's just so nice to have a memory these days that we haven't seen already worked over in print.

That night I talk to my husband—after the kids are off to their rooms. I fill him in on the radio show, the phone call with my sister, our mother's temper tantrums out there for the whole world to know about. "What are we going to do about this?"

"About what?" he says.

I am not going to act like our mother and blow my temper. At least, not right away. "This . . . this exposure," I say, because suddenly I don't know what to call it myself. "I don't think it's good for the kids."

My husband looks over his shoulder as if to assure himself there are no hidden cameras or reporters around. "We seem quite cozy here," he says. He has a quaint way of saying things in his German accent that makes it hard to get angry at him. It's as if you were to yell at someone in an ESL class who needs all the help he can get. I don't know why he calls up this tender tolerance in me when I'm just as much a foreigner as he is. "There is no need to get upset. Soon she will write another book and this one will be forgotten."

"Yeah, right. She was on the radio today talking away about Papi skiing topless in the Laurentians with all his French-Canadian girlfriends. Mami's going to hit the roof!"

"Your mother will hit the roof anyway," he says nonchalantly until he sees the look on my face. "But this is true," he says lamely, scratching his balding head, something he does when he's nervous that usually blunts the sharp edge of my anger. Tonight, it's not really anger I'm feeling. I'm out and out flabbergasted that he would say such a thing even if it is true, which it is. I know for a fact that before he read the book and had lines like that plopped into his mouth, he would never have said so of his own accord. He used to be more polite. I feel like my whole life is losing ground to fiction.

"I just won't have everyone criticizing the family," I say in a teary voice that goes dry on me before I can wring any sympathy from him. So off I go to the kitchen to fix the kids' lunches and settle my nerves. The last thing I want to do tonight is not be able to go to sleep and have to come out here and lie on the couch till all hours reading some stupid novel. I always was a reader, but now, whenever I open a book, even if it's something by someone dead, all I can do is shake my head and think, oh my god, I wonder what their family thought of this story?

I'm in there cutting up the bread into little space-food squares

the way my third-grader likes his sandwich and leaving out may-
onnaise the way my eighth grader likes hers when the phone
rings and it's my other "fictionally victimized sister," or so she
introduces herself in a grim voice. I can't say I go in for all this
labeling but my two sisters are psychologists and that's the way
they get a handle on things. Me, I just get mad.

"People have been coming up to me at work asking, so which
one are you. My therapist says this is a kind of abuse!" She goes
quiet a moment. "What are you doing? It sounds like you're hitting something."

"Just making the kids' lunches."

My sisters, I love them all, but sometimes they get on my
nerves. This one is always seeing trauma and sadness. Around
her, I purposely go shallow, hoping I'll get her to smile. "Oh, we'll
survive," I say. Maybe talking to my husband has calmed me
down.

"Speak for yourself," she says gloomily. "But I'll tell you one
thing, I'm never going to talk to her again."

"Oh, come on," I say.

"I mean it. I'm glad this is all happening around my birthday.
Because when she calls me, I'm just going to let her have it."

"I know," I say instead of pointing out that if she's not talking
to our sister, she can't let her have it. "So how are things?" I say in
a bright voice, hoping to get her talking about something happy.
Why is it that with all my sisters I always feel like I'm the therapist?

"Well, actually, there is something else. But you've got to
promise me that you're not going to tell her—"

"Hey, I'm not talking to her either," I lie. I'm not sure why. It's
as if I'm caught up in some family melodrama that I don't necessarily like. "So what is it?"

A coy pause, and then a jubilant, "I'm pregnant."

"Ay-ay!!!" I cry out, and here comes my husband, rushing into the room, the paper still in his hand. "Good? Bad?" he mouths. Recently, he observed—one of his new insights—how it's hard to tell what's really going on in my family with so much overreaction. Anyhow, I tell him my sister is pregnant and he gets on the phone and says he is delighted. Delighted?! I grab the phone back, and we gab for half an hour, the book forgotten, all those fictional doubles sent packing, my sister remarking on all the errors our mother made with us that she is not going to make with her child, and I kind of defending our mother because actually, though I don't say so, I've repeated all those sins with my own kids—except the one with the nuns and that's probably because there are no Carmelite convents that I know of in Rockford, Illinois. My sister concludes with the reminder that I am not to breathe a word of this to you-know-who.

"It seems kind of mean," I even surprise myself by saying so. I guess I'm feeling expansive, like there are really only a few big things in this world, LOVE and DEATH and LITTLE BABIES. Forget fame and fortune and whether or not someone plagiarized you into a fictional character. "I think you should tell her."

"You promised!" she says with such fury that even our mother could take lessons from her.

"Hey, I'm not going to say a word, it's not that. But I think *you* should tell her. After all, she is going to be an aunt."

"I can't believe you're saying this! I'm going to be a mother!"

"But why not tell her?"

"I just don't want my baby to become fictional fodder."

I get this crazy picture in my head—a cartoon really more than a picture—of this tiny baby being put through a big roller and coming out the other end as one of those small books that reviewers like to call a *slim volume*. But I also kind of see my sister's point—it's not just the baby, but the rest of the story will probably find its way into that slim novel: single motherhood, artificial insemination, sperm brought up from the D.R. from an area of the country where hopefully there aren't many first cousins. Just thinking about it I get goosebumps up and down my arm.

"What are you doing? It sounds like you're crying."

"No, no, I'm so happy," I reassure her, and then she makes me swear on my own children, which makes me very uneasy, that I won't mention a word of this to our sister.

Well, I no sooner put the phone down and finish wrapping up the sandwiches and putting in an applesauce for the dieter and a jellybean cookie for the little Christian when the phone rings and it's you-know-who.

"What's going on?" she says all weepy like it just occurred to her that everyone isn't ecstatic over her being famous.

"What do you mean?" I say, because if I've learned one thing in this family it's you better not let on that anyone has gotten to you first with another version of the story.

And she tells me. Mami is going to sue her. Papi has to call her from a public phone. Our eldest sister has her husband say that she's not available. "And I just called Sandi, and she hung up on me." There is a wrenching sob, and though I myself was going to kill her six hours ago, all I want to do is ease that mournful sound. I keep remembering how when we first got to this country the only way she'd go to sleep was if I held her hand across the space between our beds and told her something I remembered from being back on the island.

"Hey," I say, putting the best face on this messy situation, "I bet there were a lot of people mad at Shakespeare, too, but aren't we

all glad he wrote *Hamlet*?" I don't know why I'm saying this since
I dropped out of college in part because I just couldn't pass the
Renaissance. "But still," I go on, getting everyone's point of view
in, "imagine how you'd feel if you were his mother."

"What do you mean? What's art going to mirror if it isn't life?
Everybody, I mean everybody, writes out of his or her own experience!" And she's off into all the stuff I already heard her say on
Fresh Air. But I let her say it. For one thing, my head is going a
mile a minute, all that clunky, outdated emotional machinery
from childhood that should have been replaced years ago with
the trim, cutting-edge technology of feeling is chugging away,
and nothing short of a handful of sleeping pills is going to shut it
off. I might as well stay up on the phone instead of sitting in the
living room shaking my head at some dead novelist.

"It really hurts, you know, that my family can't share this with
me. I mean I haven't done anything wrong. I could have been an
axe murderer. I could have gotten up on some roof in a shopping
mall and mowed down a bunch of people."

I sure am glad it's me she's talking to and not one of the psychologist sisters.

"All I did was write a book," she wails.

"Everyone's feeling a little exposed, that's all."

"But it's fiction!" she starts in.

Oh yeah? I want to say. I don't care what it says on that page
up front about any resemblance is entirely coincidental, you
know when you spot yourself in some paragraph of description.
"But it's fiction based on your own experience! Like all fiction," I
add, quoting her from the radio. "I know, I know, what else are
you going to write about?" But to myself, I'm thinking, why can't
she write about axe murderers or law-firm scams or extraterres-
trials and make a million and divide it four ways, which by the

way is what the other sisters suggest she should do with this book since we provided the raw material.

"So you do understand, ay, it means so much you understand."

Oh dear, I'm thinking, if this gets out to the rest of the family! And before I know it I've opened one of the lunchboxes and I'm nibbling away on the space rations.

"Mamma, why are you eating my lunch?" It's my boy coming in to say good night. He has stopped in the doorway, hands on his hips, striking a righteous pose. He fancies himself part of The Force policing the galaxy. Catching me snacking is right up his alley.

"I'm talking to your auntie Yoyo," I say as if that's a reason to eat his lunch. Oh boy! Those little galactic-fighter eyes light up.

"I want to talk to Auntie Yoyo!" he cries out. I hand him the phone, but suddenly, the Milky Way's motor-mouth is totally stagestruck. All he can manage are little earthling grunts and murmurs. "Uh huh. Nah. Um um, yeah." His face is pink with terror and delight.

"Love ya, too," he whispers at the end and hands me the phone with such a radiant look on his face you'd think he'd gotten the baby Jesus Himself in his Easter basket.

"You got one fan here," I tell my sister.

"Only one?" she asks, straining for a light tone, but I can hear those tears just ready to rain down if I say the wrong thing.

It strikes me that what my sister wants is that look of adoration on every one of our faces. The best I can do is, "Well, you *are* a big hit with all the nieces and nephews." And then, I can't help myself, even if my own two precious babes are hanging in the bargain of my silence, I tell her that she's going to be a new aunt, that our sister is pregnant, and that she better not write about it or all my little sticks are going to fall, too.

"I have to pretend I don't know a thing?" She sounds so sad like she's just been kicked out of our gene pool or something. But I know what hurts her most is to be left out of a family story.

So, I tell her that I'm going to talk to the others because no matter what, we're sisters, and we're always going to be sisters, even though I was pissed as hell to hear her talking our stuff on *Fresh Air*, but I love her and that's the bottom line, and she's all subdued and listening and saying, well thanks, thanks, and it's like we're ten and nine again, our arms swinging in the dark as we hold on tight to each other's hands.

Have you talked to your sister?" my mother wants to know, as if *my* sister is only related to me, not her. She's already gone off the phone twice to see who's on the other line. Mami, the gadget lover—that part the book got right. She's got every conceivable option on that phone of hers. I've teased her that if the extra-terrestrials finally get through to planet Earth, it's going to be on her phone number.

"What sister?" I hedge, and then because I don't want to wimp out on my promise, I say, "She sends everyone her love." I don't know why I'm making up this stuff except I'm figuring that with a few touches here and there, surely we can get back together as a family.

"Humpf!" Mami scoffs. "Her love?! What does her love mean? She didn't even send me a Mother's Day card."

And I'm thinking, but you were going to sue her. What's she going to say? Dear Mami, happy Mother's Day from your plaintiff daughter. Or wait a minute, is the plaintiff the accused or the other way around? I should know with all that O.J. stuff on TV all the time. "It probably just slipped her mind," I explain. "She's on the road a lot these days."

"Oh?" she says, curiosity peeking out from her voice like the toe of a lover's shoe under a bedskirt. "Where's she been? Your Tía Mirta saw her on live TV. Mirta says she looked terrible like maybe her conscience was bothering her. It was one of those programs where you can call in with a question, but your aunt couldn't get through. I tell you, I want my equal time. I want my chance to tell the world how she's always lied like the truth is just something you make up. Remember the time she ran away to the Carmelite convent and told them she was an orphan?"

For the first time in my life that I can remember my jaw drops of its own accord, not in some pantomined gesture of shock. I'm pacing up and down the little stretch of kitchen promising myself that I'm going to get one of those cordless phones so I can walk off steam while talking to my family. At the very least, get some of my housework done. "You're the one who used to drive us over there, Mami, don't you remember?"

"Why would I do something like that, mi'ja? You can't visit Carmelites, silly. They take this vow of leaving the world and you can only talk to them in an emergency through a grate. But of course, if a little orphan girl is pounding on the door, they're going to open it. Thank God your cousin Rosita, who had joined not long before, recognized Yoyo right away and called me."

How can you argue with such good details? I start thinking that maybe my sister and I made up this memory of Mami threatening to dump us at the convent to make ourselves feel better about a mother suing a daughter. Anyhow, I want to hear the end of her crazy story. "So, what happened?"

"What happened? We pile in the car and go pick her up and bring her back and I'm ready to give her the spanking of her life but first I ask her why, why would she do something like this. Imagine, it's like giving her an invitation. So she says she was just missing Cousin Rosita so much, she slipped out of the play-ground to the grounds of the convent, knocked on the door, and told the head nun that she's an orphan come to see her only liv-ing family, Rosita García!" Now even Mami is laughing. "Can you believe it?"

And I'm shaking my head, no, no, because I don't know what to believe anymore except that everyone in our family is lying.

A few months pass, and things quiet down like my husband said they would. Mami drops her suit, though she's still not talking to Yoyo except through me, and poor Papi gets mugged while emp-tying his pocket change on the little metal shelf in a phone booth near his old office in the Bronx. The other sisters exchange a cou-ple of stiff birthday cards and calls with Yoyo, everything very cool like we're a New England family or something.

And week by week, the photos pour in that I've got to keep from the kids. They show a naked Sandi in profile from shoulder to living-color crotch, and on back in very neat handwriting like she's tidying up her act for this baby, she writes, four weeks and two days, five weeks, and so on, and then in parenthesis, *Eyes have formed! Differentiation of fingers going on!* And then I turn the photo over and stare and stare because it really takes an act of faith to believe that a secret life is growing in that bikini-flat belly.

"And Yoyo doesn't know a thing about it," Sandi gloats over the phone. My knees go weak beneath me so I have to go sit down in the living room. Thank God for this cordless phone I got as an anniversary gift from my husband although the beautiful gold pendant would have been more than enough. But he says this phone might save him a heart attack from always having to run into the kitchen to see if I'm yelling because I cut off my fin-gers or I'm just talking to my family.

Finally, about the twelfth week I get an irate call from Sandi. Some friend of hers just called her from Florida and told her there is a story in *USA Weekend* by Yoyo about a single mother. "You didn't say anything to her, did you?" Sandi is breathing so heavy that I tell her to go sit down, to think of the baby. But she won't be placated, and though I'd like to think of myself as having more character, I take the easy way out. "Of course, I didn't tell her."

Soon as I hang up with her, I call Yoyo. I'm all set to say a few choice things on her machine, since I haven't reached a live person at her house for months. But she answers and is so obviously happy at hearing my voice that it's as if someone let a few decibels out of my anger. Still, I'm mad enough to practically yell at her that I really think she's purposely trying to piss off everybody.

"What are you talking about?" she says in this truly shocked voice. I just wish I could see her face because I can always tell from her eyes if she's making up something.

"I mean writing about Sandi in this *USA Weekend* story!"

"Sandi?" She's rifling through her memory, I can hear it in her voice, as if she were looking for something of mine in her drawer. And then she finds it. "Oh, *that* story. What makes you think it's about Sandi?"

"There's a single mother in it, isn't there?"

"And that makes it about Sandi?!" There is the sound of laughter on the phone, not real laughter but the kind of backslapping laughter that has a dagger in its other hand. "First off, I'd have you know, Sandi isn't the only single mother I know. And number two, for your information—"

There is something fearsome about Yoyo when she knows she is right. She's not just going to tell you you're wrong. She's going to take it to the Supreme Court.

"In actual fact, I wrote that story about two and a half years ago, no, three, three years ago, that's right. I didn't have my new printer yet so I can prove it."

"Okay, okay," I say.

"But let's explore this further."

Do we have to? I'm thinking. I've unfolded the ironing board so at least I can get everything smoothed out on cloth if not in the family.

"Maybe Sandi got the idea of being a single mother from my story, you think? I used to send you guys my stories back then, so she probably read it, and said, Gee, that's a swell idea. I think I'm going to go kidnap a baby, too. You think?"

"Sandi isn't kidnapping a baby. She's pregnant."

"Precisely. *My* single mother kidnaps her baby because she doesn't want to pass down her crazy family's genes to some poor kid. Now that part isn't fiction."

Laid out in front of me on the board is my husband's favorite blue and lavender striped shirt. I put down the iron. I button it up as tenderly as if he were inside it. What would happen if we couldn't imagine each other, I wonder. Maybe that's why crazies shoot people in shopping malls: all they see are aliens instead of mamis and papis and sisters and precious babies. "You're right," I admit. "I'm sorry." To make it up to her I fill her in on everything going on in the family, including the new baby just getting his full-fledged sex organs this week. Then I can't help myself. I've got to know. "So what happened to the woman who kidnapped her baby?"

There is a pause in which I can just imagine the look of delight on Yo's face at being asked. And I know what's coming as if I had peeked ahead in a thick book to the last page. "Read my story," she says.

———

It isn't until that real baby is born on a bright December day that the family gathers face to face at St. Luke's. We pore over that little guy like we've got to pass a test on what he looks like if we want to keep him. He's a dark olive that Papi keeps saying is just a suntan until Sandi shuts him up by saying well the kinky hair must be a perm. "Dr. Puello screened the sperm," Mami assures him, and again one of my loony cartoons pops in my head. Some old guy in a sombrero with a droopy mustache is sieving sperm like he's separating egg whites into this bowl-like vagina.

Anyhow the aunties are delighted with their new nephew. I should say two of the aunts, because Yoyo isn't here. Even though Sandi later read the kidnapping story I sent her and felt pretty foolish, the grudge is on. I suppose Yo's absence is why I'm feeling blue even though a healthy baby's birth is right up there with True Love and Mami's guava flan on my scale of happiness. And something else, though I would never breathe this out loud, I feel bad that there's no father here. Call me old-fashioned, but it seems like a baby should have a *set* of parents. Look at my family. What would we do if we didn't have Papi to call us from a public phone when Mami sues us? Or when Papi disowns us, who but Mami is going to assure us that he'll get over it?

But even this considerable sadness melts away when I look into that honeydrop face, uncurl those little fists to convince him that he doesn't really have to fight the love that's pouring into him from his mamma and aunts. I know his genes are only half ours, but I've already traced every one of his features to some relation. When I put him back together again and try to figure out who he looks like as a whole, it just pops out of my mouth. "He looks like Yo's baby pictures, you know."

Sandi scowls into the baby blanket. "In the whites of his eyes, you mean?"

But Carla agrees, especially when the baby lets out a peal of angry crying, his little mouth opening so wide as if he doesn't know how to work it yet. "Same big mouth, see?" Carla points out.

We burst out laughing, and suddenly we can feel her absence in the room as if there were a caption above the bed, along with all those blue *It's-a-boy* balloons: *What is missing from this picture?*

For the umpteenth time, I tell Sandi, "I think you should call her." Carla nods. Sandi bites her lip, but I can tell she is being swayed. Her eyes have this soft-boiled look as if the room were wallpapered with pictures of her beautiful baby. Suddenly, she cocks her head at us. "I can't believe you haven't told her!"

Both Carla and I look down to hide the guilty look in our eyes.

"I see, I see," she says. "No one in your family can keep a promise," she tells her little boy. As she picks up the phone, she adds, "I guess that includes me."

And then, I could kill Yoyo, because I can tell from the look on Sandi's face that she's getting that stupid machine that says to call Yoyo's agent. Sandi rolls her eyes, and as if on cue that baby starts to cry with the big mouth of his aunt.

"Ya, ya," she coos to the baby and then in this prepared voice you use for machines, she begins. "Yo! It's me, your *real* sister number two, and I know you know you've got a new nephew who everyone says looks like you, god forbid, but I personally think he looks like our handsome Tío Max on Mami's side, though if he turns out to be as big a womanizer, I'll cut off his baboodles, just kidding, just kidding, did you hear those lungs? He's got the cutest toes without a nail on the little toe which he gets from Papi, and you know what they say about why the Garcías don't have a little toenail—"

I take that baby from her because I can just tell she's settling into a long one. It's as if Sandi is filled with nine months' worth of news that she's going to deliver now that she's finished giving birth to her son. And she's talking to a machine, for heaven's sake! I suppose it's her one chance to say all she wants without someone in the family cutting in with their version of the story.

Part 1

The mother

nonfiction

To tell you the truth, the hardest thing coming to this country wasn't the winter everyone warned me about—it was the language. If you had to choose the most tongue-twisting way of saying you love somebody or how much a pound for the ground round, then say it in English. For the longest time I thought Americans must be smarter than us Latins—because how else could they speak such a difficult language. After a while, it struck me the other way. Given the choice of languages, only a fool would choose to speak English on purpose.

I guess for each one in the family it was different what was the hardest thing. For Carlos, it was having to start all over again at forty-five, getting a license, setting up a practice. My eldest Carla just couldn't bear that she wasn't the know-it-all anymore. Of course, the Americans knew their country better than she did. Sandi got more complicated, prettier, and I suppose that made it hard on her, discovering she was a princess just as she had lost her island kingdom. Baby Fifi took to this place like china in a china shop, so if anything, the hardest thing for her was hearing the rest of us moan and complain. As for Yo, I'd have to say the hardest thing about this country was being thrown together in such close proximity with me.

Back on the island we lived as a clan, not as what is called here *the nuclear family,* which already the name should be a hint that you're asking for trouble cooping up related tempers in the small explosive chambers of each other's attention. The girls used to run with their gang of cousins, supervised—if you can call it that—by a whole bunch of aunts and nanny-maids who had wiped our bottoms when *we* were babies and now were wiping the drool of the old people who had hired them half a century ago. There was never any reason to clash with anyone. You didn't get along with your mother? You had two sisters, one brother-in-law, three brothers and their wives, thirteen nieces and nephews, a husband, your own kids, two great-aunts, your father, a bachelor uncle, a deaf poor relation, and a small army of housemaids to mediate and appease—so that if you muttered under your breath, "You bitch!" by the time it got to your mother it would sound something like, "Pass the mango dish, please."

And this was true for Yo and me.

Back there, that one was mostly raised by the maids. She seemed to like to hang around them more than she did her own kin, so that if she had been darker, I would have thought she was a changeling that got switched with my own flesh and blood. True, from time to time we did have our run-downs—not even three, four dozen people could always block the clashing of our two strong wills.

But I had a trick that I played back then, not just on her, but on all my girls, to make them behave. I called it putting on the bear. Of course, by the time we left the island, it no longer worked there, and it was only by mistake that it worked once here.

It started innocently enough. My mother had given me a mink coat she used to wear when she and my father were traveling a lot to New York for vacations away from the dictatorship. I kept it at the back of the walk-in closet, thinking maybe someday we would escape the hell we were living in, and I'd get to wear that coat into freedom. Often I thought about selling it. I hadn't married a rich man and we were always short on money.

But every time I got ready to sell it, I don't know. I'd bury my nose in that tickling fur that still held the smell of my mother's perfume. I'd imagine myself walking down Fifth Avenue with lights twinkling in the shop windows and snowflakes coming down so pretty, and I just couldn't bear to part with the coat. I'd slip the plastic cover back over it and think, I'll hold on to it a while longer.

Then one Christmas, I thought it'd be kind of neat to dress up for all the kids. So I draped this coat over my head with a bit of my face poking out, and the rest of the fur falling all the way down to my calves. I had some story worked out that Santa Claus couldn't make it down from the North Pole, so he had sent one of his bears instead.

My girls and their cousins took one look at me and it was like sheets hitting a fan. They screamed and ran. No one could be coaxed to come forward for a present. Finally, Carlos pantomined chasing me off with a broom, and as I hurried away, I dropped my pillowcase of goodies. Minutes later, when I walked back in, dressed in my red organdy, the girls ran to me, "Mami! Mami! El cuco was here!" El cuco was the Haitian boogeyman I had told them would come and steal them away if they didn't behave.

"Really?" I said, miming surprise. "What did you do?"

The girls looked at each other, big-eyed. What could they have done but avoid being mouthfuls for a monster with an appetite for their toys. But Yo piped up, "I beat him and chased him away!"

Here was a little problem that was not going to go away by

itself. Often, I put Tabasco in that mouth hoping to burn away the lies that seemed to spring from her lips. For Yo, talking was like an exercise in what you could make up. But that night was Christmas Eve, and the dictatorship seemed far away in some storybook about cucos, and Carlos looked so handsome in his white guayabera, like a rich plantation owner in an American ad for coffee beans or cigars. Besides I felt pleased with my little trick.

From then on, especially when I heard them fighting, I threw that coat over my head and went hooting down the hall. I'd burst into their room, swinging my arms, calling out their names, and they'd scream, holding on to each other, whatever fight they had been in the middle of forgotten. Step by step, I approached, until they were at the edge of hysterics, their little faces pale and their eyes wide with terror. Then I flung the coat off and threw out my arms, "It's me, Mami!"

For a minute, even though they could see it was me, they hung back, unconvinced.

Maybe it was a mean thing to do, I don't know. After a few times, what I was really trying to do was see if my girls had any sense at all. I thought for sure they would catch on. But no, each time, I fooled them. And I began to feel angry at them for being so slow.

Yo figured it out, finally. Maybe she was five, six—I don't know. All those years have mixed together like an old puzzle whose box top is lost. (I don't even know anymore what picture all those little pieces make.) As usual, I went howling into the girls' bedroom. But this time, Yo broke loose, came right up to me, and yanked that coat off my head. "See," she said, turning to the others. "It *is* just Mami like I told you."

It was no surprise to me that she was the one who caught on.

Back in my room, I was returning the coat when I noticed someone had been poking around in the closet. My shoes were scattered every which way, a hat box knocked over. That closet wasn't just any walk-in closet. It had once been a hallway between the master bedroom and Carlos's study, but we had closed it off on both sides in order to make a closet you could enter from either room. It was almost always locked on account of we kept everything valuable there. I suppose at the back of our minds, Carlos and I always knew that one day we would have to leave the island in a hurry and that it would be handy to have our cash and valuables on hand. And so, I was fit to be fried seeing signs that someone had been rifling through our hiding place.

Then it came to me who our intruder had been—Yo! Earlier, I had seen her in Carlos's study, looking over the medical books her father let her play with. She must have gone in our closet, and that's how she had figured out the fur was just a fur. I was ready to call her in and give her a large serving of my right hand when I saw that the floorboards close to the study side had been pried open and not exactly wedged back in place. I crawled in under the clothes with a flashlight and lifted one of those boards. It was my turn to go pale—stashed inside and wrapped in one of my good towels was a serious-looking gun.

You can bet when Carlos came home, I threatened to leave him right then and there if he didn't tell me what he was up to. I found out more than I wanted to know.

"No harm done," Carlos kept saying. "I'll just move it to another location tonight." And he did, wrapping it inside my fur coat and laying the bundle on the back seat of the Buick like he was going off to sell that coat after all. He came back late that night, the coat over his arm, and it wasn't until the next morning as I was hanging it up that I found the oil stains on the lining. They looked just like dried blood.

After that, I was a case all right. Nights, I was up to four sleeping pills to numb myself into a few hours of the skimpiest sleep. Days I took Valium to ease that jumpy feeling. It was hell on the wheels of our marriage having me down so much of the time. Worst were the migraines I got practically every afternoon. I'd have to lie down in that small, hot bedroom with the jalousies angled shut and a wet towel on my face. Far off, I could hear the kids yelling in their bedroom, and I'd wish I could squeeze that bear trick one more time to terrify them into silence.

Lots of worries went through my pounding head those afternoons. One of them that kept hammering away was that Yo had been snooping around in that closet. If she had seen that hidden gun, it was just a matter of time before she'd tell someone about it. Already I could see the SIM coming to the door to drag us away. One afternoon when I just couldn't stand it anymore, I leapt out of my bed and called down the hall for her to come to my room this instant.

She must have thought she was going to get it about all the loud bickering coming from their bedroom. She hurried down the hall already defending herself that she had plucked off Fifi's baby doll's head only because Fifi had asked her to. "Hush now," I said, "it's not about that!" That stopped her short. She hung back at the door, looking around my bedroom like maybe she wasn't so sure the bear was nothing but her mother in a fur coat after all.

I gave her a little pep talk in a soft voice—the way you talk to babies as you stroke them till their eyes drift shut. I told her Papá Dios in heaven could see into every one of our souls. He knew when we were good and when we were bad. When we lied and when we told the truth. That He could have asked us to do whatever He wanted, but out of all the hundred million things, He had only chosen ten holy commandments for us to obey. And one of those ten was honor thy father and mother which meant you shouldn't lie to them.

"So always, always, you must tell your mami the truth." I served her a big smile of which she only returned a little slice back. She knew something else was coming. She sat on the bed, watching me. Just as she had seen through the fur to her mother, now she was looking through her mother to the scared woman inside. I let out a long sigh, and said, "Now, cuca darling, Mami wants you to tell her what things you saw when you went looking in the closet the other day."

"You mean the big closet?" she said, pointing down the passageway that led from the master bedroom to the walk-in closet and right through to her father's study.

"That very one," I said. The migraine was hammering away inside my head, building its big house of pain.

She looked at me like she knew that admitting she had been snooping would get her into a closet full of trouble. So, I promised her that telling the truth this time would make her my and God's little darling.

"I saw your coat," she said.

"That's very good," I said. "That's what I mean. What else did you see in Mami's closet?"

"Your funny shoes," she remarked. She meant the heels with little holes pockmarked in the leather.

"Excellent!" I said. "Mami's darling. What else?"

She went through that whole closet with the full inventory of practically every piece of clothing I owned. My God, I thought, give her another decade and *she* could work for the SIM. I lay there, listening because what else could I do? If she hadn't really seen anything, I didn't want to put any ideas in her head. That one had a mouth from here to China going the long way like Columbus's ships.

"How about the floor?" I asked stupidly. "Did you see anything *in* the floor?"

She shook her head in a way that didn't convince me. I went back over the ten commandments and not lying to thy mother, and still I couldn't flush any more information from her except my monogrammed hankies and, oh yes, my nylons in a pleated plastic case. I finally made her promise that if she remembered anything else, she should come and tell Mami directly and no one else. "It will be our little secret," I whispered to her.

Just as she was slipping out the door, she turned around and said a curious thing. "Mami, the bear won't be coming anymore." It was as if she were stating her part of our bargain. "Honey cuca," I said. "Remember, Mami was the one playing the bear. It was just a silly joke. But no," I promised her, "that bear's gone for good. Okay?" She nodded her approval.

As soon as the door latched shut I cried into my pillow. My head was hurting so much. I missed not having nice things, money and freedom. I hated being at the mercy of my own child, but in that house we were all at the mercy of her silence from that day on.

Isn't a story a charm? All you have to say is, *And then we came to the United States*, and with that *and then*, you skip over four more years of disappearing friends, sleepless nights, house arrest, narrow escape, *and then*, you've got two adults and four wired-up kids in a small, dark apartment near Columbia University. Yo must have kept her mouth shut or no charm would have worked to get us free of the torture chambers we kept telling the immigration people about so they wouldn't send us back.

Not being one hundred percent sure we would get to stay—
that was the hardest thing at the beginning. Even the problem with
the English language seemed like a drop in a leaky bucket then. It
was later that I got to thinking English was the hardest thing of all
for me. But believe me, back then at the beginning, I had my
hands too full to be making choices among our difficulties.

Carlos was morose. All he could think about was the compañeros he had left behind. I kept asking him what else he could
have done but stay to die with them. He was studying like cats
and dogs for his license exam. We were living on the low end of
the hog off what little savings we had left, and there was no
money coming in. I was worried how I was going to pay for the
warm clothes my kids would be needing once the cold weather
set in.

The last thing I needed was their whining and fighting. Every
day it was the same question, "When are we going to go back?"
Now that we were far away and I wasn't afraid of their blurting
things out, I tried to explain. But it was as if they thought I was
lying to them with a story to make them behave. They'd listen,
but as soon as I was done, they'd start in again. They wanted to
go back to their cousins and uncles and aunts and the maids. I
thought they would feel more at home once school began. But
September, October, November, December passed by, and they
were still having nightmares and nagging me all the long days
that they wanted to go back. Go back. Go back. Go back.

I resorted to locking them in closets. That old-fashioned apartment was full of them, deep closets with glass knobs and those
keyholes like in cartoons for detectives to look through and big
iron keys with the handle part shaped like a fleur-de-lis. I always
used the same four closets, a small one in the girls' bedroom and
the big one in mine, the broom closet in the hall, and finally the

coat closet in the living room. Which child went into which depended on who I grabbed first where.

I wouldn't leave them in there for long. Believe me. I'd go from door to door, like a priest taking confession, promising to let them out the minute they calmed down and agreed to live in peace. I don't know how it happened that Yo never got the coat closet until that one time that I lived to regret.

I had shut them all up and gone round, letting out the baby first, then the oldest, who was always so outraged. Then the two middle kids, first Sandi. When I got to Yo's door, I didn't get an answer. That scared me, and I opened that door quick. There she stood, pale with fright. And, ay, I felt so terrible!—she had gone in her pants.

That damn mink coat was in that closet, way to one side, but of course, being Yo, she'd gone poking around in the dark. She must have touched the fur and lost her bananas. I don't understand because it had seemed she knew the fur was just a coat. Maybe she associated me being under that coat, and here I was on one side of the door, and there she was alone on the other side with a monster she was sure we had left behind in the Dominican Republic.

I pulled her out and into the bathroom. She didn't cry. No—just that low moan kids do when they go deep inside themselves looking for the mother you haven't turned out to be for them. All she said that whole time I was trying to clean her up was, "You promised that bear was gone for good."

I got weepy myself. "You girls are the bears! And here I thought all our troubles would end when we got here." I laid down my head on my arms on the side of the bathtub, and I started bawling. "Ay, Mami, ay," the other three joined in. They had come to the door of the bathroom to see what was going on. "We promise we'll be good."

Not Yo. She stood up in the water and grabbed a towel, then stomped out of the tub. When she was out of my reach, she cried, "I don't want to be in this crazy family!"

Even back then, she always had to have the last word.

Not a week later a social worker at the school, Sally O'Brien, calls up and asks to make a house visit. The minute I get off the phone, I interrogate my girls about what they might have said to this lady. But they all swear that they have nothing to confess. I warn them if this lady gives us a bad report we'll be sent back, and if we are sent back, cucos and bears are going to be stuffed animals compared to the SIM fieras that will tear us apart there. I send them off to put on their matching polka dot dresses I made them for coming to the United States. And then I do what I haven't done in our six months here. I take a Valium to give this lady a good impression.

In she comes, a tall lady in flat black shoes with straps and a blond braid down her back like a schoolgirl dressed in an old lady's suit. She has a pleasant, un-made-up face and eyes so blue and sincere you know they've yet to see the worst things in the world. She carries a satchel with little hearts painted on it. Out of it she pulls a long yellow tablet with our name already written on it. "Is it all right if I take some notes?"

"Of course, Mrs. O'Brien." I don't know if she is a married woman but I've decided to compliment her with a husband even if she doesn't have one.

"Will your husband be joining us?" she asks, looking around the room. I follow her glance since I am sure she is checking out whether the place looks clean and adequate for raising four girls. The coat closet I forgot to shut looms like a torture chamber.

"My husband just received his medical license. So he has been working like a god every day, even Sunday," I add, which she writes down in her notepad. "We have been through hard times." I've already decided that I won't try to pretend that we're having a ball in America, though believe it or not, that was my original plan on how to handle this visit. I thought it would sound more patriotic.

"That must be a relief!" she says, nodding her head and looking at me. Everything she says it's like she just put the rattle in the baby's hand and is waiting to see what the baby is going to do with it.

I shake it, good and hard. "We are free at last," I tell her. "Thanks to this great country which has offered us the green cards. We cannot go back," I add. "It would be certain death."

Her eyes blink at this, and she makes a note. "I read things in the paper," she says, bringing her braid from behind to fall down the front of her suit. She doesn't seem the nervous type, but the way she keeps minding that braid it's like she is getting paid to keep it occupied. "But are things really that bad?"

And right then and there in my broken English that usually cuts my ideas down to the wrong size, I fill her two ears full with what is happening back on the island—homes raided, people hauled off, torture chambers, electric prods, attacks by dogs, fingernails pulled out. I get a little carried away and invent a few tortures of my own—nothing the SIM hadn't thought up, I'm sure. As I talk, she keeps wincing until her hands go up to her forehead like she has caught one of my migraines. In a whisper she says, "This is truly awful. You must be so worried about the rest of your family."

I can't trust my voice to say so. I give her a little nod.

"But what I don't get is how the girls keep saying they want to go back. That things were better there."

"They are sick of home—" I explain, but that doesn't sound right.

"Homesick, yes," she says.

I nod. "They are children. They do not see the forest or the trees."

"I understand." She says it so nicely that I am convinced that even with those untried blue eyes, she does understand. "They can't know the horror you and your husband have lived through."

I try to keep the tears back, but of course they come. What this lady can't know is that I'm not just crying about leaving home or about everything we've lost, but about what's to come. It's not really until now with the whole clan pulled away like the foundation under a house that I wonder if the six of us will stand together.

"I understand, I understand," she keeps saying until I get control of myself. "We're just concerned because the girls seem so anxious. Especially Yolanda."

I knew it! "Has she been telling stories?"

The lady nods slowly. "Her teacher says she loves stories. But some of the ones she tells, well—" She lets out a sigh. She tosses her braid behind her back like she doesn't want it to hear this. "Frankly, they are a little disturbing."

"Disturbing?" I ask. Even though I know what the word means, it sounds worse coming out of this woman's mouth.

"Oh, she's been mentioning things . . ." The lady waves her hand vaguely. "Things like what you were describing. Kids locked in closets and their mouths burned with lye. Bears mauling little children." She stops a moment, maybe because of the shocked look on my face.

"It doesn't surprise me," the woman explains. "In fact, I'm glad she's getting it all out."

"Yes," I say. And suddenly, I am feeling such envy for my daughter, who is able to speak of what terrifies her. I myself can't find the words in English—or Spanish. Only the howling of the bear I used to impersonate captures some of what I feel.

"Yo has always been full of stories." I say it like an accusation.

"Oh, but you should be proud of her," the lady says, bringing her braid forward like she is going to defend Yo with it.

"Proud?" I say in disbelief, ready to give her all the puzzle pieces of my mind so she gets the full picture. But then, I realize it is no use. How can this lady with her child's eyes and her sweet smile understand who I am and what I have been through? And maybe this is a blessing after all. That people only know the parts we want to tell about ourselves. Look at her. Inside that middle-aged woman is a nervous girl playing with her braid. But how that girl got stuck in there, and where the key is to let her out, maybe not even she can tell?

"Who knows where Yo got that need to invent," I finally say because I don't know what else to say.

"This has been very helpful, Laura," she says, standing up to go. "And I want you to know if there's anything we can do to help you all in settling in, please don't hesitate to call." She hands me a little card, not like our calling cards back home with all your important family names in fancy gold lettering. This one shows her name and title and the name of the school and her phone number in black print.

"Let me call the girls to say goodbye."

She smiles when they come out in their pretty, ironed dresses, curtsying like I taught them. And as she bends to shake each one's hand, I glance down at her pad on the coffee table and read the notes she has jotted: *Trauma/dictatorship/family bonds strong/ mother devoted.*

For a moment I feel redeemed as if everything we are suffering and everything we will suffer is the fault of the dictatorship. I know this will be the story I tell in the future about those hard years—how we lived in terror, how the girls were traumatized by the experience, how many nights I got up to check on their blankets and they screamed if I touched them.

But never mind. Within a year of all this, the dictator will be shot dead by some of the very men who were in the underground with my husband. The girls will be jabbering away in English like they were born to it. As for the mink, I will exchange it at the secondhand shop on Fifth Avenue for four little-girl coats. If nothing else, my children will be warm that first winter everyone warned would be the hardest thing about coming to this country.

The cousin

poetry

Don't think I don't know what the García girls used to say about us island cousins. That we were Latin American Barbie dolls, that all we cared about was our hair and nails, that we had size-three souls. I don't deny I looked around me once I was trapped here for the rest of my life. I saw the women in their designer pantsuits loaded with gold, the little rounds of teas and parties. I saw the older tías with their daily masses and novenas, praying to ensure the family a good place in the next life while their husbands went off on business trips with pretty mistresses they pretended were wives. I saw the maids in their color-coded uniforms working way past overtime. And still, I spread my arms wide and gave myself to this island, which is more than the García girls ever did for their so-called homeland.

They came every summer and were out of here by September. They had to get back to school, I know. But still, it seemed right in keeping that they should make their exit just as hurricane season was about to start. That was their way. They'd talk and talk about the unfairness of poverty, about the bad schools, the terrible treatment of the maids. Then, once they had us feeling like creeps, they'd leave for their shopping malls and their colleges, their sit-ins and their dope cigarettes and their boyfriends in rags with trust funds in the bank. And you know what would happen? All their questions would stay spinning in my head: How could I let maids make my bed? How could I let my novio push me around? How could I put fake eyelashes on top of my real ones?

The big question that kept spinning inside me long after the other ones were laid to rest was this one: how could I live in a country where everyone wasn't guaranteed life, liberty, and the pursuit of happiness?

It was always Yo popping that question. She never put it to me directly. She did her arguing with the men, the uncles and boy cousins, who were the ones responsible, she said. Personally, I think she just liked men, liked hanging around them, pitting her mouth against theirs. But she said she was raising their consciousness, and the aunts let her get away with it. Those crazy gringa cousins could do what the rest of us would have been put away in a convent for doing. Not only that, those old tías approved of Yo's mission. I think they thought Yo was working on the men's *consciences,* just as they themselves were always on a campaign to get their sons and husbands to be more religious.

Yo would be hammering away about some book she'd read about the third world. "What do you mean, third world?" my brother Mundín would argue back. "Third world to whom?" I'd keep my mouth shut, sitting in the wicker chairs with the rest of the women, talking about, yes, our hair and our nails. But sometimes I'd turn and watch, and her eyes would wander over to me, and quick, she'd look away.

She felt guilty all right. She knew if it hadn't been for her, I wouldn't be trapped in this world. I'd be finishing my college. I'd be having *me* some first-world fun. Over the years she knew that if it hadn't been for what she'd done, I would be living a different life. And that's why she never said a thing to me about the state of *my* soul. She knew that if I *was* a hair-and-nails cousin, it was she who had made me one.

———

It all began when I was sixteen, and my parents decided to send me to the States to school. The García girls had already been gone five years, but we had stayed behind, and things had gotten really bad on the island. We were having one revolution after another as if we couldn't kick the habit of murdering each other even after our dictator was gone. Anyhow, for a couple of years, schools were all but shut down. I remember a lot of nights sleeping under the bed on account of stray bullets shattering the windows. Our pantry was stocked up with water and candles and food. It would have been a pretty claustrophobic life in that family compound, especially with the García girls being gone, except that all the people with money had built their houses pretty close together in the capital. We young people just cut across each other's yards as if there were no war going on and visited with each other.

So that now when I read about those dark and bloody years in history books, they don't seem the same years I lived through. I didn't miss one birthday party, one quinceañera party, one saint's-day party. Maybe, for lack of butter and enough chocolate, the cakes weren't as rich, and the piñatas were kind of shabby—cardboard boxes with only nuts and pencils and satin hairbands made from some aunt's old evening gown. But there was one thing there was no scarcity of, at least for me. I had plenty of boyfriends. And this, I believe, more than the revolutions and the lack of schooling and the fear for our lives, is why my parents decided to send me away to the States. They wanted to ensure that Lucinda María Victoria de la Torre was not going to go behind the palm trees and ruin her chances of a good marriage.

They shouldn't have worried, or really, they should only have worried once I got to the States. Because, as you'll remember, there was another revolution happening there that my parents didn't know anything about. It was the sixties. Even at Miss Wood's, the sleepy all-girl boarding school where the García girls and I were tucked away, we felt the rumbles of the sexual revolution going on. Those rumbles came down to our red-brick, wrought-iron-gated campus from the boys' school up the hill.

I was Carla's age, and growing up together on the island, we'd been best friends. But at Miss Wood's I was put back a couple of grades on account of the missed years and ended up in the same grade as Yolanda. Which was a little hard on me. If I was sixteen going on twenty-three, Yo was fourteen and acting like a kid, a weird kid. And I had to be related to it.

What I mean is she got in with the artsy crowd at Miss Wood's. I can't remember all their names anymore, but there were four who formed the heavy-duty core. One was a large, overdeveloped girl—*she* looked like she was twenty-three—who had to be driven in to Boston to see a shrink once a week. It was she who put her hand through a window, *to feel pain, to feel deeply alive*, which she wrote a poem about for the literary magazine. Another one of them, Trini, dyed her hair blond in mockery of the blond, preppy in-crowd at Miss Wood's. The third one, Cecilia Something, was one of those genius types, skinny with cokebottle glasses and a smart mouth. And then there was Yo, who in some ways was the oddball in the group. I mean, Yo was pretty and lively and most everyone liked her if you could get her away from Trini and Big Mama. But like I said, she was still acting like a kid, trying to get attention by making scenes out of the most ridiculous things.

For instance, we didn't have uniforms or anything like that, but we had a dress code, skirt and blouse and tied shoes to class, and something called a tea dress to dinner every night. When I got to Miss Wood's, all I had was a suitcase full of brightly col-

ored skirts and lace blouses and satin dresses that were totally out
of place. So Carla and I went downtown during one of our supervised Saturday afternoon outings, and we each bought ourselves
a couple of nice Villager outfits at the local shop that we inter-
changed and shared with each other. Maybe we did look like two
Hispanic preppies as Yo liked to tease us, but so what? She and
her friends looked like they'd just stepped out of a funeral parlor.

The headmistress called them in and told them they had to
stop dressing all in black. She ordered them to put on light pastels and plaids and tweeds like the rest of us were wearing. But
they went around with black armbands in protest, their skirts
hiked up above the knees. I mean it was embarrassing when the
in-girls in our class, the Sarahs and the Betsys and Carolines,
would turn to me, their eyes wide, and ask, "Are you *really* related to Yolanda García?!"

I probably don't need to tell you that she and her friends ran
the literary magazine, which was mostly an anthology of their
stuff with a few of us roped into submitting something by our
English teacher. The cover usually featured a sketch of someone
walking in a graveyard with a bare branch swaying in the breeze
and some poor butterfly hovering above a tombstone. The name
on the stone was fuzzed up, but the dates were clearly those of a
suicide, someone our age who had died too young. "Probably
stuck his hand through a window to feel more deeply alive,"
Heather, my roommate, suggested. She liked to read the poems
out loud.

"'And take your warm heart in my wormy arms'?!" Heather
tossed the magazine up in the air as if it were contaminated.
"Truth is, Lucy-pooh, I can't believe you're related to old Yo-gore
here." Heather had a thing about nicknames from Winnie the
Pooh. She herself was Heffalump.

We had to keep journals in English class. Everyone else on that faculty seemed like they had been let out of an old-age home to teach for the year, but the English teacher had just graduated from college with a degree in creativity. She made Carla's class write essays from the point of view of an inanimate object. (Carla did a bra.) Another class had to hug a tree and then write about what it felt like. I suppose my class got off easy just having to keep journals.

You can imagine that most of us treated the journal like a boring assignment that had to get done. But Yo and her friends carried their notebooks everywhere, even to meals—until the headmistress confiscated them, saying that it was rude to bring work to the dinner table. You'd be walking to hockey, and there'd be one of them sitting under the tree, writing away, making the rest of us have to wait to start the game. You'd go to the parlor to sit by the fire and gossip about the cute boy you'd seen at chapel, and there'd be another of them sitting on the windowsill, scribbling and giving us dirty looks as if to tell us we were being superficial, talking about boys. I'd think, why don't you go do that in your room since it's private? But no, they had to show off writing in their journal so we'd all feel less sensitive, less poetic, less deep than they were.

Well, I wasn't going to let little Yo García dampen my happiness. Sure, I missed my family and friends, and many nights I woke up panicked that something horrible had happened on the island. I also didn't especially like being in a strict all-girls school, forced to take American History and listen to Battleaxe Ballard lecture about the USA lending a helping hand to the primitive countries of Latin America. But one thing kept my spirits up: there was a boys school up the hill, and I had discovered that my talent with the opposite sex translated across cultures.

Don't get me wrong, I wasn't a flirt. Yo was more of a flirt than I was if it came right down to it, riding the surface of a boy, splashing water in his face, bailing out if he came close. But I dove down to that cool place at the bottom where I could feel the strong currents coming through their tweed jackets and wool pants, and I waited, days, weeks if need be, and they always came round. My first three years at Miss Wood's, there wasn't a cool guy up at Oakwood that hadn't come down from his high hill to call on me, his long nervous hands stuffed in his pockets, his pale face flushed as he talked on and on about his family vacation to Barbados or Bermuda, which I understood was his hazy-geographical way of relating to my heritage. I'd listen for as long as it took for him to feel interesting. And then I'd give him one of my looks, and say, well, next time you're in the neighborhood, you better drop in and visit me! In nine cases out of ten the boy was smitten.

But it was the one case I'd end up being interested in. Maybe it was the old thing my mami always said about girls playing hard to get. I liked a man who didn't instantly come to feed out of my hand. Anyhow, during my senior year at Miss Wood's, a guy I'd had my eye on for a while came calling: James Roland Monroe. Everyone called him Roe, and he was the one I fell for. The problem was, so did my cousin Yo.

Roe really was more of a Yo-type guy than my usual blond blushers with all those lacrosse badges back in their rooms. Also a senior, he was tall and slender with blue-black hair just grazing the regulation length at the bottom of the earlobes. Like Yo at Miss Wood's, Roe was part of the artsy crowd up at Oakwood, the editor of their literary magazine, and the drummer of their rock-and-roll band, the Beatitudes. He wore the usual preppy clothes but with a difference. He'd be dressed in his navy blue Oakwood blazer and gray wool pants but if you gazed down the length of his long pantlegs, you'd see he was barefoot. He hung his tie over one shoulder as a protest at having to wear one. And always there'd be a copy of Hesse or Kahlil Gibran or D. H. Lawrence in his jacket pocket to show off, I suppose, that he had a deep soul.

But you know, in his case, it wasn't a scam: the guy was deep and in demand—a guy who could fill up your whole life if you let him. That first Sunday he came calling on me, I sensed the jealous faces lined up at the windows of the dorms that ringed the circle where we walked round and round with our callers. (That's what Sunday calling hours amounted to.) Up there, Yo must have been looking down on us, thinking it wasn't fair. Not that I saw her. I had made the mistake of looking right into Roe's soft gray eyes, and an hour later when he left, I still hadn't come up for air.

Why he came calling on me, I don't know. The current revolution had ended, and we were finally having elections back home. My father was running for president—one of his many times, as it turned out. Anyhow, I became a minor celebrity at Miss Wood's, a would-be president's daughter. Don't think Battleaxe didn't give a grand lecture on the difference between democracies and wannabe democracies. But I don't believe it was my VIP status that lured Roe to take an interest in me. It was the poem I'd written for one of her crazy assignments that my English teacher submitted to the combined autumn issue of the Oakwood and Miss Wood's literary magazines. Actually the poem had turned out pretty well, if I do say so myself, one of those données, as she said the French called them, a gift from the gods. In my case, it had to have been a gift all right. I guess the gods got me confused with another dark-haired Latin American kid, my poet cousin. We were supposed to look a little alike.

I'm sure Yo was jealous when my donnée won the literary contest. It was as if I'd trespassed into her creative ken by making a big splash with my pen. What was that poem called? "Immigrant's Love Song," something like that. I still remember the first and last stanzas.

> When I left home I was lost
> as if the sea had no land,
> no place to let loose its waves,
> no dryness in which to run.
>
> But now beside you at night
> I discover a new continent,
> in your hands I find it mapped,
> in your breath I hear my anthem.

I actually thought my poetry debut would ruin my reputation up at Oakwood, turn me into one of those artsy fartsy freaks. But I got even more callers after the poem was published. Heather guessed it was that last stanza with the intimation that I'd gone all the way. She kept reading it over in a sexy Marilyn Monroe voice.

"So?" she finally came right out and asked me.

"So what?" I asked.

"Lucy-pooh!" she cried in exasperation. "So did you go all the way with some guy?"

"My lips are sealed," I said. A popular claim at Miss Wood's those days.

My confession would have been pretty disappointing. Of course I was a virgin. The whole point of sending me to Miss Wood's was to keep me pure for some Dominican macho, who had probably been doing it with the maid since he was twelve. In virgin terms, my parents had been successful.

But not in other ways. I'd gotten ideas in school. Winning that contest was only one thing among others that had convinced me I had a brain. I'd even managed a B+ from Battleaxe, who now was buttering me up. Maybe she thought if the D.R. became a democracy she could claim to have been an influence through the president's daughter. During our monthly conference, the headmistress kept encouraging me to apply to college. But what could I do? Unlike the Garcías' mother and father, who had changed their minds living in this country, my parents still didn't think girls should go to college. I was scheduled to go back to the island after graduation in June.

Then my father, who had been in D.C. talking to some senators about supporting his candidacy, came up for his first parents' weekend ever. The headmistress got him in a corner and said something like the daughter of a democratic president should be setting a good example. My father agreed, and what's more, he went back and convinced my mother that it would be the best thing for me: two years at a junior college, max. I said, sure, even though I had set my sights on the whole shebang: four years of college, a couple of years working in New York City, and then marriage. The face of that husband had been a hazy dream until Roe came calling.

But Yo stepped up to claim she had first dibs. After all, she and Roe had gone to the junior dance together. ("As friends," Roe explained.) She and Roe had spent a lot of Saturday and Sunday calling hours talking together. ("About literary magazine stuff," he assured me.) And Yo had solid evidence to back up her claim. One January night of our senior year, she came to my room to show me a packet of letters.

I read most of those letters through, and I could feel the blood draining from my face. She was right, they were love letters, full of poems that were e. e. cummings clones, not unlike the ones Roe was now sending me. But you know, instead of being mad at Roe, I was mad at my cousin for destroying my peace of mind. "Why are you showing me these?" I asked, tossing the packet back into her lap. She was sitting at the foot of my bed, and I was at the other end. Heather had slipped out of the room to give us a little privacy, but not before rolling her eyes to the ceiling as if to say, you poor thing.

"What do you mean, why am I showing you these?" Yo's eyes were full of tears she was blinking back. She had grown prettier this past year, I don't know, like she cared about the way she looked. Maybe it was Roe who had inspired her.

"I mean, you guys maybe had something going *last* year," I told her, trying to keep my voice calm. That's the way I was explaining it to myself. But I was looking at Yo now with more than a pang of jealousy, thinking, maybe she is prettier than me. "It's over, Yo," I told her as if it were for me to say so.

"Don't kid yourself, Lucy girl." She was shaking her head, smiling ironically. But there was a hurt look in her eyes. "This last letter was written two weeks ago," she said, holding up the pale blue envelope. It was one of the ones at the bottom of the packet I hadn't bothered to look at. After all, I'm not a glutton for punishment.

"Shall I read it to you?" she went on.

I looked her point-blank in the eye. "No," I said. "I'm not interested. Not in the least." Of course, I was dying of curiosity but I wouldn't let on. Plus, I knew my cousin Yo. If she had a point, she was not going to leave it alone. She'd read me that letter if she had to tie me up to listen to it.

And read it she did, sobbing, as my face got stonier, and my heart shattered like those windows in my house during our revolutions. In his last letter, Roe seemed to be answering some desperate note Yo had written him. (Of course, she made no mention of that.) "What we have is forever," he wrote. "But our love is platonic"—a word I was glad I'd learned from my SAT list. "You are still my inspiration. You are still my muse."

It made me wonder what the hell I was?

"Get out of here," I said to her when she was done. Maybe it was the gleam in her eye that made me lose control like she was gloating over how she was right. "Get out of here!" This time it was a scream. Heather poked her head in the room. "You guys all right?"

Yo looked scared. "Come on, Lucinda," she said. "We're cousins. We're not going to let Roe come between us."

"He *has* come between us," I said, hot tears in my eyes.

"Well, I'm willing to give him up," she said, her jaw all set, "if you are."

I burst out laughing. "Sorry, charlie, I'm not going to cut any deals. Let Roe decide who he wants."

She gathered her packet together and left the room with overdone dignity, brushing past Heather still standing in the doorway. As she rounded the corner, I couldn't help calling out, "May the best man win!"

Then I heard her voice calling back down the hall, "May the best *woman* win!"

The very next weekend was winter carnival, and I managed to get on Roe's team for building a huge Puff the magic dragon for the snow sculpture contest. When we were done with our part on Puff's tail, we slipped away into the woods behind the dorms, and I let him have it.

"Come on, Lucinda," he kept saying.

"You come on," I said to him. Tears I had tried to keep back were coursing down my cheeks. He was kissing them away, and damn it, I was letting him.

"You got to understand," he pleaded, "I really thought you wouldn't talk to me if I blew your cousin off."

You know what? It sounded plausible to me. Hadn't I heard Battleaxe talk about those big, mafiosa Latin American families that impeded the growth of democracies. I could see where Roe might think I'd stand by my blood rather than him. "Well, you better talk to her if you want to keep seeing me."

"Sure, sure," he said, looking down at me. Those eyes, those soft gray eyes . . . they got me every time.

"Ay, Roe, I want to be your muse, I want to be your inspiration."

"You are my muse," he said, and bowing his head so that our foreheads touched, he whispered some lines that sounded *very* like e.e. cummings:

> "and now you are and i am now and we're
> a mystery which will never happen again."

"So will you talk to her?" I asked before I let him kiss me again.

"Sure I will, Yolinda," he said. I *swear* I heard "Yolinda."

He must have talked to her because Yo didn't talk to me for almost three months, which must have been hard on her with that big mouth. Finally, we had a tearful reunion at the mailboxes on the day we found out we had both been accepted at Commodore. Though it wasn't a junior college, Yo's mother, Tía Laura, had talked my parents into letting me apply where she could keep an eye on me along with her daughter.

"We'll be together again," Yo said, wiping her eyes. When she gave me a hug, I gave her a few little taps on the back like I was burping a baby.

I should have been the more generous one, I know. After all, I was the one who had ended up with Roe. He had gotten into a college two hours from Commodore, and I was ecstatic. We'd be able to continue our romance into college and on into the rest of our lives. But you see, though I had won Roe, I had lost my peace of mind. We'd be sitting in the parlor and I'd catch Roe's eye straying over to where Yo was writing in her journal, and I'd think, it's Yo he wants. We'd pass by Yo walking around the circle, and Roe would say, "How's it going, Yo?" and I thought I could hear his blood quickening when she blushed a little and said, "So-so."

That spring there were poems by Roe in his literary magazine I hadn't seen. They were all about a love "now lost to touch but heavy in my heart." I grilled him about who that lost love was. "It's just a literary convention, Lucinda," he assured me. "Keats, Wordsworth, Yeats, everyone writes about lost love."

"Doesn't anyone write about happy love?" I asked. "Can't you start a tradition?"

"I need more experience," he said, squeezing my hand

We had talked about it, going all the way. It turned out that Roe, for all his good looks, was a virgin just like me. But at eighteen, Roe was starting to feel like there was something wrong with him because he hadn't had sex. Not that he wanted something crass and cheap, one of the townie girls who snuck into mixers with their teased hair and flashy necklines. He wanted the word made flesh, the alpha and omega meeting in an infinity of love without end. He could go on and on until I really didn't understand what he was talking about. One thing made sense to me: the first woman a man had, Roe said, would stay in his heart for the rest of his life.

But like Yo, I had been raised Catholic. Our eternal souls, if not our good marriages, hung in the balance if we gave up our virgin flower without the sanctity of holy matrimony. But looking into Roe's eyes, I could feel my insides going soft, and I worried that Lucinda María was going to go with her body.

Am I still in Roe's heart, I wonder? I tried to track him down one time, between marriages. I got as far as calling the alumni office and finding out that James Roland Monroe III (I hadn't remembered a number) was working in a big law firm in Washington, D.C., that he'd married Courtney Hall-Monroe, had three kids, Trevor, Courtney, and James Roland IV. I wondered if every time Roe made love to Courtney, he heard the lapping of the Caribbean sea, the faint rustling of palm trees? I decided not to try to find out. What if I called him up and he said, "Lucinda who?" Or worse, "Oh yes, Lucinda from Barbados, wasn't it?"

The truth is that for a long time it was Roe who was in my heart. The many men I fell in love with could all have been his double. The black shank of hair, the fatal look, the same charm I couldn't resist. Problem was, neither could other women. If my father made a career of running for president, I made one out of marrying the wrong men. But never again did I have to compete with my cousin, Yo. She didn't seem to find the same kind of man attractive anymore. Maybe because of the fiasco she brought about that ended things between me and Roe.

Remember those English class journals? All that spring of her broken heart, old Yo was writing down her collected grievances, blow by blow. Me and Roe French-kissing. Me and Roe going steady. Me and Roe applying to nearby colleges. Me and Roe planning to elope and not tell our families.

I'm just making this up. I don't really know what Yo told in her journal, but it was enough to ruin my chances of going on to college or ever seeing Roe again.

What happened was that Tía Laura, Yo's mother, came across the journal—she called it a diary—in Yo's room and read it cover to cover. They're all snoopers in our family. My parents opened every piece of mail from a boy. I wasn't allowed to talk to guys unless an adult was in the room. But no one had remembered to tell them there was a boys school up the hill from Miss Wood's. No one had described calling hours. No one had mentioned winter carnival, spring break, homecoming.

No one, that is, until Yo.

That summer Tía Laura appeared in the compound, supposedly bringing the García girls down for their annual visit. Suddenly, my mother had her eye on me all the time. My father barely spoke to me. I tiptoed around, on my best behavior, spending the evenings at home while the García girls went out on the town with Mundín, having a grand old time in their summer-vacation homeland.

Then the day came round when I was supposed to leave with them for freshman orientation. I'll never forget that morning in my parents' room, my father pacing back and forth, my mother crying, a rosary in her hands. They wanted me at home at their side, they informed me. Tía Laura had discovered a filthy diary. They knew that my cousin Yo had a big imagination. They knew that it was all invention, but still, just the fact that such stuff could be in their niece's head meant the States was no place to send their daughter. There was to be no further discussion. If I wanted an education, I could go to the local college.

I cried and pleaded and even threatened to kill myself. I sounded just like one of those literary magazine poems back at Miss Wood's. I wrote Roe, shamelessly begging him to come rescue me. But I heard nothing back for months. Finally I got a note via Carla on that same pale blue stationary. He had met someone over the summer. *And though I still love you, Lucinda*—I tore that letter up into as many pieces as he had broken my heart. I didn't want to hear about how what we had was forever. And I certainly didn't want to come across the word *platonic.*

As for Yo, we had it out when she came the following summer. She was full of apologies. I had to believe her that she hadn't left that journal out on purpose. I had to believe her that she had wanted me to come to Commodore. That she didn't hold a grudge about Roe. She must have asked me about a hundred times that summer was I happy. Did I forgive her? I told her I forgave her, sure. But I never answered her question about being happy. To tell the truth, at that point I *was* miserable. I had been ready to spread my wings and fly, and it was sort of like being an evolution mutation, all set to be a bird only to find out I was going to have to be an earth creature.

Don't get me wrong, I turned out to be a happy woman after all. I've got five beautiful kids, the oldest the age Yo and I were when Roe came into our lives. I've got a string of boutiques selling my designs faster than my factories can make them. Wife, mother, career girl—I've managed them all—and that's not easy in our *third world* country. Meanwhile the García girls struggle with their either-or's in the land of milk and money.

Especially Yo. And maybe because of her own struggles, she still feels guilty about me. Every time she comes down here and we all gather together, I catch her eye straying over to me, wanting answers.

Those times, you know what I do? I turn to her and I flash her one of my hair-and-nails smiles, a smile I know she does not trust. And I see her wincing as if it still hurts her not to know after twenty years whether it was the right thing for me to end up with the life I'm living. Whether it's all her fault the hard times I've had along the way, the bad marriages, the problems with my parents, my kids without a live-in father. And looking at her, in her late thirties knocking around the world without a husband, house, or children, I think, you are the haunted one who ended up living your life mostly on paper.

The maid's daughter

report

I was eight years old when my mother left me in the campo with my grandmother to go off to the United States to work as the maid for the García family. My mother had been working for the de la Torre family most of her life which is how she finally landed this job with the Garcías. Mrs. García was born a de la Torre and knew all about my mother's background, so when she and her husband decided to stay living in New York after our dictator was killed, she asked my mother if she wouldn't like to come help her with the hard life of being a housewife in the United States.

Mamá jumped at the chance. For years, she had been saying that she wanted to go to Nueva York. Whenever any of the de la Torres went off for an extended stay, my mother made sure she helped pack their bags. She would sprinkle in a special powder made of her ground fingernails and bits of her hair and some other elementos the santera had charged her twenty pesos to prepare. It worked. Over the years, all those little bits and pieces of my mother collected in New York and set up a force of attraction that finally drew the rest of her to the magic city.

Off she went full of promises about how our lives were finally going to change for the better. I believed her, even though, at first, my life changed for the worse. I had been living in the capital in the boarding school she had put me in so I could be near her. It was a nice enough place with toilets and electricity and uniforms and dark-skinned girls, many of whom had light eyes and good hair on account of they were the illegitimate daughters of maids and the young or old dons of important families. There was a whole hierarchy based on whether or not your father had "recognized" you: whether he had admitted that he indeed was your father and had given you his family name. I was pretty low on the totem pole as I was there only because the de la Torre family had talked the nuns into taking me in so I could be near one of their favorite maids, my mother. Or so I thought, back then.

Anyhow, after Mamá went to the States, I was sent way out to the countryside to be with my old grandmother, who ate with her hands and brushed her teeth by chewing on a piece of sugarcane. We slept in a palm-wood hut, no electricity, no toilet, no nothing. Every month we went down to the capital to the de la Torres to collect the money my mother had sent for us. Along with the crisp green bills came letters I read out loud to my grandmother as she didn't know how to make sense of those chicken scratches. Mamá's letters were full of fairytale news about buildings that touched the clouds and air as cold as the inside of the deep freeze at the colmado. There were also pictures of the four García girls, all a little older than me by one, three, four, and five years, all very pretty, with their arms around each other, their heads tilted this way and that in a friendly sisterliness that made me feel sad that I didn't have a sister, too. On the back of these pictures, they signed their names, and once, the one called Yo added a little note, *Dear dear Sarita, we love your querida mamá and we thank you so much for lending her to us.*

Well, at least they're grateful, I thought.

Five years Mamá worked for them, saving up money, coming to visit us only twice, the second time putting me back in the boarding school because she said I was becoming a jíbara like one of those Haitian children who'd never worn shoes. Well, I'd already been three and a half years with the old woman, and I'd grown attached to her, and now it was hard to go back to sleeping on a mattress, eating with utensils, and being a young lady full of pretensions. But how could I complain? My mother was working so hard to give me all the opportunities she never had. I couldn't let her down by showing a preference for the old life she had left behind.

Five years after she left, the incredible news came: Mamá had asked Mrs. García if she could bring me to the States, and Mrs. García had agreed! Ever since I had become a young señorita, Mamá was sick to death leaving me without supervision in a country of wolves. "I know what I'm talking about," she wrote in one of her letters. Later my mother would tell me the truth she had kept from me back in the old country. She was the illegitimate daughter of my country abuela and the wealthy rancher who said he owned the land my grandmother had been squatting on. As for my own father, my mother refused to name him.

The de la Torre family put me on the plane in Santo Domingo, and when I landed at Kennedy airport, there they were, all lined up and leaning over the railing, Mamá, Mrs. García, and the four García sisters. The minute I came through the door, a scared, skinny girl of thirteen, still holding the Barbie they had sent me for Christmas, with my two braids pinned to the top of my head and my pink sweater clashing with my new plaid dress (what did my old grandmother know of matching?), those girls pounced on me.

"Ay, Sarita, our little sister, Sarita!" They kept hugging me as if they'd known me all their lives. I looked over their shoulders at Mamá standing there, smiling proudly, and waiting for her turn.

When the girls were finished, I reached for my mother's hand, kissed it, and asked her blessing. I did the same to Mrs. García, who seemed pretty impressed, and later lectured the girls on the way home about how they should learn from little Sarita how to be well-behaved. There was enough rolling of the eyes in the back seat that the car should have rocked down the highway to their house in the Bronx.

From the first, those girls treated me like a combination of favorite doll, baby sister, and goodwill project. They gave me clothes they had outgrown and jewelry they had gotten that I wasn't supposed to wear in front of their mother. And all of them spent special time teaching me things. Carla often asked me how I felt about this and that (she was practicing to be a psychologist), and then she explained to me how I *really* felt. It was fun—like reading my horoscope in a magazine or hearing Abuela predict what was going to happen to me from the stains in my coffee cup. Yo and Sandi taught me how to make myself up so I looked like exciting things were going to happen to me. Afterwards we had to scrub my face because we knew that Mamá would disapprove. Fifi was more like a playmate since we were almost the same age. Sometimes she would get jealous at the attention I was getting, and Mamá would take me down to the basement where the two of us lived.

"One false step and we will be sent back."

"With your permission, Mamá," I began, "I didn't do anything—" Down came that hand in a slap across my face. Tears brimmed in my eyes, but I could not cry. Mamá had already instructed me on how we were not to make any commotion in this house.

"Don't you give yourself airs," she hissed at me, her voice just above a whisper. "Don't you think you can start disagreeing with me like those García girls with their mother!" She jerked her head up to indicate their upstairs status. Soon that gesture became a shorthand between us. Whenever she wanted to hush me or to send me packing from a room or bond the two of us in a moment of collusion when the girls were around, she'd jerk her head that way. Those García girls! Don't ever think you are one of them.

But they did treat me like one of them. Every once in a while, they'd talk Mamá into letting me go out with them. They had to tell her step by step what they were going to do—even if they then detoured drastically from their plan. Mostly, they said they were taking me to the library or a museum or a movie that was on the list Catholic girls could watch. Then instead of heading for the Metropolitan or the Sacred Heart auditorium, we went down to Washington Square in the Village and watched American kids get high. Sometimes one or the other sister would get picked up, and of course, we'd all go along. One time we ended up in a loft with two long-haired guys listening to loud music that sounded exactly like someone had put forks and spoons in a blender and turned it on high. Those guys started in that they didn't believe we were really all sisters—which is what the García girls had told them. For one thing, Sandi was fair and blond, Fifi was tall like an American girl, Carla and Yo were light olive, and I was café-con-leche with long, black hair and hazel eyes—so we looked like a ragbag family, all right.

But the girls giggled and said that we were island girls and "things happen" on a Caribbean island. Those guys came towards us, suddenly weird and nasty-eyed, but also staggering a little. They said they had a way of telling if girls were sisters. We were scared! We stood up real slow like we were in a room with a colicky baby who had finally fallen asleep, and all five of us gave each other the eye, and a little nod towards the door, a gesture reminiscent of my mother's García girls head-jerk. One-two-three—it was like we were one person breathing in unison—then Yo cried out, "¡Vámonos!" and we flew out the door, clattered down the stairs, and didn't stop running until we were eight blocks away and two flights down at our subway stop.

On the ride home, Carla asked me and Fifi how we felt about what had happened, and Sandi said if we breathed a word about what had happened we would all be in a shitload of trouble. But that Yo kept wondering out loud how those guys could tell if girls were sisters or not.

"Please stop!" Carla finally yelled at her—and it was a yell that could be heard above the rumble of the train. People looked up at us. "You're going to give me nightmares."

"You sound like you need a shrink, Carla," Yo said, so sharp and clever. No one could have the last word with her around, which is why her mother was always threatening to put Tabasco sauce in her mouth—to burn off her quick tongue. There were some sad scenes in that family.

Anyhow, that was the last of our secret trips to the city. In a week, the summer was over. The three oldest García girls were packed off to their colleges, Fifi to her boarding school, and I was left alone with the three grown-ups as if I were the one and only García girl in that family.

If it hadn't been for school, I would have died of loneliness in that empty house. The life there was so isolated compared to the island. Even when I lived out in the campo, Abuela and I woke up in the morning and went outside until it was time to go to bed. Our living room was three rocking chairs under the almond tree facing our neighbors' rocking chairs. The kitchen was a palm roof over a counter of carbon fires where a bunch of women cooked and gossiped together. The toilet was a field on the far side of the river, and the public bath was *in* that river. And in all these places there were plenty of other people.

But in that fancy area of the Bronx, everyone was locked up in a house that had a burglar alarm system and heavy drapes at the windows. Mamá had been there five years, and she said she still didn't know anyone in the houses around ours. The only people Mamá ever saw were the patients that came next door to see the psychologist, who had an office in her house. There was a lady in dark glasses and a kerchief looking over her shoulder, a woman and her skinny teenage daughter screaming at each other as they came up the walk (Mamá shook her head at them just like she did at the García girls), a man with a twisted body and horrible limp (Mamá imitated him to show me how bad), and a bunch of others. I felt all the more grateful to Mamá for what she'd been through for five lonely years, imprisoned—that's the way I thought of it—in that house with only Sundays off. I know I couldn't have stood it. But like I said, I had school to break the lonely monotony.

The public school was a bus ride away in a not-so-good area of the Bronx. Most of the kids there were American blacks along with some Puerto Ricans and a few Irish kids who'd gotten thrown out of the Catholic school. At first Mamá was going to send me to Sacred Heart, but she would have had to pay tuition, and the uniforms cost money. Also, the García girls had gone to that Catholic school before they went off to boarding school, and I believe Mamá knew that Mrs. García would think the maid was giving herself airs if she sent her daughter there.

Before I started at the public school, Mamá lectured me backwards and forwards on the whys and wherefores of what I could and couldn't do. I was to get no phone calls or bring anyone over as this wasn't our house. I was to go directly to school on the bus and promptly at the close of school I was to come back on that bus. Mamá always walked me to the stop in the morning, and she was waiting for me there, dressed in her uniform, every afternoon about four o'clock.

Stories spread at school. I was fairly light-skinned and rather pretty—all the García girls said so. In fact, most people guessed I was Italian or Greek. I had a fancy address on my report card. Kids on the bus reported that a maid in a uniform waited for me—on rainy days she carried an umbrella. When I finally knew enough English, I explained in a faltering voice that my parents (yes, I had created a legitimate family for myself) did not allow me to receive phone calls or visitors. I became the mysterious, rich girl from an island that my father owned . . . near Italy or Greece.

These were *their* misinterpretations, and I didn't have enough English to catch them in time. For all I knew, my father could well be a rich Italian or a toad-faced Greek like the Onassis guy who had married the beautiful Jackie Kennedy. So I let these lies ride, and they became the official story of my life. Who was there to set them straight?

I'll tell you who. Yolanda García. My second year at that school, she came home for the month of January. At her college, students had to do an internship or a research project off campus once during their four years. Yolanda had planned to write a report on her family in the Dominican Republic, but the political situation turned ugly, and Dr. García wouldn't let her go. She threatened to go anyhow, hijack a plane if need be, but Yo's mouth was always bigger than her courage, so of course, she stayed put and looked around for something else she could spend a month studying.

Her eye landed on me.

This was her proposal, which her parents were glad she came up with because she finally quit nagging them that if Shakespeare's parents had kept him from going to London, he never would have written his thirty-eight plays. What she proposed to do was observe my acculturation—I'd never heard of such a thing—as a way of understanding her own immigrant experience.

"Would it be okay, Primi?" she asked my mother, after she'd set up the whole thing over the phone with her advisor.

"My child, we are here at your service, you know that," Mamá said. This was her standard response to anything the Garcías asked for.

"Thanks, thanks so much!" Yo threw her arms around me. I closed my eyes, heartsick. My whole fantasy world was about to come crashing down around me.

Yo and I walked to the bus stop the next morning, Yo yakking away about what it was like for her family that first year in this country. I took a deep breath of that frosty air and let it out so I could see something of myself in this alien world of bare trees, gray sky, brick houses, side by side. Then I told Yo my little secret. I had pretended to my teachers and classmates to be part of the García family. I kept my eyes fixed on the ground as I spoke. I could have taken a test on all the cracks, doggie poo, and graffiti on our walk to the bus stop and gotten an A+ for sure.

When I finished confessing, I expected some kind of judgment.

Instead Yolanda said, "How'd you get away with it?"

"What do you mean?"

"You have a different last name, for one thing."

"I don't mean I told them I was a García. I . . . I—" This was hard. "I just made believe I live in your house with my own father and a mother who's not the maid." I could feel that tingling in my nostrils that meant tears were coming.

"Ay, Sarita." Yo had stopped walking. Her face was full of delight as if I had made up this story to please *her*. "You are my little sister of affection, and that's all anybody has to know about it!"

Why is it that if you hope for something with all your heart, and it's granted, you suddenly have this empty feeling? Or maybe it was just that relief made me feel a hundred pounds lighter, floating on air. She slipped her hand into mine. A gloved hand in a gloved hand—even a human touch was different in this country.

Every day for two whole weeks Yo went to school with me— well, almost every day. She did play hooky a couple of times when her hippy boyfriend hitchhiked down from western Massachusetts, and they snuck away for the day together. Like Mamá, Dr. García didn't believe in dating for his girls. One time when Yo got a call from this guy, Dr. García came on the line and challenged him to a duel!

At school, Yo sat in on all my classes, taking notes, talking to my teachers about my progress. Of course, they wanted to know more about me and about the family. "Sarita's our mystery student!" they said, laughing as if I weren't there. Yo would launch right in, turning my little fibs into the high art of fiction.

I think that's when I lost my joy in making believe I was someone I wasn't. I saw there was a way you could get further and further away from yourself like those García girls, who had become American girls sneaking off with boys who were more interested in getting high than in getting to know them. And did the García girls themselves really know who they were? Hippy girls or nice girls? American or Dominican? English or Spanish? Pobrecitas.

I suppose if I had had Mamá's strength of character I would have stayed in the same school and told the truth. Instead I spoke to Mamá, and after days of my badgering, she finally gave me permission to talk to Mrs. García.

That weekend while I was helping Doña Laura take down the Christmas decorations, I asked if she would mind if I went to the same school as her daughters.

She thought at first I was asking if I could go to Fifi's boarding school. "No, no," I said, "I mean Sacred Heart. I'll get a much better education," I said, which was true enough.

"Why, of course I wouldn't mind," she said, looking at me curiously. "I thought maybe your mother wanted you to be in a school with kids who . . ." I knew what she didn't want to say, in a school with black kids so I wouldn't feel so out of it.

"She says I can go if you say I can," I said, and then, quickly, I added, "but we'll need your help with the tuition." I bowed my head, ashamed to have to ask for this help.

She came down a few steps on the ladder, smiling that sweet smile you see on a mother's face when she looks down at her child. "Of course, you can count on me!" she said. "All I ask is that you keep up your grades." For a second time in two years, I reached for her hand and kissed it. "May la Virgencita be with you and each of your daughters."

She got a faraway, sad look in her eyes—like maybe the only person who might be of some help with her girls *was* the Virgin Mary. Then she climbed back up the ladder and handed me the psychedelic purple-orange-green papier-mâché star the girls had made for the top of the Christmas tree.

———

At the end of her two weeks, Yo stopped coming to school. Then it was pound, pound, pound upstairs on the typewriter her father had given her that she didn't let anyone else use, not even her mother to fill out Dr. García's Workman's Compensation forms. "That's a selfish way to be with that typewriter," Mrs. García accused her.

"It's my one and only special thing," Yo fought back. Just that would have gotten me a slap on the mouth. But Yo didn't know when to stop. "Would you let someone sleep with Papi?" Out came the Tabasco sauce. My mother gave me a jerk of her head, meaning, *Go downstairs. I don't want you to see this.*

But all in all, it was a relatively peaceful time, except for the continual pounding upstairs as if the house now had a heartbeat. I have to hand it to Yo—she worked day and night on that report. She had already interviewed Mamá and me, of course, and her parents, and other maids whose phone numbers Mamá had given her who worked in Dominican homes in Brooklyn and Queens. Sometimes I asked her about what she was writing, but it was like she was caught up in a dream or something. Her mother had to snap her fingers to get her attention. Her father would cup his hands at his mouth and call across the dining room table, "How is our little Shakespeare?"

And then, one night, Yo came racing down the stairs with her report in hand to show to us. "I'm done! I'm done!" She made Mamá touch the stack of pages for good luck, and then she read us the first page where it said that this report was dedicated to all those who had lost their native land, and especially dedicated to *Sarita y Primitiva, parte de mi familia.*

Mamá didn't know what to do with a dedication. "Thank you," she said at last, reaching for that report like it was ours.

"No, no," Yo laughed. "I have to hand this in. A dedication is just, well, a dedication."

I knew exactly what I wanted to do with that dedication. I wanted to write it over, using Mamá's rightful name. More than once, I had tried to get my mother to go back to her real name, María Trinidad. But Mamá refused. The de la Torres had given her that nickname when she was a young wild girl just hired out of the campo. "I'm used to it now, mi'ja. At this point, I'd get all confused if someone changed it. Lord knows my old head has enough trouble remembering who I am as it is." She had spent her whole life working for the de la Torres, and it showed. If you stood them side by side—Mrs. García with her pale skin kept moist with expensive creams and her hair fixed up in the beauty parlor every week; Mamá with her unraveling gray bun and maid's uniform and mouth still waiting for the winning lottery ticket to get replacement teeth—why Mamá looked ten years older than Mrs. García, though they were both the same age, forty-three.

That weekend, the Garcías went off to visit Fifi in her boarding school, and Yo went along to say hi to her old high school teachers. Mamá and I were going to leave early on Saturday afternoon to spend the night with her friend in Brooklyn. So while she did the laundry downstairs, I was finishing up the upstairs. In Yo's room, right next to her typewriter, I spotted the fancy black binder. I turned past that dedication page, and I began to read.

I don't know what I can compare it to. Everything was set down more or less straight, for once. But I still felt as if something had been stolen from me. Later, in an anthropology course I took in college, we read about how certain primitive (how I hate that word!) tribes won't allow themselves to be photographed because they feel their spirits have been taken from them. Well, that's the way I felt. Those pages were like those little pieces of herself Mamá had sprinkled in the suitcases of traveling de la Torres—a part of me.

I put that binder in my bucket of cleaning materials, and when Mamá wasn't looking, I slipped it in my bookbag. My plan was to take that report to school and hide it in my desk until I had decided what I wanted to do with it.

Late Sunday night—Mamá always waited till the last minute to come back from her day off—the two of us walked up from the subway. It was a snowy night, and at each street lamp, we could see thick flakes coming down, thousands upon thousands, like something there is plenty of for everyone. It put Mamá in a good mood, even though she was on her way back to grinding the yucca, as she called her hard work.

She had stopped at a street lamp, and like a child, she was sticking out her tongue and laughing as the flakes pelted her face. "Ay, Gran Poder de Dios" she said. "I hope your abuela sees this before she dies."

I couldn't bring myself to second a wish for my grandmother to come to such a cold and lonely country. "Why?" I asked Mamá, a challenge in my voice. The habits of the García girls were catching.

I thought maybe Mamá would strike me for the rude tone in my voice, but instead she looked directly at me. In the light from the street lamp I saw her face wet with melted snowflakes. "You are not happy here, mi'ja, is that it?"

"I'm always happy at your side, Mamá," I lied.

"The girls, they treat you well. Doña Laura has a special place in her heart for you."

"I know, Mamá, but they're not our family."

She was quiet a moment as if she were going to tell me something but then thought better of it. "What is it you want, mi'ja?" she asked finally.

I hesitated. I did not want to hurt her. I wanted her to believe she had given me everything I could ask for. "I want you and Abuela to have a nice house. For you not to have to work so hard."

My mother touched my face in the old way from when I was a child. "You keep working hard in school, and someday you'll make something of yourself, and help us out."

I felt my heart sink down to the bottom of my cold feet. I had ruined our one chance in the United States! I would not get away with what I had done. The Garcías would never believe a burglar had broken into the house just to steal Yo's report. And as my mother had once told me, one wrong move and both of us would be on a plane home to poverty and hard work.

That short block before the turn on the corner to the García house, I think I prayed the hardest I had prayed up to that point in my life. *Please God, don't let the Garcías be home yet! Please don't let me be found out!* But when the house came into view, I saw lights beaming in the second-floor bedrooms.

We let ourselves quietly in the side door, and I braced myself, but no Yo came running down the stairs to report her stolen work. No Dr. García asked my mother to try and remember who might have been in the house besides the two of us. No Doña Laura queried us on where we might have put things that had been left lying around. A miracle, I thought, a miracle has happened.

Before I went to bed, I guess I felt that thief's impulse that supposedly sends them back to the scene of the crime. When Mamá was tucked in her cot, I slipped out of mine. Inside our closet, I reached in my bookbag. The folder was gone.

The next day Yo came running down the stairs as we were going out the door. "I'll walk her, Primi," she said to Mamá.

On the sidewalk, out of earshot, she let me have it. "Why, Sarita? Just tell me why?"

I shrugged. Mamá had already told me not to insult any of the Garcías, or we would be in hot water. What could I say?

"I was panicked when I couldn't find it," she went on. "Mami and Papi helped me search all over. And just so you know," she added, her voice full of self-righteousness, "I didn't tell them where I found it."

I guess I should have said, Thank you for saving mine and my mother's hide. But the words wouldn't come out of my mouth.

"Aren't you going to at least tell me why you did it, Sarita?"

I shrugged, clutching my books to my chest as if a cold wind were blowing. But the day was unseasonably warm. Most of last night's snowfall had melted, and the streets and sidewalks had that rainy smell of wet pavement.

"I don't understand," she said finally. I could feel her eyes looking intensely at me. "I thought we were close." She left that sentence up in the air just begging for me to reassure her. But instead I kept on looking down at the sidewalk, studying all those cracks I was not supposed to step on so as not to break my mother's back.

Over the years that Mamá and I stayed on with the García family, Yo and I never spoke of this incident again. Sometimes, we had long talks, and we'd end up hugging each other, but that stolen report was always between us. It wasn't the stealing itself, but my silence when Yo asked me if we weren't close. It was as if I had broken some bond all four of the García girls had taken for granted.

The report itself Yo gave me to keep when she got it back from her professor. I can't say I ever read it, but I accepted it, and it stayed stacked on our shelf of things in the basement closet. Finally when Mamá went back to live on the island, she took it along. For all I know, the pages of that report were used by Abuelita to light her fogón that she insisted on using even after I bought her an electric stove.

I kept my promise to Mrs. García. I got all A's at Sacred Heart and won a full scholarship to Fordham, which was only about ten blocks away from the house. The scholarship was part grades and part tennis. I'd gotten pretty good at the park program Mrs. García enrolled me in to get some exercise over the summers. A few years of Nueva York nutrition and I'd shot up like Fifi and gotten some skin on my bones. Once in college, my coach wanted me to go professional, but I decided against it. Those hobby professions were for the García girls—who ended up being unemployed poets and flower arrangers and therapists. Instead I majored in the sciences—which didn't come so easy to me. But I made myself study the flow and movement of atoms and molecules with as much intense concentration as I had focused on those cracks in the sidewalk during my heart-to-heart talks with Yo García.

One day, years after Doña Laura and Don Carlos sold their house in the Bronx and moved to the city, Yo shows up at my clinic. Turns out she's in Miami, peddling her manuscript at some convention. I hadn't seen any of the García girls for at least two decades. One of my technicians comes in and says that there's a kind of kooky-looking lady asking for me.

"Show her in," I say—my heart pounding when I hear the name.

In she comes, a wisp of a woman with her long straight hair she used to wear in a braid now a tangle of gray-speckled curls.

She's still pretty, but it's a prettiness tinged with weariness like her looks weren't made for the knockabout life she's had. "Wow, Sarita, girl, pretty nice digs here," she says, rolling her eyes in that García girl way.

I catch my head involuntarily jerking up, and I feel the sharp pang of missing my mother.

And that's why she's here. She gives me a big hug, and we sit down on the couch. "I heard about Primi," she says, her voice cracking. "I didn't even know she was sick." Her eyes fill, and on account of her mascara, she has black tears.

"She had a hard life," I say in an even voice. It's one of the skills that I've cultivated over the years—keeping tight control of my feelings. "And it was especially hard at the end when your family turned against her."

"We never turned against her!" Yo stands up and paces back and forth in front of the couch. "My sisters and I were always on her side."

I have to admit she's right. Until the end, the USA Garcías never rejected Mamá. It was the de la Torre family back on the island that accused her of having lost her mind when she claimed—at the very end—that one of them was my father.

"Even Mami," Yo continues her pacing, "even she said that your mother wouldn't make up such a thing."

I recall Mrs. García's sweet smile, the special place she always had in her heart for me. Maybe she knew. Maybe that's why she let me come up from the island to make something of myself in New York. "I believe you," I tell Yo. "Now come sit next to me. You're making me nervous pacing like that."

She sits down, and suddenly we are face to face after all these years. What I'm thinking is, Mamá's dream has turned out! Her baby, an orthopedist with one of the top sports medicine clinics in the country, with a Rolex that cost four times her annual wages before she came to New York, and beside me, Yo García, starving writer, sometime teacher, in a cheap jersey dress. "Your mother was like a mother to us," she says. "Ay, Sarita, we thought of you as our sister."

It's too late now to try to set things straight. "You girls were good to us," I agree. That is only part of the truth, of course. But it's the part that I want to give her to make her feel good about the past. I can tell by looking at her that she's going through hard times. She's too skinny. There are bags under her eyes. She needs a good haircut.

I stand up—it's time for me to get back to work—and when she stands up right after me, I put my arms around her. I can feel her dry skin against my cheeks.

She's the first to pull away. "I better go," she says, looking over her shoulder, laughing awkwardly. "Your boss is going to get on your case for keeping your patients waiting."

"I am the boss," I say, smiling straight at her.

"Just like predicted!" When I look at her quizzically, she adds, "I guess you never read my report, did you?"

"I didn't know I was going to be graded on it twenty-five years later," I say right back.

She is laughing, shaking her head. It's not often someone has the last word with Yo García. "Let's not wait another twenty years to see each other," she says, picking up her coat. I nod, though I doubt I am ever going to see any of the García girls again. Mamá has died. The past is over. I don't have to make believe anymore that we are five sisters.

"Take care of yourself," I say to Yo as she heads out the door. "And say hello to your sisters."

The teacher

romance

*O*nce *in a career there comes a student*—he writes out in longhand. He is retiring at the end of this school year and has vowed never to touch a computer. The English department secretary will type up his garbled notes, and by that very afternoon a white envelope marked *confidential* will be in his box. Confidential indeed. Lord knows what his colleagues would say about Garfield's indulgence of this latest plea for help from their troubled ex-student, Yolanda García.

Dear Professor Garfield, I've got to get my life back on track. I've decided to follow your advice at long last. I'm applying to graduate schools, and I hope that you will write me a letter of recommendation one more time. I know you don't have any reason to believe that I will carry through with my plans, but who does a person turn to when all others have lost faith in her promise? I turn to you.

Fifteen years ago, Yolanda García turned up in his Milton seminar, a dark-haired, pretty young woman, an intense look in her eyes. At that point Garfield didn't realize it was the only look she had. He had assumed that with a name like Yolanda García and a slight accent to her speech, she was a foreign student, and her writing would be ghastly and her comprehension of the text minimal. But she whipped out papers that sang with insight and passion. She wouldn't leave the lines of *Paradise Lost* alone until she had tripled and quadrupled the double entendres, and Professor

Garfield had to restrain her. "That will do, Miss García. Four puns a passage is quite enough, even for Milton's Satan."

I've finally decided to get my life back on track.—How many times has she written this line, or said it in a crackly, breathless voice in a late-night call from some place where it was probably still a decent hour. But of course, Miss García would not think that here, in western Massachusetts, it could be bedtime for her old professor who was just getting on track himself after a journey to heartbreak and back.

So, what's one more time? The first letter of recommendation he wrote to the Fulbright committee was thirteen—or was it fourteen?—years ago, the fall of her senior year. *Once in a career there comes a student.* He could not think of a worthier candidate to be awarded a fellowship to go to Chile to translate contemporary Latin American writers. She was of Hispanic origin. Her first language, Spanish, would be indispensable to her in understanding the original texts. As for her English. Caramba! (Of course, he crossed out that silliness with a thick, inked line so not even the secretary could read it.) Yes, her English was flawless. Though still sporting a slight accent—that had indeed been his unfortunate verb, *sporting*—she had a native's intuitive grasp of the language of Milton and Chaucer and Shakespeare. *Gentlemen, you will not regret the choice of Miss Yolanda García as a Fulbright fellow.*

He had had to eat those words. By the time Miss García had been awarded the grant, she had become enamored of a local hippy boy and had run off with him—spring of her senior year. He, Garfield, could not believe it when the dean called him up with the news. "Garfield, you're her advisor, can you make any sense of this?" Garfield remembered a golden-haired young man waiting outside class for Yolanda, a boy of classic beauty—the girl had an eye all right. Darryl Dubois—she had introduced them—looked like an Arcadian shepherd in a pastoral. Garfield also remembered the boy couldn't put two words of his own native language together. No, the professor and advisor told the dean, he could not make any sense of Miss García's choice at all.

Her own father could not make sense of it either. The irate Hispanic man had shown up in the dean of student's office. "Where is my Yo?" he had shouted in a broken English that made him all the more pathetic. Thompson, who'd accepted the deanship only on the proviso that he get a leave every fourth year, did not have the talent for this sort of thing. What could he do but sit the man down, get him a glass of water like a child, and say, "Dr. García, we at Commodore College are as perplexed as you are. We will do everything in our power to convince your daughter to graduate in time with her class. She is one of our top students. We are mystified. We are disappointed."

According to Thompson, his tone of voice, the cadence of his short, futile statements calmed the furious man. "And Jesus, Garfield, what I haven't seen in all my years dealing with parents, this dad put his face in his hands and wept." Thompson had poured out the whole story to Garfield during their usual Friday evening at the Green Tavern. "I just can't get the poor guy out of my mind."

The truth was these students did get under your skin. They signed up for your Milton seminar or your Romantic poetry course, and before you knew it, you were not only teaching them how to scan iambic pentameter, you were also trying to save them, in many cases from their own selves. How could Yolanda García, with the highest grade point average in the department, run off with a high school dropout whose idea of literature was the ridiculous lyrics of some song by a band with the name of an animal—the monkeys or the turtles or the beetles, for heaven's sake?

Thompson told how the father had ripped up the reimbursal
check the college was returning to him for the second semester
tuition. In a thundering voice with a hand lifted, finger pointing
heavenward, like Moses (Thompson's field was religion), the
father had announced to the whole of the dean of students' office
that his daughter was dead to him. Off he went in that salmon
suit, a color no one on this sleepy campus had ever before seen a
man wearing. As for Yolanda García, her name was removed from
the list of active students. "A waste, a damn waste," Thompson
concluded at the end of the evening.

But Garfield could not let the matter drop—though Helena
again accused him of being obsessed with a student. "What about
your own children?" she scolded, pouring herself a nightcap of
straight vodka. "They're not children," he had argued back.
"They're in college."

"And so is this Jocasta—"

"Yolanda. It's a Spanish name," he corrected her. She was right,
of course. Yolanda was the same age as their eldest, Eliot. But
Yolanda was unusual—she didn't know the ropes in this culture.
Someone had to teach her. "Once in a career there comes a student," he began.

"Oh please, Jordan, spare me the bullshit."

That they never saw eye to eye—Garfield had learned to live
with. But that she had the coarse, foul mouth of a hussy when
she had been drinking was still hard for him to bear. He, for
whom words counted, for whom the world was held together by
the glue of language. "Helena, please," he protested and retreated
to his study. There he made a few calls among the locals and
found out the whereabouts of the young newlyweds.

Next day, he presented himself at the door of the rundown
apartment on the North Side, next to the town dump. At first,

Yolanda was shocked, and then grateful, embracing him and pulling him inside as if theirs were a clandestine meeting.

Once the door was closed, she seemed at a loss what to do with him. The place was a mess. The window sashes sagged, the painted wood floor was chipping, the few pieces of furniture looked as if they'd been dragged in from the dump outside. "It's just temporary," she apologized, her cheeks full of color. Her young husband was already at his bartending job, please sit down, what could she offer him?

He sat gingerly on a couch draped with an Indian bedspread of elephants linked tail to trunk, a rajah with an umbrella atop each one. A cat the color of the yellow fog in "Prufrock" observed him through narrowed eyes. Garfield expected it to open its mouth any minute and recite, "'That is not it at all. That is not what I meant at all.'"

"No, thank you," he said when Yolanda repeated her offer of refreshments. He wanted only to talk to her.

It took one or two questions before she tearfully admitted she had made a big mistake. "I mean, dropping out my senior spring," she was quick to add. "I'm not sorry I got married." She played with the band on her finger, no doubt still clinging to the hope that love would conquer all. "I only had nine more credits to go."

"Well, *that* mistake can be rectified and we will rectify it." Garfield nodded at her as if she had come in for a conference asking for his advice. "You are finishing up the semester, Miss García, and that is that." Even in this run-down tenement with wallpaper Victorian ladies with parasols, coming unglued as if in shock over the invasion of Indian rajahs on elephants—even here, sitting on a dirty sofa that smelled of cat and spilled drinks and other mistakes, Garfield observed the formalities. *Miss García. That is that.*

Didn't he always proclaim to his classes the greatness of British civilization, how even in far colonies and dim outposts the Brits maintained their impeccable manners. He himself was from Minnesota, though he believed no one could guess it from his speech. If only Helena could observe some civilities from the dim reaches of her drinking, things might be better between them.

"But, Mr. Garfield, I can't afford Commodore. My parents disowned me." She looked at him with the doomed eyes of a Desdemona whom Othello has by the throat.

"Let's not get carried away, here. We'll talk to Dean Thompson. Even if you have to take out a loan, we will get you through." The conversation was getting very personal. He checked his watch. "I have conference hours to attend to. I'll look for you tomorrow morning in my office, nine o'clock sharp."

"But—," she began, glancing towards the door as if afraid the hippy boy might show up any minute. "I don't think Sky Dancer will like it."

Sky Dancer, good God! "*That's* his name?"

She looked at him from under her brows with knowing eyes. "He changed it. He thinks it sounds more . . . " She hesitated. She had caught herself already making fun of the new husband.

"More interesting," he concluded for her. She nodded, biting her lip. To keep a smile from surfacing? "Well, Miss García, if Mister Sky Dancer really does love you, he will not stand in your way. If he gives you any trouble, you tell him—" Who on earth did he, Garfield, think he was? This young woman was no relation, after all. His colleagues were bound to talk. "You tell Mister Sky Dancer to come see me." He cleared his throat. "*In loco parentis*," he added. "I am your advisor and that is as good as family."

She bent her head, and when she looked back up at him, her

eyes were wet. "Thank you, Mr. Garfield," she said. "You've probably saved my life."

"Is that all the credit I get? *Probably*?" he teased, casting a look around. On an upended crate that seemed to serve as an end table to the couch sat the edition of Stevens they had used fall semester in the modern poetry seminar. "'After the final no there comes a yes,'" he quoted.

"'And on that yes the future world depends,'" she finished, smiling.

She graduated with honors—the degree awarded to Yolanda María García, whose semi-reconciled family was in attendance. "That's not her fucking name!" the hippy boy-husband stood up and shouted. After the ceremony, Garfield witnessed the scene on the green outside the chapel. This Sky Dancer snatched the sheepskin from Yolanda's hands and, just as Dean Thompson had described the father tearing up the reimbursal check, the young man ripped up her diploma. "If they want you to graduate, let them give you one with your fucking name." The father, who had just barely contained himself all weekend, cursed the fellow roundly in loud, furious Spanish in front of quite a crowd.

Six months later, the phone rang—a crackly, far-off voice from some dim outpost. She had gone down to the Dominican Republic and gotten a quickie divorce. She was calling from there, staying a few months to get her head together but she wanted to finally get her life on track, you know? (Yes, he knew!) And so, she was thinking of applying to his alma mater Harvard, what did he think?

"Marvelous idea!" he yelled into the line so that Helena, lying beside him, plunked her pillow over her head and groaned. "Hold the wire, let me take it in my study," he said. But he left the bedroom line off the hook, and later he wondered if Helena had listened in on the conversation. For days afterwards she was berating the girl for spending long distance money for therapy from a man who couldn't get his own life together.

Graduate school was a marvelous idea for Miss García. He had discouraged her preoccupation with "creative writing," a soft field to say the least. One could always write on the side if one wished, but one had to be trained in something substantial. She would do well to specialize in the Romantics or perhaps modern American literature since she was so partial to Stevens and Eliot and Frost. "I always thought your analyses and papers were graduate school material. As for the past, it's over. We all make mistakes. The challenge is to keep moving. 'To strive, to seek, to find, and not to yield,'" he concluded, quoting Tennyson.

"'I will drink life to the lees,'" she agreed. The echo on the wire made the quoted lines sound all the more sententious. "'To follow knowledge like a sinking star beyond the utmost bound of human thought.'"

Beyond the utmost bound of human thought, the echo came back. After the call, he could not sleep. The rousing lines from Tennyson, the voice of a special student, the bright young faces lost to him every year at graduation, the book on the Victorian discovery of the epic in diminished form he had never written—all of these ghosts taunted him in the small downstairs study below the room where his estranged wife of thirty years lay sleeping. What was a life about, anyhow? A struggle to find one's way under the cold impartial stars—who had said that? He thought of the unhappy woman upstairs in bed. *I strove to love you in that old, high way of love, and yet we'd grown, as weary-hearted as that hollow moon.* How did those lines go?

To quiet the turmoil, he sat down at his desk, and he penned then and there his second letter of recommendation in support of Yolanda García. To the Graduate Studies Program of the English Department of Harvard University. *Once in a career there comes a student.* A month later, she called to say she was back in the States, her application was completed, could he send his letter out? By all means. Months went by, a couple of conversations transpired, including the elated one in which she delivered the news that she had been accepted with a T.A. Marvelous! Then, silence. No note on Harvard letterhead, no postcard of the Cambridge quad with a scribbled greeting or promise of a letter later when things calmed down. Finally, he heard from a returning alum—their third-year reunion already!—that Yolanda García had gone back to the Dominican Republic and gotten involved in a revolution or something. Hadn't he seen her picture in *Newsweek* along with some Peace Corps kids? On the way home, Garfield stopped by the library and looked up the old issue— and sure enough, there she was, arm in arm with a handful of fair-haired young men and women and surrounded by guardias on the steps of a pink national palace. So that's where the men got their taste for suit color.

Garfield was both downcast and exhilarated by the *Newsweek* photo. He was sorry Miss García had let the brilliant opportunity of the Harvard T.A. go. On the other hand, he couldn't help but admire her gutsiness. Maybe she would be a Maud Gonne, somebody a young Yeats would write poems about.

He didn't hear from Miss García for the next two years— though he thought of her now and then, wondering what had come of her rabble-rousing on the island. During that time, his own life took what looked like a nose dive but really was a surfacing into clearer, happier waters. Helena ran off to Rutgers with that nincompoop from sociology. Given the years of disaffection and her final betrayal, the divorce was relatively amicable. His two boys wavered as to whom to side with, and then sighed with relief, realizing there was no contest here. "This is the best thing for your mother and me," Garfield told them. But he spared them the rest. *We were never meant for each other.* That would have been too brutal, to deny them the fantasy of a once happy parental past.

Still, after thirty years of shared living, the solitude was difficult. To fill the long evenings and weekends, he began inviting his junior faculty members over, young colleagues in need of mentoring, whom he would not automatically lose in four years. That's how Matthews came into this life. The new Renaissance fellow was outspoken, in need of seasoning, but decidedly brilliant, albeit with a little earring in his ear. Harder to ignore were the powerful feelings the young man stirred up in Garfield. At this late stage to find his heart inclining towards another man! Could he have been so blind? *I stumbled when I saw.* Who had said that? These days, it seemed, the glue of language was coming undone; the world as he had known it was falling apart. Still, his lifelong habits of self-control persisted. Garfield kept his secret to himself until one evening when Matthews confronted him after a student performance of Oscar Wilde.

The importance of being honest. Well, it had been their secret. Matthews had eventually gone on to UC, San Diego, unable to bear the repressed little New England campus of Commodore. It was during Matthews's time at Commodore, while he was living in Garfield's own house under the status of "boarder," that Yolanda García finally called and left a message on that horrid machine Matthews had hooked up and then taken along with him to California. It was the only thing Garfield had been glad to see go.

Hi, Mr. Garfield, wow, a machine! You, who used to hate all new-fangled things! Well, I guess we've all been through some changes. I'm back in the States, in Tennessee of all places—I love it! I'm working with prisoners and senior citizens and schoolchildren. I'll write you a long letter, promise. I just wanted to say hi and see how you were doing. Please say hello to Mrs. Garfield. And sorry about the Harvard mess. Okay? Oh yeah, this is Yolanda García and let's see, I think it's Tuesday and it's ten o'clock in the morning here. Bye!

Prisoners, senior citizens, school children. So, she had finally decided on social work. What a pity. Well, at least she had settled down and was happy.

"Who is this Yolanda García?" Matthews had asked him.

"Once in a career there comes a student," Garfield began—and stopped himself.

But Matthews was nodding. "Yep, I've had one of those." His first year out of graduate school, there was a young woman who had flipped over him. It got to be quite a problem: she would follow him home, stand outside his apartment building, gazing up at his window. Matthews thought he could cut off the crush just by informing her of his sexual orientation, but when he called her in and confessed, she didn't bat an eye. "So? I don't care." Matthews still got birthday and Christmas cards from the young woman, who had since married but continued to sign her letters, *Love always.*

"Oh, this situation is not personal in that way," Garfield informed him.

Matthews had looked at him with those kind but sharp, blue eyes of his, and in his soft Louisiana drawl that was like butter on bread, he'd said, "Jordan, it's always personal. You know that."

Too soon, Matthews was gone—San Diego, the other tip of the continent!—and the days were long and the nights were longer. But the promised letter from Miss García did arrive. She was working on a project with the National Endowment for the Arts in prisons and schools and senior-citizen homes teaching creative writing. (Oh dear. Better that than sociology, he supposed.) Furthermore she had fallen in love with a British man and they were planning to get married, and this time she thought she was making a smart choice. What did he think?

As a whole the British are a fine people, he wanted to tell her. Consider how, even in far colonies and dim outposts, they maintain their impeccable manners. And so on. But as he read her letter he was struck by how, after extolling this British man, she had asked for Garfield's opinion. Wasn't the doubt already an indication of something? But how could he ruin her peace of mind with Macbeth-like doubts. *Oh, full of scorpions is my mind, dear wife!* He was available for any *academic* advice she might need, but affairs of the heart, in that arena he had to agree with Helena's estimation of him, he was not one to talk. Hadn't it taken him most of his life to figure out who it was he could love?

And so he wrote, *I am glad you have found a suitable companion for yourself, Miss García.* As he scribbled congratulations, it was Matthews he imagined, the long aristocratic hands, the slender hips, the bony martyr's face cocked playfully to one side, saying, "'Come live with me and be my love and we will all the pleasures prove . . .'"

"Impossible," Garfield had told him when Matthews proposed in quoted verse from San Diego. "I've got a thirty-four-year career to think of, Matthews. If you had wanted to live with me, why didn't you stay here? Commodore was only too happy to have you."

"Sure, Jordan, and die a slow, painful death"—and then the unforgivable words that made Garfield place the receiver calmly and furiously in its cradle—"just like you have."

———

Over the course of the next few years, he heard from her often. Her calls were no longer requests for recommendation letters or advice, but friendly chats. How are you, Mr. Garfield? Where'd your machine go? What are you doing over the summer? Are you working on a book or something?

He supposed that she had found out about his divorce and was calling up, in part, out of concern, thinking that the lonely twang in his voice was due to his missing Helena. After his heart attack the first fall Matthews was gone, she called every few weeks, always on Sundays like his sons. "How you doin', Mr. Garfield?" Her voice resounded as she paced through the rooms on the other end of the line. She was living in a big, old house in San Francisco. (Five hundred miles north of San Diego!) The Englishman was well-to-do, it seemed, traveling all over the globe. "He's one of the ones who runs things," she laughed. He could hear it in her voice, too, a hankering for something else. "Is it okay if I send you some stuff I'm writing," she asked. "I know you don't believe in creative writing, but I need some feedback."

"Absolutely! I'd love to read what you're writing," he lied. What he really wanted to say was, now that you're settled down, Miss García (she had kept her name this time), why don't you visit the nearby Stanford campus and consider that doctorate? Think of it, you'll have your own focus in life, since obviously, this jet-age Brit isn't providing it for you.

The poems came typed but already worried with penciled-in revisions as if she couldn't stop herself from her endless perfecting of the lines. And they were quite good. Oh, the world weariness in them got old, and he could have done with a lot less of those female poems about the discovery of her own body, but the control was there in the lines, the mastery or near mastery of form. The stories were less compelling but the understanding of character and the eye for the telling detail showed promise, as he told her in his long letter back. He could not help adding, "And now, Miss García, this is my unasked-for advice. You are quite near the Stanford campus. Look up my old Harvard classmate, Clarence Wenford, *the* Wenford who edited our *Modern Poetry* text—I'm penning him a note right off."

Next time she called, she reported that she had gone to visit Professor Wenford and had sat in on his classes all day. "But I don't know, Mr. Garfield. I'm just not cut out for the nitty-gritty academic stuff—"

"Of course, you are," he interrupted. "'The fascination of what's difficult,'" he quoted.

"Yeats was writing about writing poetry, not about going to grad school."

"You have to think of your future." Garfield himself had not had the goods for a brilliant career and so could never trade his post at Commodore for one at UC, San Diego. "You've got what it takes, Miss García. It would be a waste not to use it."

There was a worried silence at the other end. Then, rather vaguely, she said, "Well, I'll see, Mr. Garfield."

The poems kept coming and the stories. Faithfully, he wrote back his letters of evaluation: *You might consider using the sonnet structure in your love poems to provide some control over such difficult material. Excellent use of stream of consciousness to convey confusion of your protagonist. Kill all your darlings, to quote Faulkner.* Then, after two years of frequent contact, the calls and letters and packets of poems and stories stopped. Weeks and months went by. Once or twice, Garfield tried reaching her. But all he got was the British husband's canned, civilized voice encouraging him to leave a message. Finally, the tearful call came that he was not all that surprised to receive. She was in the Dominican Republic again. "I'm getting a divorce. We're just not meant for each other, you know? Though, he's a good man. And it's so hard to make any real connection on this earth. I keep wondering if I'm all wrong, you know, everyone here thinks I'm making a big mistake."

She was crying now. "Let's not get carried away, Miss García," Garfield soothed her.

"Ay, Mr. Garfield. What do you think, eh?"

He looked into the dim outposts and far reaches of his heart and took a deep breath. Damn the proprieties that kept him in chains. "I think you should follow your heart, Miss García," he said at last. When they hung up, he stood awhile with his hand on the receiver as if he were still calming the distraught young woman over the wires. And then, he picked up the phone and dialed the number the department secretary had given him months ago for Professor Timothy Matthews.

Perhaps because he took the following year off, renting out his house to the new woman in classics and writing up a leave proposal to research the collapse of the stanza "as we know it" in contemporary poetry, he lost touch with Miss García. He had not left an address with the department, asking instead that his mail be forwarded to his sister in Minnesota. To his dear sister, he confessed everything with firm instructions not to give out his whereabouts. The year was a glorious interlude in sunny California. And it turned out his stay was quite a help to Matthews, who was undergoing his tenure review. The young hothead was suddenly a bundle of nerves.

"*Fait accompli,*" Garfield kept reminding him. "For heaven's sake, you've already got a book out from Cambridge and you're a first-rate teacher. What more could they want?"

"Garfield, hombre, don't take away my suffering," Matthews sassed back.

Of course, Matthews was awarded tenure, and during their week of celebration in Acapulco, the couple began to make their plans. Garfield would have to go back for at least a year of teaching after his paid leave. "It's the honorable thing to do," he argued when Matthews insisted he could just "blow Commodore."

"Oh, Jordan." The young man laid his head on the older man's shoulder. "What am I going to do with you?"

"Love me always," Garfield suggested.

"'Until the seas 'gan dry, mee love, until the seas 'gan dry,'" Matthews recited grandly. But he kept muttering, "Honorable thing," as if he couldn't quite make sense of that combination of words.

After that first year of separation, Garfield's sense of dutifulness prevailed again. Why not complete the final two years of his tenure and retire with what Matthews called "your gold watch and pat on the butt"? With long vacations together and the telephone to keep them in close contact, they could wait. But it was Garfield who could wait, accustomed as he was to maintaining control over the unruly feelings in the far reaches of his heart. Matthews, on the other hand, could not. One early fall morning of their second year of separation, the devastating call came.

"I've got some bad news, mee love." Matthews' voice was shaky on the other end of the line though he was trying to sound his usual cocky self. Garfield had been outside where he was putting away his tomato cages for the season—his old Minnesota farmboy past had not completely disappeared. Oddly, as he raced inside to get the phone, it was the face of Yolanda García that had flashed through his mind. It was far too early in California for Matthews to be up on a Saturday morning.

"What is it, Matthews, where are you?" Garfield demanded. In the background, he could hear an intercom making its self-important announcements.

"I'm at the hospital. Garfield, listen. I . . . I . . . picked up something and it doesn't look good."

He did not have to say much more. "Let's not jump to conclusions," Garfield advised, his heart beating wildly in his mouth.

"Garfield, let's face it. Mouth's full of sores, lungs sound like *Paradise Lost*, blotches all over the old corpus delicti. I'm a dead man."

"We'll get through this, we will!" Garfield could hear an unfamiliar edge of hysteria in his voice—he struggled for control. The semester had already started. How was he going to tend to Matthews long distance *and* teach his classes?

"Get yourself checked," Matthews was saying. And then he himself solved Garfield's quandry about how to be in two places at once. "Can I come die with you?"

"Yes, yes," he whispered fiercely into the line. As if in mockery, the memoried lines came to mind. *After the final no, there comes a yes.* He quoted them now to Matthews.

There was that naughty chuckle he knew so well on the other end of the line. And then, the heartwrenching sob, "Oh, God, I thought we had a lifetime."

"No more of that kind of talk," Garfield scolded, with no conviction in his voice. When he finally hung up, he found he had crushed the tomato cage he had carried in under his arm.

Out in the garden he plowed under the spent stalks of corn and dug up the last of the leeks and onions to bring in. He fixed up the boys' bedroom, putting down fresh sheets on Eliot's bed. He checked the supply of towels in the linen closet. Made an appointment for an HIV test in Boston, where he could be checked discreetly before meeting Matthews's plane. Then there was the batch of Restoration drama papers to correct. Anything to keep sorrow at bay, anything. If Garfield had developed one fine talent in his life it was that one. In a few days, Matthews would be coming home to die by his side.

Come die with me and be my love and we shall all the horrors prove.

It was the autumn of Matthews's dying—the long, slow, chilling days of his departing. *This thou perceivest which makes thy love more strong, to love that well which thou must leave ere long.* At long last, Garfield let his heart go, tending to the vanishing young man. All that could be said was said. Matthews died in his arms as Garfield read Auden out loud, and Matthews mouthed his favorite lines.

Lay your sleeping head, my love, human on my faithless arm.

By the time it was over, Garfield felt numb, unresponsive to the world around him. The box of ashes in his study was all that was left of the luminous presence in his heart—propped there between *Piers Plowman* and *Pamela*. Matthews would not like that fit, at all. Come summer, Garfield would put the ashbox out for a spell in the garden, as if it were a cage, and the little bird of Matthews might be enticed to sing in the fresh air.

Of what is past, or passing, or to come . . .

One handful of ashes Garfield had already thrown into the Pacific Ocean when he went out to vacate Matthews's condo. "Put some of me in the Atlantic, too," Matthews had requested. He had grown petulant and spoiled on his deathbed. When the worst of the winter weather was over, Garfield drove to Provincetown and hurled a stinting handful into the Atlantic.

As for the rest of Matthews. "Just throw me all over this place, okay?" he had said. But Garfield could not bear to dispose of the full contents of the box—even on his own property, not just yet. It was as if Matthews were still with him as long as Garfield kept hold of what was left of him.

Somehow, Garfield muddled through that long winter of his discontent, running his classes like clockwork with his bowtie still perky under his chin. He was "on automatic," as he confessed to Thompson. But some things had changed. He was talking openly to Thompson, for one thing. And then, how does it happen? He began to feel again. To worry over a student's absences, a colleague's persistent cough, the collapse of the stanza in contemporary poetry "as we know it." He took an interest in his sons, those young, intriguing strangers who called weekly and came by every few months.

Who would have thought my shriveled heart could have recovered greenness, the poet sayeth. Garfield's swan song, as he called the lecture he would deliver on the occasion of his retirement a year from May would be a personal meditation on Herbert's poem "The Flower." He knew the poem by heart. All winter it had kept him going. *I once more smell the dew and rain, and relish versing.*

Spring was coming again to the far reaches and dim outposts of Garfield's heart.

A full revolution of the year and already it is the first anniversary of Matthews's dying. This is Garfield's last year of full-time teaching, and he has begun untying the little knots that bind him to his routines and students. Several weeks ago, in his office, he almost threw out the Yolanda García file. It's a good thing he didn't for here again is this request for a graduate school recommendation. Of course, he will write a fresh letter, but these past drafts help. He sits in his study at home watching a fall sunset of such passionate reds that, for a moment, he is convinced there must be an afterlife. Who but Matthews would be so garish with a New England sky? Matthews, who loved opera and elaborate cakes and Mardi Gras bands and Wagner and the purple poetry of D. H. Lawrence. *My manhood is cast down in the flood of remembrance, I weep like a child for the past.*

The address on Miss García's envelope is a small town north of Boston, only a couple of hours away. She has been teaching at a private school for a year now, not a minute to herself. That's why she's finally going to take his advice and get that Ph.D. Otherwise, she'll never land a college teaching job that might allow her time for her writing. *I know, I know, Mr. Garfield, you told me so thirteen years ago.*

Yes, indeed, he told her so. But not before your own life takes you somewhere can you really go there. He should know. The letter should be easy enough to compose, what with so many previous drafts to go on. And yet he cannot seem to get past that first sentence, *Once in a career, there comes a student.*

He rereads her letter for more clues, something to convince him that he is indeed doing the right thing by her. *I've been too embarrassed to call—it's been so long. I feel like I only get in touch when I need you.*

What else are old mentors for, he wants to tell her. In fact, he *has* already told her, *Don't thank me, pass it on.* But then once in a career, there comes a student who keeps coming back for more.

Can I come and see you some weekend? I'm only a few hours away. I'd love to talk over the future. Really, I'd love to see you!

He rereads the letter one more time, musing. And slowly, like the cold knowledge that Matthews is no longer with him, Garfield understands he has failed her. *The successful student learns to destroy the teacher.* (Who said that?) Miss García should be in full flight by now. Either he has held on too long or she has held on too long. At any rate, he must not allow this situation to continue! Fiercely and finally, he pens the letter of recommendation, as if to dismiss her, and stuffs it in its envelope. She must get on with it, finish her Ph.D., be happy at long last. At any rate she is not to come back for more. He must be firm and tell her so.

He picks up the phone and dials the number she has written at the bottom of the letter by her name. But kindness overtakes him mid-conversation, and instead of telling her that this is it, he arranges for a get-together lunch at his place next Saturday. He has the letter for her to hand-carry back and some last words of advice. "Ay, Mr. Garfield, it's been so long," she says. "We have so much to talk about. But I'm doing it this time, I am." He hears the resignation in her voice.

Then, the self-doubt, "Well, what do you think, Mr. Garfield?"

He takes her through the garden as if to show her the origin of the ingredients of their luncheon. "Gee, Mr. Garfield, I didn't know you had these talents," she notes, lifting a stalk and cradling the Bella Donna tomato in her hand. The rows seem laid out with a ruler; sturdy posts hold back the raspberry canes; stones define the small herbal plot at the edge of the lettuce row. Only one tomato plant sprawls messily without a cage. "The chip on the knee of Michelangelo's David, eh?"

She seems thinner, sadder than the lively young woman who could outdo Milton's Satan on double entendres. Over the course of their lunch, it has become quite clear that this graduate school decision is the bitter pill she believes she must swallow in order to get what she wants.

"Nothing else has worked out, Mr. Garfield. It's like I've been living the wrong life or something. Can't seem to get where I want to go. Always get waylaid, you know?"

He knows. Has the life experience to prove it, as a matter of fact, but why burden her with his sorrows. He is her mentor, after all. His job is to push her out of the nest. But where will she go?

"So, anyhow, with that doctorate, some place'll hire me, don't you think? Like you said, I need something substantial. Then I can get back to the writing. It's the only thing I really want. I mean, besides true love and fame and fortune, you know?"

They laugh, and Garfield looks at his watch, his old tic returning involuntarily. He has enjoyed the leisurely lunch, the groundswell of affection that has carried them through the fleeting hours. Now it is time for her to go. The drive is more like three hours, not two. But it is he who has been delaying her departure, insisting she take this last tour of his garden. At the end of her visit, the long night of missing Matthews awaits him, the endless ache of Sunday, the waning light of another autumn.

As she rounds the last row, she kicks the ashbox Garfield has rested against a small rock and knocks it out to the middle of the path. "Whoops!" she cries, recoiling. "Ay, I thought it was alive or something."

It is my golden bird, Garfield feels like saying. I have kept it out all through the glorious summer so that it will sing to me. But he says nothing.

"What is this, Mr. Garfield?" She bends down as if to examine the contents. Quickly, Garfield lodges the box back in place and takes her hand. "Come with me, Miss García. I have something for you."

He escorts her through the sliding glass door back into his study. There on his desk is her file he almost threw out a few weeks ago. Inside, in addition to copies of his past letters of recommendation are the many poems and stories she has sent him over the years. He had been rereading them before she arrived late this morning.

"I wanted to give these back to you," he says, handing her the thick file. "They're your work," he explains when she gives him a puzzled look.

"But I sent them to you—for you to keep." She opens the folder and makes a face. "God, you should burn this stuff!"

"No, I should not. In fact, I have an assignment for you, Miss García." Garfield pauses a moment, enjoying the bafflement on her face. Until the tour of the garden he did not know he would present her with this evidence.

"What?" she says. That old, intense look has come into her eyes.

"First, I want you to give me back that letter I wrote."

"You mean this?" She lifts the envelope out of the deep pocket of her Guatemalan jacket.

He nods and takes the letter in his hand, and then in three quick jerks, he has ripped the letter into pieces. The irony is not lost on him—the men in Miss García's life always seem to be tearing up her papers. But the look on her face spells, not disgust or fear, but relief. She does not even ask for the explanation he gives her.

"You *were* right all along, Miss García. You don't belong in a doctoral program. I was wrong to keep pushing you in that direction." He waves away her defense of him. "At any rate, the past is over. And the future is before you."

They both look out the picture window as if the view outside were the panorama his words were unfolding. Matthews is outdoing himself tonight with splashes of gaudy red and orange—an extravaganza, a signaling to Garfield on this late fall afternoon that it is time.

"So what's the assignment?" she says, breaking the spell of his daydreaming.

He turns back to her, trying to remember where he left off.

"You said you had an assignment for me?" she reminds him.

"Indeed I have. You've got enough material there for a book, two books. That's your assignment, Miss García. Call me when you are ready for me to look at your final drafts."

She hesitates, the intent look on her face has been replaced by a look of pure terror. "I don't know, Mr. Garfield. I mean, I should really get something practical under my belt. . . . Most places aren't even hiring writers unless they have Ph.D.s. . . . I haven't written anything in over a year. . . ." Her excuses fade before the stern look on his face. "I don't know if I can do it," she says at last. "I really don't."

"You don't have a choice." He opens the sliding door and lets her out.

When she drives away, he watches her car go down the long driveway, until with a farewell honk, the blue Tercel disappears past a bend on the road. Then, he walks to the end of the garden and picks up the box from its rocky nest. Lifting the lid, he scoops a hand in and lets the wind take the ashes, hither and yon, until Matthews, too, is gone.

The stranger

epistle

The old woman Consuelo, what a dream she had last night! She tossed and turned this way and that as if the dream were a large fish she were trying to haul in—without success. Finally she gave a great roll to one side and her little granddaughter Wendy let out a yelp that woke Consuelo up. *¡Dios santo!* She ran her hand over her face, wiping off sleep, and maybe it was in doing so that she lost a part of the dream which all the next day she was trying to recall.

In the dream Consuelo was counseling her daughter Ruth about her predicament. Consuelo had not seen her daughter since five years ago when Ruth had come by the village with the surprise of a baby she had given birth to in the capital. Along with the infant, the daughter had brought an envelope of money. She counted out over two thousand pesos to leave with the grandmother. The rest was for a plan that Ruth would not tell the old woman about. "You'll just worry, Mamá," she had said, and then, throwing her arms around the old woman, she added, "Ay, Mamá, our lives are going to be so much better, you'll see."

And everything that had actually happened was also so in the dream. Ruth had made it to Puerto Rico on a rowboat, then on to Nueva York where she worked at a restaurant at night and at a private home as a maid during the day. Every month, Ruth sent home money along with a letter someone in the village read to

Consuelo. Every few months the Codetel man came running through town, "International call!" Consuelo would be out of breath by the time she arrived at the telephone trailer to hear her daughter's small voice trapped in the wires. "How are you, Mamá? And my baby Wendy?" Consuelo would curse herself later, for she would fall into that mute bashfulness she always suffered in the presence of important people and their machines. Words to her were like the fine china at the big houses she had worked in, something she felt better if the mistress were handling.

Then, just as with her own Ruth, the dream Ruth had gotten married. It was not a true marriage, she had explained in a letter, but one of convenience in order to get her residency. Consuelo prayed every night to el Gran Poder de Dios and la Virgencita to turn this mock marriage into a true one for her daughter's sake. He is a good man, the daughter had admitted. A Puerto Rican who wants to help a woman of a neighbor island. Hmmm. Then the letter that occasioned the dream had arrived. Even though she could not read the words, Consuelo studied the dark angry marks that were so different from the smoother roll of her daughter's usual handwriting. The man—it turned out—would not give Ruth a divorce. He was saying he was in love with her. If she tried to leave him, he was going to turn her in to the immigration police. What should she do? *¡Ay, Mamá, aconséjame!* It was the first time Consuelo's daughter had asked for her advice.

How she wished she could sit her daughter down and tell her what to do. Use your head, she would say. Here is a good man who says he loves you, mi'ja, why even hesitate? You can have a fine life! It is within your grasp! Next time her daughter called, Consuelo would have her advice all prepared. For days as she washed or swept or cooked, Consuelo practiced saying the words, the little granddaughter looking up surprised to hear the taciturn old woman speaking to herself.

Then the shock of last night's dream! It was as if her daughter were by her side listening. But what Consuelo was saying was not what she had planned to say—that much she remembered. Her daughter was nodding her head, for Consuelo was speaking wonderful words that flowed out of her mouth as if language were a stream filled with silver fish flashing in the water. Everything she said was so wise that Consuelo wept in her own dream to hear herself speak such true words.

But the devil take her for forgetting what it was that she was saying! When she had run her hand over her face, she had wiped the words away. All morning, she tried to recall what it was she had said to her daughter in the dream . . . and once or twice . . . as she swept out the house . . . as she braided the child's hair into its three pigtails . . . as she pounded the coffee beans and the green smell of the mountains wafted up to her, why there it was, the tail of it, quick! grab it! But no, it inched just out of her reach.

And then, she could almost hear it, a far-off voice. She crossed the yard to María's house after it. Almost a year ago, María's youngest boy had drowned in Don Mundín's swimming pool. María had stopped working in the big house, and even after the period of mourning, she continued to dress in black and to hold on to her grief as if it were the boy himself she were clutching to her side.

"I have had such a dream," Consuelo began. María had placed a cane chair under the samán tree for the old woman. She sat by, cleaning the noon rice in a hollow board on her lap. The child, accustomed only to the company of the old woman, hid her face in her grandmother's lap when María's boys beckoned to her to come look at the leaping lizard they had caught. "In the dream I was speaking to my Ruth. But this one woke me, and I cleaned my face before remembering, and there went the words." The old woman made the same gesture as María, flinging the rice chaff out beyond the shade of the samán tree.

"My Ruth has written for my advice," Consuelo went on. Among her own people and out of the sight and presence of the rich and their machines, the old woman found it much easier to speak her mind. "In the dream, the words came to me. But I have forgotten what it was I said to her."

María combed her fingers through the pile of rice as if the lost words could be found there. "You must go down to the river early in the morning," she began. With her long, sad face and her sure words, she was like the priest when he came up the mountain once a month to preach to the campesinos how to live their lives.

"You must wash your face three times, making a sign of the cross after each washing."

The old woman was listening carefully, her hands folded as if she were praying. The child at her side looked up at the old woman and then folded her small hands.

"And the words will come to you, and then immediately you must go to the Codetel and call your daughter—"

Just the thought of speaking into that black funnel stopped the words in Consuelo's throat. She took a deep breath and made the sign of the cross and the words blurted out. "I do not have a number for my daughter. She is always the one who calls."

María stood up and shook out her skirt. She called the child to her side and asked again how old the child was and whether she was going to school to learn her letters. The child shook her head and held up five fingers but then thought better of it and held up another five. Consuelo watched the playful conversation. A tender look had come on the grieving woman's face. It was as if she had forgotten the dream altogether.

María sat back down. The interlude with the child seemed to have put a new thought in her head. "You have gotten letters; there is an address on the envelopes, no?"

"I do not know," Consuelo shrugged. "There are marks on the envelopes."

"You must bring me the letters," María concluded. "And if there is an address, then a letter must be written with the words of advice that will come to you by the river tomorrow."

"Who shall write this letter?" Consuelo worried. She knew María could read letters, but Consuelo had never seen her write them. And once written, how would the letter be sent to the daughter?

"My hand is not good," María confessed, "but there is Paquita." Consuelo could see the same caution on María's face that she herself was feeling. The letter writer in town, Paquita Montenegro, always broadcast your business as if you were paying her, not just to write your letter, but to tell everyone about it. Consuelo did not want the whole village to know that Ruth had paid a man to marry her and was now wanting to divorce him. There was already enough talk about how Consuelo's good-looking daughter had come by the money to end up in Nueva York.

"I am thinking now," María said, interrupting the old woman's thoughts. "A woman has come to the big house. Don Mundín's relation. She is from there. She will help you write this letter and then she will see to it that your daughter receives it."

At these words, Consuelo could feel her old bones lock with fright. Before she would talk about her daughter's problem to a stranger, she would rather pay Paquita the forty pesos to write the letter and blab its contents to everyone. Again she found it

hard to get the words out. "Ay, but to bother the lady . . . what if
. . . I could not . . ." Her voice died away.

But now María seemed more determined than ever. "What do
you mean? They bother us enough when they want." Consuelo
could see the face of the boy surfacing in the mother's face—
before it was washed away by a look of terrible anger. "Sergio will
take you tomorrow after the words come to you at the river." The
younger woman grabbed the old woman's hand. "It will go well.
You will see."

Consuelo did not know if it was the fierceness in María's eyes,
but the look struck deep inside her, flushing out the words that
she had spoken in the dream! Right then and there, she knew
exactly what it was she must say in the letter this stranger would
write to her daughter.

Just as Sergio had reported on their walk over to the big house,
Don Mundín's relation was so easy. She was standing at the door,
waiting for them—as if they were important guests she had been
expecting. She was not the usual run of rich ladies, calling your
name until they wore it down to nothing but the sound of an
order. All her life, Consuelo had worked for many such fine
ladies who kept everything under lock and key as if their homes
were warehouses in which to store valuable things.

But this lady addressed her as Doña Consuelo and asked to be
called Yo. "It's my baby name and it stuck," she explained. And
what a little lady she was—you could fit two or three of her
inside Ruth and still have room for little Wendy. She was dressed
in pants and a jersey shirt, all in white like someone about to
make her first communion. She spoke easily and gaily, words just
sputtering from her lips. "So, Doña Consuelo, Sergio says you
need help with a letter?"

Consuelo prepared to say something.

"What a pretty little girl!" The lady crouched down, crooning until the child was beside herself with fear and excitement. Before Consuelo knew it, the child's pockets were full of Don Mundín's mints and the lady had promised that before they left, she would take the child out to see the swimming pool shaped like a kidney bean. No one seemed to have informed the lady that only last summer in that pool, María and Sergio had lost their boy, no bigger than this little girl.

"We do not want . . . ," Consuelo began. "We ask pardon for the molestation." Her heart was beating so loud she could not hear herself thinking.

"No bother at all. Come in and sit down. Not on that old bench." And the skinny lady pulled Consuelo by the hand just as little Wendy did when she wanted the old woman to come attend to something. Consuelo felt her heart slowing to a calmer rhythm.

Soon, they were settled in the soft chairs of the living room, drinking Coca-Colas from fancy, fluted glasses. Every time Consuelo took a sip of the syrupy liquid, the ice tinkled against the glass in a way that made her feel distracted. She kept reminding the child to hold her glass with both hands as she herself was doing.

But the lady did not seem fazed by all the breakable things around her. She propped her glass on the arm of the couch, and went on speaking, waving her hand within inches of the vase beside her. Consuelo pulled the packet of letters from the sack and waited for a pause in which she could insert her request. But the lady spoke on, a whole stream of words whose sense Consuelo could not always follow. How beautiful the mountains were, how she had come for a month to see if she couldn't get some writing done, how she had noticed that so many families in the village were headed by single mothers—"

"The child is my granddaughter," Consuelo informed her. She did not want the lady to get the wrong idea that in her old age Consuelo had been going behind the palms with a man.

"Ay, I didn't mean that!" The lady laughed, slapping the air with her hand. Her eye fell on the packet of letters in the old woman's lap. "But let's get to your letter. Sergio told me about your daughter. . . ." And off she was again, telling Consuelo all about Ruth going to Puerto Rico in a rowboat, about Ruth living in New York, working hard at two jobs. It did spare Consuelo the trouble of having to tell the story from the very start.

A silence followed the lady's coming to the end of what she knew. Now it was Consuelo's turn. She began haltingly. Each time she stopped, at a loss for words, the lady's eager look reassured her. Consuelo told how Ruth had married a Puerto Rican man, how she had done so for her residency, how the man had fallen in love. As she spoke the lady kept nodding as if she knew exactly what it was that Consuelo's Ruth had been going through.

"But now she has written for my advice." Consuelo patted the packet of letters on her lap. "And in my dream it came what I should say to her."

"How wonderful!" the lady exclaimed, so that Consuelo felt momentarily baffled as to what exactly the lady felt was so extraordinary. "I mean that your dreams tell you things," the lady added. "I've tried, but I can never make sense of them. Like before I got divorced, I asked my dreams if I should leave my husband. So I dreamed a little dog bites my leg. Now what's that supposed to mean?"

Consuelo could not say for sure. But she urged the lady to visit María who would know what to make of the little dog.

The lady waved the suggestion away. "I've got two therapist sisters who are full of theories about the little dog." She laughed, and her eyes had a far-away look as if she could see all the way home to the two sisters giving the little dog a bone.

Consuelo eased the topmost letter from the packet in her lap and watched as the lady read through this last letter Ruth had written. She seemed to have no trouble with the writing—Ruth had a pretty hand—but as her eyes descended on the page, she began shaking her head. "Oh my God!" she finally said, and looked up at Consuelo. "I don't believe this!"

"We must write to my daughter," Consuelo agreed.

"We sure should!" the lady said, pulling over the coffee table so that it was right in front of her. On it lay a tablet of clean paper and a pretty silver pen that gleamed like a piece of jewelry. The lady looked over at Consuelo. "How do you want to start?"

Consuelo had never written a letter, so she could not say. She glanced back at the woman for help.

"*My dear daughter Ruth*," the lady suggested, and at Consuelo's nod, she wrote out the words quickly as if it took no effort at all. The child came forward on the couch to look at the lady's hand dancing across the paper. The lady smiled and offered the child some sheets as well as a colored pencil. "You want to draw?" she asked. The child nodded shyly. She knelt on the floor in front of the table and looked down at the clean sheet of paper the lady had placed before her. Finally, the child picked up her colored pencil, but she did not make a mark.

"Okay, so far we've got, *My dear daughter Ruth*," the lady said. "What else?"

"*My dear daughter Ruth*," Consuelo repeated. And the ring of those words was like a rhyme the child often said to herself skipping in a ray of sunshine. "*I have received your letter and in my dream came these words which this good lady is helping me to write down here with all due respect to el Gran Poder de Dios and gratitude to la Virgencita without whose aid nothing can be done."* It was just as it had been in her dream: the words came tumbling from her tongue!

But the lady was looking at her, perplexed. "It's kind of hard . . . you haven't really . . ." Now she was the one at a loss for words. "It's not a sentence," she said at last, and then she must have seen that Consuelo had no idea what she meant because she added, "Let's say one thing at a time, okay?"

Consuelo nodded. "You're the one who knows," she said politely. It was a phrase she had been taught to say when asked by the rich for an opinion.

"No, no, it's *your* letter." The lady smiled sadly. She looked down at the paper as if it would tell her what to say next. "Never mind, it's fine," the lady said, and she marked a whole half page in her quicksilver hand and turned the paper over. "Okay, let 'em come!" She whooped as if she were urging lazy cows across the evening pasture.

"My daughter, you must think of your future and the future of your child for as you yourself know marriage is a holy vow—" Consuelo stopped briefly to catch her breath, and for a moment, she could not go on. She had begun to wonder if these indeed were the words she had spoken in her dream or had she confused them with what she herself had wanted to say to her daughter?

"And so my daughter, honor this man, and he will stop beating you if you do not provoke him for as the good priest has taught us we women are subject to the wisdom and judgment of our fathers and of our husbands if they are good enough to stay with us."

The lady lay the pen on top of the paper and folded her arms.

She looked over at Consuelo and shook her head. Her face had the stony gravity of María's face. "I'm sorry. I can't write that."

Consuelo's hand flew to her mouth. Maybe she had misspoken? Maybe this young woman, skinny as a nun at Lent, maybe she could tell that Consuelo was not speaking the correct words. For a second time, the words of her dream seemed to have fled her memory. "My daughter will make another foolish choice," Consuelo pleaded. She indicated the child with her chin in order to present proof of Ruth's errors without giving the child the evil eye by saying so. The little granddaughter, who had been studying her blank sheet for a while, bore down on her pencil and made a mark.

The lady bit her lips as if to keep back the words that were always so ready on her tongue. But a few slipped out, full of emotion. "How can you advise your daughter to stay with a man who beats her?"

"The man would not beat her if she did as she was told. She should think of her future. I have always advised her to think of her future." Again, Consuelo felt the words she was speaking were not the wonderful words of the dream that had drawn agreement even from the stubborn Ruth. In a much smaller voice, she concluded, "She has always been too willful."

"Good for her!" The lady gave a sharp nod. "She needs a strong will. Look at all she's done. Risked her life at sea . . . supported herself on two jobs . . . sent money home every month." She was counting out the reasons on her fingers like the shopkeeper counting out the money you owed him.

Consuelo found herself nodding. This woman had an eye that could see the finest points like the eyes of the child, who could thread a needle in the evening light.

"If I were you, I definitely would not advise her to stay with a man who abuses her," the lady was saying, "but, I mean, you write what you want."

But Consuelo did not know how to write. The brute of a man who had been her father had beat her good and hard whenever he found her wasting time like the child now bent over her sheet of paper. "You have reason," she said to the lady. "Let us say so to my Ruth."

She had meant for the lady's words to be added to the ones that had already been written. But the lady crumbled the sheet in her hand and commenced a new letter. The child retrieved the crushed letter, unfolded it, and ironed it out with the flat of her small hand.

"*My dear Ruth,*" the lady began, "*I have thought long and hard about what you have written to me.* Does that sound all right?" The lady looked up.

"Sí, señora." Consuelo sat back in the soft chair. This indeed was a better start.

"*You have proven yourself a strong and resourceful woman and I am very proud of you.*"

"I am very proud of her," Consuelo agreed. Her eyes were filling with tears at the true sound of these words of praise for her daughter.

"*You entered upon a clear agreement with this man, and now he refuses to honor it. How can you trust him if he so badly abuses your trust?*"

"That is so," Consuelo said, nodding deeply. She thought of Ruth's father, stealing into the servants' quarters in the middle of the night, reeking of rum, helping himself to what he wanted. The next morning, Consuelo was up at dawn preparing the silver tray so it would be ready when the mistress rang the bell in her bedroom.

"A man who strikes a woman does not deserve to be with her," the lady wrote.

"A man who lifts a hand," Consuelo echoed. "Ay, my poor Ruth . . . you should not suffer so. . . ." Again Consuelo felt the words knotting in her throat, but this time, it was not from bashfulness, but from the strength of her emotion.

"And so, Ruth, you must find a way to get help. There are agencies in the city that you can call. Do not lose heart. Do not let yourself get trapped in a situation where you are not free to speak your own mind."

And as the lady spoke and wrote these words, Consuelo could feel her dream rising to the surface of her memory. And it seemed to her that these were the very words she had spoken that Ruth had been so moved to hear. "Yes," she kept urging the lady. "Yes, that is so."

As the lady was addressing the envelope, the child held up the sheet she had filled with little crosses, copying the lady's hand. Consuelo felt a flush of tender pride to see that the child was so apt. And the lady was pleased as well. "You wrote your mami, too!" she congratulated, and she folded the child's letter in the envelope along with Consuelo's letter.

Part II

The caretakers

Sergio was called down to the telephone trailer early in the morning. A call from Don Mundín: ready the house, a woman is coming up to spend some time in the mountains.

"Just the woman then," Sergio repeated to clarify the order. A woman sent up alone. Maybe she was a mistress of Don Mundín, someone in trouble.

The house was fine, yes sir, Sergio affirmed, although already in his head he had begun the breakneck cleanup that must be completed before that afternoon when the car would pull up the long drive—which had to be cleared—the croton hedges trimmed back. The chickens had to be got out of the pantry. The loaned horse must be rounded up, and his sister sent for to tend house for the doña.

"Yes, yes, no problem, Don Mundín," he repeated with each new reminder. And then, to the crumb of a personal question. "María is fine, yes," Sergio replied, "and the children, yes."

The remaining children, he was thinking, for the youngest boy drowned last summer in the new swimming pool. Don Mundín had warned Sergio to fence off the area, to keep an eye out, but how could Sergio care for the big house, tend his own conuco plot, and be building fences where they were not needed? Besides, the boys had been reared here at the headwaters of the River Yaque; they knew not to go near deep water. But what was a swimming pool to a small child but a toy left out overnight by the patrón's children for him to play with. Danger was the river roaring down the side of the mountain. The boy must have leapt in that morning, while Sergio was out cleaning the stable, thinking that, like the patrón's children, he could splash and stay afloat. He was found hours later by his mother floating face down. She had come to collect water from the pool which she used as a large cistern for washing and cleaning—although this, too, Don Mundín asked them not to do.

"We are at your service always here," Sergio was hoping to conclude. "Perhaps we will see you and Doña Gabriela and the children up here soon." To the young patrón's credit—though María did not want to hear it—he had not returned to the house since the drowning. The weekend visits were over, the pool had been drained, the sheets and towels stored away in a closet that smelled like the forest. Sergio had heard that Don Mundín was looking to sell the place. As for his own María, she had refused to set foot in the house since the accident. Now that this woman was coming, Sergio would have to get his sister to fill in as the housemaid. Another chore to get done. And still Don Mundín chatted on.

"She wants solitude, she wants inspiration," he was explaining.

"Yes, of course," Sergio agreed, though these words were like the silverware the rich lined up on a table when all that was needed was a spoon to scoop and a machete to cut. Inspiration? Maybe something was wrong with the woman's lungs.

"We will take good care of her," Sergio promised, and then, thankfully, so he could get started on the fullest day of the last year—for the south lawn also needed to be mown as well as two handfuls of errands to be done—Don Mundín hung up.

"She wants inspiration and solitude," Sergio repeated for

María. He had gone to fetch his sister and found his wife there, working on a preparation to remove the curse of bad luck that had befallen Elena and her family.

"Go on." María scowled. "There is a belly there, or a broken heart."

Sergio shrugged, draining the last of his cafecito and putting his hat on. He could not afford a longer chat today. "I am only telling you what Don Mundín said," he concluded. That was always his amen when anyone in the village questioned something he did not care to defend or explain.

All her life María had been mounted by the santos, so that people always came to her with their problems and hopes and fears, and she procured for them the help of the spirit world. The santos would descend on her shoulders, and trembling all over, her eyes rolling as if they were marbles inside her head, María would speak in a voice not her own. The pretty Ruth must deposit a box of talcum in the crotch of a samán tree for Santa Marta if she wanted to find a good man. Porfirio better light a candle to San Judas of lost causes if he wanted his cock to win.

But after her boy drowned, the santos stopped speaking to María. It was her doing at first, as she refused to receive them in order to leave a space open for Pablito to come through that narrow shaft to her. Daily, she implored him to calm a mother's heart and let her know he had made the crossing safely. But after a year, Pablito had still not spoken to her, and when she tried to contact her santos for news of the boy, all she heard was an immense silence from that other world.

Still, her neighbors kept coming to her, and María could not just turn them away to suffer without hope as she herself was doing. And so she maintained her pretense of being in touch with the santos who could help them. After a lifetime in the village, she knew everybody's business, and just from looking clear-eyed at their predicaments, María could tell them what they should do to ease their suffering. Recently, she had begun to think that her boy's silence was God's punishment for the deceit she had been practicing on her fellow villagers.

This morning her sister-in-law Elena had summoned her for help with the bad times her family was having. Her husband Porfirio had lost his job working on the grounds of Los Pinos Hotel, which was finally closing. In the last year, tourism had been going steadily downhill. Everyone was leaving in droves, the less desperate for the capital, and the rest for Miami and Puerto Rico in rowboats. It was as if with the death of the boy all good luck had drained out of the village.

But perhaps a reversal was about to begin. Just as María was lighting a candle to draw good luck down on Elena's family, Sergio had arrived with an answer to the petition they had been making: a lady was coming to the big house. Somebody was needed to do the cooking and cleaning starting right away.

Sergio had looked directly at her, his eyes asking if she wouldn't put her grief aside at last and resume her old job. But the news of a guest at the house made her feel that knot in her heart that she could not untie. María had not been able even to look at the place since that horrible day, no less enter it and serve the patrones or their guests. Why not have Elena do the cooking and hire Porfirio to help out on the grounds? The santos were finally responding to María's entreaties, filling her head with their high, windy voices. Perhaps they would bring news of Pablito, the faintest touch on her cheek, a whisper from the row of cypresses that lined the south side of the street.

On the grounds of the big house, Sergio was following the lady around, answering her many questions. What was that tree over there called? Where was his wife and did he have any children? As they talked, they walked through the grounds, up to the tennis court and stables, then around the nursery where Doña Gabriela had cultivated her swinging baskets of orchids. They ended up at the pool.

"Wow," the lady exclaimed, "Mundín didn't mention a pool."

They were standing at the edge, looking down into the turquoise bottom littered with leaves and trash. For the last year, the pool had been used as a giant receptacle. Today during his instructions, Don Mundín had delicately avoided mentioning it, but of course, Sergio understood that the pool must be readied, too.

"Can we clean it and fill it?" the lady wanted to know, crouching down as if to look more closely at the trash below.

"The filter is broken." Sergio hesitated, seeing the lady's face fall. If the lie should get back to Don Mundín, Sergio would be roundly scolded for not having told the patrón that the swimming pool needed fixing. "But I will get the part," Sergio added.

Indoors, it fell to Sergio again to show the lady around. Certainly, he knew more than Elena, who had only been to the back door of the house before today. As he followed the lady, Sergio had to keep wiping his forehead with his hand. The summer was going to be a hot one all right. But the lady seemed not to feel the heat. She went through every room, looking out every window on each of the three floors, trying to decide which room had the best view.

Finally at the topmost floor, a tower room with windows on all four sides, she cried out, "This is it!" Far below, Sergio could see the little village, the crooked streets winding uphill, the bell-tower on the tiny chapel. The mountains loomed above, the river tumbled down. The combination of height and heat made Sergio feel dizzy.

"There is no bed here," Sergio noted, once he had recovered from his vertigo by looking down at his feet. "Begging your pardon, doña, I do not know that we could fit a bed in here."

"Don't beg my pardon," the lady insisted, smiling. "Of course, we could fit a bed here, Sergio. We'll just put the mattress on the floor so-so." She swung her arms, outlining where the bed could go.

"You're the one who knows," he said quietly. It was not for him to contradict the lady. Still, Don Mundín would be displeased if his caretaker didn't take good care of his guest. "One must remember there are no screens and there are mosquitoes."

"But look at the view!" the lady exclaimed.

And so, they carted a mattress up to the tower room and somehow crammed it lengthwise under the eastern windows. When the sun was low on the mountains, the lady called Sergio up from the yard. Elena had already been summoned from the kitchen where she was making the lady a bean soup. "Hurry, you're going to miss it!" They galloped upstairs and stood breathless at the tower landing watching the view. "Ay," the lady kept gasping, as if a man were pleasuring her.

Even after the sun was down and the shadows lengthened across the room, the lady stood a while longer. She wore a listening look on her face as if she were hearing in some far-off room her own baby crying. She had already confessed to Sergio that she had no children, that she was unmarried and meant to stay that way. Sergio had not dared comment.

"It is so *so* beautiful up here," the lady finally spoke up. "Don't you think so?"

Sergio looked out again at the village he had known all his life. Perhaps it was beautiful, but he was not sure. Beautiful was a word that one heard in the boleros on the radio or in the mouths of novela stars on the television at the bodega. "You are the one who knows, doña."

"Ay, Sergio." The lady's tone made him look her in the eye in spite of the habits of deference he had been taught by Don Mundín's family. "Do you really think I am the one who knows?"

Sergio hesitated. It was going to take some practice, talking to this lady.

That night María was surprised when both Elena and Sergio showed up after supper. In the past when Don Mundín and Doña Gabriela came for weekends and longer vacations, María and Sergio had moved into the house with their children, in order to be there providing service around the clock.

"We do not have to work nights," Sergio explained. He laughed when María opened her eyes wide at this news.

"The Virgencita has sent the answer to our prayers." Elena clapped her hands together and rolled her eyes heavenward. "¡Ay, Dios santo!"

"She is treating us like Americans," Sergio added. "You know how the Americans can only work from this hour to this hour, and if you make them work more, you have to pay them double." Of course, he would not take advantage. For one thing it might get back to Don Mundín.

"Did she *pay* you?" María was eyeing the uncapped bottle of rum Sergio had brought in with him.

He nodded sheepishly.

"Ay, ay"—María shook her head, smiling all the while—"collecting twice!"

"I told her she didn't have to," Sergio explained, "but she says it is just a tip. She says if she were staying at a hotel she would be paying a lot more."

"All I did today was prepare her a soup," Elena added. "She says she must not touch meat. She wouldn't even let me put a bouillon in the beans."

"Maybe it is part of her religion?" María suggested. "Maybe she made a promesa because of a great sorrow." Suddenly, her own sorrow flooded the room: the boy, his little shirt, his socks floating in that big blue cauldron. They were silent a moment.

"All we have to do is talk to her, it seems," Elena concluded.

"She will end up asking for a lot more, you will see." María's voice was thorned with bitterness.

"Ay, María," Elena pleaded. "If you meet her, you will see she is not like the rest of them."

"It would be good if you came to be introduced," Sergio added, capping the bottle to give sobriety to his point. "She asked many times after my wife, and how many children we have, and how old they are, and what do I feed them, and are they going to school." He laughed in a strained way.

"You did not tell her?" María's look was fierce.

Sergio steeled himself. "She would not stay. She would leave."

"He is right," Elena said, sweeping to her brother's defense. "It is past time you put this behind you."

María cast her eyes upwards. "Dios mío, give me patience. Even our sorrows have to be put aside for them."

Later that night María slipped out of bed and walked out in the yard. In the vague light of a thumbnail moon she could make out the samán her little boy used to climb. The branches were broad and low to the ground. She stood under it now and called him down, "Pablito!" But there was no answer.

All this talk of the big house and the lady had stirred up that old grief again. Before the tragedy she had worked for Doña Gabriela, cleaning house, cooking, listening to her complaints about how boring it was in the mountains without her friends. Somehow Doña Gabriela had found out that her cook received spirits and could read the future in the coffee stains on a cup. "María, come tell me what's going to happen to me today," Doña Gabriela would call from the sunny, covered patio where she liked to eat her late breakfast.

One day, gazing down at the patrona's cup, María saw the small body floating on top of the new swimming pool. She had thought, of course, that the warning was meant for the patrona's two boys, and she had cautioned Doña Gabriela to be careful of her children and still water. "You're getting me all upset," Doña Gabriela complained. "Tell me something happy. Don't you see something good in there?"

It still pained María that she had been so preoccupied with the patrona's happiness, and house, and children that she had not seen the danger her own child was in. Not even when the santos had tried warning her through Doña Gabriela's coffee leavings.

Now she wandered out of the yard and down the dark road that twisted past Elena's house towards the center of town. A dog tied outside the mayor's house barked at her, but after she spoke the Saint Francis's charm, he quieted. The village was so still, she could hear the breeze stirring in the cypresses and far off the roar of traffic on the road to the capital. "Pablito!" she called, and the dog commenced its tiresome barking again.

At the corner, she turned right, and the big house she had avoided all year came into view. Up in the tower room, a light was shining. She could see the lady sitting at a table working at something. "Pablito!" she shouted and the lady's head lifted. For a while, she sat, her head cocked, as if she, too, were waiting for his answer.

Weeks went by, and Sergio had still to fix the pool. He tried steeling himself with swigs from his rum bottle, but every time he walked down the angled floor to the garbage at the end, he had to get out quickly, overcome by his feelings.

From the beginning, Sergio had been able to treat the whole tragedy with filosofía. In fact, that black evening when Don Mundín had called him into his private sitting room, it was the patrón who had wept, and Sergio who had done the consoling. "Don Mundín, you must not get like this."

The young patrón had offered Sergio his arm. "You are right, hombre. We must go on with our lives."

"We have to go on," he had repeated countless times to María. "That is what Don Mundín himself said."

It was not that he did not miss the boy, as María accused, his little bullcalf, the silly thing. But it was not the patrón's fault that the boy had died. Don Mundín and the rest of them had their houses, their work, their own ways, and then Sergio and his family had their ranchitos, their work, their own ways, and these two worlds lay side by side, peaceably. But where they came together, there was a steep dropoff, and on that particular July morning, the boy, wandering off from the side he belonged on, had fallen down that dropoff into a swimming pool the holiday color of a summer sky. That is the way that Sergio saw it.

But now, a year later, at the bottom of that pool, a terrible sadness was welling up that would not allow him to finish the job. Several times the lady asked him, "What's up? Did you ever get the part?"

"Tomorrow it comes," Sergio kept promising. Many days, he took off early, leaving word for the lady.

Then one day, coming up the drive, he was stunned to hear the sound of water pouring into his son's grave. The lady sat reading on a lawn chair by the rising waters, looking up from her book when she saw him. "Ay, Sergio, I decided to just go ahead and fill it, filter or no filter," she explained. "Don't worry, if I get sick, I promise I won't blame you." She was laughing, as if the look on his face had anything to do with her.

Later in the afternoon, Sergio watched from behind the croton hedge, dipping into his bottle of rum to steady his nerves. Back and forth the lady traversed the length of the pool, her head lifting and then dipping back down under the water, her legs kicking. How easily—like a dragonfly—she breezed through the nightmare waters. It was not just their money he envied, but the ways in which that money cushioned the rich from the sorrows of others. María had her santos, and he had his bottle of rum, but still the pain had seeped through as it was doing now. He did not care what Don Mundín had said—he, Sergio, and his mujer María had not gone on with their lives. Their loss was a weight they could not put down.

He reached for his bottle, but the rum was gone. Furiously, he hurled the empty bottle onto the pile of trash that had once filled the bottom of the pool. And for the first time since he had rushed down from the stables, summoned by María's screams, Sergio wept for his son.

That night, María waited for Sergio under the samán tree. She was worried. According to her sister-in-law, Sergio was drinking at the big house—something he had never done. Many late afternoons, he sat behind the croton hedge where he did not think he could be seen and emptied a small bottle.

"The lady even asked me if Sergio has a drinking problem," Elena confessed to María.

"It is not the drink that is the problem," María said bitterly as if she were speaking directly to the lady.

"Perhaps it would help," Elena said carefully, "if you lit a candle for him."

But María knew candles would do nothing. The santos were not going to help her with her problem—just as they had not helped her with the problems of others for the last year.

"He is letting the bottle be his woman," Elena spoke plainly. María had noted how over the course of this month at the big house, Elena had grown in self-assurance. "Rum has become your rival, María."

Tonight as she waited, María found herself chanting the prayer to Santa Marta, over and over. She had worked herself into such a dreamy state that she jumped when she saw the dark shape turning into her yard. She called to him softly, and instead of a gruff, drunken refusal, he came, his hands in front of him in the dark, drawn by the sweetness in her voice. Tucked under his belt, she noted the small bottle.

"I am going to the river tomorrow afternoon to wash the clothes," María began. "When I get back, I will dress the boys and bring them up to meet the señora."

There was a surprised intake of breath. He reached a hand out for her, and though it would have touched only the air, she groped for it and brought it to rest on her lap, where it began to investigate the folds in her dress.

"Ya, ya," she laughed, stopping his hand. "Let's not give the neighbors un show."

Together they stumbled towards the dark house, but later, in bed, he was too far gone to give her any pleasure. She lay beside him, willing herself to stay and not prowl the streets calling for her dead child. She would climb out of her grief—if not for her own, then for her husband and her children's sake. Elena had spoken harsh words, adding the worry of losing her man to the weight on María's heart. Not that these admonitions hadn't been spoken before, but today María's bitterness had given way. Maybe all these tales about the lady's easy ways were loosening the knot in María's chest and making a space in her heart where the santos could descend and begin to speak to her again.

The next morning, Sergio was surprised to find the house open and no sign of the lady. He searched all the rooms calling out, "Doña?" and then headed down the driveway towards the village. He caught sight of her coming up the road, her head down as if she were contemplating something sad. In each hand she carried a loaded string bag.

Sergio rushed to help her. "The house was wide open," he noted in an even voice so the lady would not think he was voicing a criticism. "There have been many robberies," he added.

"I was just going to be a minute," the lady explained. "I was shopping for vegetables for a stir-fry."

"But you do not add any meat," Sergio noted after she explained what a stir-fry was. If the lady gave him just a little entryway, he would suggest that adding meat might put some flesh on her bones.

"Never," she said, watching him, her eyes crinkling with laughter. "You probably think it's crazy, don't you, a vegetarian diet?"

"If I may say so," Sergio began, but then it seemed a too-forward thing to say.

As they walked up the long drive towards the house, Sergio

noted that the hedges needed trimming again. But the lady did not seem to notice the straggly branches.

"I'll tell you what, Sergio," she was saying. "I'm going to show you what a good meal you can have without meat. I'll make you and Elena and your families one of my famous stir-fries. No, no, no, don't refuse me or I'll get insulted. Do you have any plans for tonight?"

"Plans?" Sergio asked.

"Can you come for dinner tonight?"

"Mi mujer," Sergio began, "she is coming this afternoon with the two boys to give you her salutations."

"Great! Then, it's set. Tell Elena to bring her family, too. We'll have a party. The kids can all have a swim before supper."

Sergio did not know how to tell her without sounding as if he were contradicting her wishes. "My boys," he began, turning his hat around and around in his hands, "I do not want them near the pool. They do not know how to swim."

The lady seemed surprised, and then determined like the American missionaries that mounted their revivals in the center of town and gave out sacks of rice to those who said Christ was their personal savior. "They definitely should learn how to swim," she proclaimed. "I'm going to teach them—it's something they should know, living so near a river and all. I mean, don't you think so?"

"You are the one who knows," he said quietly even though she had asked him not to say so.

Sergio was sitting with the children under the shade of the samán tree when Porfirio arrived. The lady had let him go early. The afternoon had been so wickedly hot, it would not do for him to water the plants as the air soaked the moisture right up. "It's going to be a long hot night tonight," Porfirio noted. "Maybe we should all jump in the pool with the lady?"

Sergio hushed him, looking over his shoulder to make sure the women were not within earshot. He had yet to mention the swimming lessons to María. Surely, when the lady saw the children all dressed up, she would not persist in her mission. Still, she had a will that was hard to bend once she made up her mind. To this day she was sleeping on a mattress on the floor of the tower room despite the mosquitoes helping themselves to the little there was of her to feast on.

Inside the house, Sergio could hear the women giggling like girls as they dressed.

"I'm not appearing with you in mourning. No, señora," Elena was saying. "Today you leave that behind you." Indeed when the women finally joined them outside, María was wearing her favorite blue dress from the last child's baptism.

Sergio whistled. Then he called out the compliment he usually saved for their private moments, "¡Cuántas curvas y yo sin freno!"

"So many curves and my brakes are shot!" his oldest boy shouted, imitating his father.

María lifted her head proudly. "Are we to go or are we to stand here and hear the roosters crowing?" Her hands were on her hips. But her mock scowl could not hide the pleasure on her face.

As they left her yard, María felt a tightening in her gut. She had not been back on Don Mundín's property since that dark day. Even when Doña Gabriela had sent for her before the funeral, María had refused to set foot in the house, and the patrona had had to come see María instead.

"I am also a mother. I understand how you feel," the patrona had said. She was so trim in her cream linen suit, it was hard to

believe she had borne children. Perhaps she would get dirty just
standing on the dirt floor of the hut. María had not said a word,
but she had accepted the envelope of money that was handed to
her. "For the funeral," the patrona had said. Of course there had
been quite a surplus beyond the funeral costs, and with that surplus, Sergio had rebuilt the wooden house with concrete blocks
and poured a cement floor on the ground. But on that day, when
the lady had stepped out of the house into the waiting car, María
had spit on the ground those high heels had marked.

"I wonder what the doña will cook?" she asked Elena, so as to
keep such thoughts out of her head.

"She will tell you not to call her doña," Elena coached her
sister-in-law. "She says that she is just to be called Yolanda."

"I cannot get used to it," Sergio admitted.

"Every time I prepare to say, Yolanda, I look at her, so white
and sorry-looking, and all I can get out is Doña Yolanda." Elena
was shaking her head and laughing.

"I will call her Yolanda, " one of María's boys piped up.

"Yolanda! Yolanda!" the children chorused.

"You little nothing, you be fresh to the lady and I'll show you
what a guayaba branch is good for," María scolded.

The women took the hands of the youngest children. It was
like a wake, the whole family dressed up and marching down the
streets of the village in the late afternoon. All that was missing
was the little box decked with flowers and, of course, the cries of
the mother.

The lady came down the stepping-stone path from the pool, her
arms held out in welcome. She wore a white jersey dress with
dark patches where her wet bathing suit had soaked through.
María was surprised by how small and fragile she looked. There

was a blue aura around her head that meant that she herself was feeling a great sadness. María wondered if she had lost a child, too. According to Elena, the lady was unmarried and had never had any children. But perhaps in her youth, who knows? Many were the women who came to María wanting to get a child out of their womb. But that was one job María would not do. Not since the death of her son.

"You must be María," the lady began.

"I am at your orders." María bowed her head, not out of obedience, but because she did not want the lady to see the glint of defiance in her eye.

But it was as if the lady had read her thoughts. "No, no, no, you are not at my orders"—she was shaking her head—"I don't give orders!" And then, most surprisingly, the lady threw her arm around María's shoulders. That is why minutes later when she offered to give the boys a swimming lesson, María hesitated, and then taking a deep breath as if she herself were going to plunge into the water, María said yes.

"But you boys better mind whatever the doña says or she will give you a sound beating!" María whipped her fingers together in the air.

"No, no, no," the lady protested again. "I don't hit children."

Certainly, she had made a lot of promesas—no orders, no meat, no whipping of children. Perhaps she, too, was marked at birth by the santos? According to Sergio and Elena, the lady shut herself in the tower room all day, only coming out in the afternoon to nibble at some insignificance in the kitchen and then to wander through town talking to the villagers as if everyone were a relation of hers. María recalled that first night she spotted the lady up in the tower room, poised at a table as if she, too, were listening for voices in the silence.

With the lady's permission, María found some old swimming shorts that belonged to Don Mundín's children. But when the lady tried convincing her to join them by the side of the pool, María refused, pleading dizziness from having caught too much sun this hot day. Waiting in the kitchen, however, was proving to be unbearable. Every time María heard a scream, her mother's heart skipped a beat or two.

To calm herself, she wandered through the downstairs rooms. Elena had certainly let the place go. There were dust balls in every corner, and Doña Gabriela's fancy glasses were out of the cabinet, put to everyday use. On the long, flowered couch, the cushions were annoyingly jumbled. María arranged them in a symmetrical way and slowly began climbing up the stairs, curious to see what had become of each of the rooms. Through the window on the first landing, the lady's voice came up from the garden, coaching one of the children. "Just let yourself fall back, go on. I'll hold you. I promise."

In the tower room, María found the bed, as Sergio had described it, lying on the floor under the eastern windows. She would have talked the lady out of such foolishness! A table was wedged into the corner, and on it lay a notebook scribbled with unrecognizable words. The sun was coming in through the western windows and the whole room glowed with light, so that standing there, María felt as if her santos were descending. An old ache traveled down her back just as when she used to ride her baby boy on her shoulders. "Ay, Dios santo," she whispered, looking up, but the setting sun blinded her, and for seconds she saw nothing at all.

To recover her vision, she shaded her eyes and looked down at the village below. There was the mayor's house, the mangy dog tied to the mango tree; the old woman Consuelo was sweeping her yard; and there was her own yellow house with the samán tree in front (she had forgotten to shut the back door!), the zinc roof Sergio had gotten for free by letting the Montecarlo people paint their ad on it—the sight stunned her as if she had never seen her spot on this earth before. From the pool, the happy cries of her own and Elena's children rose up, and then the voice she had been waiting for came through, clear as a bell from the tiny chapel below. "Mamá!" he was shouting, "Mamá, come and see how I can float!"

The best friend

motivation

Now that we're best friends, I hardly remember a time when I didn't know Yolanda García. I have to go back to that first year after my marriage fell apart and enter a peach-colored room where Brett Moore has gathered a group of us together to talk about the muse. That's what she has told us the group is going to focus on since all of us in there are writers or painters or musicians—and all of us are going through some sort of block.

We have our work cut out for us, Brett says, rolling up the sleeves of her plaid flannel shirt. Brett affects country manners with her clients—I think she thinks it makes them feel they're not in therapy but at a dude ranch with Brett, their cowgirl shrink, ready to rope in their neuroses and problems and brand them with names, Self-Destructive Behavior, Panic Disorder, Weak Ego Formation. Anyhow, our work, according to Brett, who has invited each one of us to join, is to track down our silences to their sources.

We will meet Thursday afternoons for a year, and we will all come to the same thing. At the back of every blank canvas, empty notebook, tin-ear composition book is an ex-husband or soon-to-be ex-husband or a bad lover or an unresponsive lover. Not that we're blaming these guys. In fact, Brett says, blaming them would be relinquishing control of our silence as we have relinquished control of our lives. Take charge, gals! she exhorts us.

Anyhow, though we originally gathered together to make contact with our muses, what we end up doing is talking about the men in our lives.

Every one of us in that group is living out some unpleasant and, hopefully, temporary man situation. There is a woman named—well, I shouldn't really give names, we've promised each other that much. Anyhow, there is a woman who keeps divorcing and remarrying the same man—I think they've gone through this routine three times. Another woman has a lover who disappears periodically—she doesn't know where he goes. She's afraid maybe he's murdering women in some other state, or something. "Then, why keep on seeing him?" we ask her.

"He's not trying to murder *me*," she defends herself.

There is a woman who has married a politician who is gay but needs a cover-up relationship. Believe me, none of us are going to vote for *him* in the next election! There are four other women going through wretched divorces, and we get to hear all about them. This actually helps me feel better, knowing I'm not the only woman who can pick the worst husband for herself. Pete's a sneak and a bully, that's the only way to put it. And it's amazing I've come out of this marriage with a full set of teeth, some self-esteem, and a healthy appetite for sex. I won't say more. After all, he is the father of my two wonderful boys.

Then there's Brett Moore herself, marching us forward, cracking the whip. Brett is out-and-out gay—short, curly red hair, hair with chutzpah, I call it, which she usually covers up with one of her incredible collection of cowboy hats. They hang on one wall of her office under a poster that shows a woman being thrown by a bronco. EVEN COWGIRLS GET THE BLUES, it reads. She has a long-term lover, whom she calls a partner, and two kids from an earlier marriage before—as she puts it—"I knew better." Sometimes

I wonder if there isn't a hidden agenda behind Brett's starting this whole group thing. Like maybe Brett thinks we should cross over and try our happiness with women for a while. I'm just guessing. But she isn't going to convince me. For the first time ever, I'm having a sex life like you wouldn't believe. In fact, Brett has suggested—whirling that bighorn lasso diagnosis—that I might be a borderline nymphomaniac.

But you got to take old Brett with a hunk of salt. Like I tell Yo, "I knew her before she was gay, when she was still wearing skirts and hot-combing her hair like the rest of us." I also knew Brett before she became a shrink, when we were both teaching at that alternative college that has since gone under. As for my being a borderline anything, the only guys I'm seeing are an Israeli guy who fixed my shower and a political activist who just got divorced himself. Oh yes, I guess there's also a computer programmer I met at contra dancing. Personally, I don't think three men with the emotional maturity, combined, of my two boys is overdoing it. Besides, I'm making up for lost time. In my forty-four years all I ever got was a buss on the lips from my high school steady, periodic goosings from my Uncle Asa, and lots of heartache from an abusive husband.

Yolanda is the group's "straight man," if that makes any sense. I mean, whereas the rest of us are tussling with men in some way, she has opted for celibacy, which doesn't make a bit of sense to me. She's thirty-five years old, good-looking, with a skinny bod the rest of us would die for. She can have any man from the small pool of decent available guys around and maybe even some from the unavailable ones who are out cruising the single scene. There's even this guy who's followed her around since college, mad for her. And she's going to hang up her sneakers and not play ball? Come on.

I suppose I should be glad—one less pretty face around, and so on. But for some reason, Yo's decision bugs me. Maybe it's my need for neatness. (I'm a Virgo all right.) I want to sort the world into male and female, and here's someone telling me that she's asexual. I suppose if I'd grown up Catholic, I'd be used to this third category, what with nuns and priests. But I grew up Jewish near Jones Beach and even as a little kid, I saw the men and women in my family holding, fondling, nuzzling, enjoying, yeah, even goosing each other. It's a wonder I married a goy from Boston whose idea of good sex was leaving the lights on.

Seems like I keep trying to talk Yolanda into getting her feet—among other things—wet again. Her first marriage doesn't even count—I mean, it lasted all of about eight months. Her second divorce is already five years old and it wasn't mean or anything. Her ex was some big-wig Englishman whom she was actually very fond of. According to her, it was as if they were both like moms on the first day of school, saying to their kids, I'll stay as long as you want me to. It took them several years to finally get the divorce. "So what was wrong with him?" the group asks.

"Nothing was wrong with him really." She gives us all an indignant look like how dare we criticize her ex. "I mean, he thought writing was eating your own head, yeah, that's what he called it, and he kept telling me that I had to get hold of myself, stuff like that." She looks up at us, hoping that's enough. And I'm thinking, compared to being punched out, what you had there was a good marriage. But then everyone tells me I settle for a lot less than I deserve. Deserve-schmaserve. It's not like we're being matched up by merit, or something.

Anyhow, all the time I'm trying to talk her into rebounding in one direction, old Brett is working on her to go in the opposite direction: has Yo ever considered that maybe what she is calling asexuality is really a revamping of her sexual orientation? It's like Brett and I are those two mothers in the Bible who want King Solomon to decide who's going to get the baby. But to tell you the truth, I don't care which way Yo goes, I just want her to make a choice for the simple reason that the road has come to a T: she is not happy.

"'Everybody needs somebody,'" I hum for her when we get together for dinner. Over the course of the year, we've become good friends outside the group. Even though I am nine years older, we do have a lot in common. We're both writers—and more importantly, she likes my poetry, I like her poetry; we both teach, and she's got something I need, free babysitting. Oh, I don't want it to sound like I'm using her, but Yo actually asked me if she could spend some time with my boys since it doesn't look like she's ever going to have any kids of her own.

"Of course, you're not," I say, shaking my head at her. "But then maybe your Catholic mami never got to the part about having to have sex if you wanna have babies."

She gives me a withering look. "You know, Tammy, ever since you started dating what's-his-face—" she calls all my men that— "your sense of humor has gone into the negative numbers."

"At least I've got one to start with," I say.

At this dinner we're discussing this date Yo doesn't want to go on. It's actually not even a real date. This rich guy who owns a very ritzy gardening magazine published locally, *Tillersmith*—I mean gardening-for-people-with-gardeners type thing—started talking to Yo at the nursery and somewhere in there she tells him how she misses seeing plants from her native Dominican Republic, and so this guy asks her over to see his greenhouse where he grows orchids and bromeliads, and now she is having a panic attack.

"But why?" I lean towards her as if to draw the good sense out of her like a magnet. "All you're going to do is go over there and say, wow, what a neat orchid, that's a terrific yucca plant. Then you can go home if you want."

She looks at me as if she's not sure whether or not she can trust me. As if what's really going to happen is she's going to go over there and this guy is going to trap her in his basement with his dormant bromeliads and force her to make love to him. So what would be so bad about that? I feel like asking her.

"Why don't you come with me? We'll just pretend that we were driving by and you wanted to see his bromeliads, too." Even she has to smile when she says this.

"I'm sure that'll go over well—you bringing a chaperone."

"You see," she says, narrowing her eyes at me, "you do think he's going to try something."

"Yolanda García," I say, laying my hands down flat on the table like I've had it with her. "I'm going to tell you the truth now and you can go blab on me to the group if you want. It's time you got over all this meshugaas about men." She's looking at me with those big intense eyes like I caught her with my high beams crossing the road. "Till you let those juices flow, you're not going to be able to write worth shit!"

Her mouth drops open and thunder *and* lightning come out of those eyes. "I thought you said you loved my poetry," she cries out. Thank God, we're at Amigo's, our town's one ethnic watering spot, if by ethnic you mean turquoise walls with orange-magenta trim and a cactus in the corner. But with those mariachi and ranchera tapes going full blast, two loud-mouthed ladies don't make a dent. Still, there's a guy I've had my eyes on since we walked in, sitting by himself, having a burrito, and I want to make a good impression.

"I do love your poetry," I say in a hushed voice. "But, Yo, face it, you haven't been writing much. You've put a lid on everything, including your muse."

By now, I'm holding her hands, and she's crying, and the cute guy, who maybe isn't so cute with sideburns that look like he's trying to prove something, has lost interest, probably thinking we're gay or something. But I don't care anymore. I'm so sure I'm right about Yo, I give it all I got. "Please, just try, okay. This guy might turn out to be a friend, and that'll be a perfect re-entry for you with men. To make friends with them first."

Big talker here. It's not as if I'm making friends with the near strangers I'm bedding down.

She wipes her eyes, and this determined look comes on her face like she's headed for the front lines of the gender war. "Okay," she says, "I'll try."

And hey, I should hang out my prophet shingle, because Yo and this Tom guy become good friends. Of course, the poor guy soon wants more. Late nights the phone rings, and I pick up my end quick, thinking something's happened to one of my boys—they're with their father for the summer. But it's for Yo, who's moved in with me before heading north for a new teaching job. I hear the longing in Tom's voice as he greets her, "I just called to say goodnight."

"Why don't you let him come over?" I ask her the following morning. Down the hall, we can hear my Israeli in the shower that he himself fixed months ago.

Yo cocks her head in the direction of the bathroom. "It takes me longer."

"Well, you don't have much longer," I remind her.

She leaves for New Hampshire in late August, and the group has decided to break up then as well. We're done with our work,

as Brett tells us. The gay politician's wife is out of the closet herself, the woman with the disappearing lover has started dating a
cop, and everyone else is in the last throes of their divorces and
writing or composing or painting like mad. I don't know what
magic dust Brett threw in the air, but even Yo and I are writing
poems again. Every few nights when I don't have a guest over, we
get in my bed like sisters and read each other what we've written.

Some of the stuff she's writing is pretty good—and I keep urging her to come to our open mike readings on Fridays at the Holy
Smokes Cafe, but she just makes a face. "It's not my scene," she
says. The Holy Smokes has gotten a reputation as a place to go
pick up someone easy. "All those guys drooling over my sestina?
No way!" She makes a face over the poem she's been reading out
loud to me.

"Such an attitude!" I shake my head at her. She has shared
some of her poems with the group, and of course, with me. But
she won't let guys near her stuff. She says every guy she ever
showed her poems to used reading them to get her to do something else—like jump in bed with them. Even her favorite professor from college kept telling her to get a Ph.D. instead of wasting her time writing.

"But you send him your stuff." I've seen a couple of manila
envelopes addressed to professor so-and-so in western Mass.

"Well, he's far away," she shrugs. "Besides, I think he's gay."

"He's still a guy!" I give her a shove with my foot. "What? Is
Brett not female?"

"Yeah, yeah, yeah," she agrees. "But gay people are different.
They're not into conquest."

"Oh no, kiddo?" I say, like I'm some old gangster guy you better listen to. "You need to come out of the woods and take a little
walk in the real world."

She gives me a coy smile, and then she says, "So does New Hampshire count as the real world?" We both fall silent, and this sadness comes over me thinking how she'll be gone by the time the boys are back for school.

A few weeks before she's to leave, Yo gets brave and invites this Tom guy over. All summer, she's dropped in on him or they've met at what she calls some neutral space for breakfast of all things. According to Yo, breakfast is the ideal meal for a date if you're not very sure about a guy. "Dinner can always stretch to bedtime and lunch can become the rest of the day, but everyone's got to go to work after breakfast."

"I don't believe you," I tell her. Here I'm always trying to think of a way to get a guy to come home with me after linguini or stir-fry, and Yo's shooing them off to go earn the bacon after the scrambled eggs.

But finally she's going to have Tom over for dinner, and I'm tickled as anything. I want her to leave for her new job having gotten over this anti-man thing. But then I overhear her on the phone, and I swear to you she says, "Just for supper because Tammy and I—we go to bed early." When she hangs up, I ask her straight out, "Have you told this guy we're gay or something?"

This little pressed smile comes on her lips like she's starched and ironed it to wear for just this occasion. She looks away, because as she well knows, I can see right through to her soul. It's the reason we're best friends.

"Well?" I challenge, and she looks up at me, the truth written all over her face before she even tells it. "I just haven't said, you know, one way or the other—"

"I can't believe you! This is a small town. You'll ruin my heterosexual reputation!" I had meant to give her this righteous scolding about using our relationship to protect herself. But I guess what I'm really upset about slips out. "I never was popular with guys before this," I wail.

And that's when she takes hold of my hands and sits down in front of me, and looks me in the eye. "Okay, Tammy Rosen, now I'm going to level with you. What I've seen going on in this house is not popularity or friendship or anything that's going to keep. You're running away from men just as fast as I am. And sure, you're still writing great poetry, but your personal life stinks!"

And suddenly it's me bursting into tears, and she's crooning over me, and I'm thinking, God, what are we, emotional Bobbsey twins or something?

I know she's right, and I finally bring it up in group, how unrenewing my relationships have been, how men have become an addiction for me, how I have to break the habit of staying on the surface with them. That's when Brett gives *me* her big all-purpose diagnosis about being a borderline nympho, and I swallow it whole without my usual chunk of therapeutic salt. Then I cry and everyone holds me, and in the days following, in a great burst of coming-clean resolution, I break things off with my Israeli, my activist, my computer guy. Afterwards, I'm as shaky as if I just gave up smoking and I don't know how I'm going to survive without a butt sticking out of my mouth.

For Yo's big Friday date, I offer to stay with my ma who's been down in the dumps since the boys left. Besides, it's open mike at Holy Smokes. I pile up all these good reasons for me to stay in Boston. Finally, I level with her. "Hey, I've cleaned up my act. Now it's your turn."

She takes me by the shoulders. "You ain't out of the woods yet, honeychile. You've been moping around like you just lost your best friend."

"Well, it's hard," I say, all teary. "And soon, you'll be gone too. I won't have any friends." Yes, folks, even forty-four-year-old women are sometimes emotional seven-year-olds.

"You ain't losing me, babycakes," she drawls, giving me a hug. It's funny how Yo, a native Spanish speaker, thinks of southern redneck talk as affectionate English. "And those other bozos were never your friends. That's what you really need, you know, a male friend. It'd be a perfect re-entry for you with men. To make friends with them first."

Is there an echo in the room? "Well, anyhow, I want you to have the run of the place," I tell her. "In case, you know—"

"Don't start in," she says, all huffy. "I've told you we're just friends! And besides, Tom wants to meet you," she insists. "You're my best friend, you know?"

And suddenly, I'm all tearful again, and I'm thinking, maybe now that I've decided to behave like a grownup woman, meno-pause is kicking in.

I don't know what it is, but something feels different about Yo the week we're preparing for our Friday supper party. Some edge that wasn't there before that makes me think she's more excited about this Tom guy than even she knows. Suddenly, her hair doesn't look right—should she part it on the other side? Aren't her legs kind of skinny, what do I think, are her legs skinny or not? Is there an exercise to build up the calves?

"In five days?" I ask her.

When she starts coming down for her cup of coffee in the morning with her eyes made up, I think: she's going to sleep with this Tom guy before the summer's over.

Me, I'm winding down just as she's getting revved up. The first few days after letting go of the guys, I thought I'd have to go to a detox unit. What would be the methadone for coming off men? Cold showers under the good showerhead they fixed? Little boys?—I'm sorry, as the mother of sons, I shouldn't joke that way. But anyhow, pretty soon, I'm loving the long mornings in my study working on my Sappho poems—Sappho, who lolls on couches reciting her Sapphics to doting devotees; Sappho, cool and in control. Afternoons I garden and sun and read the high-minded Rilke, then poetry readings with Yo every night, and finally I crawl into the big old bed where there's no one nudging me awake—all of it seems such a luxury. The ascetic's pleasures, Yo's pleasures, I begin to understand them.

But the guys don't give up that easily, which surprises me. Maybe they were getting more out of the relationship than I thought. They keep calling, when can they come over, can't we talk about it. Suddenly, it's *me* hinting that Yo and I have something going. But that doesn't stop my activist friend Jerry.

"You can't just unilaterally end a relationship like that," he announces, like it's in the U.N. charter or something.

"Who says?" I say. "You guys always bail out when you feel like it." I think of Pete running off with his secretary, insulting me not just by abandonment but by such a cliché.

"Oh please," Jerry says. "Don't make me responsible for my whole gender. I'm just as much against sexism as you are, you know that."

The truth is, I didn't know that. Where was I when he told me? Too busy taking his pants off? But I turn it around so it's his fault. "We never talked," I accuse him. "I don't even know who you are."

"Well, why don't you find out." His voice has gone all gravelly and soft, the way men's voices get when you get through to them. And then he says just the right thing. "And I want to find out who you are, Tammy. Give me a chance."

"How about dinner tonight?" I ask him. It occurs to me that tonight will be more comfortable all the way around if we are two pairs. Besides, if Tom has any wrong ideas about me and Yo, Jerry's presence will straighten him out.

Jerry jumps at the chance. "I'd love to. What shall I bring?"

"Just yourself," I say gaily. My heart already feels lighter, shedding all those wimples and veils of good clean living. Sure, I can be a nun, but it's a stretch for us Jewish girls, you know? I do add—for one thing, the group and Yo would kill me otherwise—"But, Jerry, it's just dinner, okay? I need to go slower this time. I want to become friends first."

There's a disappointed silence on the other end, the kind I'm used to hearing when Tom calls Yo in the middle of the night. Finally, he says, "I understand, Tammy. Whatever it takes."

Did I get lucky or what? And to think I almost sloughed off this mensch of a man! My new Sappho poem goes back in the drawer, and for the rest of the day, it's me trying on outfits, insisting that the basil for our pesto be fresh-picked, getting out my Aunt Joan's flowered dessert plates, driving all the way into town to Heart and Hearth to pick up those slow-burning, dripless candles that can go all night long.

We're in the screened-in back porch, having dinner, the candles flickering whenever a breeze blows in. It's one of those humid, crickety summer nights that feels as if we're way down south rather than just north of Boston. Yo and I are sitting side by side, the men facing us. Jerry, of course, is familiar to me, but I'm seeing him in a new light tonight. Especially after four glasses of wine. He's dark and gabby with a looseness and easiness to his movements that make him very sexy, though I'm trying not to think of that.

Beside him, Tom seems almost stiff—in fact his looks surprise me in a way. I thought Yo, being Latina and all, would choose someone more exotic and swarthy looking. Someone like . . . well, my Jerry. But Tom—and believe me, we can't keep ourselves from joking about Tom and Jerry—Tom has a neat blond look that makes you want to mess up his hair. Which Yo keeps doing whenever she goes by him. Later, watching her serve him a fat wedge of her guava flan, licking the syrup on her fingers, her bright eyes on Tom, I think, yep, tonight's the night.

We're discussing our pasts. Among us there are six divorces, incredible! "What's going on?" I ask the table, as if they know.

"The old connections don't work," Yo pipes up. Most of the real conversation tonight is between the two of us, the guys joining in every now and then. Sometimes, I think that it's the intensity between us they're drawn to, like the moths flapping against the screens, wanting in. "We all have to figure out new ways of relating," Yo continues.

"You said it," Jerry says, nodding knowingly. His voice is thick and slurred. It reminds me of how my boys say they've colored over the lines in their drawing book. Jerry just can't keep his voice inside the tidy pronunciation of words. I don't know how he's going to drive himself home tonight.

"That's why I went celibate," Yo says openly to the table. "I just kept falling back into my old habits with men. I had to break the pattern, you know?"

Tom looks down at his piece of flan as if studying where to cut the next mouthful. But I can tell by the tilt of his head that he is listening carefully. He has *not* had too much to drink.

"So how are you. . . . How are you," Jerry starts up again, hazily recalling where he was heading, "you know, going to get back in the saddle—" He flashes me the silliest ear-to-ear grin.

That decides it. He's too drunk to drive himself home. He's sleeping in Jamie's room tonight.

Now it's Yo's turn to look down at the table, embarrassed. "I don't know," she says. "I guess I'll know when it's time." At this, Tom gets this distant look on his face—one of those brown studies that people in the nineteenth century got into when they couldn't just come out and say what they were thinking. Suddenly, I know who Tom reminds me of besides Barbie's Ken, the guy in *Pride and Prejudice*, Darcy what's his name, who's good and wise and kind but needs some livening up. Enter our heroine, Yo García.

As for me, I'm hanging on to my good resolutions, so when dinner is long over, and those slow-burning candles are down to nothing but their wicks, I announce that I'm calling it a night. Jerry looks up hopefully at me. "Let's get you to bed, too," I say. He flashes the table a triumphant grin and grabs hold of my arm. As I kiss Yo goodnight, I whisper in her ear, "Don't worry, he's going in Jamie's room." By her baffled look, I see she's completely forgotten to police my good intentions about men.

Upstairs after a slow, swaying climb, Jerry is too drunk to put up much of a fuss. "Where are you going?" he asks when I've tucked him into the small twin bed. He could be my boy, lying there with the quilt up to his neck and his head poking up, afraid to be left in the dark bedroom all by himself.

"I'll be right back," I hush him, and I go out to the bathroom and get him two aspirin and a glass of water.

Later, lying in my bed, I can make out voices on the back porch, whispers and giggles, a voice persuading, a voice resisting but not really. I doze off, and when I next come awake, I hear the same whispers and giggles coming from the direction of Yo's bedroom. And then, much later, when I wake, the house is still, that three o'clock in the morning stillness that sends a shiver of mortality through me and makes me reach out for the extra pillow and hold on to it.

Someone is crawling in bed with me! At first, I think it's Jerry, but when I turn, almost grateful for the intrusion, I realize it's Yo.

"What's the matter?" I whisper.

"It wasn't time," she says, taking the extra pillow I've been using as my substitute man.

I'm still mostly asleep so I don't know what she's talking about right away. "Time for what?"

"You know," she says. There's just the slightest edge of blame in her voice. And I start to feel bad like maybe I pushed too hard for a breakthrough.

"Well, it's late," I say in the soothing voice I use on my kids. "Things'll look different in the morning."

Not a sound from her side of the bed. She's lying on her back, looking up at the ceiling, an insomniac getting ready for the long night ahead. And though I try to sink back into the folds of the dream I was having, before I know it, I'm wide awake as well.

"I'm sorry," she says when I turn on the bedside light to check the time on the clock. Four-fifteen. Tomorrow—or really I should say, today—is going to be a wasted day all right. "I feel like the muse is gone again," she says. She's taking those short, panicky breaths I recall from when Pete used to scare me half to death. "Like I've let a man invade. You know?"

I want to say, now come on, Yo, you're scaring yourself. But maybe it's the wine still in my head or the late night and us talking in whispers, but I know exactly what she means, how unknowingly we women give over our lives to the first needy thing: or men or children or the soufflé that won't rise or the kitten that's got a swollen paw. "I know," I tell her, "but you're not going to lose your voice. It's in you, how can you lose it?"

She seems comforted by my argument, but when I go to turn off the light, she says, "Tammy, let's read each other some poems, okay?"

"Yo, it's four o'clock in the morning!" I argue, but I think what the hell, four-fifteen, five, what's the difference. Besides, something in me always gives in to Yo's schemes—a desire to make my life more troubled and interesting, I don't know.

She tiptoes out and comes back with her folder of poems, and grabs mine from my study on the way in. And there we are reading poems to each other while two men are snoring away in another part of the house.

Or so we think. Yo's in the middle of her second muse sonnet, when I look over her shoulder, and there's Tom in the doorway, a towel like a little wrap-skirt wound around his waist. The neat hair is tussled, all right, and if earlier tonight he looked like he belonged in the nineteenth century, now he looks like he walked out of one of those plain-wrapper magazines you can't even get in New Hampshire.

"What's going on?" he says, a kink in his eyebrows.

We're both in our nightgowns with manila folders on our laps. What does he think?

"We're having a poetry reading," I say, like it's the most normal thing in the world.

But he's not taking that for an answer. He looks straight at Yo, his eyes full of twentieth-century pissed-offness. "I wake up and you're gone," he says. I can hear the anger in his voice, and I feel my heart beating hard, recalling those horrid scenes with Pete. Meanwhile Yo's gone absolutely silent on me.

"She couldn't sleep, and neither could I," I defend us. "So we're just reading to each other."

He thinks about that a moment, and when he lets out a sigh, I realize I've been holding my breath. I kid you not, but it's some kind of revelation to me that a man can get angry and not hurt anyone with it. "I guess I can't sleep myself. Can I join you?" he asks in a voice I would find hard to refuse.

I'm about to nod when Yo finally finds her tongue. "No!" she says, so adamantly that both Tom and I are taken aback. "Tammy and I, we share our poems only with each other," she adds in a kinder voice. Which is a lie, on my part. But of course, Yo has this thing about showing her poems to guys.

This hurt look opens up his face, and just for a second, I catch a glimpse of the boy inside the stiff, shy man. And I can't help but feel sorry for him. Yo feels bad, too, I can tell. Her eyes follow him as he shuffles down the dark hall, his hands behind his cute, terryclothed butt.

And though she goes back to reading her sonnet out loud— her heart isn't in it. Her voice trails away. "Your turn," she says, but I'm not into reading my Sappho poems either. It's like the muse *has* fled. "We should have let him stay," I tell her, taking half the blame.

She looks down at the poem on her lap as if it is going to tell her what to do. "I know," she says at last.

"And you know, honeybaby, until you share your work with a man, you ain't gonna feel right with him in the sack." Sappho with a Southern accent, sweet-talking some sense into Yo.

Into myself for that matter.

In a minute, she's out of bed. "I'll go get him," she says. "But it's going to change things," she adds in a warning voice. Of course it is. The minute a man enters our lives, there's bound to be trouble. But hey, like I told Yo, she's got thunder and lightning to outdo any guy. And so do I for that matter.

She comes back with Tom still in his terry kilt and an extra nightgown draped over her shoulder. "I told him he can join us," she informs me, holding up the nightie. Tom looks at her, his eyebrows lifting, his curiosity piqued—as is mine, I admit.

"Put up your arms," Yo says and climbs on my bed and slips the nightgown over his head. "Tammy, get me one of your scarves."

At first, I think this straightlaced Tom is going to hightail it out of here. But he's turning this way and that as Yo tugs the nightgown so it falls just so. All the while he's grinning away like we're playing out *his* fantasy. And I'm thinking, why this is a fantasy of mine as well. To find a male girlfriend with whom I can share my bed as well as the state of my soul.

"One scarf, coming right up," I say, grabbing my favorite, a purple silk from the basket on my bureau along with one of my lipsticks.

"Hold still," I say, outlining his lips in red. "What do you think?" I ask Yo. "A little eye makeup?"

Yo nods, laughing, and now Tom is laughing, too, the loosest I've seen the man since he set foot in this house almost ten hours ago. And the thing I'm liking about him is that he's not acting limp-wristed and silly the way men feel they have to when they're imitating girls. When we're done, Yo takes him by the hand and stands him in front of the mirror.

"You make a damn good-lookin' woman." Her arm hangs over his shoulder, pals; her nose nuzzles his neck, lovers. She, too, has calmed down from the panic attack she was having only minutes ago. "And you're not half bad as a man either."

When we have him all dolled up, we let him in bed with us, the poetry reading forgotten as we giggle and girl-talk about who has the best-looking legs. Soon we hear footsteps in the hall, moving in our direction, and there's Jerry, still a little woozy, rubbing his eyes like maybe he's seeing things. "What's going on here?" he asks.

Before he knows it, we've got him in one of my nightgowns, and he's sitting at my end, the sheets pulled up to our laps, a soft dawn light coming up in the sky. Then Tom says, "Well, let's hear some poems," and I say to Yo, "You go first," so she doesn't chicken out. And sitting here with Jerry and Tom on either side of me, listening to Yo's hesitant voice growing sure and steady as she reads along, I'm thinking, hot damn! I've found everything I was looking for in Brett Moore's group, a muse, a man I can get to know, a best friend, Yo.

The landlady

She answers the ad, comes with a little notepad, wants to know everything about the place. "Is it quiet?" she asks. "I'm a writer, you know. I got to write a book to get my tenure."

I say, "I got two kids and those two kids got a TV and a dog. But I live here. I manage." She doesn't like that. She makes a little mark in her notebook, and I'm about to tell her the place is already rented because what business is it of hers if my two kids is hollering all time. Ever since Clair left last month, seems like everything around here is acting up. The oven door's broke. The roof leaks—right into that two-bedroom, as a matter of fact. The front step rail needs fixing. Clair used to do all the small jobs, and it's not that I'm cheap, but I got two kids and my own big self to think of, and I can't go hiring some handyman for twelve-fifty an hour on account of he's got a van with his name on the side written in script.

But I need a tenant, and there aren't many left as the college's starting in a few weeks, and so most newcomers in this town are already settled in, so I say, "They're nice kids. Dog's never been a barker. Wanna go up and see it?"

She looks at her watch first like she's got an appointment with someone across town who's going to rent her a much nicer two-bedroom for a lot less than the five-fifty I'm asking for. "Sure," she says. We come out my front steps and down the yard to the entrance for the upstairs part of the house. "Sure is a neat old house," she says.

"Used to be my mother-in-law's house. She was born in this house, so was my husband. This is the old part of town."

Now her eyes are shining with a greedy light I know well. Clair gets that look whenever some pretty thing comes in the auto parts store where he works. "I like old houses," she says. "Those new condos make me feel like I could be living anywhere."

I'm liking her a lot more, so I leak out a little of the truth. "Wouldn't live anywhere else myself. But a old house's a old house, and you know, things break down from time to time."

"Yeah?" she says. "Like what?"

I'm not going to get her all worried. Besides, it might not rain for a few months yet, and then it'll be snow and the ice'll plug any holes till the spring. By that time, who knows, we might be friends or something. "Nothing particular," I say. "Just it takes a lot more work to live in a old house than those spanking new lookalike things." Why is it that when I'm talking condos I always picture Clair's little girlfriend with her shaggy haircut and spiky heels and halter top and shorts up to here.

We go upstairs, and she's telling me all about how she's not originally from this country but came when she was a kid and now she has this job over at the college. All the time I'm wondering if she's giving me some story because she's talking English better than me. So I say, "You sure picked up English," and she looks at me a moment and says, "Language is the only homeland. This poet once said that. When there's no other ground under your feet, you learn quick, believe me."

"You bet," I say.

I show her the rooms, and she's oohing and ahing, saying,

wow, wow, all the time like some kid with a cowlick back in the fifties. "Light's so good here," she says in the room that's got the leaks. "I think I'll make my study here." Then she looks over at me, her face full of color like she's embarrassed that she let on that she wants this place. "That is, if I end up living here."

We go into the front room where the sun's shining through the maple trees out front, real pretty. Makes me feel all sad remembering how it used to be with Clair. This was our bedroom when we first got married and his ma was still downstairs. Well, she likes this room too, and the little window seat, and the brick chimney that goes down into my fireplace. "There was a fireplace up here, too, but Clair—that's my husband—blocked it up. Maybe I'll open it up again." I say this like it might happen tomorrow, though really, it'd cost a prettier penny than I got in my pocketbook to do that fixing.

Finally she stops wandering around, opening closets, and comes back to me in the room she likes the most, the one she said she'd make into a study. She's looking at me funny and I'm thinking she's going to ask me can I come down from five-fifty which I'm prepared to do because I like her, number one, and number two, I figure her originally being a foreigner and all, maybe she needs a helping hand, too. But she says the most peculiar thing. "Has this been a happy place for you?"

And you know, what I didn't do when Clair moved in with that little girl-woman or when his ma, who was like a ma to me, too, died a couple of years ago of a cancer that was just like rabbits breeding inside her or when I looked in the mirror this morning and saw a fat woman dressed in a tent of fabric, I have to swallow hard to keep from crying. "It's been a home," I say, "good and bad, I can't complain."

"So not really happy?" she says, all suspicious-like.

And then I see what she's getting at. She's one of those people needs to hang a rabbit foot in the rearview of their Pinto, like that's what's going to make it run. So I say something that comes right off the needlepoint Clair's ma made when she was a girl that's still hanging in the kitchen. "This house is a home to all who come here. Honest," I add, because she's looking at me funny like I'm giving her a line. "And I'm prepared to come down to four-ninety on account of you're by yourself and you won't be using as much electric and water and sewage."

She's thinking it over, goes through the rooms one more time, comes back and says, "I've got to go pick up my friend who's coming up to help me move. Can I bring her over to see the place . . . and then give you my decision?"

What a cockeyed way to do things, I'm thinking. Then I get suspicious. I seen those boat people bringing over whole villages to Miami. "I said four-ninety if you're by yourself. Each extra person's sixty more. And I need the security, too," I add kind of stern.

I can see my tone makes her jumpy—she's a sensitive type. Like she's going to decide on whether to live here depending on if I speak to her nice and the traffic light on the corner doesn't change till she counts to five. "I just want my friend to give me her opinion," she says in a little voice like my Dawn when she wants to spend the third night in a row over at Kathy's—which she always does when her daddy's in the house.

I look at this skinny lady—she's about my age, in her middle thirties, colored like those old-fashioned sepia photographs that make everyone look like they got some Indian in them, with a long dark braid down her back, big intense eyes like people in scary movies on TV have—and what I think surprises me. I could be this person, all alone in this strange world where I'm not sure how to do things because things haven't turned out the way they were supposed to. So, I act the fool, which isn't the first time. I say, "Sure. I'll leave the door open. Just bring your friend on up and show her around. I'll be downstairs. Let me know what you decide."

And suddenly, she's giving me this hug like I've donated twenty bucks a month to a orphan in her country. "You're so nice, thank you!" She climbs in her car, a Toyota, which doesn't make me too happy her buying foreign, but then I remind myself she *is* foreign. Anyhow, she toots her horn and away she goes, and all up and down the street, neighbors I've known since I moved into this house sixteen years ago as Clair's wife peek out their windows wondering what's going to happen next in Marie Beaudry's falling-apart life.

She moves in with the help of this friend I don't know what to make of. A tall, mouthy woman in shorts and a T-shirt with no bra and a funny color in her hair that don't look right. This one don't seem foreign, very white, with a name that sounds like she lives next door, Tammy Rosen, though she explains the name is really Tamar and the Rosen's been shortened from Rosenberg when her family came over from Germany during the Holocaust. I just keep my mouth shut because I never was any good at history and I can't ever keep straight who murdered who and why they did it. But anyhow, the news is good, this lady's taking the apartment—she writes me the check right off for the rent and security deposit. Only when she signs the lease do I finally get what her name is, Yolanda García, but she says she likes to go by Yo. Tammy, Yo—that sure makes it easier. One thing I appreciate about these foreigners—and the two I've met in a day are two more than I've known all my life—is how willing they are to go along with the way we do things in this country. I mean they should, I know, but things aren't always the way they should be. Look at Clair chasing after little girls and coming home drunk to beat up on his wife and kids. I keep telling myself this when I start regretting him being gone now for almost six weeks.

What they're up to upstairs—after a couple of days of moving in and setting up—I'd give my right arm to know about, throw in the eighty extra pounds I'm carting around. There's a lot of murmuring and giggling, and then I smell it coming down through the vents, incense or something. Just as long as they're not doing anything illegal, that's fine with me. Emily and Dawn's constantly upstairs and coming back down saying they been taught to say howdy-do and I-love-you in Spanish and German and to draw horses with horns that's extinct but bring good luck. Couple of times they stop to talk to me on the porch: do I know about this Chinese class at the community center—it's not really Chinese, just some exercise the Chinese do. There's going to be a medieval fair on the green with booths and jugglers, do I wanna come and bring the kids along. Truth is, they've only been here two weeks and know things about this town I never knew. I always say no, cause I figure I'll just feel fatter and more ignorant around all those college people. But just thinking I can do things besides hankering after Clair makes me feel the best I've felt in years.

Only thing is, every once in a while I realize all over again how odd these gals are. Just this morning, I wake up early—can't sleep as usual, grinding my teeth at Clair—and I see them wandering around in the backyard. I go out on my back steps. "You lost something, girls?" Funny how I call them girls even though they're about my age. They look up guilty-like. The one called Yo is carrying a little Baggie.

"Nothing, Marie," she says. "We're just protecting the space."

This is a first. But what am I going to do? Tell them they can't sprinkle talcum powder on that sorry-looking lawn no one's mown since Clair's been gone. I just go along. "Throw around a little for me," I tell them and I come back in the kitchen and look out at them through the window above the sink. They stand talking, heads together, glancing over their shoulders at my back door. Then they come right up to the house and circle it—I follow them window to window—until they end up right by my front steps shaking out the empty Baggie.

Now I don't go in for hocus pocus one bit, but next thing I know, I hear the pickup up front, and there's Clair minus the girlfriend asking can he come inside and have a cup of coffee. Of course, I want him back, but I stand with my hand on the door like I'm not sure I'm going to let him in. Well, he's grinning, hands at his hips, looking things over. I can see what he sees: the overgrown lawn I need him to mow, the broken rail at the steps I need him to fix. Finally his eyes come to rest on the upstairs windows now hung with a wild purple fabric with half-moons on it. "I hear you got you a couple of lesbian foreigner tenants," he says.

And I don't know if it's the magic powders or just having those girls around two weeks now, but I find I have a mouth. "Well, I hear I got me a tail-chasing husband." And I turn to go in like I'm too busy to be talking to him and giving my neighbors something to talk about. "You're welcome to some coffee," I say over my shoulder, "but them girls is coming down before the one visiting goes home." I make this up—the part about them coming down, though it's true Tammy's leaving today on account of her boys is coming back from their father's.

"Well, least let me get this front yard a sec 'fore I come in," he says, and that's when I know he's here to stay. Or I should say the little girlfriend must have dumped him and he hasn't found a new one yet.

He's over at the shed kicking and cussing at the mower because the motor keeps dying on him. I call upstairs and tell the one called Yo that I sure would like it if they came down and had a cup of coffee before Tammy goes. I can hear she's a little surprised like maybe I done the wrong thing but it's also the nice wrong thing. "Sure," she says after a pause. And then she adds, "Marie, there's some weird guy throwing a fit in your backyard shed. Is he supposed to be here?"

And before I can stop myself and say it in a way that doesn't sound like I'm saying it—which is my friend Dottie's description of what they teach you over at the college—I say to this Yo, "That's my husband Clair. He wants to say hello."

A few weeks of his sorry-eyed, sweet talk, and the trouble starts up again.

One night his fries isn't fried through, another night his meat's pinker than he likes and the kids is arguing over what they're going to watch on the TV, and he loses it. Thing that's changed is I'm lipping him back, and so I'm getting pushed around a lot more, and I'm feeling it a lot more as I've started to take off the weight. Gets me to thinking maybe I put on those eighty pounds as padding against his fist coming at me. But truth is he's so drunk, all I got to do is dodge, and being slimmer, I'm quicker on my feet too. He hollers and carries on a while, but then falls in a dead drunk sleep. And seeing him lying on his ma's old bed, all tangled in the sheets with his hair thinning in back, my heart fills up with a sad sorry love for him I don't know what to do with but keep to myself.

Anyways I'm used to it, but upstairs I can hear that typewriter that's been thumping away suddenly go silent. And then I hear her crossing the room, back and forth, since our bedroom's right below where she said she was going to put that study of hers. Sometimes when the yelling starts and the kids is crying, I hear her coming down the stairs real slow like she doesn't know what she's going to do. Then, a little while later, the car starts up and off she goes. I don't know where. Sometimes she stays away all night, and I lie awake on the sofa bed or in the rocker in Emily and Dawn's room just waiting for the sound of that Toyota like my life depended on her coming back home.

Then, one day I'm out back hanging the wash, and she's coming up the steps to her place, and she turns back. She walks kind of cautious up to me, her arms carrying two big bookbags she hasn't had the sense to leave by the door. "Hi, Marie," she says, and her eyes are still the eyes of someone in a scary movie, but what she's looking at is my face. It's gone down some since Clair's last fit four nights ago, though the bruise on my right cheek looks like I went crazy with the eye shadow.

"Are you all right?" she says.

"I'm fine," I say because what am I suppose to say. I love a man who's all wrong inside, and I stay because something wrong's inside me, I guess. So I say, "How's the new job? Heard from your friend Tammy? Still taking that Chinese exercise class?" A whole bunch of questions thrown at her and all the time I'm hanging up Clair's socks and drawers and giving her the left side of my face.

"Fine, fine," she keeps saying like her heart's not in the conversation.

"How's the book you're writing for your tenure going?" I ask. She explained to me about it, which got Clair all riled up on account of me teasing him one night that I bet he didn't know what a tenure was. He didn't, and he especially didn't like being shown up. "I hear you typing away upstairs," I add cause now she's looking at those bookbags instead of right at my face like she always does.

"I'm not writing a whole lot," she says. "I can't concentrate much," she adds, and she sets them bookbags down and looks me in the face. "Marie," she says, "I hear what's going on downstairs. I think you need to get some help."

I don't know why this burns me up. Maybe I'm just waiting to yell at someone who's not going to punch me out. "I don't think it's any business of yours," I tell her, and now I'm giving her my full face which is more than my full face since it's all swole up. "I didn't say nothing when you and Tammy was carrying on."

I can tell right after I say it that I just about hit the wrong bull's-eye. She looks like somebody slapped her—all surprised and unbelieving. "What are you talking about, Marie? If you mean Tammy and I are lovers, we're not. And even if we were, that's not the same as someone beating you up."

"It's not beating," I yell back at her like I'm trying to drown out the thought. It's that he's trying to kill something inside himself and I get in his way. Course I don't say that part. "We're having a little bit of a rocky road, that's all," is what I say.

"Marie, he's hurting you. Look at your face." She touches my shoulder, and for a second time with her, I feel like I'm going to cry. So, I put a stop to this softness I can't afford to get used to inside.

"Listen here, Yolander, you just remember, you're renting this place, that's all, and what you do is your business 'cepting it's legal and what I do is mine, you hear me."

Well, her eyes get kind of dewy and her cheeks a shade darker. She picks up her bookbags, and starts to go, but then she turns back. "Marie, I'm sorry, but I just can't keep living here. I'm going to have to move."

"You signed a lease," I say, sterner than I mean to sound. Cause what I feel in my heart is this swallowed-up feeling like when Clair moved out. "You can't just break a lease," I tell her—like this is America and she better play by the rules.

"I'm going to have to," she says, and I see something in her eyes I overlooked before. I must have been distracted by her little-girl size and foreigner politeness. Those eyes of hers see clear through me to where she's going—that's why they're so intent—and nothing, not Clair Beaudry, not Marie either, not a lease or a security deposit, not God Himself with His eternal tenure to hold over her head is going to stop her. I never seen a woman look like that before, though I seen plenty of men with them surefire eyes, including my Clair when he knows just how he wants his fries.

"I hope you understand it's not you," she is saying in a softer voice, like maybe she scared her own self being so strong. "I need to get writing done, and I can't work here. It's not a . . ." She sets those bookbags down and makes a shape with her hands about the size of a baby or a womb with a baby inside it. "Not a safe space. . . . And you're not willing to get help, so it's not going to change."

"I can't change him," I blurt out. "Ever since his ma died, he just about lost himself or something. I've tried." And this time the tears is dripping right down to the ground along with Clair's underwear I just hung out.

She puts her arms around me. "Then leave him, Marie," she whispers real fierce, "leave him!"

I'm about to wipe my eyes to try to see clear through if it's something I can do. But first I want to stand here a moment and hear myself sobbing, just a sweet moment, Jesus. Then over her shoulder, I see that pickup pulling up alongside the shed, and there's Clair Beaudry glaring at his wife hugging the lesbian foreigner tenant in plain sight. He comes down hard on that horn of his, and that poor gal just about jumps out of her skin and right out of my arms.

A new kind of trouble starts, and that's Clair fighting with a pretty woman instead of trying to get in her pants.

She writes me a letter saying she is moving out on account of the place is not conducive to her working. Could she have her security deposit back? She needs it in order to move to a new place. She used up her first couple of paychecks just paying back bills and she's got nothing extra in the bank.

Well, Clair gets a hold of the letter. He's now a hawk when it comes to this Yo. After he found us being indecent in broad daylight, as he calls it, he's forbidden me to have anything to do with her and he's told Dawn and Emily he'll bust their little bottoms if they go upstairs to eat rabbit food and talk foreign. You'd think then he'd just let her break the lease and go. But no, he says she's got to stay or leave and be liable for the whole year's rent, which is what he really wants. Then he can rent it double, see, and make himself a pretty profit. Maybe even move in the next little girlfriend.

He goes upstairs to tell her this and I hear voices raised, actually hers more than his. When he comes back down he's got a list and he's madder than a hornet you missed with the swatter but got one of its teeny legs. "She's got the gumption to say she's going over to the tenant bureau to make a complaint!" He's swearing up and down our living room, and I hear her upstairs pacing up and down like the one is a reflection of the other. Now I never heard of no tenant bureau, and it turns out Clair never did either. We just rent and keep it under the table. The lease I got from Dottie who secretaried over at Century 21. So I'm starting to get scared that maybe we'll get in trouble and have to pay back all the money we ever made on the upstairs.

"Clair, why don't we just let her go," I say. "She don't belong here anyway like you said yourself."

He raises the hand with the list on it like he's going to hit me for standing up for her. So I say, "What you got there?" to distract him, and he shoves that piece of paper in my face. "Lookee that!" he cries, shaking his head, his face all red like maybe he is going to have a heart attack. There on the list is everything that's been broke down with the place since she rented it. But funny, Yo never complained to me before about any of this.

"*Broken stove fan, missing rod in hall closet, loose step on the stairs, window in bedroom is cracked.*" He's reading it out loud now in that funny voice a man puts on when he's trying to sound like a woman. "I'll show her what's broke and cracked," he yells up at the ceiling.

Then he starts collecting his tools, and I'm a few steps behind him wondering what he's up to. Turns out he told her she had no right to move out as the place is all fair and square, and that's when she said, "Actually it's not, and handed him the list of repairs. She was probably thinking it'd be her ticket out. But no, old Clair's going to fix every goddamn last broke thing, including her, "if it takes me the whole year to do it!" He glowers at me like he's got the two of us confused.

So, he's up there every day after work, fooling with some small job or other. Minute he bangs on her door, she's out of there and in that car. Lots of nights she just never comes home. Sometimes I hear him wandering around up there like he's doing more than repairing the busted light in the front bedroom. And I get to feeling sorry for her. I start making this plan in my head that I'm going to get me a job and pay her that security myself and then move out on her tail. But it's all daydreams for now, cause I won't even go out of this house till I have enough of this weight off where people aren't going to stare.

Which is why I shop at the Safeway late, you see, and that's where I bump into her one night, pushing her cart with her two big bookbags in there and a bottle of wine, with the front baby part full of jars of things I always wonder who on God's earth eats them anyhow, artichoke hearts, hearts of palm, coconut milk, stuff like that. My own basket's heaping, which embarrasses me on account of I can just see people looking at me and looking at it and thinking, Uh-huh, Uh-huh. But I guess I've slimmed down considerably because Yo acts kind of startled when she sees me. She comes right up with those powerful eyes of hers and says, "Oh, Marie, I don't see how you can stand by and let him do this to another woman."

That hits right where I'm weakest and so I make myself look strong. "Look here," I say, "I got nothing to do with it. I told him to let you go." I look down at all the things in my cart I'm buying for him, his beer and cigarettes, the frozen pizzas he likes when he's watching the Sunday games, and I feel like throwing them all out. "He don't listen to me. What can I do?"

"I suppose nothing," she says, not harsh or mean, but like someone sizing up the situation and seeing you're licked. "And I'm trapped, too, until that paycheck comes. . . . Then I'm out of there! He can sue me if he wants," she adds.

I lean in towards her like maybe Clair's coming up behind me and I whisper, "He ain't going to sue you, so don't worry about that part." I want to give her that little peace of mind. Course I don't tell her why he wouldn't sue. That we don't report that upstairs income.

She looks at me a minute, surprised, I guess, that I've spoke up against Clair even if it is behind his back. Then, as she's getting ready to push off, she says to me, "Ay, Marie. You deserve better, you know."

Them words is like she wrote them in the air, and I can't help seeing them everywhere: on the label of every bottle and can and box on the Safeway shelves. As I'm driving home, my heart feels the lightest it's felt since I gained the eighty pounds.

It's as I'm unloading and wondering where the hell is Clair's pickup—that I see that quick zigzag in the sky. My first thought is them words are going to be flashed up there in bright lights, but of course, a minute later there's that rip of thunder, and then that rain starts coming down.

I swear I don't think once about them leaks on the roof. All I have in mind is the clues I'm starting to put together that Clair's after new tail. The daily shower, the cologne in his hair, his disappearing most nights after he works on the upstairs repairs. I stand in my kitchen, piecing it together with the needle and thread of those words Yo spoke to me. *You deserve better, you know.* What I don't know is what I'm going to do with this new idea when I'm through thinking on it.

It's real quiet in the house, just the sound of my two girls fast asleep in their bedroom, the refrigerator kicking in every once in a while, and that rain coming down like it's trying to tell me something I can't make out. When I hear the car out front, I turn off the lights and go to the front window. It's Yo coming home with her bags of books, dodging the rain as she comes up the steps, then back down for the grocery bag. I hear her upstairs putting things away, walking around, and then I hear the cry. Two seconds later she's pounding on my door, and she don't say a word when I open it, but grabs me by the arm. "It's late," I say. "Can't it wait till morning?"

"I want you to see this." And she's crying, crying hard.

I'm all scared that maybe she's poisoned Clair and he's dead in her shower stall, though it would serve him right. Upstairs, we quick go through the living room and hall, and then she stands aside while I step into the room she made into her study. That rain's come down and wet her papers and run the things written in ink and made a soggy mess of all her books.

"Oh sweet Jesus," I say.

"I'm going to kill him," she says as she drops down on her knees and starts picking up papers, wrapping them in paper towels. I'm on my knees, too, helping her, both of us crying—like fools—cause really paper is just paper when you come to think of it. Of course, this means a lot more to her than me. But I'm crying over things ruined long before this.

Then I just got to tell her. "Yo, I knew about them holes in the roof."

She's got a stack of papers in her hands, and she's looking down at them like they're going to tell her what to do with me.

"I'm sorry," I say, real soft. Then, I tell her what I been deciding downstairs. "I'm leaving Clair. I'm getting me a job."

Now she's looking straight at me like she's trying to figure out if I got it in me. And it scares me half to death to see she believes me.

"I'll pay you back your security," I promise, but she don't seem satisfied with just that, so I ask her, "What else can I do?"

She thinks on that while we finish up the job, and I'm getting a little worried on account of she's a flatlander and a foreigner both, and maybe she's going to ask for a lot more than the trouble deserves. "Okay," she says, standing up. "I want to go downstairs now and have you show me what belongs to Clair."

"Now wait a minute," I say. "You're going to be out of here and I'm going to get killed."

"No," she reminds me, "*he's* going to be out of here." And then, she goes real quiet and looks at me sharp like she's cutting through something that's been holding her back. "Marie, you've got to wake up. Talk to your Dawn. You can get enough on that guy to put him behind bars."

Well, it's like she's turned me upside down and shook my heart out of my mouth. "You don't mean . . . sweet Lord!" And that angry love starts coming up just plain old anger for once.

"Come on," I say, and I lead her downstairs through my house to the bedroom. We go through everything in Clair's closet and drawers, throwing his things in a pile on the floor, me tossing some of my own big sizes that I hope to God I never got to wear again. Then we stuff it all in garbage bags and haul them out to the porch. Every once in a while I get this sinking feeling, wondering how I'm going to keep going, but all I got to do is pass by the girls' bedroom and I get new gasoline.

When that whole front yard is wall to wall with Clair Beaudry's things, we come inside and get ourselves a cup of coffee. It's like we got to do something a little normal after the weirdness of this night. Then we wrap ourselves in blankets and go out on the porch like it's summertime and we're going to watch the fireflies.

We sit out there waiting for that old pickup and Clair Beaudry's face when he sees all his belongings where they belong. The rain beyond the porchlight is coming down on his boots, his belts he's used on the kids I don't want to think what for, his tools, his big bottle of English Leather, and all his sorry clothes tangled together like someone tried to make a ladder to escape out of a fairybook tower. Makes me kind of sad to see the waste of what could have been better. Then I'm just plain scared like I just landed someplace I've never been inside myself.

I look over at Yo, who's sitting there with her head down, listening to that rain like it's reminding her what was written on them ruined pages. I put everything I got into listening, too, but all I hear is the taps, splats, and pings of the rain coming down hard on Clair's things.

The student

Lou Castellucci had made good. Tall, handsome with the winning smile of a pro whose team is headed for the championships, Lou had won almost every game he had played in his life. In high school he had been a star football player, taking his small town team to the State championship first time ever.

His high school prowess had won him a full scholarship at a small liberal arts college, where he played less impressively with each succeeding year. But then, football was no longer his game. His attention had been caught by other things. His senior year he became interested in writing and in a tall girl with a mess of pretty blond hair, Penny Ross.

He had not been able to attract Penny's attention although he had tried to put himself in her way. He had taken The Contemporary Novel on the off-chance that Penny, an English major, might be in the large, popular lecture course. She hadn't been, but the class had turned out to be Lou's favorite. He was sorry now that he had so doggedly pursued his computer science major. He envied the kids who were English majors and sat around in black turtlenecks, smoking, and intensely discussed the meaning of a book. They really got into it, and it made Lou feel, listening in on their conversations in the dining hall or lounges, as if he were, well, not that smart, not that sensitive, not that vital a human being.

Spring of his senior year, Lou signed up for a writing work-shop. If he could write novels like the ones he had read, he could wow her and anyone else. But it wasn't just to wow her that he took the course. Writing was the new game he wanted to learn to play. When that guy Updike or that Mailer guy wrote a book, it was a touchdown at the end of each chapter. Sometimes as he read, Lou would catch himself, making a fist, pumping his arm forward as if to say, Go, Mailer, go!

The teacher was supposed to be a known writer but not one Lou had ever heard of. She was a Dominican-American-USA-Latina—or whatever she had explained she was during the first class. Her pretty olive color made Lou think of honey in a jar. Lou had never before known a Hispanic person without ten pounds of shoulder and chest pads on him and a teeth guard in his mouth and a helmet on his head. The couple of Hispanic guys here on the team had an attitude that Lou didn't like. Christ, it hadn't been him who made their daddies pick grapes or what-ever.

Anyhow that first day, this lady was real friendly. Said she wanted you to call her Yolanda or Yo or whatever you liked and talked about writing as a game you played for the fun of it, not just for the deep meaning. It made Lou feel better sitting in that circle, his big hands sweating all over this poem Yolanda passed out. They were going around the circle, having to say what they thought of it. Skinny, brainy girls found things in that poem that made Lou feel like a whole different poem had been handed to him. His neck started to get hot, and he wished he'd taken a lec-ture class instead of putting himself out there this way.

When his turn came, Lou said that maybe he just didn't have the background, but this poem seemed, to him, a lot more simple than everyone else had said. Yolanda's eyes lit up, and she kept nodding her head like one of those little dogs with a spring in its neck. She asked him how did he read this line and that line, and Lou did the best he could with it. "Yeah-yeah, yeah-yeah," she kept saying, and flashing her eyes at him. The writer types looked at him as if he were some kind of authority. Everyone, even the deep-thought girls, began nodding. Lou wished he'd taken his baseball cap off.

He wrote a lot of stories for this class. First one, he got back all marked up in pencil to make him feel as if everything were just a suggestion, but he got the gist of it. Big note at the bottom said, *You expect me to believe this?* He read his story over about a spy caught in a war zone, and he had to agree with her. A bunch of crap. Some episode he'd seen on TV. He thought he could put a new twist on it by having the spy wake up at the end and the whole story be a dream. In the note she said he should write about what he knew, and so in the next story, he wrote about a big football hero who gets paralyzed from the waist down in an accident and, in order to free his girl from marrying him, he commits suicide. This time the note at the bottom read, *Please come see me.*

In conference she explained she meant writing stories out of his own life. He pushed his cap back and looked down at his palms as if to reassure himself of a lifeline. "That's kind of personal," he told her.

"Yeah-yeah," she nodded enthusiastically, "stories *are* personal." The way she said it was like he was Helen Keller and she'd finally gotten through to him that *water* meant water.

It was wild talking to her in that little office. Everything he said, she tied into something she'd read. She kept climbing up on her chair to pull down this book and that from her shelves. She read him long passages of something someone famous had said that was supposed to contradict what he'd said, and kept looking up at him so hopeful. He finally said, yes, he'd try writing like she said.

Later, a buddy told Lou the woman was on a seven-year tenure track. Lou didn't really understand how this tenure ring worked. All he could think of was the racetrack his stepfather Harvey had taken him to when he was still a kid. Hyper horses sprang out of their stalls when the gates lifted, giving it all they had, to the finish line. But seven years, Jesus! No wonder some of these profs were a little odd after going around in circles for so long.

Lou had a hard time writing his next story about his dad leaving. He gave the kid in the story a different name and colored his hair yellow and his eyes blue. He told how his mom fell apart and had to be hospitalized, and how Uncle Harvey started coming around. Course, he changed Harvey's name to Henry. One day, the kid betrays Henry by telling some friends that Henry isn't his real father. Story ends with the little kid seeing the pain go through Henry's face like a crack in china.

That day in class when they got to his story, Lou felt woozier than a pregnant girl on a roller coaster. Everyone waited for Yolanda to say what she thought and then they all fell in with her that the story was really great. Of course, soon after the praise, the "suggestions" followed. "One little thing that did bother me," they always began, and then everyone tore Lou's story apart like it was now meat for the dogs. But at least when he got the story back from Yolanda the final note read, *You're onto rich material here!*

Lou had finally gotten the hang of this story game, and he was on a winning streak now. Story after story he wrote, this Yo lady was treating it like Hemingway in the rough or something. Kids in class returned his stories with smiley faces, going on and on about how this or that part was really awesome. Then, the last story he wrote for class, he just about put himself up on that computer screen like an X-ray of his chest with a dark shadow for his aching heart.

The story was about the only game Lou could ever remember losing. It happened when he was twelve. That Saturday afternoon, Harvey was right behind the team's bench, as always, rooting for him. Then suddenly, Lou's father had showed, first time Lou'd seen the old man in ages. He was loud and obnoxious up in the bleachers. "That's my kid!" he kept shouting at the crowd.

As Lou got more and more into the writing, he forgot his fears. It was the last quarter, score tied, and his team's turn to make a final touchdown. But as he ran towards the arc of the descending ball, he couldn't think straight, worrying about what would happen after the game, if he'd go up to his dad or Harvey to be congratulated. Losing his concentration, Lou tipped the ball into his opposing teammate's hands. The visitors scored the last touchdown. Afterwards, he sat with Harvey in the car and bawled like a baby. As he wrote the story, Lou realized he hadn't cried because he had lost the game for his team. His father had left without so much as saying hello to him.

Even now, Lou could feel his goddamn eyes tingling!

But the amazing thing was you could write a story about losing and feel like you'd won. And one other thing he had learned writing these stories. He had to put himself out there more. After all, he'd taken a chance with this course, and it had been pretty terrific. He would ask this Penny girl out to dinner, and if she was dating someone else, let her up and say so. He would take the job he'd been offered even if it wasn't a big-time company his friends had heard of. He had liked the people who interviewed

him, low-key and real, and they made sports equipment he believed in.

In conference, over his final folder, Yolanda told him how
much she liked his last story. She sure was glad he'd taken the
course. She hinted at how she'd had a tough time herself. She'd
been divorced (it sounded like more than once) and kicked
around for a while. What saved her was she could write books,
and she just kept writing them and writing them, until something inside settled down.

"Wow," he noted. He had really wanted to ask her if she was
okay now. Some little thing she said hinted she was lonely. "I
mean, it sounds like you've written a lot of books."

"Not enough," she said, twirling a strand of her hair like it
wasn't curly enough already. "My first-year review board feels my
publications aren't *substantial* enough. They want a major publisher." She said the word *major*, rolling her eyes, like Lou would
understand.

"Well, I think you're terrific," he said, shifting in his chair.
Now he was the one getting nervous. What if she thought, you
know, like he was coming on? Quickly, he added, "A really terrific
teacher."

She laughed. "Thanks," she said. "Anyhow, I've got six more
years to prove myself in the major leagues. Tenure," she pronounced, in the solemn voice of a diagnosis of a terminal illness.

"Wow," Lou said to be encouraging.

"I'm doing short stories for now," she explained. "It's been hard
to concentrate on something longer this year. There's a lot going
on." Yolanda sighed, on the verge of saying more.

But Lou cut the talk short. His old habit of not getting in over
his head was automatic by now. He put out his hand and shook
Yolanda's and thanked her for everything. "Gotta go," he said as if

he had something to do besides hang out this sunny spring afternoon drinking beers with his buddies in the cemetery behind the
dorms.

That afternoon, he kept thinking about her, and during a lull
in the yak, he asked if any of his buddies knew this Yo person in
the English department. One know-it-all guy Lou didn't like
much had the scoop. García had been living in a run-down old
house that burned down. She was single but had some out-of-
town, pothead boyfriend.

"So is she going to marry him or what?" Lou wanted to know.

"What am I? Her counselor or something?" The guy got a
laugh from everyone. He was a guy who worked for laughs, so
you could never trust what he said. He went on. "Someone told
me she's been having some troubles, you know." He spun small
circles by his forehead with his index finger. Some of the guys
laughed.

Lou defended her. "She's not crazy, she's real fine."

"Man, I'm not saying she's not fine," the buddy returned,
pumping his hips as if that was what Lou had meant. "I'm just
telling you what I heard, okay?"

Lou's roommate intervened. "Speaking of what we've heard.
Anybody know if the rumor on Ross is true?"

Lou didn't let his face show his interest. The guys knew about
his crush on Penny Ross. They knew Lou hadn't asked her out,
that he worried she'd be over his head, never sure of her dating
status since she was always hanging out with Philip Ballinger of
the Black Turtleneck, who co-edited the literary magazine with
her.

Same guy who knew the dope on Yolanda had news to report
here too. Goddamn guy should start a Dear Andy column or
something. He held his thumb down. "Ballinger and Ross broke

off," he announced. "Ballinger's balling the Contessa." He twirled his arm elaborately like someone greeting royalty. The Contessa was an Italian beauty whose Papa owned a line of spaghetti sauce and pasta products. She had a beautiful face with pouty lips and elaborate headbands that looked like tiaras in her dramatic auburn hair. The editor went in for hair, all right. And looks. But unlike Penny Ross, the Contessa seemed totally unapproachable. She dated only the richest, brainiest guys on campus, and them she treated with a dispassionate, affected air as if she were saving herself for something better, and these little American boys were her equivalent of sleeping with the gardener.

Later, his roommate prodded Lou about Penny. "This is your chance, Castellucci. We're almost out of here. It's now or the fifth reunion, and by then, she might be married with babies."

That night in the dining room, they were sitting at their usual tables, and Penny Ross walked in with a bunch of girlfriends. "Go for it," his roommate said. Before he knew it, Lou had left his own untouched tray behind, broken into the line, reached for Penny's tray in her hands, and offered, "Can I buy you a real dinner?" She gave him an assessing look as if she wasn't sure what to make of his invitation.

Briefly it flashed through Lou's head something he'd heard his buddies say after they'd seen Penny marching at some rally. She was a feminist. He thought of the word in the same tone as Yolanda had pronounced *tenure*. "Do I know you?" she finally said.

"This is a way to get to know me," he blurted. His goddamn hands were shaking like a goddam car with a bad fan belt.

But then, fate or something was on his side because the Contessa walked in with the editor, and Lou could see by the tightening of the muscles on her face that Penny had seen them too. He didn't necessarily like being the spare, but, hey, when you had a flat, the spare became the regular, right? Sure enough, Penny slipped her hand in the crook of his elbow and gave her head a pretty toss. "Let's get to know each other," she said. As they passed by his table of buddies, Lou lifted up the tray in his hand and waved it like a trophy for a game he'd just won.

For their fifth reunion, Penny and Lou brought baby Louie, and a load like you wouldn't believe. Lou just about had a heart attack every time they packed to go somewhere. Seemed to him that the amount of luggage you brought should bear some direct proportion to your body size. This little tyke's Portacrib and playpen and box of Pampers and extra bag of clean clothes and handbag of rattles and stuffed animals with lullabies inside them just about took up the whole back of the car and some of the trunk. He had stopped saying anything, though, because every time he did, Penny would burst into tears and accuse him of not loving his own son.

As if anyone could love a kid more! Maybe he wouldn't have felt so attached to this kid if things had been going better with Penny. First two years had been like a corny movie. He'd find love notes in his briefcase, and when he'd go on business trips, there'd be chocolate kisses and once a package of ladyfingers in with his underwear. He'd risen quickly in the company he joined after graduation, SportsAMER! With his good looks—he still worked out at the gym and ran his daily five miles—and his personable, persistent, but non-pushy manners (the same three p's Lou plugged to his team of salesmen), Lou was everyone's winner. Recently, he had been promoted from regional sales manager in the northeast to Vice President of Marketing, with a relocation to Dayton, Ohio.

That's when the trouble started with Penny. He was doing a lot of traveling to coordinate nationwide markets. Penny was understanding at first, but with each lonely, unemployed month in Dayton, she became withdrawn and nagging. She changed her name back to Penny Ross Castellucci, even though he'd bought her a real nice luggage set with just PC on it. Nothing seemed to please her, least of all getting pregnant.

She had awful morning sickness, and then a hard, uncomfortable pregnancy. Lou had asked to stay put in the home office till the baby was born, but he couldn't be spared from minding the national accounts. In fact, Lou was busier than ever. The bad economy had hit the company hard. SportsAMER! just couldn't compete. With a kid coming, expensive house and car payments, Lou could not afford to lose his job. At the back of his mind, of course, was what he most dreaded losing—his marriage with Penny.

After she'd gotten pregnant, she stopped being interested in much of anything. She sat around, reading all the time, like that kid was going to be an Einstein and his brain cells had to be pumped full of info. Many nights arriving home to a darkened house, Lou would climb the stairs to their bedroom. There, in a warm circle of light from the bedside lamp Penny would be reading. "I'll be with you in a sec, honey, I only have a couple of pages left."

But then she'd read on and on, way past the end of the chapter.

Penny had nagged and nagged about going to their reunion. It'd give them their first vacation in almost two years, she'd see her native New England again, and they'd get a chance to connect with old friends. Lou cringed. He wouldn't have minded going when he was on top of the world, but now, he didn't want to feel like a loser among his old-time, successful buddies. On the other hand, this might be an opportunity to network with some of those guys, put out his feelers, who knows, maybe even land another job. And even if a job lead didn't come of it, the reunion would give Lou the chance to show off little Louie to the fellows. None of those guys had had the balls to get married yet, much less have a son. If nothing else, he had sure beat them all to fatherhood.

That Saturday afternoon of reunion weekend, Lou took Louie on a tour through his alma mater. Penny had gone off with her girlfriends to play tennis, and the buddies went golfing, a sport Lou only pretended to like because SportsAMER!'s golf line was a big seller. He begged off playing ("Gotta babysit, guys!"), and instead wandered the campus until he found the old bookstore, open for the alums and stocked with memorabilia, a rocking chair with the college's insignia, a mug with the college's insignia, pennants and even a yuppie espresso cup set with the college's insignia. He bought little Louie a college sweatshirt he'd take a few years growing into and a college bib he could dirty this very day. Then he moved on to the book section to get a present for Penny, and there it was on a shelf of books by faculty authors: *Return from Left Field,* by Yolanda García. So she was still here! He bought the book, and once outside, while Louie slept on his blanket in the shade under a tree where Lou and his pals had downed many a beer and exchanged many a leer at the young coeds passing by, he began to read.

The book was a collection of short stories. In a brief introduction she wrote pretty much what Lou remembered her saying during their last conference. How these stories had kept her going through some pretty dark days. How all these stories had been in one way or another gifts from her family and friends and students over the years. How she'd like to thank so and so, and so and so. Lou ran his eye over all the names hoping to find his own, but there was no mention of the young football player who'd learned to take risks in her class. Obviously, he hadn't made too much of an impression on her. And why should he? Hadn't he been the one to cut off their last meeting when he sensed she had needed to talk with him? And what would she have said? Maybe something not much different from what he would say now to her about his own loneliness and fears for this marriage.

He skimmed through the book, reading first paragraphs to see if he'd get hooked by any one story. It was a diverse bunch all right. In some of them, he thought he recognized a certain character or situation, probably because she'd told them some of these stories in class. Then he got to the title story, the one that began, *That morning, Tío Marcos was so nervous, he put juice in my cereal instead of milk, he boiled my egg soft instead of hard, he went out to get his paper and came back empty-handed saying, 'Now what was it I was going to get?' It was the day of the Little League State Championship, and Tío Marcos had been training me since the day he walked into my life, six years before, and replaced my father.*

Lou's eye was caught like a fish in the hook of the print. This was *his* story, his goddamn story, right down to the kid at the end sitting in the car, his face in his hands, bawling. Only difference was this Yo-yo lady had made all his characters Hispanic, changed the sport to baseball, and written up the story nicer than Lou had been able to write it.

Lou combed through the rest of the book, reading the stories that sounded familiar. Maybe she'd lifted stories by other kids in the class? Jesus, maybe they could bring a class action suit together? He looked for her picture in the back, but there wasn't one. A brief biography mentioned that Yolanda García had written numerous works of fiction, that she taught at this college, that she was living on a farm in New Hampshire with her cats, Fidel and Jesús. Lou remembered the story he had heard from his buddy five years ago. Yolanda was having emotional problems. Well, she sounded settled down now, so he didn't have to feel protective of her. It crossed his mind that she must be on her next to last go-around on the tenure track

He was re-reading the story so intently, Penny's voice made him start. "Looo-oo, Looo-oo!" She was calling him from the window of the dorm they were staying in, waving and laughing! Her pretty hair hung down like the girl in the fairytale they'd be reading little Louie in a few years.

She was waiting at the dorm room door, and her face lit up again when she saw Lou and the baby. "My two boys," she greeted them, taking the baby. Lou hadn't heard that lightness in her voice in a while. He put his arm around her shoulder. "You having a good time, sweetheart?"

She smiled warmly, her eye wandering by force of habit to his book. "What you reading?" She cocked her head to one side and read the name on the spine. "I remember her! Must be good. I called you five or six times before you heard me!"

He thought of telling Penny about the plagiarized story then, but watching her, happily nuzzling the baby, he held back. Years ago, when she had been co-editor of *Musings* along with—what was his name?—Lou had submitted a couple of the Henry stories to the magazine, including this one. He had been too afraid to do so under his own name, so his roommate had sent them in like they were his. A note had come back from *the editors*, saying that the stories did not quite work. They were a little too maudlin. *Maudlin?* Lou looked it up just to be sure. *Maudlin?* What the hell was wrong with being sentimental? That rejection note had made it even harder for Lou to ask Penny out.

So for now, he kept his secret to himself. He could feel a close-ness growing between them, and he didn't feel like admitting this small failure to her. Instead, while the baby napped, they made sweet, silly love in one of the small twin beds like in the old days. From the room under them came the clowning thumps of one of the envious alums.

During the president's cocktail party, Lou kept an eye out for Yolanda. He had brought the book in Louie's diaper bag for her to autograph. He wouldn't say a thing to her about the title story and see if she acknowledged she had lifted it from him. He didn't know where he'd go from there. It was like he remembered when he was writing a story. You never really knew what the ending would be until you'd written yourself right up to it.

The chairman of the English department came up to Penny to meet her little boy. He was heavily freckled, and so his skin looked like a tweedy continuation of his jacket. "And this is my husband," Penny said, turning to Lou, who stood holding the dia-per bag, plastic cradle seat, and Big Bird rattle, grinning at the chairman who didn't remember him. After some catch-up be-tween Penny and the chairman, Lou asked after Yolanda García. "She's up for tenure in the fall," the chairman informed them. "We're very hopeful," he said confidentially. "She's published a new book with Norton, and she seems happy here now."

"She wasn't happy before?" Lou asked. Yolanda's little crime made him feel intimately tied to the secrets in her life.

"It's hard for our young women professors, a remote place like this, a good old boy network firmly entrenched—"

Penny was nodding away like the chair was talking about her. In fact, he sounded just like Penny when she complained about living in Dayton and wasting her life away. "Not to mention that being a minority in New Hampshire is no picnic—" The chair threw up his hands. "Anyhow, she has done well. Says her students have saved her—quite enthusiastic about her classes."

Lou felt like saying, Let me tell you just how *quite*.

Penny and the chair looked at him, sensing he was about to say something.

"Yolanda García is a plagiarist," he would start. He had a sudden picture of her standing on her desk the first time he had come to her office, reaching up for a book on her shelf. Her legs had surprised him, skinny like a schoolgirl's, a faint, white, endearing scar just below one knee. He remembered, too, her fingers, nervously tugging at her hair, the nails bitten back but still painted a bright red. That she should paint her nails red, and then, bite them off! And her lipstick, she never could get it on right, so she looked as if she'd just eaten something messy and red. Suddenly, Lou knew he wasn't going to tell on this Yolanda García he had pictured in his head. Details, she had always said, the goddamn details could break your heart.

And so he said, "As one of her ex-students, I can tell you she was terrific!" His marketing vice president voice put extra punch in his recommendation. The chairman lifted his pale eyebrows.

"I didn't know you'd taken a course from her," Penny said, looking at him with surprise. "You took a writing course?"

Lou nodded. "My favorite course, too. Made me wish I'd been an English major. Not to mention I would have met you a lot sooner!" Lou laughed, and the chair laughed. Everything had worked out so well for his star student.

Driving away the next day, they waved to their friends. Once on the highway, Lou looked over at the silent Penny. She was turned towards the window, one of her wistful moods that could so easily turn dark. It had been good for her to be with her friends, but she was readying herself for the long days with a little baby and no companionship but a pile of books. He thought of how Yolanda had said her students had saved her, and he wondered what he could do to make Penny happier.

"Baby asleep?" he asked, hoping to engage her in the one subject in which she was always interested.

Penny nodded. "Little guy's exhausted."

Lou looked in the rearview mirror, and sure enough, baby Louie lay pooped out in the car seat. "Tell you what, why don't you read us one of those stories? Get our minds off leaving."

"You're really turning into a reader." Penny picked Yolanda's book out of the carry-on bag beside the baby and opened to the table of contents. "Why don't I read all the titles, and you tell me which one sounds like a story you want to hear."

It was not hard for him to decide, of course, and Penny began the story, *Return from Left Field*. Her tense voice relaxed as she read paragraph after paragraph. She turned pages eagerly, smiled and sometimes chuckled. "*That was the first failure in my life, and I can't say it prepared me for the rest.*" She read the last sentences. "*But whenever they've come, I've thought of sitting in that car, looking out at that deserted diamond, thinking, I'll never get over this. And Tío Marcos leaning over and saying, Don't worry, Miguelito. You'll return from left field.*"

Penny closed the book and stroked the cover with her open hand. "That was a sweet story," she said. There was no irony in her voice.

"Really?" he said. "You didn't think it was just a little sentimental?"

Penny shook her head. "It took risks, if that's what you mean. That's what I loved about it." She was defending that story as if it were little Louie or something.

His heart was making such a racket in his chest, he was sure she would hear it and tell him to quiet down, he was going to wake up the baby. But instead she reached over and squeezed his hand. "Funny, but that story reminded me—" she began.

"Yeah?" he said, grinning, on the verge of telling her.

As Lou listened, her voice opened up into a story of a remembered childhood loss. Out the window, the landscape blurred into the emerald green of a playing field. "Wow," he kept saying.

The suitor

Dexter Hays wants to go down there and visit Yo while she's in the Dominican Republic this summer. She has stopped in for a weekend at his place on her way to the island, and he has been trying for two days nonstop to convince her.

But she says no. He has to understand that, down there, women don't have lovers out in the open. Down there, he'd have to clean up his act. Throw away his joints, get a nice pair of pants. Her aunts would try to convert him. "It's different, Dex. I mean, people are still old world, down there."

"Baby, baby," he says, shaking his head, so in love with this bright colorful bird that has flown into the cage of his middle age. "You realize the way you talk about this place is the way my mamma used to talk to my baby sister about her private parts. *'Now, Mary Sue, you mustn't let anyone touch you down there.'*" He mimics his mamma by pitching his accent half a note more southern.

Dexter is tall and skinny with just a trace of the buck teeth his daddy paid a lot to fix. His daddy also paid a lot to send Dexter up from Fayetteville, North Carolina, to Harvard, but that didn't take either, and inside of a year, Dexter had dropped out and joined, not just a hippy commune, but a Yankee hippy commune.

"Poor Daddy," Dexter drawls, shaking his head. "That about did him in."

Yo laughs, taking his face in her hands, cooing over him in Spanish, so he believes that despite what she says, she really does want him to come and visit her down there this summer.

"I'll behave myself, I promise," he promises. He hates the way his blond, babyfine hair stands on end with electricity. He runs his hands through it, clamping the cowlicks down. But still she looks doubtful. "What is it, baby? It's my accent, isn't it? I'm not good-looking enough? You wanted Rhett Butler and you got Gomer Pyle?"

"Ay, Dex, come on. You know if you come, everyone's going to assume we're getting married."

"Maybe we *will* get married someday," he suggests. This is the most excited he's been about a woman since Winnie Sutherland sat in front of him in fifth grade with her two braids tied with blue ribbons, and he couldn't help himself. Out of true love, he yanked at those ribbons and the dark ropes of her hair came undone. Winnie Sutherland ended up being his first wife. "You're still that kid pulling on my braids," she accused him when she sued for divorce ten years ago. "You're never going to grow up!" It is still a matter of pride with Dexter Hays that he's as much of a live wire now as he was back in the fifth grade. Who wants to grow up and be Winnie Sutherland's second husband? Donald What's-his-face is a fat dough-boy type guy who looks like he's not done yet the way his skin is so pasty white. But Donald is also a rich man, some big accountant with an aggressive silver Mercedes with windows you can't see in and a swimming pool shaped like Winnie's hourglass figure in their fenced-in backyard.

But Dexter Hays's time is coming. He can feel it in the air. This Yo lady is Missus Right, all right. Another maverick, another fly-by-the-seat-of-your-pants person with the added pizzazz of being

Latin. In the movies Spanish ladies have roses tucked behind their ears and low-cut peasant blouses with little crucifixes like hexes above those heaving bosoms, yeah! They met at a rally in support of Nicaragua or maybe it was Cuba—one of the two. Even though Dexter doesn't really follow the news, he likes going to these rallies because he's likely to meet people with whom he feels simpatico. Ex-hippies who never forgot their roots as flower children to become big-time CEO cogs in the wheel of fortune. Most guys his age make him feel like maybe he's wasting his life being a free spirit, the Donalds riding their air-conditioned German cars from one safe place to another. Anyhow, at these rallies there are naturally lots of natives from these countries, and Dexter has always had a weak spot for Latin women. Yo is right up his ethnic alley.

They've been having a long distance relationship—every weekend he flies up to New Hampshire or she flies down to D.C., where he lives. And already he is sure he wants to marry her in the not too distant future. "So maybe we *should* tie the knot," he continues, testing the waters. "It'd solve the problem of explaining who I am to your mammy and pappy."

"Whoa!" she says, laughing. "It's only been five months, Dex," she reminds him. "Twenty weekends, in fact—which means we've only really known each other forty days."

"And people say girls can't do math." Dexter makes a joke of it. But hey, it hurts to be rebuffed even if he's trying to get away from all that male ego stuff Bly and his buddies are always howling in the woods about.

"We're not teenagers," Yo continues as if he is some teenager who needs a lecture. "And I don't know about you, amorsito, but I want to be sure this time around."

"Well, I *am* sure!" he says, a bit huffy. Ambivalence is for northern girls whose daddies sent them to psychiatrists instead of riding camps. "We're perfect for each other."

"Ay, Dex," she coos over him again, kissing his eyes shut.

But this time he's not going to let himself get romanced out of what he wants. "Come on, Yo-baby," he persists. "Why can't I come down and visit you?"

"I told you. It's a bad time for scandal in the family. My uncle's running for president again."

"I'll campaign for him, swear to God. I worked for Jesse Jackson."

"Well, Dex, I hate to tell you but there's no comparison."

She has told him it is a democracy down there, but she claims that the word doesn't mean the same thing as here. She has told him her uncle is a good guy, but that he is surrounded by advisors and military thugs she doesn't trust. "You get the picture," she says.

Dexter rolls his eyes. "It's like I'm going out with Caroline Kennedy or something."

Yo laughs. "More like one of the crazy Bobby Kennedy kids." She's filled him in on how she and her sisters have been disowned a couple of times each for going their own way, how the family holds them at arm's length, loving them to bits but still hoping and praying to set them straight. "My aunts tried to marry me last year to this old, alcoholic Dominican guy. He looked seventy. Can you believe it? It would have been like being a nursemaid. But I guess I'd have proven that I could be a self-sacrificing wife after all."

"So just marry me and take care of me and you can still have good sex—"

"Dex!" She slaps him playfully. Every time she talks about all this disowning stuff and aunts with rosaries wound in their fingers and suave uncles running for president, it's like he has fallen in with the Mafia or something. He gets a charge from all the intrigue that seems to be going on always in her family. Whenever she comes down to visit him, he can't answer his own phone because her father might call. She's supposed to be doing research at the Library of Congress and staying with a friend, presumably female. "I just don't get why a grown woman can't do what she wants?"

"I can do what I want," she argues. "But why rub it in his face? He's seventy-two years old—what's the point? Let him die thinking that I regained my virginity after my divorces."

Sometimes he laughs, but sometimes, like now, he confronts her. "Aren't you supposed to be a feminist? How can you let your daddy tell you what to do with your body?"

"He's not telling me what to do with my body," she says, annoyed. "I'm just not telling him what I'm doing with it, okay?"

And then she goes into this big thing about cultural differences, that hey, he can't touch with a ten-foot pole. Once he tried to tell her that being from the South was like being from another culture, but they got into a heated discussion about slavery, and he came out responsible for all that the black folks had suffered. Only recently, he read about slave wages on sugar plantations in the Dominican Republic. But he has decided to keep his mouth shut for now. After all, he's working on a straight-up invitation to come and visit her down there.

Maybe because he is so caught up in trying to convince her, he forgets and picks up the phone when it rings. Yo lunges for the receiver, but it is too late. Dexter has already said, "Howdy there."

A heavily accented voice challenges him, "Who is this?"

"This is Luigi's Pizza Parlor, mister," he says quickly. "We're having a special tonight on the pepperoni. Can I interest you in a large."

"O," the father says in a small, pacified voice. "Pardon me the wrong number."

Pardon me the wrong number! Kisses on his eyelids and amorsito for a pet name. Sometimes the woman's libber, sometimes the Spanish Inquisition. Man, what's he doing falling in love with this complicated spic chick in the middle of his life? But then, when has he ever done anything the easy way, as his father was always one to ask.

A couple of weeks into her stay down there, Yo calls him up in the middle of the night to complain. "I can't stand it," she says, "the aunts are driving me crazy. They want me to go to confession."

"What for?" he asks. He has some vague notion that Catholics do things in small wooden closets with priests.

"They think this time my uncle will win the election if we're all reconciled to God."

"So go, Yo-baby. Just get in that little closet and ask the priest if he wants to do something else besides confess you."

"Dexter!" She sounds truly annoyed. Usually she laughs at his jokes. The place must be getting to her.

"Well, come on back, then, baby," he offers. As far as Dexter is concerned the world is pretty simple. When the shit hits the fan, you turn the fan off. That's why he quit college. Everyone was always trying to be so smart. Back and forth they'd go in those overheated classrooms. But what other options are there besides turning off the fan? "Come on home to ole Dex, honey."

"What do you mean, *home*," she snaps. Her English has already picked up the lilt of an accent. "This *is* my home."

He's also not going to touch that one with a ten-foot pole. She hasn't lived there for a quarter of a century. She works here, makes love here, has her friends here, pays taxes here, will probably die here. Seems to him all she goes down there for is to get confessed or disowned. Still, when she talks about the D.R., she gets all dewy-eyed as if she were crocheting a little sweater and booties for that island, as if she had given birth to it herself out of the womb of her memory.

Well, he has made up his mind: he's going down there whether she'll have him or not. "It's a free country," he tells her.

"Not exactly," she answers, and then adds, "Don't you dare, Dexter."

But those four words, as his mamma and daddy well know, are like turning the key to Dexter's ignition. By the end of the week, he has bought a ticket, put in for ten days off at the hospital where he's a nurse, and stashed enough reefer in an empty baby powder container in his dopp kit to guarantee smooth sailing through the turbulences of Yo's family. When he calls her up to let her know he'll be there tomorrow, a suave man's voice answers in perfect English. "Right oh," he says as if Dexter had called one of the British islands instead of the D.R. Then it dawns on him that this is probably the uncle running for president. "Good luck, sir," he says before Yolanda comes on the line.

"Right oh," the uncle says again.

Dexter informs Yo of his imminent arrival. He can hear a gasp, quickly covered over by a phoney *oh really*, and *thank you for letting me know*, so the uncle must still be in the room. It is quite apparent when Yo is alone again. "I'll kill you, Dexter Hays. I truly will."

For a moment he wonders whether to take her seriously. In the movies, if you cross them, Latin ladies are capable of anything. But here he is making the same mistake she makes. Yo is as American as apple pie. Well, let's say, as American as a Taco Bell taco. She claims the litmus test is if you say Oh or Ay when you smash your finger with a hammer. There've been plenty of times when she's bumped into something going to the bathroom in his unfamiliar apartment in the middle of the night and let out a "shit!" He wonders what that proves about her, if anything.

But Dexter knows Yo is not going to hack him down with a machete at the airport. "Your uncle's running for president, remember. You don't want to ruin his chances by committing murder on the eve of elections, now do you?"

"Are you trying to blackmail me?!"

In her voice, Dexter hears the whetting of something sharp. He backs down. "No baby, I'm courting you. I miss the hell out of you. I've cut off my ponytail. I've taken my birthstone out of my ear. I'll cut off my balls and come as your girlfriend if that's the only way."

"A lot of good that'll do me," she says in a voice struggling to stay stern. He can feel her swaying like one of those palm trees in a hurricane wind on the weather channel. It's true that Yo is never at a loss for words, but Dexter is the world's smoothest talker. The head nurse in the ER likes to say Dexter thought up the talking cure before the shrinks cashed in on it. "I'll pretend I'm just a friend, okay. I'll go to confession with you. I'll do whatever you want. Just let my starving eyes feast on the sight of your beautiful self."

"Well," Yo sighs. In the background Dexter can hear the sound of firecrackers going off, or maybe that's the sound of gunshot. For a crazy moment, he wonders if he'll get out of this alive. "I'm going to say you're a journalist friend," Yo is saying.

"You've come to cover the elections for your paper. Bring your tape recorder."

"It's a tape deck," Dexter reminds her, and as soon as he says so, he could bite off his tongue. All she needs is one excuse to cancel his leading role in the plot she is cooking up. "But I could go buy a tape recorder. Wal-Mart's open till ten."

"Dexter, just bring the tape deck, okay. All you've got to do is turn it on. Just as long as the tape's moving."

"Okay, okay." He agrees to the rest of the conditions she lays down for him. But when he hangs up, he has an uneasy feeling that he has been dating someone with a personality disorder. He has never really liked Yo's lying to her family. He himself told his parents what was what back in high school, and then again when he dropped out of college. Take it or leave it. But at least her family fibs are understandable, the good daughter trying to spare her parents grief. You don't have to be old world Latino to understand that. Look at his sister Mary Sue, pretending to obey Mamma's dictums about what not to let a guy do down there, meanwhile hottailing it all over Carrboro where she now lives, the divorced mother of three precious little girls, who do not—no one's going to talk Dexter into it—do *not* look like each other in the least.

But this is different. Yo's fabrications are not just about saving somebody's feelings or her ass. It's as if the world is her plaything and she can just pick up the facts and make them what she wants. He begins to doubt everything she's told him. Is her uncle running for president? Is she really Latin and unmarried with a teaching job in New Hampshire or an undercover agent with the FBI with a husband and five kids in Maryland? Suddenly the world seems very complicated, a world which is not simply black and white, but a shifting interplay of shadows, so unlike Dexter's bright lights and rockets' red glare.

Dex is all eyes as the limousine glides up the driveway past the guard at the gate. Beside him, Yo lifts a hand absently in acknowledgement just like someone in a tickertape parade in the States. "Hot damn, honey," he says, throwing his arm around her in a proud way.

"Dex." She nods towards the chauffeur. "Remember."

He gives her an exaggerated wink as he removes his arm. In the rearview mirror, he can see the chauffeur gazing back at him. He winks at the young man who responds with just the slightest nod of the head. Dex wonders if he is supposed to tip the guy to keep his mouth shut? It's as if he has wandered into a gangster world and hasn't yet figured out what the rules are.

But Yo has already filled him in on the lay of the land—he'll be staying at her aunt Flor's pool house. Yo is over across the garden at her aunt Carmen's house. "Is the garden well-lighted at night?" Dexter asked, pretending innocence. Yo threw a warning glance in his direction. They were still at the airport where she had met up with a handful of cousins who happened to be arriving on the same plane. "I told you everyone's related down here. The place is a fishbowl."

They'll be staying in town for a week in the family compound; then, the day after the elections, they'll head north for a weekend on the coast. Lucinda, one of the cousins Dexter has heard a lot about, has told Yo about this discreet resort that none of the old guard would go to. It's too far removed and très funky, owned by a French couple—the husband offers massages, *personal or non-personal*; the wife takes off her bikini top at poolside and not just to go belly-down on a canvas chair. Most crucifix-hung Dominican women would scatter at the sight. But there is what Yo calls her "hair-and-nails cousins" who are not fainthearted and who are actually cooking up a little feminist revolution of their own under that cloud of hair spray and eye shadow. Among them, old Lucy fox, whom Dexter claims to be already half in love with just from hearing Yo's stories.

"But how'd you manage to get us up there free and clear?" Dex is intrigued.

"I'm your guide." It's her turn to wink. "You're a journalist who wants to see how democracy is working in remote areas of the country." An odd smile comes on her lips, the smile of someone who might be actually enjoying her fibs.

Again that uneasy feeling creeps up on Dexter. Doesn't the family catch on or are they morons or what? He wonders if a man should be president who can't see through a niece with a history. "Your family really bought the story?"

"Of course, they bought it." Yo rolls her eyes at him. "It's all one big story down here, anyway. The aunts all know that their husbands have mistresses but they act like they don't know. The president is blind but he pretends he can see. Stuff like that. It's like one of those Latin American novels that everyone thinks is magical realism in the States, but it's the way things really are down here."

And with that little intro and a squeeze of his hand, they arrive at a large, elegant ranch house with sliding jalousie doors opened to the outdoors. A couple of maids in salmon-colored uniforms with white collars peek out the back door and wave at Yo. Then an aunt comes down between the orchids that grow on both sides of the covered entryway. She is wearing the bright campaign button that shows the uncle's handsome face pinned on her bosom and trailing a brood of nephews and nieces all sporting buttons. One little tyke has a whole chest of them as if they were medals. "Welcome"—the aunt smiles warmly—"welcome to the land Columbus loved the best, Mister Hays!"

For a moment he wonders if he can carry it off. Such a nice lady with a smile to light up the world. But the words come out of his lips without effort. "Oh please, call me Dexter. I'm so glad to be here. I'm such a supporter. And I think our country must be told about the strides that are being made towards democracy just south of our borders."

He has said too much. Everyone seems taken aback by his little speech. The maids start giggling, and one tiny dark-headed girl, a replica of Yo, is tugging impatiently at his arm. Perhaps they all know already who he is, and the pretense is just pro forma to make everybody feel at ease. Just like these democratic elections which—he heard on the plane—will be patrolled by tanks on the streets.

Okay, he thinks. I get it. Go along with the story. Don't try to make it real.

The garden is well-lighted at night, white Chinese lanterns posted at intervals on the cobbled path. But every time he sets out towards the bright mecca of Yo's bedroom, Dexter lands in the arms of another uncle, patting an abrazo on his back, asking him if he is getting everything he wants. It is an odd question to be asked just on the brink of achieving his desire, but yes, he answers heartily, everything is fine, thanks a bunch.

And night after night, these uncles or cousins or whoever they are somehow swing him around and lead him into one or another covered patio with a trellis of dripping bougainvillea and a built-in mahogany bar. Maybe it is the same place, maybe not. One patio is so much like another. The compound is a maze of paths and of plants that seem caricatures of the ones he knows in the States. Dexter has never seen such hibiscus, the blossoms as big as dinner plates, and the rolled-up fronds of ferns are as thick as elephants' trunks. The uncle or cousin or man-servant offers him a shot of rum or a Presidente for good luck for the campaign, and Dexter ends up so boozed up, he can barely stumble his way back to his own room in the pool house, thrashing through hedges and bringing down a rain of those Goliath hibiscus.

The next morning at breakfast, he sees the look on Yo's face, as if he has failed her somehow. As if again he is taking the fiction too seriously, pretending to be a journalist by night as well as by day.

"It's not that," he whispers to her when they are alone for a moment. "It's like your uncles have this radar. They keep cutting me off at the pass!"

She shakes her head. "Ay, Dexter. You've just got to outsmart them." But he can't seem to—even when he tries a new route and ends up stumbling into one of the innumerable little swimming pools on the grounds, soaking his nice new pair of pants. As the dogs commence their wild barking and several night watchmen converge, beaming flashlights at his face, Dexter has a brief image of Winnie Sutherland, shaking her head at him. She is right. He's never going to make it in this adult world of smooth operators. He might as well just float on his back and squirt chlorinated water up at those fuzzy, far-off stars.

On election day, Dexter is caught smoking behind the pool house by Lucy the fox and her flock of little ones. She is herding them to his pool, each one wearing a bright teensy bikini, Lucinda's no bigger than those of the children, although hers is somewhat modestly covered by a short kimono. With its diaphanous silken folds the robe seems more erotic to Dexter than the bright patches of spandex Lucinda has on underneath. A maid, swathed in white and carrying a pile of towels, brings up the rear.

"Buenas, Dexter," Lucinda greets him. Her face is all made up. Looking at her from the neck up, it is hard to believe she really means to go swimming. "Being a bad boy, eh? Sneaking a cigarette!"

Quickly, Dex shifts the joint from his pincer-like hold to the cigarette mode, between middle and forefinger. He wonders if he is going to get away with it. From what he has heard of her, Lucinda surely knows the difference.

"It's not good for you," one of the older girls pipes up in a slightly British version of English. "Mami gave it up. Didn't you, Mami?"

Lucinda nods in mock seriousness. It's hard to believe old Lucy fox would give up anything fun, Dexter ponders.

"It smells funny," the miniscule Yolanda clone declares, making a face. She has spoken in Spanish, but Dexter has understood her words perfectly. Either his high school Spanish is holding up better than he thought or the wrinkling of that button nose is all the translation he needs.

"It's an American cigarette," the older know-it-all girl pipes up again. Wisely, Dexter stomps out his cigarette on the ground, grinning and nodding at all the pretty girls. They are giving him the once-over like grown-up girls, his skinny legs poking out of his second-hand-store Bermuda shorts, his fly—which he notices is undone. Even though he is a grown man with a dopp kit full of dope and unused rubbers, he feels out of his league with this suave little flock.

"Where's Yo?" Lucinda asks, looking over his shoulder as if Yolanda might be hiding in the hedges behind him.

"Oh, she likes a few hours to herself in the morning to write."

Lucinda rolls her eyes behind the false eyelashes. Dex catches a resemblance—a glamour girl Yo, a *Reader's Digest* condensed version of a thorny literary novel.

"I don't mean, you know, real writing. She keeps a journal, that's what I mean."

"Tell me about it," Lucy sighs. "Well, come on and join us then, won't you?" Half a dozen pairs of the sweetest chocolate brown eyes double, triple, sextuple the invitation.

But on down the line, Dexter catches the long-suffering look on the young maid's face. It gets him every time—some Southern guilt re-emerging so that he wants to rescue the servants in their color-coded uniforms. "Por favor," he insists, reaching for her towels. The maid shakes her head shyly. "No, no señor."

This one is wearing all-white which means she is a nanny. One of the aunts explained the system to him. The cook wears gray, though she has a dress-up version with a white collar and apron; the nanny wears all white; the two pantry maids, whatever that is—Dexter first understood panty maids—have salmon uniforms with white collars; the cleaning maid's uniform is all black, though she, too, has a dress-up version with a white collar. "Are you going to put this in your article?" the aunt wanted to know.

Just yesterday Dexter gave away the tape deck to the chauffeur. Why keep it for a pretense? The presidential uncle is on the road all the time. Dexter doubts he'll ever meet him, much less get "an interview" out of him. None of the family seems bothered that the journalist is not doing much journalism. So be it. Anyhow, his peacock-blue and orange Hawaiian shirt Dexter passed on to the gardener, who wore it on his way off the grounds on his afternoon off. One of the aunts seeing the gardener go by commented, "Ay, Dios mío, look at that pimp shirt Florentino is wearing." Oh well, it is obvious to Dexter that he will never ever fit into this family. It's like being on a movie set with a crew that is suffering from amnesia and thinks this is real life.

Meanwhile, things with Yo are deteriorating. This story he told

Lucy about Yo needing a few hours for her journal writing is just that, a story. If nothing else, Dex is getting the hang of all this storytelling. This morning early, Yo snuck into his pool house room. ("See, it can be done!" she boasted.) His eyes had lit up. A prebreakfast reunion between the sheets, yeah!

But no, Yo had come to discuss something. They were due to leave tomorrow for the coast, but things were bound to be crazy for a few days after elections. Why not cancel the resort and stay here for the rest of Dex's visit.

Dexter's face fell. All these long, awkward days in the compound, he has been fantasizing about that French hotel lady baking her titties in the tropic sun. Except, of course, that lady has Yo's face, and hands and feet, and so on. "But I thought you wanted to have some time just the two of us together." Dex hated the whine in his voice.

"What do you mean? We're spending the whole day together here!" She was turning and turning a bangle on her thin, tanned wrist. He wanted to kiss that wrist. He wanted to show her how much he had missed her this long month of her return to the nineteenth century. Why—if she's so good at storytelling—why can't she figure out some sort of fib by which she has to have sex in order to stave off an incurable disease? If Dexter can be a journalist from the *Washington Post*, can't he just as well be an M.D. from the Centers for Disease Control?

"Tell you what, Dex. I promise I'll come *here* tonight, okay?" She was looking around the room as if casing the joint for tonight's subterfuge. But Dexter wasn't satisfied. He had gotten ambitious in his fantasies. He wanted him one of those personal massages. "I'll give you one of them tonight, too," Yo grinned. "Come on, Dex, amorsito. This way we can be supportive of my uncle after the elections."

"I haven't even seen your uncle yet. Besides, he's got a whole damn army of tanks out there to support him."

At that Yo's jaw had dropped and her face lit up in indignation. "I can't believe you said that!"

"Just joking," he added, lifting his hands up as if to show he was unarmed.

His jokes did not amuse her in the least, she informed him. She was sick, vomitously sick ("There's no such word," he countered), sick of his picking on her family. They weren't perfect, but still they had been so nice and welcoming to him and this was his thanks.

"But you criticize them yourself all the time!" he countered. "And need I remind you," he continued, "that they're not welcoming *me* but some fictional journalist from the *Post*." His grievances seemed suddenly deeper than he had realized. The annoyance he had felt at not being able to tell them he was a nurse, to wear his earring and use the rubberbands on his wrist for his ponytail now reached down and tapped the still-searing rejection he had felt when Winnie Sutherland informed him she was leaving him for Donald the Doughboy because he, Dex, was a loser, a guy who would never find himself. "I gave myself a goddamn makeover to please you and your fancy family and you can't even take off three fucking days for me."

"Please don't curse at me," Yo said with a great deal of sudden dignity. She stood as if proudly dusting herself off.

They were headed for a bad fight and he didn't want a bad fight in a country where he didn't really know anyone else but her. He needed to calm himself and her down. A joint sure would help right now. He made the mistake of suggesting it.

"Great! Just what my uncle needs, drugs on the premises. Where are your brains, Dex?" She shook her head at him in utter exasperation.

And then he said exactly the wrong thing, but this time, he did it on purpose. "It's like you haven't grown up yet and moved away from your family."

"That's such a gringo thing to say! Why should I want to move away from my family? And what? Live like you, all separate and lonely without any real connection to your history?"

"Is that what you have, a *real* connection? What about all your pretense and lying?"

"Ay!" she cried, slapping the air in his direction. She was by the door now, that hot temper he'd also seen in Latin ladies in the movies flashing in her eyes. And suddenly, seeing her there so mean and ornery-looking, he was not so sure any more about the joint apartment with batiks on the walls, the mattress on the floor, the dark-headed little girl and matching boy, the family vacations to Yosemite. "I shouldn't have come down here," he admitted. "I should've just stayed home."

He doesn't know if she even heard him say so for she was already storming out of the pool house. He waited a few minutes, hoping that she'd come back and apologize for changing plans on him, at the very least come back to make one more point. Finally, he snuck out the back way. It was while he was behind the hedges by the pool house path, soothing his aching heart with a joint that he was caught by Lucinda the fox and her gaggle of little Yo lookalikes.

"So are you going to join us?" Lucinda is peering over her shoulder to where Dexter is still standing trying to persuade the maid to let him carry the towels.

"Sure," he says, and falls in behind all those cute fannies. But today, he can't enjoy them. He feels as if the cage of his heart has swung open and the bright bird he thought was his has flown away.

———

Late that night Dexter sets out once again through the maze of the compound grounds to find Yo. Thank god for the garden lanterns as most of the house lights seem to be off, everyone fast asleep—if that's possible. Periodically, there are blasts of fire-crackers or gunpowder or perhaps thunder—it is after all a cloudy night, no sign of a star up in that murky sky. It amazes Dexter how much this place has spun its web around him that the last thing he would think of is real thunder, what would seem most natural. The blasts are probably practice runs for a revolu-tion. By now, the election results must be known. This afternoon, when he tried to book a seat out for the next day, the young lady on the other end of the phone said, "You are confirmated but please to telephone to see if the plane leaves tomorrow."

"*If* the plane leaves?" Dexter had challenged the heavily ac-cented young lady. "What kind of a confirmation is that, sweet-heart?"

There was a moment of silence and a sigh he was meant to hear. "We have the election results tomorrow," the young lady explained as though he were a very small child who could not understand the simplest thing.

That evening, he had tried getting Yo alone for a moment to tell her he would be leaving the next day, but the compound was flooded with well-wishers dropping in to wish the family luck. The uncle was still out on the road campaigning somewhere, but he was due home that night after the booths closed and before the tanks began to roll on the streets of the capital. Everywhere there were clusters of guests around big-screened televisions the like of which Dexter had seen only in downtown bars in Atlanta. Maids in uniforms of all colors and stripes had been enlisted to pass around serving trays of what looked to be Velveeta cheese on small squares of white Wonder bread. "Delicioso," Dexter enthused each time he refused so as not to hurt their feelings. One country's delicacy is another country's junk food was all he could think.

Beautiful women looped their arms through his and asked him what he thought of their crazy country, and he smiled, aware of Yo's eyes on him. "Nicest folks possible," he kept saying. "Especially the ladies."

At one point, Lucinda and a whole gang of adult cousins set out in a caravan of cars to check the mood of the town. Somehow he had gotten roped into going—though later when all the cars disembarked at Hotel Jaragua, he realized Yo was not along. There were drinks and dancing, and later at Lucinda's request, he whipped out his American cigarettes, a brand not unknown to the D.R. cousins. By the time the group got home just before midnight, the firecrackers or gunshots had started. Dexter had fallen instantly asleep only to be startled awake by a nearby volley of something. That's when the determination to find Yo seized him. They should, at the very least, have a parting tête-à-tête—as close as he's ever going to get to anything French on this island. Maybe he could also prove to Yo and to himself before he left that he could outsmart the uncle system.

Up ahead in a kind of gazebo bar, a string of lights burns. A solitary figure leans against a post, looking out at the dark garden in a musing pose, a drink in his hand. Dexter is about to slip through a break in the hedge beside the path, when the figure calls out something in Spanish.

"No hablar español," Dexter calls back, afraid that the figure might draw a revolver and shoot this intruder wandering around the compound in the middle of the night. "Soy Dexter Hays," Dexter adds, hoping this is an uncle he has met before for one of those captive nightcaps.

"Dexter Hays . . . Dexter Hays." The man is sorting through some memory Rolodex trying to place him. He gestures for Dexter to come on towards the light so he can place the stranger's face.

Once Dexter draws near, he recognizes the handsome older man, a face now famous by repetition on buttons, newspapers, billboards, posters, TV. "I'm Yo's friend," he elaborates, offering the man his hand.

"Right oh," the uncle says. "The journalist from the *Post*. How about a drink? I'm having a quiet nightcap before pandemonium begins."

Dexter is impressed that the man would use a word like *pandemonium*—as if he has some sense of irony about this whole presidential campaign he is caught up in. As if secretly under the Donald-like exterior of success and know-how, there is a touch of a free spirit like Dexter's inside the suave uncle. A man after my own heart, Dexter thinks. And suddenly, on the eve of his departure, Dexter wants someone here to know who he really is. "Actually, sir, I'm not a journalist," Dexter admits.

"Oh?" The uncle looks at him with curiosity; a smile crinkles the corners of his eyes. The skin of his face is so evenly smooth that Dexter wonders if he leaves his TV pancake makeup on full time. "You're not here with the CIA or the USIA or the FBI or some such thing, are you?"

"No sir," Dexter answers, laying on the Southern accent to make himself sound more ignorant and likeable. "I'm here because . . . well, because I'm Yo's compañero." He tries out the Spanish word. "Or I'm trying to be," he concedes.

So there, Dexter is thinking. He downs the rest of his rum drink, bracing himself for the slap on the face or the challenge to a duel or whatever it is they do.

But the elegant uncle is chuckling. "Well, young man, I guess we both need some luck. May we both win!" He clinks glasses and finishes his drink and then with a slap of an abrazo and a nod in the direction of a bedroom with its light still on, the presidential uncle is gone.

Outside the bedroom door, Dexter listens a moment before tapping lightly. A chair scrapes against the floor. "¿Sí?" a voice calls out, a voice that can still tug at his heart.

He turns the knob and the door opens into a small room lined with bookshelves that are filled, not with books, but with vases and ceramic ladies with baskets on their head and other knick-knacks. A couch has been converted into a bed, a pillow propped up by one of the armrests. Next to it, at the desk, Yo sits, a lamp shining on the notebook in which she has been writing.

She looks startled to see him here, and for a brief moment, Dexter thinks she will say, my hero, you did outsmart the cunning uncles. But instead her face tightens.

"What do you want?" she asks, watching him closely. Dexter feels the way he did back at the pool with all the little girls looking him over.

He sits on the armrest of the couch, his eyes glancing down at the notebook page where he catches the familiar curves of his handwritten name. "Baby, baby," he says, kissing her hands, "what's happening?"

Her face relaxes into a softness he knows is just before tears. "I thought you'd fall in love with my family," she says in a teary voice. "I hoped you'd be happy here."

For a moment he feels the same temptation to tell a story that Yo must feel. To say, *Of course, I can be happy down here. I can fit right in with the smooth uncles and cousins and manservants more* sophisticated *than I am. For you, I can turn myself into a Dominican Dough Boy and let the chauffeur drive the Mercedes.* But Dexter knows he is too old for anything but a surface makeover. "I do like them," he reassures her. "They're interesting and gracious. . . . Lord, they even remind me of my folks with their Southern hospitality. But honey baby, I left home twenty years ago. I don't want to go back."

"But your family—" she begins.

"My family is you and me." He kisses her forehead. At the moment, it seems the right place to kiss.

"I couldn't live that way. I couldn't understand myself without the rest of the clan to tell me who I am."

"I know," he nods sadly. It's as if he has finally knocked at the right door. Cinderella answers, and the shoe fits, but he's in the wrong fairytale. His prince is supposed to wake up a sleeping beauty, not fit shoes on a waking one.

"What are we going to do?" she asks him. Her look is so open and trusting as if she believes that he, Dexter Hays, could make up a happy ending to their story.

"How about one of those personal massages?" he teases. But the sad look on her face mirrors the sadness in his heart. Neither is really in the mood.

"I wonder," she wonders aloud, "if we would have figured all this out if you hadn't come down here?"

And so, on this, their last night together, they lie down on the small couch and fall asleep to the booming of firecrackers. Some time much later, as light is beginning to seep in through the jalousies, Dexter hears the phone ringing with the call that informs the presidential uncle that he, too, has lost.

Part III

The wedding guests

He would like to say, friends and family, we are gathered here to celebrate this coming together of Douglas Manley and Yolanda García, which means—as you can see—the coming together of rich lives and many stories, the coming together of all of you.

But he does not like to wax eloquent outdoors. It is one thing to sound the high notes under the arched cathedral ceiling in the vaguely luminous light of St. John's and an altogether different thing out here on this hot May day in the middle of a field next to a sheep farm and under a grove of hickory trees that keep dropping their plentiful nuts (the squirrels will be happy this year) on the assembled guests.

In front of him stands his old friend, Doug, whom he has known and not known in the way it is in most friendships, full of their disclosures and abeyances. Been with him through the settled years of his first marriage, the seemingly settled years, the church building committee meetings for the new roof, the battered women's center in the basement—boy, did they have to fight the old guard for that one! Watched him grow in stature if that is a correct phrase for a shy man who is willing to help with the food tent at the bazaar and to read the second reading, which is generally quick and easier than the first reading with its hard-to-pronounce Old Testament names, but who would prefer not to

come up to the altar and receive a Parish Angel pin for his contri-
butions to St. John's. Watched as a weariness descended upon
him, an absentness that he had meant to talk to Doug about, but
never did even after the rumors leaked through the guard he as a
minister kept up against such ways of knowing things. Prayed
with him and for him when Doug himself came with the news,
vows broken, a marriage foundered, a house built on rock shifting like the sands. And then the hard years, the embattled years.

He would like to say, Doug, here is the promise of renewal.
Here is the helpmeet, the ram under the bush that spares you
from sacrificing your happiness.

But again, it must be almost eighty degrees even under these
shades trees. Beyond Doug and Yolanda's shoulders he sees the
hazy mountains indeterminate in the heat. He should be brief.
But he would like to say some of these things.

Close to her father, biting her lip, is the child of that first marriage who is now adrift between families and fighting back tears.
He would like to say, Corey, it will get better, I promise you. There
is an end to grief, a still point in the turning world. But the most
he would get from a young teenager if he spoke in this churchy
way would be a fuck-you. He recalls pouring the water of spirit
over the creased little forehead, the enraged howls, the legs kicking under a christening gown that was far too pretentious for this
bit of person, and he recalls, too, how when he intoned her
name, a sudden quiet descended on the tiny features as if this
were all she had been waiting for, her place in the world which is
now being taken away from her.

He does not really know what to say to her.

And flanking Corey as if to bolster her in this, her moment of
knowing that it will not be the happy story she wants—her mom
and her dad reunited, egg hunts in the attic—are her grandpar-

ents, Doug's mother and father with their older, tired versions of
the granddaughter's face, of Doug's face. Sweet simple people.
Always the phrase comes to mind, the salt of the earth, and of
course the beatitudes, blessed are the meek, blessed are the clear
in spirit.

Here and there he spots the familiar faces he has come to
know over the course of twenty years in this New Hampshire
parish, Doug's friends and family whom he has met at church
suppers and supper parties, at hospital bedsides and grave sites.
Known their crises of spirit, their good works and their not-so-
good works. In their light pastels, seersucker jackets, and cotton
sundresses; their quiet grace; their modulated, educated voices
(this is, after all, a college town)—this is the flock he has struggled to shepherd. Of them and to them he could—for the most
part—speak what is in his heart.

But then with flashes of bright color and with loud voices, and
with the sound—he almost wants to say—of tabor and harp like
the daughters of men in Genesis six, verses one through four,
who draw down from the mountains the serious men with offers
of tender meats and sweets, come the family and friends of Yolanda
García.

Among these, her people, he feels tongue-tied and pale. All
afternoon, there have been spats and reconciliations as they gathered and mixed on this meadow, the father and mother upset
with one of the daughters, a weeping sister hugging an old aunt,
two friends screaming oh-my-god hellos. He has heard whispered words that are almost biblical: *disowning, redeeming herself,*
my blessing, die in peace now. He knows from the gossip they have
passed on to him before he put on his robe hanging on a hook in
the van, before they knew he was "the priest" (the family are all
Catholics, he believes), that one of Yolanda's exes is here, that he

will be reading a Rumi poem, that the attractive darker-skinned woman is the maid's daughter, that the best friend in the snug black leotard with a distracting lace bodice has brought a whole therapy group along with her. Among these there is a gay woman and another gay woman and two little babies, how did this happen? The world is full of mystery and happenstance. God bless, God bless, is all he can think to say to these people. Perhaps that will calm them down, perhaps with just the right words he can bring them together, a momentary congregation on this New Hampshire hillside on a hot day at the end of May.

And in the midst of this clamorous clan, this kaleidoscope of colors, wanders the bride herself, Yolanda García in a gray tunic and pants. She seems almost subdued amid this tintinnabulation and emotional commotion as if she were trying to put all of these people together in her head, a quilting of lives, a collection of points of view.

By the cooler of spring water Doug's parents have set up, she stands for a moment by herself and looks over at him. He recalls—how could he not?—that she did not want a church wedding. That when he asked her at the counseling session before agreeing to perform the ceremony if she believed in the Lord Jesus Christ, she looked at him a long moment, and answered, Yes and no.

And that same look is in her eyes now along with a look of puzzlement as if she were wondering how she will carry this off, the ceremony and the life afterwards. And the look both entreats and challenges him, *So, man of God, what can you say to me? What is the good word?*

Friends and family (he would like to say), we are gathered here both to relinquish who we were and to celebrate what we are becoming. This is our mission on this twenty-ninth day of

May nineteen-hundred and ninety-three: we who have been a seminal part of the earlier lives and loves of Douglas Manley and Yolanda García have come here to create their new family.

If one more of her sappy sisters comes around and asks me how I feel, I think I'm going to scream. What am I supposed to say, I'm having a great time watching you all play Mister Potato Face with my life!

Let's give Corey a new mother. Let's give Corey a new set of relatives. Let's give Corey a whole new happy family she can be a part of.

And then this one old aunt, I mean she must be blind, starts talking to me in Spanish. Yeah, I've had a couple of years in high school and I've gone to Guatemala with my *real* parents, but I'm not going to let on that I understand what she's saying to me. She goes on and on trying to figure out whether I look like the Garcías or the de la Torres. And then, I realize she thinks I'm her grandniece and that I came all the way from the Dominican Republic to attend this stupid wedding.

Like please, like por favor, would you stop breathing your bad breath on my face or I am going to scream.

This middle-aged hippy-type guy finally comes up and pulls me away. "Howdy there! You must be Miss Corey?" He's got a Southern accent that sounds made up. I nod, just waiting, arms folded, like you want to make something of it, buster. "I'm Dexter Hays, at your service." He kisses my hand. It is kind of cute. He hands me this purple balloon with a happy face, which he then proceeds to tie on my wrist.

"Will you be my date for this wedding?" he comes on to me.

I want to say, Get a life, get a good haircut, and a job or something. So I just say, "Excuse me, I've got to find my dad," and quick I turn away, keeping my head down cause, man, the last thing I want is to make eye contact with some other dumb person who's going to ask me how I'm doing.

And boy, it's my lucky day, my lucky year, my lucky life. I bump right into her, and for a minute, I think, jesus christ, she looks just as scared as I am.

"How you holding up, Corey?" she asks. She knows better than to put her arm around me, though it looked for a second like she was going to do just that.

"I'm fine," I say, all business. "I'm looking for my dad."

And boom there he is throwing one arm around her and one around me. "How are my two lovely ladies?" he says, which just about makes me throw up. I try to shrug his arm off but he keeps holding on. "Dad!" I say. "Let go!" He better let go or else.

I'll stand on this hillside and scream. I really will.

If this isn't the prettiest bunch of babes I've seen north of the Mason Dixie, my name ain't Dexter Hays. I came with a bouquet of purple Happy Face balloons for the bride, but I've been giving them away to these fair ladies. So many dearly beloved varieties gathered together here: slim Latin ones with knowing eyes and sunkissed skin; ladies hitting their full-bodied, mid-life stride; handsome ladies who prefer ladies—ah what a loss to me; and then the blond, long-legged yankee ladies with no makeup and a fresh clean look on their all-American faces.

Of which this pretty Corey-girl is one, poor baby, looking so sad. I tried to cheer her up, but she's a workout all right. Yo better start growing some of that thick skin she never could seem to graft onto her too-sensitive self. She's going to need it. But hey, she always wanted family in a big way, uncles and aunts and in-laws and cousins twice and thrice removed and friends who are relatives by what she calls affection. Well, this whole hillside's crawling with her dream come true, which usually comes as a package deal with a nightmare or two.

So who am I in this gathering, the sandman with a case of bad dreams? No sir. It's been five years since I've seen Yolanda García and it would have been the rest of our lives if it hadn't been that the Grateful Dead were giving a concert about twenty minutes from here. Over the last five years, we've kept in touch on and off but mostly off recently. So I call her up, and her number's been changed, and so I call up the new number, and this guy Doug answers, and I'm about to say, "This is Luigi's Pizza Parlor. I got a large pepperoni here to deliver to the Albatrosses, can you give me directions to your house?" But I think, what the hell, I was there before you were, buddy, so I say, "This is an old friend of Yo's, is she there?"

And he says, "I'm sorry, she can't come to the phone right now. Can I take a message?"

I'm ready to tell him to go screw himself, but then he adds, "She's writing," and I know he's not just trying to put me off. So I leave my name and number and a couple of hours later, there's old Yo on the line, saying, "Ay, Dexter, it's so great to hear your voice. What have you been up to?"

"What have *you* been up to?" I put in because I hear some major changes just in the way her voice stands up for itself. "You sound real happy." No matter what my daddy says, I got more couth than to add, *for a change.*

"Ay, I am so, so happy, Dexter, I feel so blessed."

And as she tells me how she's finally found this really wonderful man (so what was I, chopped coon liver?), I'm standing there going, "Well, that's terrific!" But you know how it is, you want your ex-heartthrobs to be happy, but you don't really want to hear about it. I guess in the bottom of my silly heart I always like to think of my past ladies as still burning a flame for me. Hell, I'll settle for a pilot light, cause I do declare, ole Dex just has not had staying luck when it comes to the gals. My daddy says it's my own goddamn fault. He says I never have really wanted to settle down. And though I wouldn't want him to hear me say so, I think he may be right.

So, anyhow, when she's caught me up on her new life, she turns it over to me. "But you tricked me, Dex. I asked you first. What are you up to?"

And so I end up telling her why it is I'm calling, I'm going to be nearby at the Grateful Dead concert the last weekend in May, and she starts to laugh, and says, "Dexter, honey. I'm getting married that Saturday. Why don't you come to the wedding in the afternoon before the concert. It's going to be out in the country on this piece of land we bought next to a sheep farm. . . ."

She goes on, waxing lyrical I guess is the way to put it, and I'm trying to listen and roll a joint at the same time on account of I've got this raw place in me I gotta fill with something. Sure enough, once I get the thing lit and take a few deep draws, I feel a lot better about all this happiness going Yo's way. So maybe that's why I end up promising as I say goodbye, "Sure baby, for old time's sake. I'll be there to kiss the bride!"

Kiss the bride, my eye, if he gets near Yo one more time I'm going to go over there and pop all those silly balloons he brought tied to his hand. (What's he trying to do—upstage the groom?)

First thing he does is come up and say, "You must be the lucky man!" Which I am, but I don't want him telling me so. So I put out my hand and say, "Doug Manley, Yo's husband," though technically, I should say, Yo's soon-to-be husband. But I want to put this guy in his place right away. Well, he's not about to let me. Out goes his hand and this cocky grin lights up his face. "I'm Dex, Yo's ex," he says.

Then Yo comes up and he starts giving her these Lordy-lord, I-declare shakes of the head, and hmm-umms like he is speechless at the sight of her. Now I'm not an easily agitated man, but I don't like this one bit. When he turns to me—as if he really is asking my permission, and says, "May I kiss the bride?" I shrug, sure, but then he keeps on giving her a peck every time she goes by. "Hold on, mister," I want to tell him, "it's not a blanket permission."

I'm glad everyone else is here. Of course, Corey looks as if she's going to cry, and there's no use trying to include her because if you do, she says she's going to throw up, and if you leave her alone, she says she's going to scream, or maybe it's the other way around. She has already given me her decision. It's going to be full time with her mom and some weekends with Yo and me. When I say, so how many is *some*, she says she's going to scream *and* throw up if I try to pin her down.

The sins of the father are visited upon the sons and the daughters. But don't kid yourself, they come rebounding back to you. Luke and I have talked about it. So many times those first few lonely years after the divorce I'd drive by St. John's and see the light on up at his office, late night, at least for a small town, ten o'clock, and I'd park and go up, and he'd put aside whatever sermon he was working on—he does love a good homily—and say, "How's it going?" He would know I was having a hard night—that's why I stopped. Sometimes he'd show me examples in the Bible (Isaac and the ram of happiness, the dove with a sprig of hope in its beak) and sometimes he would just speak from his heart, which were the best times.

And that's how, once, he ended up telling me about this project St. John's was going to do in the Dominican Republic along with some other churches, building houses in the poorest villages. Did I want to go?

It was summer, Corey was due to come to me that month. I didn't even have to think about it. I said, sure. Soon as I got home I pulled out my atlas, and I was surprised—such a big, self-important name, The Dominican Republic, for this little amoeba shape like something under a microscope that might just glide away.

So Corey and I flew down. We felt somewhat prepared as she and her mother and I had once been to Guatemala for a long vacation. But in the Dominican Republic we were based in this mountain village, living in tents, about sixteen men and ten women from churches all over the United States. At first, the villagers just eyed us as if they weren't sure what we would ask of them in return for this godsend of new houses, especially since we were Protestants. This one guy in our group who knew Spanish well explained to them that our building them shelters didn't mean they had to renounce the Pope. The villagers seemed more at ease after that, though they kept saying that before they signed any papers accepting our contribution (something the IRS and Uncle Sam required) they wanted to wait for the arrival of this person named Yolanda García.

So that is how we met—in a little, godforsaken village with Yo giving us the third degree about what we were up to and then telling the villagers that yes, it was safe, they could go ahead and sign their X's on the dotted line. I guess they hadn't known how to read the forms and were too ashamed to say so. Anyhow, later I found out that she'd been coming to this village for the past few summers and had gotten to know a lot of the villagers. These last two weeks, she had been off in the capital because her lover had come down to visit from the States. You can guess who that lover was, Mister Dexter Hays.

The funny thing was that down there Yo and Corey really hit it off. I suppose there was no jealous sense yet that this woman might become a part of my life. And this is what I keep remembering when the going gets hard. A sprig of hope in the dove's beak.

We had just finished the last of the houses, and all the villagers had gathered to celebrate under a thatched gazebo that sat in the center of the desolation they called a town. These old guys brought out the crudest instruments. One of them was a can with punctured holes over which he ran a small steel rod making a rasping sound. Another was an accordion that looked like it'd travelled all over Europe with the gypsies. Then there was a drum made out of a hollowed-out tree trunk, and maracas fashioned from gourds with the dried seeds still inside.

These guys started playing a merengue with a beat that would beat any band north *or* south of the Rio Grande. Yo and Corey were snapping their fingers and moving their hips to the beat, and suddenly they were out on the floor together, just the two of them, dancing, Corey like she'd been doing it since day one. After a few minutes, they each pulled in someone from the village, and started dancing with them. (Yo chose a guy, Corey, of course, another girl.) After a spin, they paired up those two villagers, and selected another two, danced with them, mixed them up, and soon the whole village and all the volunteers were dancing in the gazebo and spilling out to the streets of the village. I was sort of hanging back in the sidelines, because no matter how infectious the sound of that merengue was, I'm the world's worst and most self-conscious dancer. As soon as Yo and Corey each released their last partners, they looked around to see who was left, and except for the musicians, it was just me slinking away behind the town cistern.

"Hey!" Yo called, and Corey dragged me to the floor, and then the three of us were holding hands, dancing merengue, and laughing our heads off. After a rousing chorus, the musicians got up and led us through the winding streets, all of us dancing, as if we were some sort of procession, blessing the new buildings and our coming together to build them.

Of course, that's a far cry from what's happening here. Looking out over this hillside at everyone in their separate clumps— just like the sheep in the field beyond—and catching the look on Corey's face and Yo's furrowed brow, I feel doubtful but also hopeful that everyone will have just as good a time now.

Except for this Dexter fellow. Him I'd like to see lifted up by that bunch of balloons on his wrist into the sky and dropped down some place far away from here. Maybe that village in the Dominican Republic, yeah, right on top of one of the houses we built.

At first, I thought, no way.

But then I thought it over, and I guess I wanted to see them all once again. The García girls. Except for Yo, who dropped in at the clinic last June, I hadn't seen any of them for over twenty years.

But it was more than that. Mamá died last year, and I'm still grieving. I know I have to get a whole new point of view about life. You have to when you lose someone who's been hiding the view of the grave from you, a mother, a father, a beloved aunt or uncle. The older generation. Next thing you know, you're the next in line to die, and the wind blows strong in that direction.

So I was shivering and alone. Mamá was my last real tie to the island, and now that she's gone, I really have no reason to keep going back. I have a busy practice, and whatever free time I have, I'm on the courts. (I've managed to maintain my 6.0 rating.) So why go back? What little family I have left on the island is so poor and illiterate that I can't bear to face them. Every month I still send down a bank check to our village. When I first enlisted the courier service they couldn't even find the place on a map, even on the new detailed maps that include all the coastal resorts marked with beach umbrellas and little red sailboats.

The invitation was actually not from her parents but from Yo herself. And it wasn't fancy at all. She'd bought it at one of those card stores, a fill-in-the-blank type thing. Come to such and such a meadow beside the thus and such sheep farm on the last week-end in May for a big gathering and exchange of vows. An address in New Hampshire. (I had to stop by Waldens and buy an atlas to see exactly where New Hampshire was. I knew it was north of New York City, but how north? As far as I'm concerned fifty states is too many to keep straight. They should combine them into five or six provinces. That would make it easier for us poor immigrants who have to memorize them for our citizenship exam. It's the one section of the test that I didn't get a 100 percent on.)

The problem was I knew I'd be seeing more of the family than just the Garcías at this wedding. There were bound to be some of those upper crust aunts and uncles up from the island, though I wasn't sure if they would still be showing up for the García girls' marriages. (There've been seven so far.) To that old guard from the D.R., I'll always be the maid's daughter, no matter how many degrees hang on the wall and how many receptionists you have to talk to to get through to me.

And there was this added thing: this would be the first time I'd face them since my dying mother let it be known that I was related to the de la Torre family by more than her employment.

I flew into whatever city it was that has an airport close by, called a cab, and the dispatcher says he can't tie up one of his cars to go that far out. "Why don't you call Dwyer's, they got limos and there's no weddings or funerals in town today." So I call Dwyer Car Service, and they say, sure, we'll take you there. An hour and a half later I roll up to this meadow in a stretch black limo with a little guy in a uniform opening the door for me.

And this is what's interesting, very interesting. Every time some of the García de la Torre clan go to introduce me to the groom's side of the family, they hesitate. "This is Sarita Lopez . . . the daughter . . . of a woman . . . whom . . . we were very fond of." And I'm thinking, go ahead and say it. She's the daughter of the maid who used to clean our toilets and make our beds and calm our rages and wipe away our tears.

And then, please, go on with the story: she has made something of herself, the daughter. She got her B.S., then went to med school, and now owns one of the leading sports medicine clinics in the country. Sometimes, in fact, a patient will come in from the Dominican Republic, and I'll have to smile because I recognize the name. Some "uncle" on my father's side with a tennis elbow or shinsplints. Someone who would deny me if I presented myself as his niece, but here he is asking me to operate on the cartilage in his knee.

Anyhow, I *have* come a long way, baby, as the cigarette ad says. But you know, I'd give it all away, I would, the clinic, the club championships, to get that hard-working, dark-skinned, tired old woman back.

"I miss your mami so much," Yo is saying. She has thrown her arm around me—like she's been waiting to do that to someone and so I'm getting the benefit of an even bigger affection than what she actually feels for me. "I wish she could have been here. But I'm so so glad you came, Sarita. If you hadn't, it'd be like one of the García girls was missing."

It's one of those lies that the heart feels is true but the head knows is a bunch of crap. Still, for the moment, I let myself believe it. And the truth is these four García sisters are the closest I've got to family, to people who are like me: all of us caught between cultures—but with this added big difference, I'm also caught between classes, at least when I go back to the island to visit.

"Ay, Yolanda," I tell her, feeling a little teary myself. "I wouldn't have missed it for the world." But then, I glance over her shoulder at a clutch of her fancy old aunts and dressy cousins whom my mother used to serve cafecitos to on a silver tray, and I feel my self-confidence drain away as if all those degrees and patients are nothing but a story I made up about myself.

The groom comes up, a nice-looking man with a sweet, shy face. A farmer's boy, Yo tells me later on. Sharecroppers from Kansas who stayed and scraped the bottom of that dust bowl. Poor simple folk, not unlike my island family. "Ay, Doug," Yo says, "come meet the baby García sister."

And that man takes both my hands like I'm some dear person, and he doesn't have to say a word to make me feel I'm a part of whatever is going on here.

Dios santo, but I believe I recognize her in that lavender suit, with a kind of Givenchy collar, Primitiva's daughter, the one who looks like a model and became a doctor.

The way that girl showed up the García girls. God moves in mysterious ways.

I would go up to her and introduce myself: "I'm Flor de la Torre. Your mother worked for me for many many years. As a matter of fact, it was from my house that she left to go to the United Estates when the Garcías moved up here."

I treated her very well. When she left, I gave her an old winter coat of mine that I kept for traveling to New York to go shopping. It was February and I knew what awaited her when she landed.

She was my size back then, a tall handsome woman with cinnamon-color skin a little darker than the daughter's and jet black hair that matched her dark eyes. She had been with the family forever—each of us sort of inheriting her when a new baby arrived or we fell ill with a flu or threw a big party. Primitiva was everyone's right hand.

But she began nagging that she wanted to go to Nueva York. Some of the family felt she was being ungrateful, but I understood. This would be an opportunity for her. And she had a new little baby to think of, too.

Finally her chance came to join the Garcías, and Primitiva was so happy to go.

And to tell you the truth, by then I was happy to see her go, too.

My husband Arturo always had an eye out for pretty women, not unlike that blond, pigtailed guy (I recognize him from somewhere . . .) who is going around here flirting with all of us ladies, offering us those silly balloons. Anyhow, Arturo's eye would often come to rest on Primitiva as she stood by the sideboard waiting to serve the coq au vin or pudín de pan or when she was bent over cleaning the indoor pond or up on a ladder oiling the jalousies. But that's as far as it ever got. As he himself put it, he was a lover of all arts, including the natural art displayed on a beautiful human face or chest or, I suppose, a backside.

But then, after all we did for Primitiva, helping her out in every way we could—from that winter coat to tuition for the girl at a private colegio, you can imagine how much it hurt when she came out with that preposterous story about my husband being that girl's father!

And you can imagine how much it hurts me now to see her arriving here in a limousine with a chauffeur as if she were trying to show us all up. I would have thought Yolanda would be more sensitive to family feelings—though come to think of it, perhaps she does not know the story. We tried to keep it quiet. Such a scandal, for one thing, and for another, my husband was no longer around, God be with him, to explain as he always did to me that appreciating beauty was not the same as enjoying it.

I'm trying to ignore her or to just concentrate on the Givenchy suit—or is it an Oscar de la Renta?—the nicely coordinated pumps. But my eye keeps wandering up to those familiar eyes, the curve of that jaw, the way she swings her arms like Arturo when she walks.

It could be coincidence. Besides, it takes more than a man's thing to make a family. It's something you have to give yourself to, heart and soul, so you forge a link nothing in the world can break. Look at the García girls. Had they not been family, do you think I would have let them near my children?

So even if she has the de la Torre dimple in her chin and the hazel eyes from the Swedish great-great-grandmother, even so, she is still the maid's daughter, no relation to *my* family at all.

I am pretty surprised to see old Dexter Hays here. And he is pretty surprised to see me too. "Hey, Lucy, you foxy lady, you. How ya doing?"

I want to say, "Fine, fine, got any of those American cigarettes on you?" He was a chain joint-smoker back when I met him—five, six years ago when Papi was running for prez. Old Dex came down to the compound to visit Yo, who was trying to pass him off as someone from the American press. Anyhow, the air around that pool house where Dex was staying was so thick with the smell of marijuana I was afraid the gardener would get high just from cleaning the pool. Dex finally left in a huff, and Yo told me later they had broken up.

Anyhow, here Dexter is, resurrected, and running around with balloons as if he's the groom who has had too much to smoke, and the ceremony hasn't even started. For the last half hour, he's been talking up the maid's daughter—my first cousin, if I am to believe the gossip. And from looking at poor Tía Flor's face I'd have to agree with what the campesinos say, gossip is how God spreads the little news we might have missed.

At least none of *my* exes are here. It'd be just like Yo to invite old Roe up here to read an e.e. cummings poem and talk about how it was really Yo he was in love with. What does she think a wedding is? A lemon squeeze?

We used to have those every summer when the García girls came down. The girl cousins would gather in a bedroom, and we each had to say what we liked and didn't like about each person. Sometimes we did a co-ed lemon squeeze with Mundín and the boy cousins, but that wasn't as much—I wouldn't exactly call it *fun* since lemon squeezes were never fun. But when the boys were along, lemon squeezes never got off the ground. I mean, Mundín would say something like, "Okay, Yo, I guess I don't like—I don't know, let's see, I don't like, okay, I got it, your big butt."

"But Mundín, I don't have a big butt!"

"Hahaha! Gotcha there, didn't I?"

Remember we were all in our early teens, and you know what they say about boys maturing much later than girls. At forty-one, Mundín's still going on sixteen.

Anyhow, the next summer after my parents found out via Yo's diaries about my keeping company with Roe at boarding school and I was grounded on the island, we all gathered for a lemon squeeze. It'd been a while since we'd had one—I mean we were all about eighteen and had really outgrown them by then, but I suggested one for old time's sake. Yo must have sensed something because she kind of backed off and said she thought lemon squeezes were mean-spirited. That even though we were supposed to say both what we liked and what we didn't like, it was always the didn't like part that everyone seemed to fix on.

And I said, "Oh come on, Yo. Just make believe you're writing in one of your journals and let it all hang out."

She looked at me with a kind of questioning look. It was finally dawning on her that I knew how my parents had come by their information.

"I'll start," I offered. "Let's see." I looked straight at Yo. "You know what I hate about you, Yo García. I hate how you snitched and made it look like you were just being creative. How you used your pen to get back at me. How your writing is one big fucking excuse for not living your life to the fullest. I hate—"

"Hey," Sandi, the prettiest of the sisters, interrupted. "You're being kind of mean, Lucinda. It wasn't Yo's fault Mami went snooping in her diary."

But I couldn't stop myself, I kept right on. I mentioned every goddamn last thing I couldn't stand about her and then I made some things up. What was surprising was—given her big mouth—how she let me do it. Like she knew she had to accept this punishment from me. And I wanted to punish her. I wanted to destroy any relation between us. If there's such a thing as divorcing brothers or sisters or family, I wanted to divorce my cousin.

Finally when I ran out of things, I burst into tears. But it wasn't what you might think, penitent tears, no. They were tears of fury because I knew for all I had said, I couldn't destroy the fact that we were still family.

"Come on," Sandi urged. "Hug each other and make up."

Yo reached for me, but I said, "If you touch me, I'll scream!"

She backed off. She was crying, too. Then she said something that made me forgive her—in my heart—though I've kept her guessing to this day. "Remember, Lucinda, I was in love with Roe, too. But that doesn't mean I would try to hurt you. In fact, I wrote all that stuff down so I wouldn't hold it in my heart against you."

I was still too mad to let her know I believed her. Instead I laid on the guilt. "I hope you know you've changed my life forever."

"I know," she said with a heavy sigh like a burden had descended on her shoulders.

Her arm comes around my shoulders now, and she nuzzles her face in my hair. These García girls are too affectionate. "Lucy, honey," she teases me. "You getting ready to catch my bouquet?" Just last week I announced that I'd be marrying my fourth in October. Of course, this bouquet business is a joke since Yo is dressed in a very unbecoming pajama outfit, and she's not doing anything traditional like carrying flowers.

"I don't know if we should be catching each other's bouquets," I say. After all, I'm thinking, we two seem to have had the worst luck with men.

But she takes it a different way, as if I were referring to that old wound. I see it on her face, and maybe that's why she pops the question one more time. "Hey, Lucy. You are happy now, aren't you? I mean things turned out okay, after all?"

I give her a long look because I've withheld this admission for so many years, I don't even know how to tell her. I look out at this hillside and this crazy group of people, a stepdaughter with her shoulders all squared for battle, Dex out there trying to pick up a date, an explosion or maybe a celebration about to happen, and I think, she needs all the luck she can get.

So I tell her, "I'm happy, Yo. I wouldn't change one thing in my life, not the highs, not the lows."

We hug, and it's as if that old burden has slipped off her shoulders the way Yo says, "Thanks, cousin, I needed to hear you say so."

But all this hugginess makes me squirm, so I try to get us onto a new topic. "Tell me, Yo, what are those animals over there?"

"Sheep," she says, and then she has to add her smart two cents. "You're such an outdoor girl, Lucy-cakes! What'd you think they were, big bunnies?"

"You're heading for a lemon squeeze," I warn her.

"I know," she says, smiling this nervous smile. "I'm getting married."

I don't think I've seen Yo this nervous since that time way back when she had her first post-divorce boyfriend Tom over for dinner. She'd been through two failed marriages and five or so years of self-imposed celibacy, and she was as jittery as a virgin on a prom weekend. We were living together that summer, Yo and I, and some people in the neighborhood had their questions about that.

I had some lovely men back in those days before AIDS made us all cautious lovers. There was an Israeli guy, a plumber, an ex-priest, and of course, dear Jerry, who since married his therapist.

Everyone was seeing therapists back then. As a matter of fact, Yo and I were part of that therapy group Brett Moore assembled called Looking for the Muse. What I remember most during those sessions was Brett Moore and me sort of fighting over Yo's soul—whether she was going to go the gay route or not. I had no problem with Yo being gay if that was what she was. But I thought Brett was projecting her own preferences onto Yo, who was really floundering back then. I should know, as her best friend, I heard it all: how she wanted to know what she was meant to do with her life, how she felt torn between giving herself to art or to political action, how she didn't know if she was meant to love men or women. Yo was never one to take the big questions in bite-size, chewable portions. It was always *What is my place in the universe* instead of *where can I park the car and not get a ticket* or *what apartment can I rent that includes the utilities.*

Old Brett still doesn't know when to quit. She comes up to me and says, "Who's that hot-looking chick Yo's all over?" Brett has a locker room mind when she's not in her office practicing therapy.

I say, "Brett, dear, that happens to be Yo's cousin Lucy-Linda to whom I was just introduced."

"So?" she sasses, taking off her cowboy hat. This one's got a red band either as a festive touch or in support of AIDS research, I don't know. "Ever heard of kissing cousins?"

By now we're just doing this joking out of some kind of habit. As we're talking, I hear one of the babies start to cry. "How's Mimi?" I ask her. Her partner Mimi and she both got artificially inseminated by the same donor's sperm, so technically those two kids are sisters, but they don't really have a father but a donor and their aunts are really each other's mommy's lover. Try to explain that to those old Dominican grande dames sitting under that hickory grove stirring the air with their hand-painted fans.

Funny how many different kinds of family I can see just on this hillside. And that's what I want to tell Yo when she comes up to me and Brett, looking a little down at the mouth.

"Pretty overwhelming?" Brett suggests, feeding her her lines.

Yo rests her head a moment on my shoulder, not saying a word. Then, she looks up at us and sighs. "I guess it was unrealistic, thinking everyone would really come together and have a good time here." In her pretty gray Indian tunic and pants I helped her pick out, she looks less like a bride and more like some guru groupie who has just flunked her transcendence exam.

"What do you mean?" I ask her, looking at Brett as if we're both in charge of this patient together. "Everyone's doing fine. You shouldn't be worrying about us."

"That's right, this is your wedding!" Brett adds. Mimi comes up and adds her two cents: two howling babies. "I've got to change them," she reports wearily to Brett. "Do you have the keys to the car?"

Off they go together, a dozen or more pairs of Dominican eyes on them. And I'm left consoling Yo.

"I mean," she goes on, "you'd think for one day only, my family would not get into some tiff about something, my aunts could try to be nice to Sarita and stop staring at Brett and Mimi, and Corey could maybe crack one tiny smile—"

"Hey, hey," I say, making the time-out sign. "It's going a lot better than you think." It's true, pastels are starting to cluster around bright-color dresses, dark skin by fair skin; strangers' children approach the old, beckoning tías who take little chins in hand to tilt the small, bright faces this way and that, trying to figure out a resemblance in the family. And isn't that Corey chasing after one of the García kids? Finally, as if letting his high jinks go and accepting the blow of an old flame going out, Dexter Hays releases what balloons he has left to the heat-hazy sky.

A quiet descends on us as if this is a sign.

And then Doug is coming towards us, his face radiant as he looks at Yo, who smiles radiantly back at him. "Luke says to gather everyone together," he says.

I give her a pat on the butt as I've done many times before over lesser things. I'm nine years older than she, so sometimes I'm mom as well as best friend. Though soon this, too, will end. And don't think I'm not feeling wistful knowing that I'll be relinquishing my place as Yo García's best friend.

Shouts rise up from the far northeast corner of the field. Just as everyone was beginning to gather together under the hickory trees for the start of the ceremony, some argument seems to have erupted.

He wonders if he should go down and referee or stay here and religify (a phrase he heard a black preacher use on NPR about a month ago, a phrase he wishes he could use without sounding as if he were caricaturing the man's black English), stay here and religify the wedding site by laying one stone on another stone, creating at the very least a makeshift altar in this unhallowed grove. But the shouts grow in intensity. Maybe his mere presence will calm whatever hot tempers have flared or frayed nerves have snapped in this unseasonably hot weather. But surely, Yolanda's tropical-island family—for he assumes the problem has arisen among her guests—surely they are used to conducting themselves civilly in much hotter weathers.

The aunts are the first to rise from their folding chairs. Thick-fleshed and antique as they seemed, they are amazingly nimble on their black patent-leather heels. They move swiftly over the pasture to join the growing crowd of guests forming a ring around whoever it is fighting.

He looks around for Doug to ask how they should proceed, but the groom is absent. So, as a matter of fact, is the bride. The therapy group, which had been conducting a kind of impromptu session, seated on the hay bales Doug's parents laid out for chairs, rises up as if at a signal, and walks across the field en masse. Midway, at the sound of a female scream, the group breaks into a run. He cannot help noticing how middle-aged women run, their bodies like heavy bundles they are afraid might drop and the contents spill or break.

Only the old men, Yo's father and a retired professor of something, are left conversing on their fold-out chairs by the spent lilacs. "I always say to my children from Dante," the father is saying, "'There is a tide in the affairs of men. . . .'" He recites in halting English.

"I believe that's Shakespeare, Mister García—"

"It is Dante," the father insists. "I know how to say it in German, Spanish, Italian, and Chinese." He renders the quote in two of the four languages before the shouts interfere with the multilingual recitation. "Let us check the tide," the father nods to the professor, and the two men sigh as they, too, rise to their feet. They walk down the field, arm in arm.

He follows a few feet behind them, his white robe clinging to his trousers—there isn't even the whisper of a breeze. The shouts have diminished, and now he can make out Doug's voice saying, "Calm down, we're making it worse. Now will everybody please stand back."

As if Moses himself had spoken, there is a parting in the sea of cotton and seersucker and bright silks. And that is when he sees what has happened. A young ewe with two lambs bawling beside her has gotten her head stuck in the wire fence that separates the two fields. She must have tried to climb through to greener pastures, and then, at the approach of some of the guests, pulled back only to lock herself in the electric wires. On the dirty white scruff of wool around her neck there is a necklace of blood. Every time she bolts, she gets another electric shock.

Doug tests the wires, but jerks his hands off. "Someone go turn off the battery! Down there, at the northeast end of the field," Doug instructs. As everyone turns a circle trying to figure out which way is north, Dexter, the balloon guy, dashes off, the tail of his tie-dye shirt lifting as he hurries down the hill.

He cannot help thinking of those deer he has caught with his headlights on late-night mountain roads that lift their tail signaling danger before they disappear.

"What should I do?" Dexter shouts up, and Doug shouts down, "Just turn it off!"

Doug taps the wire, then grabs hold of two strands. "Okay, everyone, stand back!" But his first yank is unsuccessful. The ewe lets out a pitiful wail that sounds almost human.

"Is she okay, Dad, is she?" Corey has been the only one not to obey her dad's orders and back off. She kneels by the sheep, holding the wooly head in her hands as if to keep the ewe from strangling herself.

"That a girl, Corey," Doug says, "just hold her firm."

The old aunts in their elegant black dresses commiserate over the fate of the poor animal. One of them turns to the darker-skinned woman beside her and asks in accented English, "Are we to have it for the barbecue?"

He would like to say, this is the sheep that the Lord has sent to gather us together on this hillside. This is the promise made to the sons and daughters of Abraham.

Suddenly with a second yank, Doug pulls the wires apart and the ewe leaps forward into the field. Close behind, through the gaping hole follow the two bleating lambs. The aunts stampede to one side afraid that the animals will bite. One of the glamorous Dominican cousins whose name he cannot recollect crouches behind the returned Dexter, who is hamming it up, arms out, as if keeping monsters from causing a damsel damage.

And now, it is the children who are out of control. For how can they contain their delight at seeing their own frisky selves mirrored in these gamboling lambs? They chase after them down the length of the field, crying out for them to stop. It takes a good ten minutes before parents have rounded them up. The exhausted ewe catches her breath at the bottom of the field where the woodline starts.

"She'll find her way home," Doug reassures everyone.

"Oh, Dad, can we get one, can we get one of those lambs?" Corey pleads.

The weariness on Doug's face, which he has noted on and off all afternoon, lifts like the balloons that still hover above the windless field. "If you live here, Corey, you can have a whole farm of them next door." Doug cocks his head at his daughter, then despite her disgusted shrug, he grabs hold of her and kisses the top of her head. "Give us a smile, lambkins."

If they were at St. John's, now would be the moment he nods to the usher to ring the second bell. Instead he lifts his robed arms in a gesture he realizes, too late, is theatrically biblical. "Friends and family," he says, "we have a ceremony to perform."

"Right oh," one of the elegant uncles says, throwing his arm around Doug.

He leads them up the hillside toward the deserted hickory grove, aunts and cousins, his own parishoners, the therapy group, the sisters, the two old men, Doug's parents—his flock now, each and every one of them.

—But no, wait. Up on top of the hill, someone is standing by the folding chairs and hay bales, an angel in a silver tunic sent to the poor shepherds to say, "Do not be afraid. Sing a joyful song to the Lord. You are all His people."

But then the angel comes forward a few steps, and the word becomes flesh, Yolanda García!

As he watches her gazing down at them advancing up the hillside, he has an uneasy feeling that she might bolt like the ewe into the thicket on the other side of the road. He closes his eyes for a moment and when he opens them, she is still there, lifting her hand in welcome as if she has been waiting all her life for them to gather together here.

The night watchman

The notice arrived in the hands of the dwarf boy who came up on a mule to José's fields on a day so hot José had taken the late morning as well as the afternoon off. "What does it say?" José asked, unfolding the sheet he had already carefully removed from the envelope after washing his hands.

The boy shrugged. "Don Felipe said it was bad news, that is all I know."

"Coño, muchacho," he warned, swinging at the boy. But it was the mayor Felipe who deserved a cuff for sending a boy like this up into the mountains, bringing bad luck to the yucca plants.

José unfolded the notice again and narrowed his eyes, concentrating. Somehow it seemed that if he looked at the paper intently enough, the meaning would communicate itself to him. But all he saw were the neat, furrow-like rows of print, and an insignia on top with the flag. This would have to be a government notice.

His mujer came to the hut's entrance and peered out, squinting.

"I have to go down to the village," he spoke calmly. Xiomara was carrying his seventh and it would not do to get her agitated and end up with a monstrosity like this dwarf for a child. Not that José wanted or needed another mouth with seven other children, including Xiomara's nephew, and her mother and father to feed.

He called out to his oldest to saddle the mule. At first, the boy did not move from where he lay under the ceiba tree, numbed by the heat. But as soon as José made the motion of standing, the boy was on his feet and running away to the field behind the hut where the mule had been let to graze.

Down in the village the bad day got worse. Felipe explained that the notice had gone out to all campesinos on the south side of the mountain who were squatting on government lands: the fields were to be flooded when the dam being built north of here was completed. Inhabitants must be evacuated by the end of the year.

"What is a man to do?" José asked in his quiet voice. When he was younger, some of the men in the village had called him pajaro for talking in a woman's voice. But he had suspected it was more than his voice that bothered them. José could turn any woman's head, a fact he had known since he was a boy of twelve and Doña Teolinda had asked him to undo the hook on her brassiere and then do the work of the brassiere himself. "I have ten mouths to feed. We cannot live on nada."

"There might be an opening for the postman job if Guerrero doesn't get any better. But . . ." Felipe looked straight at José as if trying to decide something about him. Perhaps he was still not sure whether José had come down the mountain for added news or because he could not read the letter at all. "But the postman job would require knowing your letters."

"Is there other work?" José said by way of an answer.

"I hear talk"—Felipe shrugged as if not responsible for the rumor he had heard—"that a relation of Don Mundín's has come to the house again this summer. She might need a gardener, a night watchman."

"I need work for longer than the summer—" José began.

"I understand," Felipe nodded. "But you talk to her, you get a job, and maybe she is satisfied and talks to Don Mundín and they take you down to the capital to work on their gardens there."

The prospect sent a jolt of excitement through José even in the midst of the bad news he had just received. Coming down the mountain it had entered his mind again, the possibility of getting his papers and going to work in the States. The old people on the northside farm, the Silvestres, had two grown sons, both of whom had made it to Miami in rowboats, without papers, and gone on to work in factorías and restaurantes, marrying portorriqueñas and getting their papers. Every month, they sent home money, so that the old people had a small generator that ran a television, a radio, even a cookstove like the rich people down the mountain.

"Go talk with this woman," Felipe urged. "Tell her your predicament. You know how women are."

Yes, José agreed, though it had been a long time since he had known a woman besides Xiomara. The slave life he led didn't allow him the time or the money for such distractions. Looking down at his callused hands—the dirt packed under the nails, the battered thumb he had smashed in the cane grinder years back— it was hard to imagine them doing anything else besides working the soil his grandfather and father had worked before him. What other talents did they have? Briefly, he recalled his young hands, softer, cleaner, still untried, working Doña Teolinda's pale breasts. "Yes," she kept saying as he touched where she told him, "yes, that's just right."

At the big house he explained to Sergio, the short, muscled caretaker whose mouth was rich with gold fillings, why he was here. His farm was being repossessed the first of the year, and he

would need a job by then. But if he could find work now, he
could manage this last harvest at the farm what with three big
enough sons—

"It is not up to me." Sergio held up a hand to stop his flood of
reasons.

"Is there a need?" José asked in his small voice that always
pacified men like Sergio or Felipe. It made them feel, José understood, that their self-importance was being recognized. "Perhaps
there is something I can do?"

Sergio shrugged. He did not know of anything that needed
doing. José could see that the caretaker was looking him over as
if he, José, were a lower class of human being. He had not
changed from his work clothes, and the shoes he had brought for
show were still in the paper bag he carried with a cold plátano-
con-queso-frito wrapped in a plantain leaf in case hunger caught
him on the road. Sergio seemed to have forgotten, along with the
Sandovals and Montenegros, the Lopezes and Varelas, that they
themselves had come down to town from dirt-poor farms up in
those mountains.

A handsome woman appeared at the back door, a bunch of
keys in her hand. José had passed her several times in town, and
like most women she had gazed upon him admiringly. Now she
nodded a warm saludo.

"My wife, she is in charge of the house," Sergio said by way of
introduction. "And my sister does the cooking. Porfirio, her husband, he helps me with the gardens. So, you see, everything is
taken care of." Sergio lifted his hands helplessly. He turned to his
wife and explained the situation in a way that was already concluded: José wanted a job, but there was no job to be had.

"He should talk to the lady," the woman said when her husband had finished.

"And bother her when she has just arrived?" Sergio said with temper in his voice.

They were speaking of him as if he were not there, so José walked off a little ways in deference to them. As he stood waiting, he lifted his eyes to the largeness of the house. Up on a second-story balcony a lady was looking down on their gathering. Her face was painted up so that she looked like someone on the television the old people had showed him, a face watched by many people. "¿Qué hay?" she called down. But it was not for him, José, to say what was up.

"Can we help you with something, doña?" Sergio called up. His face had changed—instead of the harshness of someone in charge, it was now full of concern and smiles.

"No, nothing." The lady pointed. "But him, what does he want?"

Sergio waved in dismissal. Nothing for her to worry about. "I will take care of it."

"I want a job," José called up, this was his chance. "I have ten mouths to feed." Though his was a quiet voice, the lady heard every word of it, for the next thing he knew, she was saying, "I'll be right down."

And down she came, a noodle-thin lady. Poorly fed you might guess, but she looked bright and frisky like someone with a full stomach and more of what she liked stored in a locked closet. She was looking him over, but not like Sergio's wife or the other women in town, not with the interest of a woman looking at a man, but as if she were taking his picture with her eyes.

"What can you do?" she asked him.

Without meaning to, his eyes strayed to her small breasts. Surely she had not given suck to a child, as small and high as they were for a woman who looked to be in her ripe years. When he caught himself looking in the wrong place, he glanced down.

He could feel her own eyes, following his gaze to his bare feet. And maybe that more than anything is what won her heart—for when he said he could do anything at all she wanted, she said, "We'll find something for you to do, right, Sergio?"

"You're the one who knows," Sergio conceded.

That very night José began his job as the night watchman at the big house, eating the plátano Xiomara had packed for him as well as a plate of arroz con habichuelas Sergio's wife María left him for his late supper. The next morning he appeared at his hut, his eyes heavy with sleep, but his heart light with the good news that a lady at the big house had hired him. He was to be paid more money in a week than he had earned in a month farming this maldita tierra.

It was the first time José had cursed the land his father and his grandfather before him had farmed. Xiomara made the sign of the cross, and then placed her hands on the roundness of her belly to ward off the evil eye.

From the first, the lady intrigued José. She was supposed to be Don Mundín's relation, but what that relation was, no one was sure. It was said she came summers to work in privacy, but no one had seen what private thing it was she was doing except sitting at a table upstairs looking at the mountains.

Soon José knew her full story, for the staff was only too eager to inform him. They had known her since she first started coming eight summers ago. She was so easy and kind that María, who had left the house after her son had drowned in the pool out back, would return to work whenever the lady came down. Recently, she had married a husband, un americano, but it was well known that they were not good at satisfying their women. There was the added proof that she would not be having any children—or so she had told María, who told Sergio, who had the habit of sitting with the watchman and reporting the day's happenings before going home at night. Now that the lady had shown a liking for José, Sergio's attitude towards the hick farmer had changed significantly.

"You will not guess why she cannot have children?"

"She is too old," José guessed, although he had assessed that she had six or seven years before the change would come over her.

Sergio shook his head importantly, his eyes closing with the pleasure of knowing the answer. "The husband had himself fixed years back de propósito." On purpose.

"No, no, no." The two men shook their heads in disbelief.

"Like a steer," José added. It pained him to think of it. "Do they cut the thing off or—how do they do it?"

Sergio slapped José on the arm and almost fell off his chair shaking with laughter. José smiled so as not to spoil the care-taker's fun, but the truth was that he took no pleasure thinking on the suffering of another man.

Surely that was why the lady had come to the mountains alone this summer: to recover from the grief of a husband missing a vital part. But then, why had she let him do it? According to María, the husband was already fixed up by the time the doña met him. Then why marry him? José had wondered. But the lady had not explained this to María although it seemed she had shared most of her private business as if María were a friend, not a servant.

For days afterwards, José could not get the castrated husband out of his head. He had not spoken about the matter to Xiomara, afraid of its effect on the son in her belly—and he knew it would be a son by the way she carried him low in the cradle of her hips unlike the high-riding girls. Rather a dwarf boy with everything intact than a normal-looking one with his manhood missing. He tried to put the matter out of his own mind because it offended him to think of a man coming to this eventuality.

But when the lady wandered into the yard one night, looking for company, the maimed husband was the first thing that came to José's mind. She asked him to please sit down and continue his supper, and then, though she said she would be getting on, she herself sat down on the stone bench and began to question him. What was that smell in the air? It seemed to be coming from that bush over there. Did he know what it was called?

In the backyard floodlights that Sergio had instructed him to keep on all night, José made out the small, twining bush. "We just call it the bush with the strong scent at night, doña," he told her, because the other name for it was not something one could say to a woman of her class.

"Doña!" She wagged her finger playfully at him. "Now, José, I've asked you all not to call me that. Why can't you just call me Yolanda?"

He kept quiet, not knowing what to say. She had corrected him several times, but her bare name did not seem respectful enough. Finally, he recalled what Sergio always said when the lady made her unusual request. "You're the one who knows—"

"If one more person tells me I'm the one who knows, I'm going to scream!" she threatened, fisting her hands. The silver bangles on her arms clanged prettily like coins in a pocket. For a moment he worried that the lady would become hysterical, but her face seemed only to be pretending to anger like the faces in the old people's television. Then, as suddenly as she had scowled at him, she flashed him a bright smile. Maybe she was a little touched—these quick shifts of emotion. "Say after me, Yolanda," she requested.

"Yolanda," he said in his small voice.

"Louder," she ordered. Each time he said it a little louder—for it was not his habit to allow his voice to go much louder—she laughed as if it were a trick he were delighting her by performing. José found himself enjoying making the lady laugh as if he were giving her pleasure even if it was of a different kind from the pleasure he had given Doña Teolinda years back. But then again he could not recall Doña Teolinda ever asking him to call her by her Christian name as this little lady had.

Nightly now she came outside and visited with him, talking for hours, asking him what he thought of this and that. It seemed suddenly that one could have an opinion about everything and anything on God's green earth and even outside it. When he looked at the stars, did he see shapes or did he just see stars? Did he believe in God and who did he think God was, anyhow? What would he do if he had a million dollars? Did he believe, and tell the truth now, that men and women were equal? Did he think that what the country needed was a democracy—and painstakingly she explained what that was—or some version of socialism like they had over in Cuba? She had to explain that as well.

In the mornings, as he rode the mule up the mountain, his head spun with the many things that he had worked over the night before. It was like a drug, this thinking, affecting you in ways that made you not yourself. Or maybe this was who he really was, he pondered. At the door of the hut, Xiomara greeted him, each day looking bigger than she had ever looked. Or maybe now that he was so used to looking upon the little woman, it was his pregnant wife who seemed distorted.

"How is she treating you?" Xiomara asked him one morning.

"She is making me feel like a man," he replied, without thinking. But as soon as he had spoken, he saw splayed on her features that flash of woman's jealousy. "Ay, coño, not that, mujer," he scowled in disbelief. "She asks for my opinion and we discuss things."

But over the next few days as he prepared to go down the mountain for the night, he was aware that he was taking special care to dress in a clean shirt, to run his damp fingers through his hair and tamp it down, to polish his one pair of shoes and then, upon arriving at the gate, to dismount the mule and put them on so that he would arrive fully dressed in case the lady was still outside, walking in the garden. Perhaps Xiomara's jealousy was not so far off the mark. It was a kind of entering and knowing a woman, even if you were at the other end, inside her head instead of between her legs. And the truth was that he, José, knew more what the lady thought about any number of things than he knew what Xiomara thought about a handful of things—but then again, he and his mujer were not in the habit of wasting talk. Except in love making. Then, he would whisper the palabritas Xiomara liked to hear that would make her open to him. With this lady, all he had to say was her name, pure and simple, Yolanda, and she smiled warmly back at him.

But still it bothered him that her husband was castrated. She never brought it up, and observing her closely, he could not see that she was especially morose or that she clung to him with her eyes in that needy way of an unsatisfied woman. But she did pore over Elena's girls and chase Sergio's youngest boy around the yard with a water gun as if she were a child herself. That was how her hunger showed, José decided. She was starved for the child her husband could not give her.

One night after hearing her speak at length about Elena's girls, he blurted out the question he had been meaning to ask her. She, who was so good with children, would she not want one of her own?

Instead of the usual smile of pleasure at being asked a question she could talk about, her face became serious. "Why?" she asked him, and before he could answer her, she went on, "Do you know of someone?"

He did not quite know what her meaning was. "Someone to . . . give you one?" he hesitated. What would Don Mundín say about one of his relations coming up to the mountains to go behind the palms with one of his workmen?

"Yes," she nodded, "I've been wanting to adopt. But my husband, he's not so sold on the idea. Still, I'm sure if I found a baby who needed a home, my husband would reconsider."

José nodded, finally understanding. She wanted a child to raise, the way Xiomara was raising her dead brother's boy, the way that Consuelo had taken in her daughter Ruth's mistake. What a lucky child that would be, raised by this lady and her husband, living allá in the land of money with every convenience and nice clothes and a mind sharp and alert like this lady's. Now José could see why the lady was here for the summer. "So, you have come to find a child."

"No, no." She was shaking her head, smiling again as if the cloud had passed that had made her face so long and sad. "I'm working on a new book, writing, you know."

He nodded, though no, he did not know. But he did not want to tell her so. Just as having no children and a husband who could not pleasure her might be her shame, not knowing his letters was his.

"But if I found a child . . ." She closed her eyes and breathed in like a lady he had seen on television smelling her sheets. "A child who needs a home . . ."

He spoke before she had even finished, before he himself had thought through what he was promising. "I know of a child," he said in his quiet voice.

She reached out and touched his arm. "Ay, José, do you really?" She was looking at him with such naked need, as if she were no longer the mistress of the house, but a woman, like other women, wanting something from him.

"A man should be proud to please a woman like you," he began, testing to see if she would say something about her need for a man that was not being satisfied. When she remained quiet, he understood that he had stumbled upon some border she was not ready to cross. "I mean no disrespect," he added. And then to get her talking again, he asked about the work that she was doing. What was it exactly she was writing?

As if he had unstoppered a bottle, the words flowed out of her mouth. She was a writer of novels, stories, essays, and her favorite, poems. Did he know what they were? He shook his head no. Quickly, in one of those sudden shifts of mood, she stood up and recited something she called a poem she had known when she was a child. The same soft look was on her face as when she talked about Elena's girls or Sergio's two boys. "That is very pretty," he agreed. He was surprised to see her suddenly look away with color in her cheeks as if it were she, not the poem, he had complimented.

They spoke a while longer about her work. But before turning in that night, she again brought up the other matter. "Let me know, José, about that child."

"I will see what I can do," he said, looking away. He did not want her to see the worry that had entered his head—he had promised her a child, but of course, he could not give away his son without first asking Xiomara.

José had never seen Xiomara as furious as she was the following morning when he made his suggestion.

"¡Azaroso! ¡Hijo de la gran puta! What do you think a child is, something you can buy and sell—" She threw the slop bucket at him and wouldn't let him come in the hut, so that finally, in his exhaustion, he sent his oldest boy inside to get him the hammock to string up between the two samán trees by the river.

But even as he lay cooled by the breeze coming up from the river, he could not sleep. He was in a fix now for sure. His mujer had thrown a fit that would mark that child so that even if Xiomara could be convinced to give it up, the lady would not want it. And what a fool he was to even breathe the thought, *if Xiomara could be convinced*. Wasn't it obvious how women were worse than a hen with her chicks! It went beyond reason, really, because if Xiomara sat down and thought about it—as these last few weeks of being asked so many questions had trained José to sit down and think about things—Xiomara would see that this was an opportunity that did not come in a lifetime to most people. Their child could be raised with all the privileges and comforts of los ricos. Their child could receive an education and help his poor padres and brothers and sisters.

But there was another part José could not explain to Xiomara. He, José, would like to give this lady the pleasure her husband had not been able to give her: replacing her barrenness by placing his own flesh and blood in the cradle of her arms.

Through the weave of the hammock he saw that a visitor had arrived. Xiomara came out, a hand at her forehead, and motioned the dwarf on his mule to where José still lay resting by the side of the river. Just watching the dwarf riding up on the path made José uneasy. What bad news was the town sending up to him now?

But it was a message from the lady. "She says to forget what she spoke to you about. She says the whole thing is off." He shrugged as if to say—before he could be cuffed—that he did not know what the lady meant by such a remark.

José sat up. He was released from his predicament, but instead of relief, he felt a great disappointment. Already he had seen his boy driving a big car up the mountains to the farm he had purchased for his brothers and sisters.

"She sent you for this?" José asked the boy, who threw out his undersized chest proudly. His head was far too big for his narrow shoulders. But gazing upon him, José did not feel his usual disgust. His own son might turn out like this. He might as well accustom himself to looking upon a disproportioned thing.

"Pepito," he said after the boy had told him his name, "Pepito, let me ask you this. What would you do if you had a million dollars?"

The boy seemed stumped by the question. He sat on his mule, scratching his head and looking around him as if for a clue. But José did not have to think long what he would do with money like that. Lying here, gazing at the green rows of yucca plants, he had felt the hopelessness of his situation: he and Xiomara and his brood of children had nowhere to go once they left this land his father and his grandfather before him had farmed. Already he pictured the moving mountains of water released by the dam. By next year, this field he was standing on would be underwater. And the boy in Xiomara's womb would know nothing of this loss but turn his little head and smile at the sound of his mother's voice—whoever she was.

———

That evening when he arrived, the lady did not come out to greet him as she usually did. José watched and waited, curious as to what had caused the lady's sudden change of heart that could not wait until that night for their talk. When Sergio stopped in the yard for a cigarillo on his way home, José mentioned he had not seen the lady stirring in the garden.

"The doña is not herself tonight," Sergio agreed. "She was calling the husband this afternoon." Sergio had the full story from Miguel, the operator at the Codetel office. There had been a fight on the phone. The lady was raising her voice and crying. "Maybe the husband is getting sick and tired of this separation," Sergio suggested. "But you know how women are when you cross them."

"Yes," José agreed. After the dwarf had left, he had gone back to the hut and mentioned to Xiomara that the lady had sent word she did not want a child, after all. But this only made Xiomara angrier. What did he and this lady think? That money could buy the only thing the poor could have for free, their own children?

Later when Sergio and the others had left, José circled the house, craning his neck at the windows, hoping for a glimpse of the lady. Up in the tower room he could see a light was still burning. Finally, when it looked as if she would not be down at all, he entered the house and climbed the stairs, calling, "Doña," to formalize his coming into the living quarters without permission.

She stood at the top of the narrow stairs, looking down at him on the landing. "¿Qué hay, José?" she asked just as she had asked him the first day. But tonight she seemed a much older lady, tired and sad. "Did you get my message?"

José nodded. "There was no hurry."

"I just didn't want you to tell someone and then have me disappoint them." There was a pencil still in her hand, and her hair was gathered back as if she were focused on an important task, and even a lock of curl falling on her face would be a distraction. It was the way Xiomara bound her hair before she gave birth or beat the husks off the rice. "I hope you didn't go to any bother."

"No bother, no," he lied. For the next few days he would be sleeping in the hammock. Then Xiomara would begin to take him back. In a month, the lady would be gone, and by the end of the year the guardias would escort him off his land. Yes, there was a great deal of bother coming, he wanted to tell her. But what could she do about his flood of problemas? Already her husband had refused her own plans. She herself could not get what she wanted.

As he was turning to go down the stairs, the lady called him back. "Come up here a minute," she said, pushing the pencil into the gathering of her hair. From the front, it seemed as if the implement had been driven through the back of her skull. "I want you to see what I do."

The small tower room had large, open windows on all four sides. Had it been day, José could have looked out to the south to the plateau in the mountains where his own hut sat amid the plowed fields. The table set up under these windows was stacked with books, more than he had ever seen all at once. A lamp shone on the sheet of paper on which the lady had been writing.

"My books are all in English, or I'd give you one."

He said it straight out, what he had been ashamed to admit to her: "I could not read them. I do not know my letters."

She looked at him with a pained expression. It was the same expression he had noted on Xiomara's face when he first told her that the lady did not have any children. "You mean, you can't read?"

He bowed his head and caught sight of his worn red loafers. How could he have thought these shoes would make him feel like a big man?

"Sit down," she said, pulling up a chair she had emptied of her papers. "We're going to start with your name, José."

Every night she brought him up to the tower room or came down to the garden with her pad of yellow paper. First, she wrote down all the letters, so that he began to recognize some of them on signs in the village or on the boxes and cans of the bodega. Then she spelled now one, now another word, and left these sheets of paper for him to study the rest of the night and the days following. But though he tried to brand these marks on his brain, he had not made much headway by the time she was ready to leave in the middle of August. He still could not read the notice that he had stowed away in the hut under one of the eaves. He could not make out the sign in front of the post office that announced—so he was told—the death of Guerrerro. And when he brought the doña a small handful of soil from his farm for her to take back with her to the States in remembrance of her country, he could not read the sheet of paper she handed him.

"It's a poem I wrote you," she explained. "It's got my address on it. Write me when you can read it."

After she left, he was tempted to take it down to the village letter-writer, Paquita, or to show it to the wise María, but he did not want to share these words that the lady had given him. Even unknown, they were his only. And so he stuffed the letter together with the notice under the eaves of his hut. When his little girl was born, he named her Yolanda, because that and his own were the only two names he had learned to write by heart.

The third husband

The first week they are back, Doug has to brace himself. It has happened before so he knows that she will come back to their life here in New Hampshire, but slowly.

He can't tell her so, of course. Or all the little sticks will fall for him—an expression she has taught him from the island. Or he'll be accused of not wanting to listen to her pain—an expression she has picked up from therapists in this country.

Lordy lord. That's what they say in Kansas, where *he* is originally from.

The minute they are in the house all the spirit waters have to be changed before she can relax or even unpack her suitcase. Don't ask her why. At certain windows there are saucers filled with water, again don't ask her why. Two years ago he didn't know what spirit water was and he still doesn't know what it is because you can't ask her straight questions about it.

"That's not true," she'd say. "You *can* ask questions, but you're asking me so you can laugh at me."

"I'm not going to laugh at you," he promises. "I'm just curious."

But still she doesn't really say.

First time he encountered one of those saucers he thought maybe she'd forgotten her coffee saucer on the window sill. He took it and rinsed it out, and next thing he knows she's storming up to the bedroom with the saucer in her hand and her eyes flashing outrage.

"Did you wash this?!"

He'd been reading in bed, getting ready for an early turn-in, and a cuddle which is how he likes to suggest sex since women get so riled up if they think you just plain want to have sex. And there she stands acting as if he's some old Greek god who has eaten one of the children.

"Why, yes," he says, sitting up slowly, already thinking through what he might have done to that saucer he shouldn't have. "It was just a saucer left on the sill." He gestures in the direction of the easternmost window that looks out on the splendor of the mountains. It is the first window to catch the light at sunrise.

"Please, please," she says almost in tears, "don't ever touch my things."

"I never do," he says, glancing over at her bureau with its little jewelry tray and half dozen framed photographs of her whole crazy family.

"I don't mean my possessions." She is shaking her head. And that is when he gets his first lesson on how there have to be spirit waters in the new house and how she will be setting up "little things" he mustn't touch. And if he ever runs into something buried, please not to dig it up.

"You mean a body!" He lets his eyes go big and buggy, mugging some goofy kid he saw in *Our Gang* over forty years ago. She doesn't mean a body. She means power bundles, the remains of spells, mal ojos that need to be dispersed, and so on.

She is not a wannabe witch and she is not a leftover hippy. If you stand her pedigree right next to his, he should be fanning her with a palm leaf or carting stones up her pyramid. These superstitions—he mustn't call them that—are part of her island background, though to this day he has yet to hear one of her aristocratic old aunts talk about evil eyes or the spirits.

So every time they get back from the island—all this spirit paraphernalia has to be nailed down. Then, there's bound to be some homesickness, and then, finally—he really can't figure out what breaks it, she's out in the garden asking him what is this weed called, and why do you put cages on tomato plants, and oh Cuco, come and look at this amazing, amazing butterfly.

But the re-entry this time is surprisingly smooth. No big deal about the spirit waters or the lighting of candles before the gaudy Virgencita, and the regrets she voices are mild, and more in the order of wishing they could get better mangoes in New Hampshire. She seems to have forgotten the baby she wanted to adopt—just like that, calling him up, Couldn't she bring a baby back? No thanks, he'd told her over the phone, and he'd braced himself for months of hearing how sick for a child she was. But she seems really glad to be home, keeps humming "Home on the Range" and saying thank you, thank you, as she walks around the house revisiting each room. In fact, he is the one reminding her that those mango seeds she smuggled in should be started in water, that the little Baggie of dirt some campesino gave her for luck should be emptied in the garden, that the saucer of spirit water in his daughter's bedroom is empty and needs to be refilled.

She stands at the landing, a hand on her hip, grinning at him. "How do you know that's spirit water?"

He knows this: whatever he says will be enjoyed. Cuco, she calls him when she's in one of her good moods with him. An island endearment that means bogeyman. "I know it looks like the spirit water we almost got divorced over."

"Listen to that exaggeration. And I thought it was just us

Latins that exaggerated." She is addressing that imaginary Latino audience that moved into the house with her like an extended old world family.

"So, what's in Corey's bedroom?"

"Sweetening waters. Great for stepdaughters," she says, and prances up the stairs.

Lordy lord, he thinks, if Corey should ever know Yo is putting spells on her. She will be home sooner than Yo knows and that saucer better be out of there.

At the bedroom Yo is standing at the door blocking his way. Maybe now is the time to tell her.

"Hey, big boy." She is playing a secondhand Mae West. Most of Yo's imitations of certain period film stars are imitations of Doug's imitations since he's the one who grew up with television in this country. "Come up and see me sometime."

Corey flies from his mind. It's been a long, lonely summer.

Later, lolling in bed and sweet-talking, which is one of the things he missed most this summer, he tells her. Corey is coming to stay with them for two weeks before going on to her mother's.

He feels her stiffen beside him. "She was really excited when she called." Doug is going to pitch this one high and hopeful. "I think she is probably coming around."

"How so?" All the play has gone out of her voice. Corey has refused to stay with her father since he remarried two years ago although she also insists on having her own bedroom in the new house. She likes Yo, she says, but it's just hard for her to accept her father being with someone else. Yo hates to be referred to as someone else. "I have a name," she tells Doug when they're alone, and she rattles it off, "Yolanda María Teresa García de la Torre." But to Corey, she just says, "I understand how you feel."

"How so," she is pressing him. "How so is she coming around?"

"Well, she picked Spain to spend the whole summer, didn't she?"

"How is that supposed to be coming around?"

She is sitting up beside him in bed. Whatever he says now will be the wrong thing, that he knows for sure.

"You're Spanish and . . ."

"I'm not *Spanish*! I'm from the D.R. People in Spain would probably think of me as a . . . a savage." Her face looks savage. The dramatic, overdone expressions. Sometimes she is not so pretty.

"Stop exaggerating, Yo," he says and suddenly, he leaps out of bed. Later she will say she forgives him precisely because it was such a wonderfully spontaneous and unusual move for him. He grabs the sunrise saucer, and dumps it over her head.

Here comes Corey. Just turned sixteen, and trying to look the part of the sophisticated world traveler in her beret and vest. Oh, là là. "That's French, Dad," she tells him, head held high. But when they leave the crowd of other kids and their parents, he sees that scared look in her eyes. A needle in the heart to see it still there. He knows it has taken a leap of faith for her to venture so far from home, and now, to return and try the waters at her father's house. He remembers the nervous little girl, waking up with nightmares in the middle of the night. This was before there were any problems in the marriage, so you couldn't say—the way some therapists later did—that the kid was picking up the tension. But Yo has offered this explanation: maybe Corey has a clairvoyant streak and was seeing into the future, her father with someone else.

On the long drive north from the airport, they catch up. Her summer was awesome. Her Spanish mom and dad and sister and brother all made her feel a part of their family. "It's not like this country," Corey informs him. "People there still basically stay in their original families." There is a pointed silence. They pass a stretch of woods already beginning to turn—and it's only the end of August. "It's a Catholic country for the most part, that's why," Corey concludes, turning what would have been the barbed comment of six months ago into a lesson on culture. He is touched by her gracious little effort.

They've gone through every possible family topic and he's caught her up on all family members on his side, and she's talked about the trip her mother and stepfather made to Spain to visit her, but she still has not asked about Yo. "We just got back from the D.R. ourselves, you know?" Corey nods. "That's right, I told you on the phone. Yo was there most of the summer, writing. Let's see, what else," he says, "we're really happy you're going to be with us a few days. You and Yo can yak away in Spanish." The image is so farfetched that it almost makes him weepy, exposing as it does the raw hope. Yo has already told him that Spanish people and Dominican people don't even speak the same Spanish.

"She always says that the first few days of re-entry are the hardest. You're neither here nor there." He looks over at Corey, for she has not said a word. It can't be that after two years he still can't mention Yo or she'll pout. She is looking out her window, struggling with something on her face. When she turns to Doug, whatever it was has been replaced with a tentative smile. "I wouldn't call it hard," she offers. "It's now when you see things you missed before, you know?"

He has to agree with her, he says. He is so glad Yo isn't here or he would be turning himself into a human pretzel, saying, yes, it is the hardest time those first days, but oh isn't it wonderful how you see things in a new way.

———

By their third supper together, Doug has had enough of Spain and the D.R. Let's talk about China, he wants to say. Let's imagine the sunny grape arbors of central Anatolia.

"The weirdest thing happened today," Corey begins, and instantly Doug and Yo are too attentive, too grateful any time Corey joins in the conversation. "There was this collect phone call. It was a man from the D.R. José, he's a farmer or something?" She looks over at Yo, who says, "José!"

"He's going through a hard time," Corey continues. "He lost his job and he's being thrown off his land or something. He left a number. Says he'll be there tomorrow afternoon, to call him."

"Your Spanish is pretty good if you could get through all that!" Doug says because he doesn't know what to say. Who is this José character and what's he doing calling here collect with his troubles? "Do you know who this guy is?" he asks Yo.

"He was the night watchman at Mundín's house. Where I spent the summer up in the mountains writing. The village you and your dad went to," she adds for Corey's benefit.

"Well, after he was done telling me all about himself and what I should tell you and where you should call him and all"—there is that roll of the eyes Doug knows well, a sign of impatience she learned from her mother—"he asks me who I am, and I can't think of the word for stepdaughter—do you know what it is?" She turns suddenly to Yo.

Yo thinks a moment, and then shakes her head. "You know, I don't think I've ever heard it. People there don't usually get divorced, so all that vocabulary of melded families—I just never hear it."

"Like in Spain," Doug offers.

"Anyhow, I didn't know the word for stepdaughter so I just tell him I'm your daughter—" She says this without a hitch. There is a sunny moment in Doug's head. He imagines them all calling out goodnights like *The Waltons* before they turn in tonight.

"—And he starts asking me like am I married and how old I am and how nice of me to talk to him and how I have a good heart and he can tell I'm pretty by my voice—"

Yo and Doug are both shaking their heads in disbelief.

"—and finally, he just like right out asks me if I would marry him and bring him to the States!"

"What a guy!" Doug says. "Proposing to my daughter on my nickel."

Yo, too, is taken by surprise, a surprise in layers, she will tell Doug later. First surprise is that the guy would dare call her at all with such an enormous request. Then, that this same José might have had a little something going for her. And that *now* he's going after her stepdaughter over the phone.

"I told him I was too young to get married, and so he asks me how old I am, and I say sixteen, and he says that's old enough." Corey giggles.

"The man has no shame," Doug is saying.

"He sounded really, really nice!" Corey casts Doug a righteous look. She is at that age when all need and sorrow are little kittens. He better keep his mouth shut or he'll be cast in the role of the mean farmer with a sack wanting to drown the whole litter. He looks towards Yo hoping she'll throw her weight on his side, call this José a rascal, but no such luck.

"He *is* a nice man. Probably desperate. He's so poor." Yo recounts her visit to José's farm up in the mountains. The skinny naked kids, the sad hovel, the barefoot pregnant woman who would not come out to say hello. She and Corey are dewy-eyed with sympathy. "So you can see why people really want to get out."

"Like my little wife here," Doug jokes to lighten the mood. Both women blaze looks at him that could start a forest fire.

Yo is explaining to Corey how there is a whole phoney-marriage business now. You pay some American citizen to marry you because then she can "ask" for you and you can get your papers. Once you're here, you get a divorce. "People are paying up to three thousand bucks just to be married on paper."

"If they're that poor that they have to get out, where do they get three thousand dollars?" Corey wants to know.

"Corey, girl," Doug says to her, "that is a brilliant question." He can see the color heightening in her face, but after a moment's study, he knows it is not because she is pleased by his praise. He has embarrassed her. She thinks he is making fun of her. "It *is* a smart question," he stresses, "seriously."

"He didn't offer you money, did he?" Yo asks her.

"No." Corey shakes her head slowly at first, and then more vigorously. "He didn't mention money. Just said he would like to marry a girl who was so nice and spoke such pretty Spanish."

Lordy lord, Doug thinks, but this time he keeps his mouth shut.

The next day at supper there is a report from the soft underbelly—as Doug has started calling Yo and Corey for being too tenderhearted. The soft underbelly called the number José left, which was the number—Doug recognizes it—of the Codetel office in the mountain town where Yo spent the summer. José was not there.

"The guy who runs the Codetel office says José was there yesterday," Yo is explaining to Doug. Just beyond her through the big picture window, the mountains are picking up fall colors. But the sky is still that high-blue summer-evening sky that makes him want to lift up his arms in a corny, born-again Christian way. "But get this, the Codetel guy says José left for the capital this morning, saying he was going to the States."

"You suppose he's going to show up here?!" Corey is full of girlish excitement. Of course, if a weird man showed up at the house, Doug knows who'd have to answer the door and send the man packing, too.

Next supper, there's yet another progress report from Corey. A call this afternoon from the capital. It was José. Again Corey spoke to him since no one else was home. "He's coming to New York. He wants to know what to do once he lands here."

"What kind of a salary did you pay him this summer?" Doug asks Yo. "I mean a ticket costs a mint."

"Maybe he's borrowed some money from Mundín?" Yo is puzzled, too. "But he'll need a passport and papers, and he can't even read."

"Really?" Corey says, and in her eyes, Doug sees the flash of disappointment. She's been building up this fantasy of a gallant Spaniard who recites poetry by Lorca and has black, shiny, greased-back hair like a model in one of her teen magazines he likes to look at.

"Anyhow, I told him when he gets to New York, just to call us collect, and we'll figure out something."

Doug's mouth has dropped. "You told him what?!" And as he says it, he knows his tone is all wrong. That it is absolutely totally necessary for his daughter to maintain her dignity in front of Yo, and here he has made her feel like a fool in front of her stepmother. She runs out of the room in tears.

"Ay, Doug, why'd you do that for?" Now it's Yo, looking as if he has hurt *her*. And out she goes on Corey's heels, and a little later, tiptoeing to the landing on the stairs, he hears them both talking in those cooing voices of women behind closed doors. Well, thank God for that, he thinks, heading back downstairs. He has a mind to call this José character and tell him, sure, come on up to my house, cause scenes, bring us together as a dysfunctional family. Where did he learn this kind of vocabulary? All those years of marriage counseling, he guesses.

Two calls in as many days and Doug forbids Corey to accept any more collect phone calls from the D.R. She offers to pay for every last cent of those damn phone calls and for her braces and for her summer program and for ever even being born, okay?! There are shouts and raised voices. For, of course, one thing leads to another and soon Corey has opened up the Pandora's box of the failed marriage. Daily now there are scenes, the throats of doors ache from slamming. Yo confesses to Doug that for the first time she feels like she's the one from a buttoned-down, stiff-upper-lip family.

And she has a theory about what is going on. They're under a spell. And she has traced it, too. That soil José gave her! No wonder she was reluctant to bury it in her usual spot, finally letting Doug do it in his garden. Doug being the one who handled it, the spell falls mostly on him. And the one protection he might have had, she reminds him, the spirit water in Corey's room, he made Yo remove so there wouldn't be any problems with Corey.

When she is done explaining it all in such a rational, mapped-out way, Doug can't help but ask, "So what do I do?" as if for a minute, he believed it was true.

They are bound to José as long as those grains of soil are here, and so they must be removed from the property. Then they can act generously or judiciously, however they want to act, but it won't be out of spirit manipulation. "But I've already poured out the little bag!" Doug explains. "I can't pick out those grains. I can't even tell them apart."

"We'll shovel a great big circle into a bag and take it up to the mountains," Yo says.

"Okay, okay," he agrees. He is not going to tell her that he's already plowed under the garden. Those grains of soil are everywhere casting their little spells, making Corey hysterical half the time, spooking Yo, and just plain driving him crazy.

It's like they're Bonnie and Clyde planning a getaway, how they're going to dispose of this soil. It'd be easy enough if he could just take the garbage bag to the side of the road and dump it, but no, she wants it at a safe distance from the house. So, it's settled, when they're driving Corey to her mother's next Saturday, they'll take it along.

"You mean, dump it at her house?" Doug has this image of his ex-wife looking out the window and seeing him empty what she'll assume is his trash in her backyard. He smiles in spite of himself.

And there is a naughty look in Yo's eye, too. "I suppose we better not." She laughs. On the mountain they will be crossing to get over to the interstate, there is a little park, a bench or two, a Robert Frost plaque. That's where they'll dump the soil.

"Before or after we drop off Corey?"

It'll be dark on their way back. Not as easy to dispose of the bag. "Let's wait and see," Yo says. Doug can tell she is tempted to include Corey since the two of them, anyhow, have been having a good visit.

They will see, he supposes, how things go for the next three days. He knows very well the phone calls have not stopped, but Corey is now reporting them to Yo, not to Doug. She keeps aloof from him, treats him as if they are in a sitcom together, and she is acting the part of his child. Bright and polite, but if he tries to give her a hug, or put his arm around her, she dodges him. He stops trying. Yo accuses him of moping around and wasting this valuable time with Corey.

"It's not my fault your friend put a spell on me," Doug says, half joking.

Yo looks at him as if he is miles and miles away, and she is not sure she is hearing him correctly. "No one's put a spell on you," she says at last. She's changed her mind about the soil. Poor José wouldn't do such a thing. Corey has gotten the whole story in the last few phone calls. José lost his night watchman job. He is desperate and has gone on to the capital, hoping to find someone who will sponsor him to the States. Yo feels sorry for the guy. Maybe they can do something to help him out.

"You mean, marry him to Corey!"

"Oh, Doug, why are you so purposely thick-headed sometimes," Yo says in a teary voice. Now she's the one hurrying upstairs, wanting some quiet time, which is how some therapist taught her to say she is not talking to him. Instead of the human pretzel, he's turned into the big oaf in everybody's way.

Left downstairs by himself, Doug goes up to the window. It is a black slab, too dark now to look out at his garden—what he likes to do at moments like this. Somehow those straight brown furrows soothe him like the little farm plots seen from an airplane do. Instead, he sees his reflection, a much younger man, all dramatic shadows and planes. It is him years before anything has happened, Corey is a baby in his arms, his wife is making faces at her, he has planted their first garden. The moment is so perfect, it does seem madness or witchcraft to allow anything to threaten their happiness.

He hears the steps coming down the stairs, and then stopping at the door. He turns to find a surprised Corey frozen in mid-step. "I thought you'd gone to bed," she accuses him.

"No, that was Yo," he says, wanting to say so much else. But how does he ask his own child to forgive him for the unforgivable sin of falling out of love with her mother? He lingers a moment but seeing that she is waiting for him to leave so she can pour herself a soda—for even filling that small need in his presence is too much of a letting down her guard—he departs the room. "Buenas noches, Corey," he calls out from the stairs. After a long silence, he gets a grumpy, "Night." So much for *The Waltons*.

Saturday, while Yo and Corey are out shopping for the ingredients for a paella, which, it turns out, is eaten both in Spain and the D.R., the phone rings. There is a garbled, official, foreign-sounding voice on the other end. It is an operator asking Doug if he will accept charges.

At first, Doug is tempted to say, No! Tell this jerk to stop calling my house and causing trouble. But curiosity lures him on. "Sure," he says, "I mean okay, sí."

"Look here," he starts, but all he hears at first is himself echoed back, *look here*. He stops and in that silence, a man is speaking, asking for Doña Yolanda or la señorita Corey.

"No está," Doug says, and then he wants to say who he is, but he can't think of the word for husband. He does remember the word for father, though. "Soy padre de Corey."

The man says something rapid and grateful-sounding that Doug doesn't understand. It's time to lay down the law. "Corey no matrimonio." And furthermore, he adds, these calls are "muy expensivo. No llamar, correcto?"

There is a long silence. And then, like the air being let out of a tire, Doug hears, "Sí, sí, sí, sí . . ."

"No puedo salvar mundo," Doug adds, feeling guilty even as he says so. His whole childhood was full of Lone Ranger dreams of saving the world. Now he doesn't even want to accept the charges on an SOS call.

"Por favor," he says, and then, thinking he's sounding like he's waffling, he adds, "Policía," to put a punch into what he is saying. As he expected, José hangs up.

Back out in the garden where he is fertilizing, and pruning, and potting, and getting things ready for the first frosts, he hears a terrible sound, a cross between a human cry and the trumpets of those angels that are going to descend on the last day to sort out the good and bad souls like laundry. Looking up, he sees the sloppy V of geese headed south for the winter. And to them, since there is no else around, he finds himself apologizing.

A wonderful but punishing peace has descended on the house. Corey is back to being the daughter who used to sit on his knee and ask him why stars didn't fall off the sky like raindrops or snow. Yo is on a high. Corey is looking so pretty. Corey makes her feel better about not having her own child. Corey has really grown up so much. Far be it from Doug to suggest Corey still has some growing up to do.

"She's coming along. Like you said," Yo says, smiling fondly at him.

There are no more phone calls. The soft underbelly seems to have gone hard as nails—not a word about José. Just as there hasn't been another word about that island baby. Sometimes Doug has a feeling that these enthusiasms Yo picks up are momentary inspirations she eventually deletes from the rough draft of her life.

"I wonder why he hasn't called?" Doug dares to introduce the subject during their last dinner together. His guilt is making him talk like that guy with the albatross around his neck. "Maybe he got to stay on his farm, you think?"

Corey shrugs. She has gone on to new concerns; her school starts Monday, the day after she gets to her mother's. Her friends have found out she's back, and they've all been calling her. Perhaps, Doug thinks, José has tried to call but hasn't been able to get through.

"I bet Mundín gave him his job back." Yo called her cousin, explaining José's predicament. "Anyhow, there's nothing else we can do for him from so far away."

"What do you want to do about the soil?" he asks Yo that night. The problem of bad energy in the house seems to have been solved all by itself. Normally, he would take this occasion to point out to her that this business of spells and spirits is all a bunch of Dominican malarkey. See, things resolve themselves in their own good time. But he doesn't feel so righteous anymore. What does he know of the magic that connects people and tears them apart. It might as well be spirits.

Yo says she'd just as soon leave the soil here.

But he has already packed it up like she said. Is she sure she isn't going to want him to dig it all up again when the next disagreeable thing happens?

"Sounds like you want that soil out of here," she teases.

To tell the truth he does want that soil out of here—even though he knows damn well José's soil is plowed throughout the garden. But this dark plastic bag has come to represent all his troubles here these last two weeks, all the fury pent up in his child, all the loneliness of missing Yo for two months, all his anger at the country that keeps claiming her and taking her away from him, which is why, he knows it now and without the help of a therapist, thank you, why he was so angry at the intrusions of José's calls.

He says, no, if it's okay with her, it's okay with him to leave the soil here. . . . But the next morning, he packs the bag in the trunk and hurls it into the dumpster behind the hospital. There, a few years ago, a newborn baby was found, bawling, wrapped in those brown paper towels of public restrooms. It was traced to a young girl who was so terrified her parents would find out she wasn't a virgin, she opted for murderer instead.

But that baby survived, Doug is thinking as he stands by the dumpster. Sometimes the grandparents bring him into Doug's office, and the little boy is a sunrise of smiles and cooperation. There isn't a mark that Doug can see with the naked eye or with any of his instruments—not a mark on him of his horrible arrival on this planet.

And that is what Doug is hoping as he stands by the dumpster—for the deposit seems to draw something from him, a prayer, a wish, a goodbye. Maybe Corey will be all right after all. Por favor, Corey, felicidad.

On the ride down they make plans with Corey. She will come to visit them during her fall break. She'll spend Thanksgiving with her mom, since over Christmas she and Doug and Yo are already planning this wonderful trip to the Dominican Republic.

"It'd be so awesome after being in Spain!" Corey has pulled herself up so her arms rest on the back of the front seat. It is the way Doug remembers her during car trips as a child. She'd stand on the back seat and lean forward into the front seat, wanting to be a part of everything going on.

"You'll meet my whole crazy family," Yo is saying. "Maybe Mundín will let me borrow his mountain house again."

"I'll get to meet José," Corey offers. They are telling this story together, the story of the Christmas trip to the island.

"I'd like to meet José," Doug says, and both women look at him as if not sure he is being facetious.

"Really, Dad?" Corey has thrust her head even further into the front. If he turns to her now, he could probably plant a kiss on her cheek.

"Sure, I've been thinking maybe we should buy some land there. Maybe José would like to farm it for us. For a salary," he adds, "a good salary."

The soft underbelly is happy. They like the ending he has given their story.

All fall Doug jumps a little whenever the phone rings. Often it is Corey calling to find out how you guys are doing, reporting that she has already gotten a two-piece on sale and a pretty terrific sundress that makes her look skinny. Yo's spirit waters have gone to seed, if that is a proper term for them, who knows. The saucers sit empty at their windows and one day when Doug looks for them, they are gone. "The house is pretty well protected now," Yo explains when he asks after them. It's odd how he finds himself missing them.

When the frost hits, the garden wears a silver coat, which by midday the sunshine melts. The leaves fall every which way, a beautiful mess, leaving the hillsides bare and skeletal and scary. The soil hardens, and the land braces itself for winter, all browns and grays, a clenched look. Doug misses the garden most these months, before he can begin to plan the next garden in February, sorting his seeds, paging through a stack of catalogues. Fall is when he starts watching TV and cooking and wondering where his life is going. This year, he daydreams, a kind of mind travel, as if he has another simultaneous life going on long distance.

He is on the island on a mountain farm in an upper field by a roaring river. They are planting the yucca in long even rows. He is helping another man whose face he does not see, or maybe the other man is helping him. When Yo hands him his soup dish at dinner, they have almost gotten the whole southwest corner finished. "Where are you?" she wants to know.

He is not one to think of fanciful ways to say things so he surprises himself when he answers her, "Everywhere you are."

The stalker

All I have to do is look into your bookjacket eyes and I can see all the way back

to that roadside quickstop in western mass where you are wearing a pea green uniform and hairnet and grilling burgers and dogs and dipping fries in their wire basket and I am touching myself as I can see through the pea green fabric to the dark panties

and afterwards walking out and looking up I see the stars shift into a connect-the-dots spelling of your name which I do not even know is your name yet—yolanda garcía—the whole name down to the little accent over the i

which tell me was not a sign .

which is why I was not surprised in the reading room when your face stared back at me from today's SUN TIMES with the announcement that you are going to be at a bookstore on michigan avenue at eight tonight reading from a new book which I have not seen though all others are already in my possession

I call the bookstore. I say, I want to go to the reading tonight, do I need a ticket, how early should I come and how long will it last and is there parking nearby—all these busywork questions before I slip in the one I want an answer to

is there any way I can get a hold of ms. garcía as I am an old friend of hers whom she would like to hear from I am sure

—there is a hesitancy on the other end

—a catch of the breath with which I am familiar as I seem to incite this kind of reaction in females

of a certain age and intelligence and looks which in this instance I cannot verify as I cannot see this clerk but I would guess she is a petite brunette with a turned-up nose and a cute look she is trying to fight with eyeliner and all-black loose-fitting clothes

so I am not surprised to hear her recite the expected I'm sorry but we are not allowed to give out this kind of information but there will be an opportunity after the reading to talk to the author

so I say, of course, how can you give out this kind of information as you don't know me from auden and for all you know I could be an ex or an axe murderer or an ex axe murderer (hahaha) but she does not laugh just listens real hard like she might be trying to make out some telltale background sound that she can later tell the police about so they can trace where I might be calling from

Let them come down michigan and on down the long avenue of the years over the need the fear the loneliness the pain on the train out to elgin to the brick two-story, THE BRIDGE OVER TROUBLED WATERS, says the sign, flashing their badges at mark who leads them upstairs

to my room where they knock and the nicer-looking one says, excuse me but we are trying to find a certain walt whitman, without blinking an eye, without thinking but this name has already been taken up by a famous poet of the nineteenth century

saying instead, yep, walt whitman—at least that's the name he has been going by for the last five years and before that it was

billy yeats, and before that george herbert, gerry hopkins, wally
stevens

(as if you might listen if I were one of your resurrected heroes)

and I say, come in, and they step into the life of the boy with
the pouring problem who at five is rushed to mass general
unconscious from a rubber-hose beating

because, she says, this boy is out of control I give him the box
of frosted flakes and the bowl and he keeps pouring until the
whole box is empty and there are flakes all over the floor the
same thing with the carton of milk until it is running off the sides
of the table the half-gallon wasted the talcum powder, too, the
entire ammens container sprinkled over himself and everything
else

and he knows better but does it to get at me and that is why I
have to take my hand to him for you have to understand he is not
right in the head since the day he was born the spitting image of
his father who has never seen his son's face unless maybe by
some weird coincidence he spots a dark pretty boy on the street
in a bus riding up an escalator and thinks that little guy sure
looks like me

she says all this to the doctors and they put it down in their
records and put me where she can't get at me for a few years

until I am a boy without a pouring problem on my first weekend with my mother

doing unto her cat her miniskirts her panties her makeup as
she has done unto me

which sin I repent me of which sin I have confessed time and
time again to the state employed and underemployed the coun-
selors the therapists the social workers the officers the chaplain
the advocate the psychiatrists and even to mark—all of them
paid ears and not the one person I want to hear me out

and say, it wears a human face
yes, it wears a human face

I leave the house, telling mark, I'm off to my shelving job at chicago u. and, yes sir, I'll be back by the nine o'clock curfew maybe even before

my shopping bag filled with your books which I have dismembered and reassembled so that not one page is the way you wrote it, sentences spliced into different stories and the list of your thank you's in back mixed in with your iambic pentameters and your eyes popping up in the white margins, every word tampered with until

you sound like the babelite you are, writing your gibberish and pretending there is any word of truth to it

and for snacks, a pack of lorna doones ah yes lorna doones and the state-owned boarding school and the hall of cots and the late night visits of our rough-voiced big-handed monitor with the pack of lorna doones

and a bar of monterey jack for the one bright spot of rosemarie who brought one back every time her papa took her out

and my hunting knife that folds into itself, cute as a boy's toy, in the bag

Looking for where you might be staying

walking round and round the glassy storefront where the cute bookstore brunette (I can see her now) scans with her magic wand the books someone has piled on her counter

pass three cappuccino bars two bagel shops a card store a small cafe called cachet and count five little boutique dress shops two shoe stores a deli with sausage links like nooses for sale in the window and four parking garages like the little gal on the phone said there would be

sharp wind blows off the lake
a snowflake and another snowflake no two alike so they say
going further and further out
and I am in luck as I find the big westin where you might be
staying about twelve blocks away from where x marks the spot

It is easier than I think
I go up to the desk and say, I am a reporter from the SUN TIMES
here to interview the author yolanda garcía

this black spic, a spic and spade (hahaha) with a little name
tag saying he's mr. martinez like I can't tell looking at his brown
face and the pencil-thin mustache above his fat lips

doesn't blink an eye but types you up in his computer and
BINGO! he is on the phone saying the interviewer from the SUN
TIMES is here

and I hear your surprised little voice saying, who?
and the guy puts me on, shrugging, she wants to talk to you
straightening up my voice, saying oh-so-politely, sorry to
bother you, ms. garcía, but my secretary set this up with your
publisher so I'm sorry to hear you didn't get word and I sure do
hope you can squeeze me in as we've planned a big feature article
for sunday with color photos and we think this will sell lots and
lots of your wonderful books

wow, you say, impressed, but see, nobody told me, in fact, my
publicist purposely left the afternoon free so I could visit with my
sister who came all the way down from rockford just to see me—

unless—and your hand is over the speaker and your voice all
garbled—and then you're back on saying unless you don't mind
interviewing me with her in the room

and now it's my turn to hesitate and wonder can I carry it off and
sure enough I feel an extra rush to think there will be two of you

no problem, I say, and then you say the room number

———

Which at first I think is your joke on me, having figured out who I am, and no way are you going to be in room 911—the call-for-help number—the number you dialed the night I sat outside your door at the top of the stairs, knowing you had no other way out as the fire escape was only built later after the fire

which was ruled arson and which they tried also to pin on me sitting there crying and begging you to let me in

and you were screaming on the other side of the door, get away from me, leave me alone, I don't want to have anything to do with you, you scare the hell out of me with all your crazy letters and your following me around and going through my trash and picking out things and appearing on my doorstep with your crazy talk that I am your other, your soulmate, your doppelgänger, I am not, I am not, I am not, do you hear me, I swear, billy or george or gerry or whatever your name is, if you don't leave this minute as much as I hate calling the pigs on anyone I will dial 911 and you are going to be in hot water as I'm sure you've got a record trailing you from somewhere

and I pleaded saying, please just open the door and let me in for five minutes you can time it and throw me out when my time's up but I need you, I need you, I need you to hear me tell you what I've been through

and this fat lady with a knocked-around face came out from downstairs saying, you gotta leave her alone if she don't want to talk to you

and I could hear your voice on the phone saying, there is a man out there who has barricaded me into my apartment, who has been following me around for fifteen years on and off

and no, officer, no

and I could hear your thoughts in your head thinking, *I know how you guys think if you get raped you must have cockteased the guy, if you get mugged you must have provoked the guy, if you get stalked you must have put out your pretty hooks, but no, I have never slept with him, never talked with him more than five minutes that night fifteen years ago when he walked into the damn quickstop where I was working and told me he had no money but was hungry so I made him an angel on horseback which was a hot dog sliced down the middle with melted cheese inside and bacon wound around the whole dog and I don't know who named it that or why cause why would an angel with wings need a horse but see even this detail of what he was fed whose naming I had nothing to do with he read as a sign—and the only time I can think that I talked to him for more than five minutes besides that first meeting was at a bar where this guy I was married to and I were having a fight and so when this crazy guy sat down on my other side I just let him go on and on about how a force had sent him to be with me*

    and other crazy things like that, and I admit, okay, I admit that I let this crazy guy go on so my husband would see how somebody could go mad with love over me

    but I never ever again capitalized on his madness, I swear

and I could hear your voice on the phone saying, can't you hear him, officer, yes that's him pounding on the door and shouting I have to let him in

so please, oh please, send someone down to 20 high street, a big gray two-story building with a falling-down porch up front where you've been before when the guy downstairs went berserk when he found his clothes in the yard but I'm the apartment on the second floor with the narrow staircase coming up to my door and that's where he's been for the last hour, so I can't get out, but please you or someone else stay on the line with me while you get down here as I'm terrified because now he is throwing his whole body against the door and what if it breaks and he gets his hands on me?

———

get off on the eighth floor as I don't want you waiting at the elevator then quick running down the hall and locking yourself and your sister in

a little maybe vietnamese maybe korean girl with her cleaning cart parked in the hall next to an open door nods and goes back into a room with the tv blaring a soap

from room to room she watches the world turn and fall apart

pretty little gal with her long hair pulled back in a black ponytail which makes me want to take all the doll bottles of her shampoo and pour them out in a tub and turn the faucet on full blast and climb into that steaming fragrant soapy water and have her rub me good and hard and should the hunting knife slip out of my bag and she jump back alarmed, I'd say, do not be afraid as evil is always a choice and you know what waylays it and allays it and as a matter of fact slays it

take a guess

and maybe she doesn't know much english because she looks at me funny as she comes out of the room and sees me standing here perusing her little soaps and clean face towels and phone message pads and ballpoint pens—maybe she doesn't understand my english

but still in her own funny tongue she knows the answer she knows what holds the darkness she brought with her to this country from the killing fields of vietnam or salvador or korea or wherever she left behind a village burnt down, the men begging pleading oh please in the name of god allah jesus christ buddha coca-cola the shouts the screams the naked kids running around with worms coming out of their behinds—

she knows that even here hundreds of thousands of miles away that evil will break down her door and burst into her head and make itself right at home—unless she tells someone she loves or could love what she has been through—

but now she is looking at me with a hesistant catch-of-the-breath not-so-sure smile so I take up one of her pens and jot down the BRIDGE OVER TROUBLED WATERS number saying, any time you want to talk—

but already she is backing into the room, shaking her head, saying, no english, mister, and that scared look in her eyes I can never get through

so I head for the exit door and climb up the one flight of stairs to you

I knock and you open and before I get out hello I'm the reporter from the SUN TIMES I see the same scared vietnamese-girl look in your eyes and you try to shut the door on my face, but I'm already inside

slipping the bolt locking you in a neck hold and yelling at your sister who has sprung to the phone

you touch that and she gets hurt

so your sister throws up her hands and says, no, no, no, no, look I'm not calling anybody but please don't hurt her just take our money and even my wedding ring and this pendant my husband gave me for our twentieth anniversary which should be worth lots as he is still paying on it

I loosen my hold and you are touching your neck and coughing with your back to me and I give you a little nudge and say very gently, why don't you go sit on the bed there next to your sister

and you do as you are told, the two of you side by side holding hands on that flowered bedspread that matches the drapes the two paintings the lavender carpet—a room not unlike rooms

I have known in institutions I have known where anyone can
briefly live a businessman a poet a woman who will be operated
on for cancer after her test results are in a woman who has beaten
her child a woman waiting for a lover

a woman calming her weeping sister saying, it's okay, don't
worry, really, he's somebody I know from the past, who will not
hurt us

but your voice trembly over the last statement as if you are not
so sure

Your face older, thinner, marked with lines where before it was a
smooth moon pulling and pulling at the tides of my deep need
for you

and your hair short now and wild with curls and speckled
with gray instead of the long thick rope of your braid I tried to
cut off with a pair of scissors after the first restraining order after
the fire after the time in brookhaven

and your hands bony and troubled and your shoulders thin
and wingless

feeling cheated to have you before me but not have you before
me as I would want you before me a worn-out woman a soulmate
become mortal

I sit down opposite you on the other queen-bee bed

I take off my coat, I pull out your books from the bag—you
are both watching closely—the lorna doones, the monterey jack,
and of course the knife

which when I press on the white eye pops open and you both
jump

and this time your sister does not cry

but makes terrified animal noises little whimperings and
whines

so I cut you each a slice and offer it to you with the point of the knife

and you take yours with a shaky hand and hold it as if it is poison contagion the atom bomb

until I say, you are not going to waste it, are you, this is my body this is my blood (hahaha) and with little nibbles you slowly eat my offering up

I've waited a long time for this moment, I begin, a long time— marking the numbers in the air with the knife—twenty-five years, ten years since I last saw you or didn't see you on the other side of the door then fifteen years before that

which adds up to a quarter of a century suffering on account of one bitch after a quarter of a century suffering on account of the other bitch who put me away for pouring out her frosted flakes

which is no more no less than calling the cops on a guy for trying to talk to you for they caught me going down the stairs took me down to the station they fingerprinted and interrogated me and then they let me go but they were watching me and when a week later the fucking house you lived in burned down you must have told them you thought I did it because they dragged me in and by that time they had some other dope on me and off- ed me to brookhaven for trying to cut off that braid you used to have, remember

stand up and let me show your sister how long that fucker was

and you stand up turn around give me your back and I press the blunt side of my knife just above your little ass

and your sister gasps

and I say, wouldn't you say it came down to about there

and you say, feeling the knife, you say, yes, about there is right

Then slowly you turn and face me, your hands held out, small, star-like, pleading

I just want to say I'm sorry I never meant to cause you pain I want to explain why—

and I scream, shut up, bitch, shut up, don't come at me now with your sorrys your fucking oh-if-I-knew-back-then-what-I-know-now

but in a soft voice a sweet rosemarie voice a voice hard to resist you say, oh please

Please don't make me shut up as I feel terrible

because seeing you here—I know you are going to think I'm lying to you, that I'm just saying this stuff to get out of a tight spot—but seeing you here, I see that you were right when you said you were my soulmate, my other, my doppelgänger or whatever it is you used to call me

but you see you used to say it in a scary way that made me run away which I'm not saying was your fault don't get me wrong

just that the style of a person and the tone of voice can make all the difference

for supposing you had come without that needy desperate look and without that spooky thorazine voice

saying, you are my soulmate my life your name belongs among the stars—

I might have listened I might have helped I might even have fallen in love with you for my husband—yes I am now married to a big strong man who should be coming back any time now from the art institute—he says pretty much the same things to me

and it feeds my soul it fills my heart to hear him in his calm sure voice saying so

but believe me, you are not the first whose style and tone just don't go with mine as I was married twice before once to this hippy guy and once to this british man

and though both guys meant well and loved me with all their heart and I loved them with all my heart

still their styles just rubbed raw where I was sorest

and maybe that is a shabby excuse though I'm not blaming you as I am sure no matter the style you project or the tone of your voice you have a good heart as I can testify you never laid a hand on me never tried to hurt me only that one time yanking my hair to cut it which I'm not saying was wrong because how else can you cut a braid but by pulling it away from the head and my sister and I we can both see that you came here to share your cookies and cheese and get your books signed which I really appreciate

for to tell you the truth one of the reasons I was so scared of you was that you were facing bravely and openly yes I can see that now bravely and openly a dark and fearful part of yourself that I was too afraid to face unless it was on paper

which is why I write books as my way of giving you yes you my way of saying, take this as maybe it will help for a moment to hold back the terror heal the wound make a brief stay against the confusion—

shut up! I scream, I told you to fucking shut up, lunging from the bed

and putting the blade to your throat and saying, do you think I don't mean it, bitch, and the sister begging you, please please please, and finally you shut up and I sit back down and cut myself a piece of monterey and wolf it down and I don't know maybe it is the taste of this cheese rosemarie used to feed me but I start to rock myself and feel the fear and the pain and the old old tears

---

And gathering my voice
  to say finally after so many years to say
  what I would have said—
  but every time I tried to talk to you everywhere I followed you
you shut the door you ran off you let your boyfriend come shove
me around you called the police your husbands called the police
you put your fingers in your ears and screamed, go away you're
crazy and you're scaring me
  you would not listen though just a few months ago I heard
you on the fucking radio talking about the importance of stories
how after food and clothing and shelter
  stories is how we take care of each other and all this bunch of
crap
  —and I hurl one of your books at the window but of course
the hotel glass is hard and thick and suicide-proof and the book
lands on the carpet and another book and I tear out the pages of
a third and pull open a fourth to show you what I have done
  the pages all sliced and tampered with
  —and you gasp, oh my god! and that is when you start to cry
  holding your sides and sobbing
  which makes me want to puke cry take to the streets fly out
the window as what good does it do when the boy is beaten the
cat is beaten the village burnt the books destroyed the shank of
dark hair in my fist and it still hurts
  so I say, I say
  —stop stop for I swear to god I'm not going to hurt you as I
give you my word which I have never done before
  —and look as a sign of my good will I am putting away the
knife picking up your books leaving you the lorna doones
renouncing my rough magic
  —but before I go away I want you to do something for me

which is to sit there quietly yes like that yes without crying just calmly truly hearing for once what I tried to tell you for years but you would not let me

   and you glance at your sister with a look of not believing
   you take a deep breath
   you look at me with a look that sees all the way back to the beginning
   okay, you say, okay, I'm listening

The father

Of all my girls, I always felt the closest to Yo. My wife says it is because we are so much alike, knocking her head with her knuckles as she says so. But that is not why I feel closest to Yo, no.

She looks at me, and I know that she can see all the way back to when I was a boy in half trousers raising my hand in that palm-wood schoolhouse. *What color is the hair of God? When you reduce a sum by its shadow and multiply it by its reflection, what will you get?* Our teacher, who called himself Profesor Cristiano Ilumi-nado, spouted his wild questions. Soon after I passed on to the higher school, the mad professor was hauled away to the asylum to eat mashed plantain and sleep on straw and contemplate the mathematics of the stars. But, and this is the point of my anec-dote, I was the only child in that classroom raising my hand to answer those impossible questions.

And Yo sees that one hand waving when she looks into my eyes. So that I am blessed—and sometimes cursed—with a child who understands my secret heart. I should not say child any-more, for she is a grown woman who is already preparing herself. When she looks at me these days, she can see that fresh-dug hole in the mountain cemetery near the town where I was born, the flash of the river between the trees.

She writes me one, two letters a week. Sometimes she includes an old black-and-white photo with those scalloped edges as if all memories deserve a little lace doily to lay on. A young handsome man sits with a young lady in a crowded booth in a bar sixty years ago. With those pasting papers which were invented for her because she always has to put her two cents on everything, she writes, *Where was this taken? Who is the girl beside you? Were you really in love?* She strikes right for the secret heart of that young man!

Most of the things she asks I tell her. I run the past through a sieve of judgment in my head, and if there is no harm, I give her the full cup of my life to drink from. Some little things catch in that fine net, and I leave them out or I make a broad statement. But then the next letter arrives full of interrogation: *Papi, you say you had to escape the island because you were in a revolution in 1939 and I can't find any mention of it in the book. You say that you were in a log-cabin hospital at Lac Abitibi near the Laurentians and I look on the map and Lac Abitibi is nowhere near the Laurentians. Are these just lapses of memory or did you make the whole thing up and if so why?*

And then I have to explain, sieving everything over again. Until the next letter arrives, and I explain some more, and after a while, I lose that quality control. Before I know it, I've told her the whole story I did not want her and the others to know.

Is that really so? I ask myself. Don't I want to be known before I go? And perhaps Yo sees that secret desire, stronger than all the other secrets in my heart, and that is why she keeps asking.

Suddenly, the letters stop. At first, I think she is very busy with her writing and teaching and the new husband who is a very nice man. Then two, three weeks go by, and still no letters with the impossible questions I love. I ask my wife, who is now talking to Yo after forgiving her for writing the last book, I ask her how is our Yoyo doing. My wife is the one always calling the girls even to ask them did they finally get the stuck window closed, how long do they stir their rice pudding. Usually my wife puts me on at the end to say, "Well, your mother has already told you everything so I will just say goodbye." But with Yo, because of our many letters, I always shake my head when my wife offers me the phone.

"Doug says she is sad," my wife says. "I guess she went to a lecture at the college and this famous critic said that those baby boomers who never had children are committing genetic suicide."

"Why go to a lecture like that?" I ask. Sometimes I think my children never use their brains to figure out what is good for them, only to be smart.

"Papi, she didn't know what the man was going to say ahead of time. Anyhow, Doug says she is depressed. Maybe Sandi's new baby stirred things up. She's been telling Doug that women in the Bible who never had babies were said to have a curse on them."

"That is an exaggeration." I shake my head, which is a safe thing to say when anyone tries to prove something with the Bible. But then I start to think that perhaps if I were a woman, I would feel the same way. Perhaps if I had all the equipment and I never used it, there would be a sadness, like letting part of myself go to waste.

So I write her. I say, *my daughter, your father is so proud of you. You have created books for the future generations.*

I do not mention that I know anything of her feelings. I try to say my praise so that she sees that her books are her babies, and for me, they are my grandbabies.

In the middle of the afternoon at the oficina where I still go for

a couple of hours, she calls me. "Ay, Papi, I just got your letter."
She sounds a little weepy, so I go and close the door. For a
moment, I worry that maybe the nice man is not so nice. Over
the years with my girls, I have had to brace myself for bad news.

"It meant a lot what you said," she is saying. "I'm sorry I
haven't been so good about writing lately. I've been kind of
down." And then she is crying and telling me about the Bible and
the famous critic—everything all mixed up so that if my wife
hadn't already told me I would think the critic was someone
famous in the Bible. I try to calm her down by offering the old-
country solution of going and breaking the man's knees. But that
just gets her more upset. "Ay, Papi, come on. It's not his fault. I've
just started to wonder, you know, did I go down the wrong road?
Did I make a big mistake?"

"We all have our destiny," I tell her. And suddenly she is very
quiet for she can hear it in my voice—the way we can with people when they are talking from deep inside what they know.
"Look at your father in 1939 having to run away to New York
with no money in his pocket."

"I thought you ran away to Canada? I thought you had two
hundred and fifty dollars saved up?"

"The important thing is I never thought I would get to be a
doctor again. All my education lost. But that was mi destino. And
even though everything went under in those years, that is what
finally came up.

"And you, my daughter," I add while she is listening so close,
"your destino has been to tell stories. It is a blessing to be able to
live out your destino."

"But many people are writers *and* mothers too."

I say what we always say to our children. "You are not many
people."

"But how can I be sure this is my destino? It's easy for you because now you can see you were right about yourself. But people often fool themselves, you know." The *buts* of depression, hitting their little horns against everything we set up to make ourselves feel better.

There is nothing to do when those *buts* get going—as my old professor well knew—but offer a magical solution that can't be knocked over. So, I tell Yo I am going to give her my blessing when we see each other for the Thanksgiving. "That is in the Bible, too," I remind her. "The father giving his blessing. That is what makes the curse of doubt go away."

"You're going to give me your blessing?" She sounds excited. This is the daughter who would prefer getting the blessing in the will over and above the house in Santiago. The shares in Coca-Cola.

So I remind her, "All my girls will get my blessing. But I am going to give you a particular one."

"You mean like with your hands on my head." The fun is coming back in her voice. "Are the heavens going to open and a voice say, This is my beloved Yo in whom I well pleased?"

"Something like that," I tell her.

After I hang up, I rehearse in my head how the blessing will go. It has to be in story form for Yo to believe in it. And so I will tell her the story of when I first realized her destino was to tell stories. She was five years old. It is a story I have kept secret because it is also a story of my shame which I cannot disentangle from it. We were living in terror, and I reacted with terror. I beat her. I told her that she must never ever tell stories again. And so maybe that is why she has never believed in her destiny, why I have to go back to that past and let go the belt and put my hands on her head instead. I have to tell her I was wrong. I have to lift the old injunction.

———

I had already been living ten years in exile in the States when I met the girls' mother. This, too, was my destino. A cousin of mine invited me to a party a friend of his was throwing at the Waldorf Astoria. At first, I did not want to go. I was a political exile and a gathering in a grand hotel like the Waldorf was bound to be filled with rich Dominicans in New York City on shopping trips. But I went. Ten years so far from home, and I was aching for the sound of our creole Spanish, the taste of ron punch or To-Die-Dreaming, the look of our pretty women. Maybe my principles had dulled on the hard edge of loneliness. Anyhow I went, and sitting out all the dances was a lovely señorita sneezing into a borrowed handkerchief—an oasis! for I had not one but two medical degrees. Not that I needed either one to diagnose that she was sick with a head cold. We spent the evening talking about her symptoms, I taking the liberty, under the guise of collecting her medical history, of finding out every-thing I could about her.

I have to stop here. My wife, she does not want me to tell about her. She says the minute I put the story out there, Yo will write it down. So I am not going to say about all the little notes back and forth; how the romance grew; how I called her mon petit chou because that is what the French name their sweet-hearts; how my wife's mother did not approve of me because I didn't come from a fine family; how her father approved of me because I was a fine man which was pedigree enough for him; how my future wife went back to the Dominican Republic when her extended shopping trip was over; how we were both heart-sick with the separation; how her mother finally relented and agreed on the marriage; how we married and I returned to the island to live under the wing of her powerful family; how we had the four girls.

And now that the story is caught up to where my wife has had the four girls, she can slip out of the story into her anonymity. From time to time I have to bring her in to say her lines but I will keep that to a minimum so as to respect her feelings. I've tried talking my wife into a different point of view, telling her what Yo has told me in letter after letter: "What is the point of shrouding yourself in silence? The grave will do that for you for all eternity."

But that always starts a fight between us. My wife accuses me of siding with Yo. She says all she wants is three things on her tombstone, her name, her date of birth and death, and this summary of her life: *She had four girls. Enough said.* She claims she wants that *enough said* engraved on the tombstone, which I think does not become a deceased person. It is the wrong tone altogether. But my wife only insists on this particular eulogy when we are arguing about Yo and her stories. So I think when the time comes, she can be talked into something a bit more flattering to herself and others.

Adored Wife, Beloved Mother, Treasured Grandmother, Friend to One and All.

Not long after we were living on the island I became involved again in the underground. Although there had been a supposed liberalizing of the regime, which is why I had been granted a pardon, nothing had really changed. If anything, things had gotten worse. A secret police system called the SIM had been established, and people were disappearing left and right for the most minor things. One of our neighbors was overheard to say that the maldito hike in the price of beans had to stop. Next thing we knew, he was found, his mouth stuffed with rags, his feet tied to a concrete block at the bottom of the Rio Ozama.

Sometimes I get confused as to what exactly happened. I don't think it is only because I am now an old man. It's also because I have read the story of those years over and over as Yo has written it, and I know I've substituted her fiction for my facts here and there. Many times I don't even realize I've done so until I get together with my old cronies from the underground. I'll say to one of them, "Maximo, hombre, do you remember that secret closet you helped me build in the new house?" And Maximo will look at me funny and say, "Carlos, you better get that cholesterol checked."

The undoctored truth is that I joined the underground. That I got some of my wife's family involved. That in my own small way I committed subversive acts. But I was being extremely careful. As a pardoned exile, I knew I was being watched. I did not volunteer for the big things. But when someone who was working his way west to the border had to be hidden for a night, I offered my house. When pamphlets from the exile groups had to be distributed, I did so from the different clinics where I worked. Regularly, I met with my cronies at a barra on the Malecón, planning our strategy for when we would strike. And I kept an illegal gun. But to tell the truth: I was not hiding that gun to blow the dictator's head off. No. I used to love to go hunting for guinea hens up in the mountains near Jarabacoa. The campesinos I treated for free in the rural clinics were always paying me back by showing me the best places. But the BB guns the regime allowed took the whole pleasure and precision out of the hunt. So I kept my .22 oiled and ready and hidden under a loose floorboard on my side of the walk-in closet.

I say *my side* as this closet opened onto our bedroom on one side and my study on the other. It was a safe place to store anything because no one was allowed into my study, not even the maids. My wife cleaned that room herself, with the excuse that Don Carlos was picky about his things. It was where, if there was a family problem, we went to talk. I could not keep track of the

whole house, but I had scoured this room aplenty, and I was certain it was free of bugs.

Into this room would wander my little Yo. Often I found her
under the desk with one of my medical books. She loved turning
the see-through pages, undressing the naked man of his skin,
then his veins, then his muscles, and finally when she had only
the skeleton left, going into reverse and fleshing the man to life
again. She was intrigued by the photos of rare diseases, seeing all
the things that could go wrong in the world, and knowing that
her papi could fix them. "My papi can do anything!" she would
brag to her cousins. "He can put in eyeballs. He can make babies
come out of the stomach." It was sweet and simple worship, a
very endearing trait of our children, before they turn into adoles-
cents who need to destroy us in order to grow up into young men
and women.

One time I asked her why she was interested in the sick people. "A pretty little girl like you should be out having fun with
your cousins."

She looked at me, and even back then I felt she could see right
through to the bottom of my heart. "This *is* fun," she asserted
with a serious nod of her head.

"But what are you saying?" I had noticed her lips moving, an
endless mumble going on as she turned the pages.

"I am telling the sick people stories to make them feel better."

My face lit up with pleasure at knowing that one of my children had inherited that sense of magic I had learned from my old
professor. "What stories might those be you are telling Papi's
patients?"

"The ones in the storybook."

My wife's sister had brought the girls back a book from New
York which she read out loud to them from time to time. It was

all about a young lady with a little cap and a sequined bra and long baggy pants who was trapped in a sultan's bedroom and who told him stories to keep herself alive. I knew what was going to happen before her head was cut off, and so I didn't think the book was appropriate for my girls. But when I complained to my wife, she said this book was famous literature and no one had ever come to harm getting a little education. I could have cited two or three dozen people of our acquaintance who had disappeared because they knew more than they should, but my wife was already riled up enough those years. Until we emigrated to this country five years later, she slept at night only if she took two or three sleeping pills.

Every time we caught Yoyo in my study, my wife wanted to punish her for disobeying orders, but I stepped in as I rarely did. I argued that maybe it was our child's *destino* to be a medical doctor, and we should encourage this. So we allowed her to go into my study and look at one book at a time after showing it first to me. The sexual diseases volume I put on a high shelf she could not reach even standing on tiptoe on the desk.

But as usually happens when you permit the forbidden, Yo lost interest in her forays into my library. One reason was the new attraction that had arrived down the block at the general's house, a small black-and-white television. I had seen one years ago at the World's Fair in New York before we had moved back to the island. Now they were being sold commercially. Or I should say, about a hundred sets had been allowed to enter the country, and those close to those in power were permitted to purchase them.

We didn't have one, and even my wife's family, who could have afforded one, didn't have one. It would have been a silly luxury for the programming was very limited: the one television station was state-owned and state-controlled. Every day there was an hour of news from the national palace, mostly speeches by El Jefe, or so I heard. I only saw the box once when I went to pick up the girls at the general's house. The general and his wife were very cordial, older people who had never had their own children and so doted on my four girls. But I knew from my compañeros in the underground what General Molino was capable of, and so when he gave me his arm in an abrazo, I could feel the hair on the back of my neck rising like a dog's hackles.

What my girls most loved to watch were the American cowboy movies which were dubbed by a deaf person, I think. Years later, when I saw an episode of Rin-Tin-Tin in Spanish, I spent most of the half hour laughing. The lips and the words just didn't go. Barks would sound a few seconds after Rin-Tin-Tin barked. Same with the gunshots, so that the villain would be clutching his bloody side and falling in a cloud of dust before you heard the bang-bang-bang of the gun. But my girls loved their cowboys, and so every Saturday, they went over to the general's house to watch those silly movies.

The particulars of what happened over there one Saturday afternoon have all become jumbled together in my head. As I said, this memory has been my shameful secret, and when you do not tell the story, everything mixes with everything else. So, sometimes when I reach down for a fact what I get is my wife's red organdy cocktail dress that she was wearing that Saturday evening when Milagros, the girls' nanny, came back with the girls from the general's house. But other times what comes up are the arrests and denunciations that began to intensify that year when the regime gave free license to the SIM. And sometimes what I remember is how those floorboards had been disturbed one Saturday morning when I went into the study to clean my illegal gun and get ready for a Sunday of guinea hunting.

The box of medical books that had secured the floorboard had been moved to one side. These were oversized books that did not fit on the shelves, and because they had a lot of pictures, I assumed that Yo had been scavenging through them. The floorboards had been lifted and then not fitted back exactly the way I would have done it. But the wrapped parcel was wedged firmly in place, and so taking great gulps of air to calm my beating heart, I convinced myself that I was safe. My cache had not been discovered. But for sure I had to get rid of the gun as a precaution in case the SIM came to search the premises.

Somehow my wife found out about that gun—or maybe I told her? One way or another, she figured out that I was involved in the underground again. She became tragic. Afternoons, she lay in bed with terrible migraines full of presentiments. We were on the eve of our extermination! The SIM were at the door! We would be at the bottom of the Rio Ozama by dawn! She was on the edge of hysteria, and it was the children who felt the brunt of it. Yo especially seemed often to be in her pajamas and banished to her room for offenses that when my wife recounted them to me seemed very minor.

Mostly it was her storytelling that got her in trouble. One time—I can laugh about it now—her grandparents went off to New York as they often did on the pretext of some illness only American doctors could treat. My Yo spread the story among the maids that her grandfather and grandmother had been sent away to have their heads cut off. By the time we cleared it up, the cook had fled in terror that she, too, might be decapitated for fixing the meals of traitors.

"You must not tell such stories!" My wife shook her by the arm. By now, my wife could see the harm that had come of that crazy storybook. It was not just the stories themselves, but the habit of storytelling that our little Yo seemed to have picked up from the lady with the bra and baggy pants.

Soon after that wild story was when it happened. That Saturday night we were headed for a big party at Mundo's house next door. A big party meant there would be a perico ripiao band, lots of food and dancing, and at least one drunk jumping into the swimming pool in an attempt to prove he could walk on water. The girls were still over at the general's watching their cowboy movie as we got dressed. My wife had put on the red organdy dress that she had not worn since her Waldorf Astoria days, and suddenly she was the sneezing señorita all over again. For the first time in a long time, she was relaxed and playful. In fact, we had used the empty house and the peace and quiet to get reacquainted under the covers. We were just getting ready to cross over to Mundo's when we heard the girls and Milagros coming up the driveway.

They came thundering in the room after only a little knock, which we had taught them was good manners. Of course, they always forgot the second part of the lesson, waiting for permission. Only Yo, I noted, was hanging back at the door. "How is my little doctora?" I teased for I was in a good mood and pleased with all five of my beautiful girls.

That was when Carla blurted out, "Ay, Papi, you should hear the story Yoyo told."

"Yes," said Sandi. "General Molino told her she must never say things like that!"

My wife's face drained of color so that the rouge stood out unnaturally on her cheeks. In the calmest voice possible, she said, "Come tell your mami what it is you told General Molino."

By now Milagros was at the door, wild-eyed, and shaking her head at the child. "Doña Laura, that child. I tell you. I don't know what devil gets in her mouth. Dios santo, keep us from trouble, but that girl is going to get us all killed."

Yoyo's face was a picture of shock. It was as if she were finally realizing that a story could kill as well as cure someone.

It took some calming down before we could get the story out of that riled-up old woman. It seems the general and his wife and Milagros and the girls had been watching a cowboy movie. Yo was on the general's lap—which surprised me as Yo did not take to the general the way the others did. She was always coming home and saying that the general had too many rings on his fingers that scratched her, that he tickled her too much and trotted her too hard on his knee. Anyhow, this Saturday, when the cowboy shouldered his rifle to shoot the outlaws, the general had commenced his baiting. "Ay, look at that big gun, Yoyo!" He was poking her here and there with his forefinger. And Yo came back with a child's boast, "My papi has a bigger gun!"

"Oh?" says the general.

And Milagros reported she made eyes at the child to unsay what she had said. But no. Once Yo was inside a story, you couldn't stop her. "Yes, my papi has many many big guns hidden away where no one can find them."

"Oh?" says the general.

"Don Carlos, the man's face was white as that sheet there on your bed."

"Yes, Milagros, keep going."

"Then this one, she says, my papi is going to kill all the bad people with those guns. And the general says, what bad people, and this one says, the bad sultan ruling the land and all the guards who protect him in his big palace. And so the general says, you don't mean that, Yoyo. And this one gets like she can get, you know, and gives the general a big serious liar's nod and

says, yes, and El Jefe, and maybe you, too, if you don't stop tickling me."

There was a wail that came out of my wife's mouth the like I
had never heard before. Terror flashed in my children's eyes. The
three innocents began to cry. The culprit tried to dash out of the
door.

But Milagros caught her by the arm and brought her over to
me. "Milagros," I said, "would you please take the other children
to their baths." By now, the girls were clinging to their mother,
who sat at the edge of the bed, sobbing into her hands. They
shrieked and pleaded that they did not want to go with Milagros. Finally I had to stand up and take my belt off and threaten
them with a pela if they didn't stop their crying and get washed
up. This threat was as far as I'd ever gone in carrying out a punishment.

When the door shut, we went at Yo like an interrogation team.
What exactly had she said to the general. Nothing, she wailed.
She had said nothing. "Let us go over it again," my wife said, her
voice a mixture of fury and fear. "Do you want your papi to give
you a pela you'll never forget?" But imagine, the child was just a
child, and once alerted that she had done some terrible wrong,
she was too frightened to speak except safely to repeat the lines
we suggested to her.

And we were frightened, too. We could already hear the little
coughing sound of the Volkswagen, the bang at the door with
the butt of a revolver, the shouts as a gang of thugs flooded the
house knocking things over. We even went so far as to think it
through—that we should not go to the party next door and im-
plicate my wife's family. We could see ourselves being shoved into
that black Volkswagen, my wife in her red organdy dress that
would stir up who knows what ugliness in these animals, my

children screaming, rounded up as hostages to elicit confessions from me.

And all because of a child's goddamn fairytale!

I think that's when I saw that the child had to be taught a lesson.

We took her into the bathroom and turned on the shower to drown out her cries. "Ay, Papi, Mami, no, por favor," she wailed. As my wife held her, I brought down that belt over and over, not with all my strength or I could have killed her, but with enough force to leave marks on her backside and legs. It was as if I had forgotten that she was a child, my child, and all I could think was that I had to silence our betrayer. "This should teach you a lesson," I kept saying. "You must never ever tell stories!"

She sunk her head in her mother's lap, bracing herself against the next belt lash. She was sobbing, her little shoulders shaking. I, too, felt like crying.

But my fear was greater than my shame. I stormed out of the bathroom to my office where the incriminating rifle lay hidden. Under the pretext that I was going to attend to an emergency at the hospital, I drove that gun over to the house of a certain compañero. To this day I persist in my secrecy and do not mention his name. I suppose it is one of those lingering habits of the dictatorship when we censored all our stories. That is what I explain to my Yo. She has to understand about her mother and me. When she writes a book, the worst she worries about is that it will get a bad review. We hear beatings and screams, we see the SIM driving up in a black Volkswagen and rounding up the family.

That night was probably the longest night of my life. When I returned, I found my wife sitting at the edge of the bed, rocking herself back and forth. Hour after hour, we waited in the dark bedroom, lifting the jalousies every time we heard a car drive by the road below. Next door, the band started up, there were happy shouts, a splash in the swimming pool. Sometime around eleven, a maid came over with a message from Don Mundo to get ourselves over there. We thought up some excuse: my wife had a sore throat, I had an emergency. We did not sleep a wink. When dawn came and it looked like the SIM were not going to show up after all, my wife finally dozed off. The old general must have decided to let the incident pass as a child's silly story.

But now that the fear had diminished, the remorse grew in my heart. I went down the hall to the girls' bedroom where Yo lay sleeping, her thumb in her mouth, her hair twisted into a cowlick on top of her head. She had kicked off the sheets during the hot night, so I could see the ugly marks on her legs. I sat down on the edge of her bed, and I tried but I could not speak. It was as if the injunction of silence I had laid on her had fallen also on me.

She must have felt a presence beside her because she stirred awake. Raising her head a little, she focused on me, and what her face showed was terror, not delight. She backed away when I reached for her, and when I forced her to come to my lap, she began to cry.

Perhaps I told her back then that her papi was so sorry for what he had done. I don't know. In my memory of the moment, there are no words. I hold her and she cries, and then, in a furious flash, forty years go by, and she is on the other end of the phone, tearful, saying how can she be sure it is her destino to tell stories.

I have promised her a blessing to take the doubt away. A story whose true facts cannot be changed. But I can add my own invention—that much I have learned from Yo. A new ending can be made out of what I now know.

So let us go back to that moment. Let us enter that small,

green-tiled bathroom that will have a fictional hidden closet behind the toilet in stories to come. I am turning on the shower. Her mother sits down on the toilet seat to hold Yo for me. It sounds like Isaac pinned on the rock and his father Abraham lifting the butcher knife. I lift the belt, but then as I said, forty years pass, and my hand comes down gently on my child's graying head.

And I say, "My daughter, the future has come and we were in such a rush to get here! We left everything behind and forgot so much. Ours is now an orphan family. My grandchildren and great grandchildren will not know the way back unless they have a story. Tell them of our journey. Tell them the secret heart of your father and undo the old wrong. My Yo, embrace your destino. You have my blessing, pass it on."